The Adar Remnant

The Adar Remnant

Plague of Souls Book Two

SIMON BARRON

MP

MP PUBLISHING

The Adar Remnant

First edition published in 2020 by

MP Publishing
12 Strathallan Crescent, Douglas, Isle of Man IM2 4NR British Isles
mppublishingusa.com

Jacket designed by Jonas de Ro.

A CIP Catalogue for this title is also available from the British Library

ISBN 978-1-84982-287-9
10 . . . 6 . . . 2 1

Also available in eBook

For Dad

With Special Thanks, As Always,
to the Biscuit Gang

In pace, ut sapiens, aptarit idonea bello.

In peace, like a wise man,
he appropriately prepares for war.

Ironforge Loft (12,124')
Fool's Camp
Mashtock
Eagle's Reach
Abnavil
Cold Point
Blue Gate
Stroming Blod
Mashtock Town
Cyne
Jow
Shen Utah
King's End
Miller's Brook
Jow
High Crossing
Ho
Miller's Folly
Fendale
The Waile
Adar
Shen Utah
SHENMADOCK
Eladreen's Heart
Druidale (Elven Springs)
Eden Realm
Eden Falls
de Hayne's Grief
Thes
Fort Beufort

Bright Star
Bright Star Lake
Daemon's Pass
Brantyl
FREE CITIES OF BRIADRANON
Blood Vale
Choat City
Krasital
Shallow Well
Seer's Fall
Sunrise Point
9,124'
IPSICA
Taal
Otack
North Ka
South Ka
Wahib City
Corfel Scar
5,421'
4,745'
Watchman's Lott
Lovers Fall
Hightower

Prologue

Winter fast approached. The ozone stench on the northerly winds grew stronger with every passing day, and soon, a heavy swathe of snow would adorn the northern duchies of Shenmadock.

It was dawn. On bended knee at the side of a road leading to the outskirts of some sleeping Mashtock town, Soora adjusted his boots. His had been a long and solitary trek from the wild Northern Territories, but for some time now, he had been passing through more populated areas. Mashtock was the northern-most duchy in Shenmadock and, Soora knew, rife with banditry and violent crime. Yet he was not worried about travelling alone.

Soora was well aware of his own capabilities with the twinned swords nestled snugly in the crossed scabbards on his back. Should someone choose to attack him, they would soon discover that they faced an opponent who had lived almost his entire life without concern for his own well-being. He imagined he knew better than anyone that Death waited around every corner. And when Death came calling, Soora would welcome her with open arms, for she was no stranger to him.

He heard footsteps approaching from behind and reached for his rucksack.

"Mornin', traveller," the new arrival slurred. "Dangerous to be out here on your own; someone ought to help you look after that heavy-looking bag of yours."

Soora remained on one knee, his right hand hovering above his belongings. The morning dew had softened the dirt track beneath their feet. Behind him, Soora could sense the rattle-strain of a bowstring pulled taut, further back than the man who'd spoken and slightly to the left.

So, there are two, at least.

"Perhaps you should let us keep it for you. Indefinitely-like. Just to ensure you don't get robbed," the speaker said amiably, eliciting a humourless laugh from his comrade.

"Nice one, Feg. You're funny in the mornings. Can I shoot him now?" The man sounded a bit simple.

From his crouch, Soora looked darkly over his left shoulder, fixing his eyes on the bowman. He stood less than ten feet to the rear, a short bow aimed squarely at Soora. The robber's next smart comment died in his mouth.

"Look," said Feg, who stood nearer to Soora and brandished a long-bladed knife. "You know the drill, traveller. We own these roads. You pay our levy with coin, gems, or blood—it's your choice. We don't make the rules; we just benefit from them. You understand?"

Soora took a deep breath, exhaled, and let his gaze drop to the ground in apparent resignation. Once again, it came to this; he never seemed to have a choice.

"Good. Jeson, keep him covered." Feg took one squelching step forward.

Soora rolled to his left, away from his bag. When he came up, he had drawn one of his short swords and hurled it backhandedly at the bowman.

The blade thumped into the bandit's face, breaking his jawbone in two and bisecting his windpipe. The bow fell from his hands, the arrow flicking off at an odd angle.

"Hey!" Feg rounded on Soora, his face ripped with fury. Without waiting, Soora lunged at the bandit, drawing his second sword. Ducking under Feg's clumsy swipe, Soora slipped the blade across his unprotected lower abdomen, careful not to cut too deep.

The bandit dropped his sword and clutched at his innards as they spilled from his sundered belly. The desperation of his cry was sickening as he dropped to his knees in the soft earth.

A call went up from a copse of trees to the east side of the road, and Soora spotted another two figures rushing toward him. As before, one was armed with a bow, the other bearing a sword this time. The first assailant nocked an arrow and stopped to take aim.

Quickly sheathing his own sword, Soora ran across the road, snatching up Jeson's dropped short bow and retrieving the arrow.

A whistling shaft from the approaching bowman thumped into the ground behind him. Kneeling, Soora loosed his own shot, taking the bowman in the throat. The man dropped backward, a jet of crimson erupting into the air.

The last bandit jumped over a low drybrick wall and rushed Soora, his blade held high. As the strike came down, Soora dropped the bow and deflected the attack with his wrist bracer, turning the tall man. Using his weight against him, Soora grabbed his enemy's sword wrist and pulled it down. With the man stumbling forward, it took a simple twist of the wrist and a shove to punch the man's sword through his own skull. With a gurgling breath and a spasm, he died.

A light rain had begun to fall, dense, misty drizzle collecting in bubbles on Soora's waxed leather armour. The precipitation created an eerie blanketing silence that permeated the whole area, interrupted only by the panicked whimpers of Feg, who continued his vain struggle to retain his intestines. His face was grey, and his arms shook with the onset of shock as he lay on his side.

Soora strode over to the bandit leader and picked up Feg's abandoned knife. Without preamble or ceremony, Soora reversed his grip and plunged the long blade viciously through Feg's lower face, smashing his jaw and pinning him to the floor, undoubtedly slicing his tongue in half too. The whimpers increased, but he was dying quickly now. His guts covered his knees, and blood flowed freely into the mud.

Soora looked around at the devastation these robbers had caused to themselves and felt no guilt or remorse whatsoever. He was incapable of remorse. These men had died as a direct result of their own ill-advised actions, and even Soora's reluctance at having to send them to hell's door couldn't change that.

Reaching down, Soora carefully selected one of Feg's dislodged teeth, placing it in a pouch on his hip. Then, one by one, he collected a similar prize from his three other victims. As with almost every other aspect of his life, he didn't understand the ritual of collecting a tooth from each of those he had slain. It had simply always been the case for as long as he could remember.

The four teeth collected and dutifully stowed, he retrieved his weapons and bag before turning toward the small town ahead of him.

He fancied a bath.

Part One

Whispering Tongues

If you reveal your secrets to the wind,
you should not blame the wind
for revealing them to the trees.
Kahlil Gibran

Chapter One

Black Snake Venom

The eagle-owl soared through the flat blackness of the night, her ear tufts ruffling in the crisp air of the coming winter. Cutting through the frigid sky, the eagle-owl circled around the spires of the Shen Utah Palace, starting her descent toward the hunting grounds north of the river. Below her, the pinprick fires of a restless city burned; the chaotic, sprawling mass of mammals sending unnatural thermals up beneath her speckled wings.

Picking up speed, the eagle-owl—one of nature's most efficient hunters—dropped a wing and cut through another thermal, arrowing toward the ground.

Mottled feathers shifted in the wind as the buildings of the city rushed up, the bird of prey whistling through the air above the rooftops. In the shadow of the eagle-owl, another predator scrambled across a loosely tiled roof, dislodging one, which fell to the cobbled street below with a smash of betrayal.

The spy slid down another slope of slate as the pursuing guards on the street responded to the sound of the fallen tile. Voices called out a direction.

Cursing to himself, the spy caught the edge of the roof as he slid off the end feet-first. Planting his feet against the wall, he pushed away and fell through the chill air to land heavily on his back upon the flat roof of the grocery store behind him.

The young man rolled to his feet and checked his rib pocket, finding the fragile, stolen vial still intact. Heaving a sigh of relief, Click took to his heals. The streets below glowered with torchlight, like the iridescent glow of deadly jellyfish glimpsed through the surface of the sea, gathering for the kill.

Jumping from roof to damp roof across another narrow alley, he landed lightly on his feet and scrambled along the thin watershed peak. The next building was much taller than the rest. Even Click wouldn't be able to reach its roof.

Running down to the ledge, Click jumped away, dropping through the cold air. He clutched his head and tucked his knees as he burst through a shuttered window across the gap, the crash of splintered wood giving his position away. But Soriana at least smiled on him for once—the building's owner clearly wasn't wealthy enough to afford glass windows.

Landing heavily on the floor of a small and uninhabited bedroom, Click grabbed up a large plank from the broken shutters and jumped to his feet.

Elsewhere in the building, he heard someone call out in alarm at the sudden and unexpected sound.

He pulled open the only door from the room and rushed out to the end of a hallway. Without hesitation, he ran down the corridor. On the right stood a doorway, and at the end of the landing was a flight of varnished wooden stairs leading down into the blind dark.

As Click sprinted toward the stairs, the door on the right swung inward and a fat man with pink jowls stepped out into the hall. His eyes almost jumped from his skull at the sight of the intruder. A burly arm swung out, aimed at Click's head.

The boy skidded on his feet, dropping toward the floor. The man's arm cleaved the air above his face. Click slapped the plank onto the floor and landed lightly on it as he headed over the lip of the top stair. Riding the plank like a sled, Click shuddered down the stairway, the fat man barking curses at him from above.

When he hit the bottom stair, Click put his feet out, halting his fall with a jarring impact and discarding his impromptu sled, which clattered off and slammed into the door ahead of him which swung back to reveal a first-floor bedroom. He ran through the doorway and across the room, exiting through another tall, glassless window. The screams of the awoken children echoed through the night.

Easily clearing the window ledge, Click came to land on a rickety balcony that overlooked a broad courtyard. More voices resonated through the night-clad streets below him, and the sounds of the fat man clamoured closer in response to the screams of his children.

Searching frantically, Click spied a length of rope secured to a pulley screwed into the nearby window frame, built for hanging out washing during good weather. He grabbed the cord, looped it twice round his hand, and lashed out with his dirk, severing the rope at the wall. With one jump over the railing, Click was yanked through the night air with alarming speed.

The flagstones of the old courtyard rushed toward him as the length of cord pulled taut, swinging him forward and to the right. Landing more clumsily than he'd have liked, Click stumbled to the ground, the air blasting from his lungs and his dirk skittering away into the darkness, lost. He heard the glass of the vial in his tunic scrape along the stone floor. He rolled to secure the precious bottle and looked over his shoulder at the nearest lane entrance.

Silhouetted by the torchlight further down that passage, a privately hired armed guard emerged into the courtyard.

Dressed all in black and remaining perfectly still, Click was almost impossible for the guard to spot—until the fat man of the building above poked his head out of his child's bedroom window and began bellowing for help. A white arm pointed at Click where he lay prone on the flagstones of the square.

By the time the guard had spied him and called out his location, Click was already up and running for the short, humped bridge that spanned a section of the river ahead.

The previous owner of Click's secreted vial, Jorus the apothecary, had been cautious. The hired guards had been waiting outside the chemist's building when Click exited. He had climbed to the roof as the alarm was raised, seeking to make good his getaway. So far, Click had made good distance from the building with the vial in his possession, despite all the hired thugs. All he had to do was reach the sanctuary of The Lows, which even the hardiest of mercenary guards would balk at entering.

Click sprinted across the bridge as the report of a fired crossbow echoed through the night. The steel bolt glanced off the wall of the bridge beside him with a *zing* and a little burst of sparks. As he disappeared around the next narrow corner, another bolt thumped noisily into a merchant's sign swinging above Click's head as he crested the rise and ran down the street beyond.

Now in an environment that was a perfect fit for a member of the underworld guilds, the apprentice Whisper blended into the darkness of the lanes and alleys of High Market. His pursuers were lost in the warren of the old town, and Click made good his escape, with only a few bruises to show for his troubles.

Not much more than an hour later, Click entered a small tavern, having safely stashed his vial of poison.

Wandering between the few occupied tables toward the bar at the back, Click wiped his brow, though his face was now clear of perspiration. He still felt the rush of adrenaline from the chase, and his breathing remained fast and shallow. He forced himself to take a single slow breath as he arrived at the counter. The barkeep looked up.

"Hi, Dad, can I have a mead?"

The Father poured the youngster some weak mead and set it on the counter with a wry smile, despite the knowledge that his patron was only fifteen years of age. Even in The Lows, the taverns were reticent to serve the stronger booze to youngsters, though those of the underworld guilds were afforded far more leeway than others. "Busy night, my lad?"

"It had its ups and downs," Click said. The Father knew better than to expect details.

Known to the children of The Lows as The Father, the barkeep was not Click's paternal father. Click's natural father had been an assassin, a member of the Black Cat Guild, and it had been a long time since Click had seen him. A very long time.

A bear of a man, The Father had earned his nickname through his propensity for always ensuring the children of The Lows had a place of rest from the dangers of the streets when they needed it. He never asked questions and only ever sought to give sage advice. His tavern, The Comfy Pig, had a reputation for exquisite food, and the main common room was often bustling with patrons. The Snug Room, however, was reserved for the likes of Click and his friends.

Of course, the fact that The Father had once been a cleric in the Order of Aga, Goddess of Protection, might also have had something to do with the acquisition of such a nickname.

Click was The Father's opposite in appearance. Where the man was tall, broad, and topped by well-combed black hair, Click was slight, slender, and constantly tousling a mop of blond hair. It was a habit he had.

"Your friends are in," The Father told him, indicating a shaded table in the corner of the already considerably shady Snug Room. "That rake Galvan was good tonight," he confessed, visibly reticent to award the troubadour too much in the way of plaudits.

"I'll tell him."

"Please don't. That little room is barely big enough to fit his head in as it is!"

Click picked up his drink with a laugh and ducked into the Snug Room to join his friends, drawing a hand down his face as though he could wipe away the fatigue that easily.

Taking a seat at the darkened table, Click smiled at Martin Galvan and Delgado. Both were travellers from the Free Cities of Briadranon, far to the east, and had settled in Shen Utah some years ago, immediately finding themselves at home in the Shenmadock capital. Over the years, the troubadour Martin had earned a decent reputation for his performances in establishments such as The Comfy Pig. With a quick smile and shaggy brown hair, Martin was an immediately likeable man.

"How did it go?" Martin asked Click.

"Jorus had a surprise or six waiting—surprises bristling with swords and clubs—but I got what I went for."

"So, it's true, then? Jorus is poison-making?"

As a force of habit, Click looked around the small room before replying, despite knowing The Snug was as secure as any place in Shen Utah for such conversations. "I don't think so; at least, not wholesale. I broke into his place easily enough, and it took me scant minutes to find the vial of poison, but it was the only evidence of poison-making I found there. None of his apothecary equipment lends itself to that art in particular, and there were certainly no signs of the usual collection of . . . ingredients one would expect to find if he was making a habit of this."

"Eye of newt and all that?" Martin quipped.

"Something like that."

"I suppose if he was making poison, he'd know it was against guild law to brew *that* poison in particular, right? Are you sure he didn't just hide it better?"

"If you're creating Black Spider Venom poison, you'd normally need a clutter of spiders from which to draw the venom. You can't import some of the venoms needed; the virulence diminishes quickly once drawn. His place simply isn't big enough or in sound enough repair to have made accommodation for that."

The group at the table sat in silence for a moment. Black Spider Venom was one of the most notorious and iconic poisons known in Shen Utah. The name of the poison—whispered at the best of times—was actually a bit of a misnomer, for it was not drawn from the fairly common black spider, whose venom was no more harmful than a bee sting. Instead, the poison was carefully developed by combining many different types of venom from more than a dozen species of spider, under innumerable chemical states. The "Black" in the title was derived from the strange occurrence in the unfortunate victim of the poisoning, whereby their blood was sometimes seen to blacken scant seconds before death. Administering the poison to the body by a shallow graze or scratch would make the victim incredibly ill, and kill the frailest of victims; but if the poison was delivered directly to the bloodstream, death was a painful and rapid certainty. The infrequent colouring of the victim's blood, which to the practiced eye was often a dead giveaway that poison had been administered, was seen as an acceptable risk should a quick and certain death be desired. In fact, the effect was sometimes intended to serve as a chilling warning.

"He must be making the poison somewhere else, then?" Martin asked.

"I don't buy that, either. By my reckoning, this is the only poison he's got. The ingredients and apparatus required to make it even in this small a quantity would be far too expensive. It seems most likely that his customer requested the poison, and he planned only to facilitate the import and sale."

"Middle man?"

"Indeed. One thing's for sure—whatever Jorus was intending to do with this Black Spider Venom had him nervous enough to hire guards."

"He's worried about the guilds finding out he's trading in poisons without their consent, and a banned poison at that." Martin shook his head. "That's a real risk for him to take."

"And hired goons are an expensive solution. It suggests his customer is paying Jorus enough to afford those guards. They weren't brilliant, but they were good enough to make me sweat in my escape. He doesn't earn that kind of money selling wart salves." Click took a long draught of his mead and wiped at his lips.

"Well, it's a moot point now that you've half-inched his stash," muttered Delgado. The big easterner's voice had a stronger accent than that of Martin Galvan, and it was sometimes difficult to follow every word.

A former slave-fighter, Delgado was an impressive figure. Though he stood easily over six feet tall and was broad as a house, he was actually a fairly timid character. Apparently, he had not raised a hand in anger since being released from slavery many years ago, although his very presence and appearance dissuaded would-be attackers from trying their luck.

"It's the Sinecure's problem now," he added. Click only nodded, reluctant to confess the fact that he hadn't actually handed the evidence over to his Guildmaster, as guild law would demand. "Have they replaced Faragwin yet?" Delgado asked.

"Gareth," he said.

"Good choice," nodded Martin. "Steady guy."

Each criminal venture in Shen Utah fell under the auspices of a number of guilds; thieves, thugs, assassins, whores, and spies—termed the guilds of the Glimmers, Pillars, Black Cats, Wheels, and Whispers respectively. Click was still an apprentice Whisper, and his Guildmaster was Malian. Each of the five Guildmasters sat upon the Sinecure, along with the leader and criminal master of the underworld, Swindle. If the Sinecure had a kingpin, Swindle was it.

Faragwin, Guildmaster of the Glimmers, had become the latest guild member to disappear in the small rash of punishments following the death of the Temple Shredder and the sinking of the mysterious treasure ship at the King's Docks of Shen Utah not so long ago. Faragwin had betrayed the honour of the Glimmer guild and sold one member out to the advantage of another. Betraying guild law, Faragwin had passed knowledge of the treasure ship to an apprentice, Grimlaw, later revealed to be the Guildmaster's bastard son. The vessel, heavily laden with illegally imported and volatile naphtha kegs, had been scuttled with Grimlaw trapped aboard. Grimlaw had gone to a watery grave, along with the rest of the cargo—a fortune in gold and gems.

The upshot was that the Glimmers had elected a new Guildmaster—Gareth, the former Night Watchman and a fair man. Another development was that Acaelian the Glimmer, one of Click's closest friends, had left the guilds of his own volition and had likewise disappeared.

Pulling his attention back to the table at The Comfy Pig, Click finished his warming mead and pushed his tankard away, suddenly having lost his taste for even the weakened booze. He took his leave of Martin Galvan and Delgado, left with a nod toward The Father, and stepped out into the cold and lonely night.

Sooner or later, he was going to have to offload the Black Spider Venom before it was found in his possession. His contact wasn't an easy man to get in touch with discreetly, but he'd have to find a way.

Chapter Two

Thoughts of Home

On the other side of dawn, far across the city in an entirely different part of Shen Utah, a soldier of the City Guard absentmindedly picked at the ties of his chest cuirass as it lay discarded against his knee. He was thankful to have it removed, though the coolness of the morning air chilled his sweat-soaked cotton undershirt. Still, Dale ignored the odd shiver. He was deep in thought . . . again!

Morning had fully broken, and the sun was now concealed behind fast-moving clouds. It would be an indistinct day season-wise; one of those days when it was impossible to discern autumn from spring. The daylight would be a flat, pale blue, the threat of rain showers constant. Dale disliked such days. Never a lover of a particular time of year, he simply liked the change of season. He had waited with anticipation for the golden turn from summer to autumn, and now revelled in the metallic taste in the air that only came with the approach of winter.

Unlike Dale, his comrade Guardigan was fond of the summer months, blossoming in the solstice revels and the celebrations late into the honey-coloured evenings.

"What are you thinking about now?" Guardigan asked him, noticing his reverie. The two sat together on the allure of the eastern battlement, having finished their sentry duty less than half an hour ago. It was the last of their midnight duties for the week, pointlessly walking the ramparts in the depths of night. Despite the absence of threat to the city of Shen Utah, soldiers of the City Guard would always walk the ramparts, relentless in their vigilance.

Unlike the City Watch, the City Guard were soldiers of the Shen Utah army and were entrusted with the defence of the city from any external threat. The care and protection of those *inside* the city proper, and the enforcement of Shen law, was the responsibility of the constables and watchmen of the City Watch.

Dale looked up from his fidgeting and glanced at Guardigan. "Nothing much," he lied. "Just tired of walking past these bloody merlons, I guess. Sick of wearing uncomfortable leather armour for no good reason."

"Tell me about it." Guardigan suddenly grinned. "But hey, finally we can get us a drink tonight! I've been chaffing at the bit for a slug of Grig's ale."

"Even Grig's? That's a desperate state of affairs. *Slugs* might actually be an active ingredient!"

Guardigan laughed, and the pair fell into silence once more. After a while, Dale looked up from the rampart and stared behind them into the city, out across the affluent area of the East End and farther on to where the Shen Utah Palace stood at the heart of Temple Link. Seabirds circled the spires that reached skyward like fingers yearning for the heavens. "What do you think your friends at home are doing this morning?" Dale asked, with a failed attempt at nonchalance.

Guardigan's head slumped forward in resignation.

"What?" Dale protested.

"I knew your brain was cooking something! Why is it important what my friends at home are doing? I haven't been home for more than a decade now. Most of my friends from that life are probably dead. My real friends are here now—like Grig the Ale-master, Penny the Wheel Mistress, and even you, Dalian the Bloody Contemplator."

Dale laughed, starting to gather his gear. It really was time they vacated the battlements. Tardiness was frowned upon, especially on the quarters of the wall overlooking the richer areas of Shen Utah, like East End, the High Wall Area, and Temple Link.

"If I was to answer your question," continued Guardigan as they descended the stone steps and reached the street, "I would say Grig is probably looking for cheap fertiliser to lace his ale with, Penny will be honking out some well-earned snores after a busy night ensuring the pleasure of the city didn't go ignored, and you are asking me questions you have absolutely no bloody interest in hearing my answer to. So, would you tell me what's really on your mind before I punch you in the face?"

Not for the first time, Dale was pleased to count Guardigan amongst his friends. If not particularly smart, the man from the north was wise, despite his frequent curses and coarse conversation topics. A little blunt and direct at times, Guardigan fooled most onlookers into counting him a belligerent, mindless foot soldier. In truth, his lengthening years had lent him impressive wisdom and sabre-sharp intuition. Unfortunately, these virtues were often hamstrung by open cynicism.

"I've never regretted joining the Shen Utah City Guard," said Dale. "I left my village when I was young with the express intention of joining the army, and now I'm here. I'm only twenty-two next spring, and I have achieved the minimum that I intended to. But—"

"But it's not everything you thought it would be," Guardigan finished for him. "Your romantic vision of being a Shen Utah soldier never included wasting your time traipsing up and down these city walls dressed in stinking leather armour, while the nearest enemy forces were hundreds of miles to the south with no chance of ever leaving their own barbarian lands, never mind reaching these walls. That about cover it?"

Dale watched his own feet.

After a good distance, the pair walked beneath an ornate, tall archway and into the morning throng of the Temple Link markets, having to shove their way between hawkers and shoppers. Dale kicked a rotten apple from his path and finally said, "I was brought up on stories of legendary battles, brave heroes, and inspirational victories."

"Most softies from Unedar were!" Guardigan himself was ironforged, a man descended from the warrior people of the frozen mountains—the tallest of which gave the people their name. They had long established traditions that first-born sons were always held in high regard as fighters, always served as soldiers or warriors of the clan. Dale was cut from different cloth.

"My favourite stories were of Arlon, the Hero of Thes, who singlehandedly fought back the barbarian horde at the River Thes. Imagine my excitement, knowing I would serve under Arlon here in Shen Utah! But all I find is a city obsessed with its own history and politics, merchants-made-nobles busily betraying one another in some ruthless bid for one-upmanship, the details of which I mostly just don't understand. And I've never even seen Knight Marshall Arlon—never clapped eyes on the man!"

Guardigan smiled. "You sound like a spoiled child deprived of his toys." As Dale went to react, Guardigan put his free hand up in supplication. "Don't start! All I'm saying is that you are slowly becoming aware of certain realities, and it is obvious that these things are being seen by young, idealistic, dare I say naïve eyes.

"Arlon of Thes is now Knight Marshall of Shen Utah. Despite his own comparatively young years, he has weighty responsibilities to this realm. Ironically, his achievements at places like Thes and Boyareen thereafter are the very things that have brought this responsibility to him. I imagine he often finds as much frustration with his plight as you do with yours. Men like Arlon are fated to face such sacrifices and compromises until they die." Guardigan stopped and fixed him with a meaningful stare. "Admire men like Arlon, my friend; even aspire to be like them, for they are great men. But never envy them, for whatever you would give to fight alongside them, they would pay double to be back here alongside us."

Dale knew Guardigan could see the confusion and frustration written on his face.

The older man slapped the slender youth on the shoulder and forced a grin. "We don't have a bad life, you whoreson! Let's get a few hours' sleep, and then I'll buy you a flagon of Grig's finest slug fertiliser, just to prove my point!"

Despite himself, Dale laughed and followed the bullish Guardigan toward their barracks near the area known as The Lows. Yes, he liked the ageing man; somehow—impossibly—he reminded Dale of home.

Knight Marshall Arlon of Thes gripped his sword firmly, sweat beading on his brow as he stalked his opponent. His enemy stepped in and flailed a little wildly with his longsword, betraying his tiredness as he cleaved a blow at Arlon's face with alarming speed. Arlon held his ground on light feet, his weight perfectly balanced, parrying twice and drawing his opponent in before thundering his shoulder into his face. The man staggered back under the charge and then toppled over in his fatigue. Before his opponent's arse hit the ground, Arlon's sword tip was at his throat.

"I yield!" his sparring partner yelled. As Arlon stepped away, Carpion wiped a trickle of blood from his top lip, tears welling in his eyes from his possibly broken nose. "Do you ever fight by halves?" Carpion complained, before quickly adding, "Marshall."

Arlon replaced his blade in the rack on the wall, wiped his tattoo-covered hands on a cloth, and then offered his right to Carpion. He hoisted him to his feet, examining the badly bruised nose. "Of course not, Cousin," Arlon said. "What would be gained from that? If you are to fight, fight wholeheartedly. Not to do so is to become weak, and we can never know what threat lurks just around the corner. If we do not remain prepared, vigilant, and strong—"

"The next time you face a man intent on ending you, his job will have been made that much easier," Carpion finished for him, repeating a mantra that had been drilled into them endlessly as youngsters. "Were they Artimus's words?"

Arlon squeezed Carpion's nose with both thumbs, straightening the cartilage with an alarming crack and more tears.

"There; just as pretty as before," he said as Carpion growled against the pain. "And I think you'll find it was Sergeant Wareing's lesson."

"Of course! Hell, he was a tyrant in the making!"

Both men's nostalgic thoughts thankfully went unvoiced as a shout came from the other side of Arlon's private courtyard.

"Sire!" Immediately, Arlon could tell it was an interruption he would resent. Leaving his elder cousin to tend his wound alone, still muttering oaths, Arlon strode to meet the messenger. "Sire, Councillor Fargil requests your presence."

Arlon nodded once and indicated he would follow.

"Despite your love of the bow, you are still a skilled swordsman, Carpion," he called over his shoulder. "Just try to control that anger of yours; it makes you powerful but vulnerable when you're tired. Your handsome nose can't afford many breaks."

"I'll beat you one day . . . Knight Marshall, sir!"

Walking the long corridors of the old palace to the Council Chambers, the mahogany-panelled walls lined with oil paintings of innumerable nobles of varying repute from throughout Shenmadock's history, Arlon thought upon his sparring session. Marginally taller than Arlon but not lanky, strong but not heavy, Carpion was the very picture of a storybook ranger. His humour often fluctuated between quick-wittedness and cutting darkness, though only Arlon and Carpion's closer friends got to see this. His charismatic but brooding nature coupled with his good looks made him a much sought-after companion for the ladies of Shen Utah society, but for those outside the palace, he was a mercurial figure . . . even dangerous.

Having grown up together, Arlon counted his elder cousin as his best friend. He reminded Arlon of a simpler time, when they had been young soldiers together—perhaps the period in his life that he had last felt he truly belonged somewhere.

Entering the Council Chamber, a sheen of perspiration still on his brow, Arlon remarked to himself that he would never master the skill of sparring in *this* particular environment.

The Council Chamber was a massive circular hall with a vaulted ceiling and ornate accoutrement that betrayed its previous life as a royal audience chamber, before the fall of the Shen Utah Royal Family and the cessation of the monarchy. The centre of the chamber was flat and circular—made up of broad flagstones with ancient, faded patterns—from which rows of seats climbed to the outer pillars above. Stretching between each tall pillar were thirty-two stained-glass windows, each depicting moments of greatness from various reigns. During the overthrow of the monarchy, many overzealous rebels had wanted to smash the windows and replace them. The only thing that had halted the hammers was the inability to satisfactorily answer one simple question—*Replace them with what?* And so, the original windows had remained, still projecting glorious colours around the grand chamber.

In the centre of the floor stood a speaker's dais, raised on a marble plinth and adorned with exquisitely sculptured relief-work. For now, the chamber was empty save one lonely figure standing at the dais.

Councillor Fargil awaited him, a flush of concern colouring his ordinarily pallid features. Arlon often found himself liking Fargil, but he was still a politician, and that kept him wary.

"Councillor, you seem agitated; how can I help you this morning?" the Knight Marshall asked, crossing his meaty arms, the continuous tattoos and the angry scars beneath them creating a confusion of colour.

"Sire," Fargil began.

"How many times, Fargil? My name is Arlon. If you must use a title, make it Marshall. 'Sire' is for a liege. I'm not a king. I forgive the palace staff such transgressions because old habits die hard, but I won't have members of our council supplicating themselves so."

"My apologies, Marshall."

Arlon smiled. It was just this type of reluctance to assume even such a simple level of familiarity—such as the use of first names, even in private—that kept Arlon wary of politicians like Fargil. It made him think they were either hiding something or after something, usually both.

"There is still no word from the East," Fargil finished, worry knitting his brow.

"This is not such a grave concern, surely." Arlon stepped around Fargil and moved to a table, upon which rested fresh fruit and a jug of water already set out for the council meetings later that day. He lifted one of the fine-meshed nets—designed to protect the fruit from pests—picked up an apple, and took a hearty bite. "What was the last we heard?" he asked around the fruit.

"A relay messenger returned a week ago to advise of Lord Handee's arrival at Hightower on time," Fargil said. "We were expecting a second message two days ago, hopefully advising that Lord Handee had left Hightower and was set to return in due course. No second message has yet arrived."

"Fargil, you're going to make yourself sick worrying about every little thing. Winter approaches, and from what I am told, it is to be a bitter one; perhaps the messengers have simply been delayed. And at any rate, this would not be the first time the Senior Lord chose to lengthen a visit, particularly to such a distant city as Hightower. It has been some time since Handee and Reinhart have had a chance to talk at length. If anything, a delay could be seen as a positive thing."

"Yes, Si . . . Marshall. I see your point. However. . ." He paused, obviously not comfortable reiterating his point. Short for a human and of lengthening years, Fargil usually struck the pose of a quiet but wise old man. His sunken eyes, hollow cheeks, and grey hair hinted at sleepless nights and stressful living. Fargil pressed his palms together and closed his eyes for a breath. "Still, I would like you to address the Council of Lords to notify them of the possible delay."

Arlon's smile broadened knowingly, but any genuine humour fled the expression. *So that is it.* Always there were matters to attend to in the Council of Lords. Handee was the Senior Lord, but not the only lord or councillor by any stretch of the imagination.

The council was attended by the duke of each of the five duchies of Shenmadock—Mashtock, Jow, Shen Utah, Unedar, and Choat. If at any time a particular duke could not attend—which, of course, was the majority of the time—then their many representative councillors, often ever-present in the capital, attended in their stead and represented their duchies in person. Councillor Fargil was one such councillor, in constant attendance for his Lord Cordon Vale, Duke of Mashtock. Despite his duchy's proximity to Shen Utah, the ageing Lord Vale rarely left his lands to attend the council, and so it fell upon Fargil and his less-experienced aides to press Mashtock's concerns.

In addition to these lords and councillors, there were many officers of the Council of Lords who held authority for certain responsibilities that kept the nation running. These officers of the nation were appointed by the five dukes and did not so much represent the concerns of a particular duchy, but of a specific facet of government—everything from security to sewerage.

In all matters of dispute, Senior Lord Handee—one of the five ducal lords—held mediator status over the council. This essentially afforded the Senior Lord the power of veto, so Handee's absence would always be felt.

Arlon imagined Fargil was in the crux of an argument with a council colleague in Handee's absence, and wished for the quick return of his Senior Lord for arbitration. An officially ratified delay in the return of the Senior Lord would mean an official delay in mediation, effectively affording Fargil a stay of execution until either Handee returned or Fargil's own duke attended council, which was, of course, highly unlikely—and even then, there were never any guarantees that a resolution could be found without mediation. Handee's deputy in such affairs, Shen Utah's Councillor Ludovic—himself a lord by hereditary title—was unable to wield veto power. His vote was only comparable to one of the other four dukes. Deadlock in the council required Senior Lord Handee to release it.

The upshot was that there was no concern for Lord Handee's well-being in Fargil's request; it was all just politics. "You may address the council yourself and advise them that Lord Handee will most probably be delayed up to a week, should you wish," Arlon said. "I have no problem with that."

"My most sincere gratitude, Knight Marshall. I shall do so this afternoon. I thank you for your wisdom." Councillor Fargil bowed low and left Arlon alone in the Council Chamber. At the door, he stopped and turned back, saying, "Perhaps you are quite correct—Handee and Reinhart are old friends who have not had reason to share time in recent years. They would have much to catch up on."

"I am sure it is so," Arlon agreed. Fargil nodded with an uncertain smile and left. The tall Knight Marshall finished his apple, tossed the core in a wastebasket nearby, and then strode over to one of the rows farther up from the floor and took the weight off his legs. He let out a breath.

After the Battle of Thes on the Shenmadock border with Boyareen—when Shen Utah forces had desperately repelled a mighty barbarian horde—Arlon's life had accelerated beyond his control. In truth, Arlon was no hero, though he was now hailed as one. They'd even erected a statue of him outside the Shen College, for goodness' sake!

Before or after that most famous victory over the Boyareen horde, which had sent the barbarians scattering to the desert winds, Arlon had never lost a battle, be that as foot soldier, captain, or commander. Yes, he was proud of such achievements; they spoke well of his ability, but that didn't make him a hero. Some of the things he had done in order to win those battles, he was dread to think of now. It made him sick to his stomach to remember . . . especially Thes.

Turning his mind away from the past, he considered his current predicament. Senior Lord Handee had left the city of Shen Utah—the nation's capital that stood upon the northernmost border of the duchy of the same name—a month before, leaving the Council of Lords to look after itself. Every year, Handee travelled to some portion of the Land of the Lords. He held it high on his list of responsibilities.

Duke Reinhart hadn't attended Shen Utah for three years, instead entrusting his duchy's representation to Councillor Horvarth, a capable if inexperienced politician, according to Handee. The ducal capital of Unedar, Hightower was not a large town by any means, but the fact that Unedar bordered Shenmadock's neighbour Ipsica made it strategically important for the entire nation, even in times of peace. Handee was no fool; he understood Duke Reinhart's importance.

And so, late this summer, Senior Lord Handee had travelled south to Fort Beufort to attend the elven festival of autumnal equinox, and had then travelled further east along the coast to visit with Reinhart at Hightower Keep. Arlon believed Handee's intention had been to return home well before the winter solstice revels in the city of Shen Utah. He could still keep to that schedule, although with these delays, it was increasingly unlikely. As Fargil quite rightly pointed out, the fact that Reinhart and Lord Handee were age-old friends made the apparent delay a little easier to understand.

Arlon laughed to himself. *Friends in politics!* Even the great Senior Lord Handee considered Arlon a friend, if the wemik's own words were to be believed. And yet, Handee insisted on leaving Knight Marshall Arlon to babysit the Council of Lords by himself, while he partied with elves and got drunk with dukes!

The purpose of his position as Shenmadock's Knight Marshall was primarily to ensure the Defence of the Realm. It was an archaic title, a legacy of the ages when

Shenmadock was ruled by a royal family. It was his responsibility to ensure Shenmadock and its people were properly protected, although only a fool would threaten such a power.

Unfortunately, the Knight Marshall was also afforded executive powers when the Senior Lord was absent from the seat of power. That meant Arlon was expected to attend the Council of Lords, and even some meetings of councillors, to mediate as best he could. If a decision could be delayed until the Senior Lord returned, then it would be. If something was pressing enough to demand immediate attention, it fell to the Knight Marshall to mediate in the Senior Lord's stead.

This strange legislation of executive power was a leftover from more violent times, when the duchies themselves were independent nations and constantly at war. The Knight Marshall's executive power had been necessary to prepare for war—a theatre of decision-making that a young Arlon understood. Politics, mediation, and decree, he did not. Nor did he have any real inclination to learn. Arlon was no politician. Perhaps that was why Lord Handee had insisted on having the Hero of Thes as his Knight Marshall. Arlon was sure it was a shrewd move on Handee's part, but being in his prime at thirty, Arlon felt his own life had been highjacked or purloined somehow.

The most intrinsic portion of this archaic law concerned the difference between absent and Absent, with a capital A. The term in this context didn't mean simply that the Senior Lord hadn't returned to the city on time. As for what it *did* mean? Arlon had always intended to read up on this precise legislation, but had never found the time or suitable motivation. He regretted that now. He sensed that the longer Handee spent away with his friend Reinhart, the more likely it was that the subject might come under scrutiny, sooner rather than later.

Arlon laughed once more, bitterly this time. Rubbing the heels of his colourful hands into his eyes, he braced his elbows on his knees for a moment's rest in solitude, or so he thought.

"A man sits alone, laughing to himself," came a feminine voice from the shadows above and behind him. "Surely this can only be the onset of madness."

Arlon recognised the voice immediately, and a chill scurried up his spine. It was not a pleasant sensation. Suddenly he felt as though his un-armoured back was exposed to ranks of archers.

"If anyone were to suffer brain malady," Arlon replied, "this cursed room would be the place to make it so." He was careful to keep his tone neutral.

"Do you not rise in the presence of a lady?" asked the voice, closer now, though he had not heard her approaching footsteps.

"Do you not announce your arrival?"

"Where would be the fun in that?"

"No games today, Marta, my friend. I am tired."

He heard the creaking of the bench behind and to his left as Lady Marta took a seat. Lifting his face from his hands, Arlon looked over his shoulder at her.

Beautiful beyond human reckoning, Marta had been his friend during childhood, when he had been tutored in the College of Shen Utah, as well as trained as a soldier in the local city garrison. She had been pretty as a teenager, with hair the colour of pale gold and features of perfect symmetry. She had grown into a slender, beautiful woman of alarming determination and terrifying ambition.

"I love this room," she told him. "Such power." The awe in her voice was clear.

"Apparently the power is supposed to be afforded to the people who attend this chamber, not the stone and mortar themselves," he replied, his discomfort growing. He caught Marta's flowery scent on the air.

"Men like my father, you mean."

Lord Karl II of Jow was one of the five dukes of the Council of Lords, and one who rarely missed a meeting. Jow was the ducal capital of the rich and powerful duchy of the same name, which bordered Shen Utah to the east. Mineral deposits traded in from the Choat Mountains had led to Jow producing some of the best weapons in history, and their weapon-smiths had been at the heart of the expansion of the Land of the Lords. In these more peaceful times, Jow's influence was somewhat waning, although the constant unrest in the lands of Mashtock to the north kept the neighbouring duchy in solvency. Weapons were always desirable, perhaps even necessary, and trade between Mashtock and Jow was frequent. Only Choat's weapon-production capabilities were comparable to Jow's.

When Arlon had been appointed Knight Marshall, Lord Karl had made no secret of his desire for Arlon to wed his daughter Marta, seeking to take advantage of their childhood friendship. Such an alliance between the city of Jow and the Knight Marshall of Shen Utah would be a dream for his duchy.

Unfortunately for the corpulent lord, Arlon was common-born and had never felt the compulsion to marry for social or political advancement, and it had been a long time since he had felt any real affection for Marta. He had little family wealth, no surviving parents, and few political powers. Yes, he held the deeds to lands in the west, but they were nothing compared to the lands that most merchants-turned-nobles owned these days.

Lord Karl couldn't influence Arlon to wed for political reasons, which probably annoyed the noble, who was used to getting his own way. Perhaps for that reason, Lord Karl was proving hard to dissuade, and Arlon was sure the spoiled brat in Marta was partially responsible. She didn't want him; she just wanted what she couldn't have. And of course, she wanted the power and prestige he now appeared to represent.

Lord Handee had revealed to Arlon some time ago that Lady Marta shared her strength of ambition with her father. Of all the lords upon the council, the Duke of Jow coveted the position of Senior Lord more than any other; he had made no secret of that fact. However, considering that Lord Handee was a wemik, a rare quadruped species rumoured to live for centuries, Karl was unlikely to achieve his ambition. Arlon was sure that rankled the duke, too.

"What do you want, Marta?" Immediately, he regretted the wording.

"Oh, you know, my prince."

"Why do people insist on referring to me as royalty?"

"But you are *princely*, my love." He ignored the compliment, knowing it to be a trap. Marta changed the subject when she realised he would not take the bait. "So, Handee is absent without leave, I hear."

"You mean *over*hear," Arlon scolded calmly.

"Oh, my sweet—politicians whisper loudly." Arlon was well aware of the myriad meanings in those few words. "So, the Knight Marshall must preside alone for longer than he'd wish." She pouted for his benefit, shiny but thin lips curling into a dangerous smile. "You need not be alone in *everything*, you know." Suddenly her eyes changed and her face became lustful, seductive.

Despite his resolve, he felt himself react. He was only human. But he was reviled by his own weakness. Arlon could liken it only to the feeling of being drawn toward the edge of a cliff by the sickness of vertigo.

"Lord Handee will return in short order, my lady. Then this city can get on with whatever it is that swells both the coffers and the bellies of fat merchants and greedy aristocrats." He stood, angry with himself for allowing the outburst to betray his real thoughts. "And I can go back to doing what it is I am good at."

"And what is that, my heroic prince?" she asked, moving toward him. Standing on the step above, her eyes were almost level with his. "What do *you* desire, warmonger?"

Warmonger? After all these years, she knew nothing about him. "I thought to maybe find a wife, have some children. Perhaps even return to King's End and breed some horses."

Marta's eyes ignited with urgent desire as he spoke of marriage, her pupils dilating, her cheeks and the slender lines of her neck flushing with colour. The corner of his mouth lifted to a subtle smile, devoid of humour, revealing his trap. Suddenly her face was ice cold and furious. Perhaps he *was* learning a little of the world of politics.

"I must beg your leave, my lady," Arlon said, stepping back before turning away and walking calmly from the Council Chamber.

"Don't play with my affections, you low-born soldier thug!" Marta barked. "One day, when this nation has grown tired of its heroes, when you come crawling to me on your fattening belly seeking my hand, I won't be waiting for you!"

"The heart wants what the heart wants, m'lady," he said to himself softly as he passed through the huge doorway and out into the long corridor beyond.

Chapter Three
Expedition

Carpion awaited him outside the palace gates, a chilled flannel clutched to his nose. He was a slender man who never seemed to gain weight no matter how hard he worked or how much he ate. His shock of dark blond hair was closely cropped about his neck and ears, for he hated to have hair in his face.

"It's not broken," Carpion muttered to Arlon, before removing the cold compress from his face and breaking out a grin. Whether his nose was broken or not, his eyes certainly showed signs of bruising. He might have a couple of black eyes to brag about tomorrow.

Arlon clapped his cousin on the shoulder and ushered him away from the palace steps, across the old grounds toward the grand outer gates that led to the expansive squares of Temple Link, the affluent cultural and religious centre of Shen Utah, which surrounded the palace.

Passing through the gates, Arlon spared a glance at the heraldic emblems that hung from each of the long wall sections. Each of the twelve emblems represented one of the oldest and most revered regiments of the army, from the great tactical infantrymen of the Unedar Pointmen to the swift knighted cavalry of the former Shen royal house, known simply as the Red Knights in honour of their crimson uniforms. Their emblem, which hung in pride of place to the right of the gates, was a blood-red shield bordered in gold and topped with a simple crown. Only a few honoured regiments still bore such a crown, signifying those who had once so loyally served the monarchy.

Loyalty, thought Arlon bitterly. *Few know the truth!*

They left the colourful display behind and exited the palace, nodding to the sentries in passing.

Though it was early in the day, autumnal clouds already obscured the low-hanging sun, and it threatened to be one of those days that never grew bright. It had been a short and bitter autumn, and yet many citizens were abroad on the cobbled streets surrounding the palace, most heading in the same direction as the cousins.

The Temple Link markets provided less for the functional shopper than the collector of luxuries and antiquities. Arlon couldn't spot a single item of everyday use exchanging hands as he and Carpion wended their way between the rich shoppers parting with too easily gotten gains and leaving with ill-conceived tat.

In recent times, the city had suffered. Even those inhabitants of the comfortable region of Temple Link and the East End had felt the terror of the Temple Shredder, a serial murderer who had prowled the streets of Shen Utah, horribly murdering women of loose morals. The nature of the crimes had been gruesome beyond reasoning, and the degree of degradation incomprehensible.

But the murderer had been caught and killed hardly a week ago, down a lonely street in the depths of The Lows, felled by his cousin Carpion's lone arrow. In part due to his enigmatic manner, Arlon knew there was more to the story than Carpion would ever share, but he also knew not to press. His cousin had such wide-reaching contacts that it was sensible Arlon didn't know the details.

"Where are we going, Cousin?" Carpion asked him as they struggled through hawkers and punters revelling in the euphoria of relief that now filled the void left by the terror of the Temple Shredder's reign. "You were never the type for shopping."

"Agreed," said Arlon simply. He led Carpion away from the swelling markets, just as some of the stall-owners recognised Arlon for who he was and started calling his name, pressing their goods.

After a short distance, they passed two City Guards standing at the southern gate of the city, both of whom snapped out smart salutes. Once they passed beneath the ancient gate and were beyond the walls, Arlon relaxed.

Though outside the city proper, the press of the population was no less in evidence. During the reign of the last de Hayne monarch, King Gerimond de Hayne, the populace of Shen Utah had far outgrown the city's capacity. Thanks to the efforts of Gerimond's predecessors, Shenmadock had successfully established rule over the direct neighbours of Shen Utah, effectively ending centuries of conflict on the city's doorstep. Those neighbours were now sovereign duchies like Choat and Unedar.

So young Gerimond had spent the vast majority of his inherited treasury, filled mostly by the fruits of previous conquests, on expanding Shen Utah. Outside the walls, the cleared glacis and the lands beyond—which had once operated as clear lines of sight for archery towers—and slanted "batters" used to repel besieging infantry forces had been converted to housing and civil facilities. Numerous communities had relocated to the new regions in the shadow of Shen Utah's impressive walls, and what had once been fertile, arable land became a crowded residential area. Farmers, millers, and granaries alike were pushed farther afield, and the face of the landscape changed forever.

The audacious move that took more than forty years to complete was intended to secure Gerimond de Hayne's name in the annals of history. And that it did, though perhaps not in the manner he predicted. The people thrived and grew in the new environment, and a number of independent centres of education and apprenticeship developed to accommodate the swelling populace.

Beyond the gaze of the Royal Family and their loyal City Guard, a desire for a new system of governance grew in the foulberg outside the city and in the markets and docks near the river. King Gerimond de Hayne's selfless move had unwittingly created the perfect cauldron for revolution fuelled and driven by those who had come to command real power in the city—the merchants.

During the ensuing rebellion, the Royal Family was quickly and ruthlessly overthrown. Their rule was usurped by ambitious merchants, aristocrats, landlords, and disgruntled nobles elevating themselves from simpering vassals to influential republicans.

Ironically, very little had changed in the years since the fall of Gerimond de Hayne. If anything, bureaucracy and argumentative politics had slowed the functions of government down. Shen Utah operated today much as it had under a king's rule—just a hell of a lot slower, and at the whim of many self-serving aristocrats who commanded great wealth.

Many of the extended Royal Family—cousins, nieces, and nephews—had escaped the city unharmed, but the principals of the household were executed during the revolution. The elder princes, King Gerimond's three sons, had led the Household Guard in the defence of the palace, along with a few loyal household staff, but sheer weight of numbers meant their resistance was ultimately doomed. The many betrayals perpetrated that night were the final nail in the coffin.

Gerimond's wife, Queen Aurora, had been stabbed to death defending her youngest child and the royal grandchildren. All those innocents were thrown from the tallest towers, their frail bodies smashing on the flagstones far below.

Well—all except one lone survivor, who had been spirited away from the assault through a network of secret tunnels in the ancient tower, though Arlon knew that knowledge was hardly commonly held.

Before the crazed eyes of the baying crowds, under a starless sky, King Gerimond de Hayne's skin had been flayed from his chest and back. He had been disembowelled and then burned beneath the shadow of the palace—all while the priests of the temples closed their doors and averted their collective gaze.

The torture and mutilation of Gerimond was something that neither Arlon nor Carpion had ever been able to level with. The king had saved many thousands of lives by relieving the strain upon the city's population and alleviating their suffering just a decade before. The rebels' actions had gone beyond mere ingratitude; they made no sense.

As they walked, Arlon said, "Shen Utah has endured a difficult time."

"Indeed," Carpion agreed. "Months under the threat of the Shredder have done little to alleviate a growing autumnal depression."

"And on the very night you rid the city of that foul murderer, a vessel exploded at the harbour wall, sending a fortune in gold to the bottom of the harbour and calling into question once more the safety of the city."

"Not to mention losing *someone* a tidy penny." Carpion nodded.

"The fact that no one has claimed that fortune still bothers me. I was sure a reputable owner would have done so by now. That can only mean the owner was less so."

Carpion's mood darkened for a moment, a mirror to Arlon's. "You're not about to lecture me on my methods, are you?"

"Of course not. You are Captain of the Watch; you have your own thoughts on how this city is policed, and I have no complaints about your ability to deliver, regardless of your unusual thoughts about Shen Utah's need for an underworld."

"I know it sounds crazy, Arlon, but the city would eat itself from within were it not for the Sinecure and their leader, Swindle."

Arlon knew that the criminal hierarchy of the Sinecure and the name of Swindle were merely titles; Carpion probably had no idea as to the true identities of the criminal guild heads, and especially Swindle. Whether he would do anything about it even if he *did* know, Arlon didn't want to ask.

"Why do you speak of these things, Cousin?"

"More unsettling times lie before us," Arlon admitted.

They took seats near a well at the centre of a small square, a few hundred yards from the walls. Children of the neighbourhood played nearby as simple folk went about their business. No one paid them any attention apart from the odd glance toward Arlon's colourful arms. Rare it was for a man in the livery of the city to be so extensively adorned with sleeves of tattoos.

Now that they were amongst the simpler dwellings of the foulberg, Arlon finally spoke his mind. "People of power always attract hatred," he said quietly. "You told me that once, remember?"

Carpion sipped at a cup of water from the well. "I did. If I recall correctly, we were talking of Gerimond, the slaughtered king, at the time. Why do you mention it now?"

"It was insightful of you."

"I'm very wise." His younger cousin smirked.

"More a rare moment of clarity, I fear."

Carpion laughed. "What's your point, Arlon? It does annoy me when you're so circumspect. Stop talking around what you want to say and just spit it out!"

"I just . . . don't want to be left holding this baby any longer than is necessary."

Carpion nodded. "*This baby* being the Council of Lords?"

"I hate politics. I wish Handee would return."

"Considering you're an orphan, you've certainly developed an attachment issue with the Senior Lord. What do you want me to do?"

"Handee has been delayed on his return. A second message was expected to advise that he was journeying home, but there's been none." Carpion's brow was knitted in concern. "I don't fear for his safety. His entourage is more than capable of protecting him. I would just like to have some kind of idea when we can expect him, before these rabid-dog politicians have me for supper, or before Lady Marta has me wed!"

"Oh, such a hardship!" Carpion mocked. "Having the most beautiful woman of the city draped across one's every word! I'm sure that sleeping beneath silk sheets gives you a rash, and wiping one's arse with solid gold only affords a man piles!"

"Would you like me to put a word in for you with Marta?" Arlon asked.

Carpion's face dropped in terror. "Don't you dare! She's a harridan in the making!" He put a protective hand across his crotch. "She'd have Carpion 'fries' for supper!"

As their laughter petered out, they spent a moment enjoying the fresh air and peace away from the clamour of the city. Arlon took a breath. Carpion really was the only man in a position to keep this next part quiet, such was his litany of responsibilities: Captain of the Watch, Honorary Commander of the Wayfarer regiment, Commander General of the City Guard. Carpion had served his time in the army, even training for a time at the infamous Hightower Point, wherefrom the Unedar Pointmen acquired their name. Being one of the most decorated commanders in the army certainly made it a sensible appointment for Carpion to lead both the City Watch *and* the City Guard—though his rank within the Wayfarers was somewhat unusual.

Officially, the Wayfarers were a scouting regiment and so actually part of the navy, and it was a rare thing indeed for a single officer to command regiments within both services. Still, Arlon considered it a stroke of Soriana's good fortune, for it meant he had a commander of all three vital regiments he could trust.

"Take some men," Arlon told his cousin. "A few Wayfarers, augmented by some of the City Guards whom you know personally. No more than a dozen, I imagine. Make them men you can rely upon, men you can trust completely."

"I trust no one *completely,* Arlon; you know that."

"Well, as close as you can get to it, then. Be sure you have four fast riders. Leave before sundown and push hard for the town of Adar, near the ducal boundary with Unedar. The village is Lord Handee's last call en route to Shen Utah.

"Check with the small garrison there, and if you see no sign of Lord Handee, wait for him there. When he approaches, send one of your fast riders or a messenger pigeon to let me know. Instruct your riders to come to me and me alone. I don't want the likes of Lord Karl or Marta getting wind of any of this. It will only cause them to start lobbying for support, trying to undermine Lord Handee's position and pass things through the Council of Lords without his ratification.

"I know little of politics," admitted Arlon finally, "but I know the council can't afford such nonsense."

Sometime later, Guardigan and Dale made their way quickly to the drill square, the latter trying to get his gear into some semblance of order. The winter sun was westering, and twilight painted everything a slate grey. The pair's plan for a night of drinking and whoring had been scattered by a hastily delivered summons from Captain Carpion, ordering them to muster at the southern barracks of the Shen Utah City Guard, ready to travel. The life of a soldier was full of such pains.

Dale could see Guardigan was seething at having his plans waylaid. He grumbled endlessly during their walk to the drill square, cursing anything from poor fortune to a street cur for this turn of events.

Dale could scarcely contain his excitement. Finally, they were being asked to do something more than just pointlessly patrol the allures of the city walls.

"You know, you being so jolly just winds me up more!" Guardigan growled as they entered the grounds of the barracks.

Ancient, squat buildings with tall, narrow windows surrounded a drill square that was larger than most City Guard barracks would need. But this was the place most new recruits trained. Dale himself had trained here, and the smoothness of the broad flagstones under his boots acted as a reminder of forgotten days. Rumour had it Arlon of Thes himself had trained on this very square, years before.

Guardigan hoisted his gear higher on his back. "I can't believe you'd rather be going for a bloody horse ride than lying in a Wheel's warm arms, chock full of ale and low intentions. You make no sense, boy!"

The voice of the captain calling them over saved Dale from trying to explain. The slender Captain Carpion was in a group of soldiers whose number Dale and Guardigan's arrival swelled to a round dozen. It was clear they were gearing up for a long ride; a number of lackeys from the stables strapping provision packs, tents, and water bags to a couple of pack horses.

"Come on, you two," Carpion urged them. "We're waiting on you."

Guardigan grumbled an unintelligible—probably derogatory—reply, and Dale stopped to finish sorting his pack out. The captain ordered the men to take a knee, and Dale was surprised to see Carpion had suffered two black eyes recently. He chose not to mention it.

"I hope you've nothing pressing to do over the next few weeks, lads, because you're going to be busy. We're off on a little ride. I want you to travel as light as possible, save for the camp equipment and provisions we're bringing. We'll eat in the saddle during the day, and hunt whatever we need for the evenings." The captain indicated five of the group who were dressed differently; *Wayfarers,* thought Dale excitedly. The nation's finest scouts and hunters. "Oats and dry bread will suffice should the game prove elusive, though I doubt that'll be the case.

"We're not likely to meet any aggression, unless there are bandits abroad who are tired of living and fancy having a pop. Bring weaponry appropriate to that, but no heavy armour. The swifter our ride, the more successful our mission, so padded or leather armour will suffice. You'll find anything you're missing in the barracks. We've enough provisions for the next week, and we'll restock at our destination for the return leg."

"Where the hell are we going?" Guardigan asked, obviously still miffed. Dale figured Guardigan's long service and good reputation meant he could address the captain in such a fashion. It was certainly the case that his outburst drew a smile and not a scowl. Perhaps they knew each other better than he'd thought?

Even so, this was a little too close to insubordination, even for him. It was common knowledge that Carpion was cousin to the Knight Marshall and commanded impressive authority in his own right. Anyone else would most likely have been disciplined for such an outburst. Perhaps that was what Guardigan had hoped for; upsetting the leader of the expedition might ordinarily have seen him thrown off the mission, but if that were his intention, he was to be disappointed.

"Thank you for the input, Sergeant; I was just coming to the reason I've chosen to curse myself with your company for the next few days." Captain Carpion smiled crookedly. "We're crossing the ducal border into Unedar—all the way to the village of Adar, to be precise." The remainder of his words were lost on Dale as his mind swam.

Adar! His home! Only that morning Dale had spoken of missing it. Unable to control himself, he interrupted the captain. "Is there a problem in Adar, Captain?"

Carpion fixed him with a glare. "It's his home," Guardigan explained with a sideways nod.

"My family still abides there," Dale added.

By Carpion's tone, he appreciated Dale's interruption even less than Guardigan's. "Why do you think I'm bringing you? And no, there's no problem, soldier. We're simply looking for Senior Lord Handee's delayed messenger. Your knowledge of your home region and its people may prove valuable." Carpion then went on to finish his orders.

With his initial fears allayed, Dale's excitement swelled again. He was going home!

Chapter Four

Plans

Shen Utah's Whisper guild was unforgiving. Most criminal organisations were; such was the nature of the beast. The guild of spies—whose membership numbered in the single figures even at its height—had once been influential and powerful in the city, but those days had seemingly died with the de Hayne Royal Family. The monarchy knew the benefits of a well-organised flow of information. Most de Hayne monarchs, by all accounts, had even relied on such for the security of the state. Unfortunately, an aristocratic republic seemed unwilling to afford such affluence to the enterprising traders of information and secrets—perhaps because protecting one's secrets and information was the fastest way to ensure one's position of profitability remained strong. Either way, things had changed over the years, and not for the better.

Whisper Guildmaster Malian was not known for his patience, usually a fundamental virtue for a spy. As a group, spies frequently relied on mind-numbing patience to glean the most valuable information, but Malian was quick-tempered and even sometimes rash, to say the least.

From his stiff-backed seat, Click watched the Guildmaster closely. The man was in his late forties, perhaps even older.

His hair, which would have been jet black in his prime, was now greying at the temples and thinning on top. His face was creased with frown lines, and his frame was angular and gaunt. The dead-eyed Guildmaster glanced around the taproom in the basement of the Sleeping Troll, one of many protected taverns in The Lows, the basement of which was held in reservation almost exclusively for Whispers and their clients.

Click had been surprised to find almost every Whisper in the city sitting in the tavern basement, including most of his fellow apprentices. In total, they numbered just over a dozen, but they were rarely seen on the same street, let alone every one of them in the same room!

The murmuring in the taproom ebbed away as Malian glared, his gall rising visibly at being kept waiting. Finally, he lost his patience and slammed an empty tankard down on the nearest table. The crash certainly got the room's attention. Click heard the pewter crack.

"That's better," Malian said with a humourless grin. Even sitting at the back of the room, Click was able to hear his menacing voice quite clearly. "This is the second gathering I've called in a week, and I'm sorry if these demands are placing pressures on you all." Click could tell he wasn't sorry in the slightest. "However, this is a critical time, these messages are vital, and this latest instruction to you all warrants a break from tradition.

"In my last message, I expressed the Sinecure's concern regarding the sinking of the vessel in the harbour some days ago. I am professionally compelled to impress upon you all that discovering the details of this action has now become your primary *whispering*. Any information regarding those responsible will be paid for at triple rates."

No one even mumbled in response, despite the promise of a princely sum for a single *whispering*. Malian traced the room with his flat gaze, seemingly trying to lock eyes with every Whisper there. "I want no confusion. This should be your first concern; for many, it should be your *only* concern. All other clients and jobs take a back seat."

Click was still just an apprentice, but if he was able to provide key information like this to Malian, it would both win him more money than he had ever seen and would surely lead to his acceptance as a fully-fledged Whisper. Being mid-teens, this would be an impressive feat, one he was already close to achieving. Learning his stealth skills from the best Glimmer there was, Acaelian, had aided Click well.

Riches and success—a heady combination. A shame, then, that this would not be Click's route to either. The fact was, whoever had owned the scuttled ship or its valuable cargo would have to be a client or associate of Malian, for why else would the Guildmaster be behaving in such a strange way? It smacked of desperation. Whoever they were, they were clearly both powerful and dangerous enough to rattle Malian, and this made Click nervous for two reasons.

Firstly, Click already knew the answers Malian sought, and more difficult questions would surely follow as to why Click had kept the information to himself until now.

Secondly, and worse, just how was Click supposed to avoid certain death if he told the guild that it had actually been *him* who had scuttled the ship, fully laden with gold, gems, and illegal explosive naphtha? They'd ask even more questions, which he still wouldn't answer, for to do so would be to betray his best friend. No, if he confessed, then they'd sell him to the scuttled ship's owner, who would cut his throat—if they didn't do it themselves. After all, the natural conclusion would be that Click had known Grimlaw the Glimmer was aboard the ship at the time, and subsequently killed during the sinking.

An eye for an eye, a life for a life.

And so, he sat in silence as the meeting ran its course. When it came to an end, he noticed a handful of Whispers remained to enjoy the opportunity to interact with those they seldom had the chance to see these days, but Click had no interest in that. He left the basement of the tavern and disappeared through a shaded side door onto the meandering, filth-strewn, frigid streets of Shen Utah. He wandered for some hours before finding himself once again at the King's Docks, where he took a moment's rest at the edge of the working docks, the westering sun cold and distant overhead. He sat upon a wall that overlooked the river, his feet dangling, just as his friend Acaelian had done on many occasions when he needed to think. Secretly, Click hoped that sitting on the wall might somehow trigger an appearance by the mercurial elf, but it wasn't to be; he was long gone.

Click looked forlornly at the spot where the ship had sunk to its watery grave on that dark and fateful night not many moons ago. Another ship was now alongside at the harbour wall, for the devastation to the destroyed ship had been so extensive that the timbers had been sundered, the masts splintered, and the cargo spread across the deep harbour floor, thus not inhibiting other vessels coming alongside. A fortune lost to the waves that still carried a rainbow hue from the split naphtha casks. Powerful men never forgot a thing like that. They would want vengeance.

Suddenly the hairs on his neck stood up and a chill scurried down his spine.

Someone approached.

Click rested his hand on the grip of his new dirk tucked into his belt as a figure stepped around the wall to his left side and stood with his toes at the very edge of the wall. Even with his peripheral vision, Click could see the man was overweight, and a stolen glance revealed eyes like pickled eggs, but there was a sharp keenness to his features that showed he was more cunning than he might first seem.

"Hello, boy," the man said without looking at him.

"I'm not for sale," Click said derisively, alluding to some of the more exotic members of the guild of Wheels—boys who sold themselves for a higher price for the scandal their trade would cause their clients.

"Nice," huffed the new arrival with obvious distaste. "I'm Constable Foord of the City Watch."

Oh great, thought Click. He felt the muscles in his legs bunch, ready to take flight. He forced his expression to remain neutral as he replied, "What do you want?"

"No call to be rude, boy, and don't even think about running. I'm not here to bring a guild rat like you in. My time is more valuable than that."

"Then what do you want?" Click repeated, even more keen to take flight. Still, he remained dismissive and flippant as he added, "You can see I'm busy sitting, right?"

Foord laughed. "You guild rats are all the same—so fast at running your mouths off!" Foord's laugh petered out in a heavy wheeze. "You're not as funny as your friend Acaelian, though."

Click looked sharply at the constable. Foord smiled knowingly.

"We both know who arranged for that ship to have an accident that night," Foord said, indicating the harbour with a jut of his jowly chin. "And we both know the elf did it all so that he was free to help bring down the Temple Shredder. It doesn't take much for a man of even average intelligence—"

"Don't flatter yourself."

"—to work out that his closest friend would be sure to know what really happened here that night."

"I haven't seen Acaelian since the Shredder got killed," Click admitted truthfully. "I don't know where he is."

"I figured that would be the case; it would appear he has up and disappeared. But I'm not looking for him. Even a talent like Acaelian can't be in two places at once. He can't have scuttled that ship and helped bring down the Shredder too. It's just not possible. I'm looking for his accomplices, or one of them, at least."

"Even if he had accomplices, they'd not betray Acaelian's trust to you, so you're still wasting your time."

"For a spy, you seem to have a knack for missing the point."

"I'm not a—"

"Oh, don't bother. I've heard it all before. Let me cut to the chase. Acaelian actually did me a massive favour that night, for which I owe him many thanks, but in doing so, he and his accomplices"—Foord flipped him a pickled-egg glance of accusation—"will surely have attracted the attention of powerful enemies—namely, the owners of that ship you lot scuttled. There's nothing I can do to help any of you, but you can help yourselves. You see, Acaelian has powerful friends, as well as enemies—whether he's disappeared or not."

The fat man took a couple of steps as though to leave, and then said, "Believe it or not, we're on the same side. You'd do well to follow me." And then he did walk away, turning up a street leading away from the King's Docks.

Click remained under the distant white sun for a moment, considering his options before deciding his position was untenable. He had to follow Constable Foord and take his chances.

Keeping a discreet distance, the spy moved among people going about their early evening business, ensuring he kept a mark on Foord's back. The constable, to his credit, never once turned to see if he was following. They travelled south for more than half an hour, wending through broadening city streets toward Temple Link.

Click stopped at a corner of a busy market half-filled with marketers and patrons braving the cold. Stalls of bright colours, normally resplendent in the summer days, were made dull by the flat light of approaching winter, and the dour colours of warmer clothing only served to bleed any vibrancy from the scene.

Foord approached a street vendor to purchase some unhealthy snack, leaving Click wondering what to do next. Watching the grease dribble down Foord's chin, he was beginning to understand where the man's corpulent build had come from.

As he was laughing to himself, Click suddenly sensed the presence of another. He was too slow to react, however, and a powerful hand gripped his elbow from behind, stopping him from drawing his dirk. A rich voice sounded in his ear. "Don't draw that, boy. I wouldn't like to have to run you through."

Click relaxed, for he recognised the voice. He turned to see the tall Carpion looking down on him. The hand released his arm. The captain of the City Watch had the beginnings of two black eyes.

"What happened to you?" Click asked with a laugh.

"I forgot a lesson I learned years ago."

"To duck?"

Ignoring the joke, Carpion asked, "Do you have something for me?"

"Here." Click reached into his tunic and retrieved the vial of Black Spider Venom he had stolen from the apothecary at Carpion's behest. He handed it to the taller man carefully and then quickly secreted the small bag of gold he received in payment. "He wasn't brewing it himself, though," he told the captain. "I think he must have bought it in."

"So, it was a one-off?"

"Seems that way. And would have paid a tidy sum for it, too, enough to convince him to act against the rules of the guilds and to hire those goons who chased me halfway across the city. Anyway, only foolhardy assassins mess with poisons like this, and even then, extremely rarely."

Carpion nodded. "Jorus might find himself in more trouble than it was worth. See if you can find out who ordered it."

Click smiled. "For a fee, of course?"

"Of course."

"It's probably worth mentioning that, while no one in the guilds knows of this yet, there are rumours. Sooner or later, someone will work out something's afoot, especially if Jorus has to import some more to honour his contract."

"Huh," Carpion said, "good point."

"Malian has everyone tearing around looking for those who sank that ship, but this poison won't escape his attention forever."

"We'll cross that bridge when we come to it. For now, head over to the table in the corner," Carpion told him. Click immediately saw where the captain meant; a lone figure sat in the cold afternoon shadows, cradling a warm drink between gnarly hands, languid steam spiralling from the cup. "Join the old man. He needs company."

With that, Carpion stepped out from the corner behind Click and walked across the expanse of the half-empty market to the café area, taking a seat at the table adjacent to the old man. Click hesitated and then followed. Constable Foord had taken his snack and disappeared; clearly his work was done.

As Click approached the table in the diminishing light of dusk, the old codger looked up and smiled slyly. Immediately Click could sense this man was dangerous. Though he looked an unimaginable age and dressed in a vaguely dishevelled manner, Click could still sense strength in him . . . or was it threat?

"Sit," the man said, not even bothering to put on an aged voice. Only Carpion would be able to overhear them. "It's really starting to annoy me how easily these guttersnipes are able to see through my disguises," he said to Carpion.

"Young eyes don't look through the fog of prejudice," the captain replied.

"You mean he's not yet smart enough to be fooled by it?"

Carpion laughed by way of response, shaking his head at the older man's interpretation.

"Well, either way, not many people would see through a disguise like this so quickly. You must be a fast learner."

"So I've been told," Click admitted.

"We have a mutual friend," the stranger said. "Unfortunately, neither of us seems to know where he has gone. Events have transpired, and I need the assistance of someone with his particular skill set and recent experience."

"Like I told your pet, Foord, I've no idea where Acaelian has gone, and I probably wouldn't tell you even if I did."

"There's no need to be abrasive. I believe you. Trust me when I tell you, if I don't know where he is, you've a cat in hell's chance."

"Then what am I doing here?"

"If you are indeed as quick a learner as you say you are, then I think you're just the boy to deputise for him. No doubt you've worked closely together."

Clearly a veiled accusation that Click had been Acaelian's accomplice. He began to protest, but the man waved his assertions away. "This is in your interest, too, my friend. I feel I should explain something. It was I who passed the job of robbing the ship in the harbour to Acaelian. In truth, I told him that under no circumstances should the cargo on that ship be allowed to reach its destination. From that point of view, I can't be mad that, instead of stealing the contents, he chose to blow the bloody thing up. It is an inconvenience for us all now that such a thing has happened. But one can't unscramble an egg. The difference between a simple theft and an act of sabotage is significant for some people. In one of those two circumstances, the slighted party might one day dream of regaining their loss. Not so in the other."

As the man spoke, Click became more and more concerned. From what Acaelian had said before he'd disappeared, it had seemed clear that the man who had pointed the elf in the direction of the laden vessel could only have been Swindle—leader of the Sinecure and criminal mastermind of the Shen Utah underworld.

Click now sat speaking with the most powerful criminal in all of Shen Utah, and probably all of Shenmadock. Add to that fact the presence of Carpion, captain of both the City Watch and City Guard, and things were looking pretty dicey.

"The gold and jewels that sank to the bottom of the harbour don't concern me. I have enough money. Precisely who it *does* concern is that which concerns me, if I'm making myself clear."

"Kind of."

"I knew there was a huge amount of gold and jewellery on that ship—anyone in my position of responsibility would know that—but the presence of that much naphtha in a vessel alongside the King's Docks is a worry to everyone, especially considering I can't find a single person who knew about it. I want to know who it belonged to and where it was bound, and you're going to find out for me."

"How am I supposed to do that, exactly?"

"You're a bloody spy; you work it out. As a lead, you might want to visit the harbourmaster's offices—preferably when they're unmanned. When you get something, take it to Constable Foord. Normally I'd have you bring it to Captain Carpion here, but unfortunately, he has more pressing matters to which he has been called to attend. Even I can't order the captain of the City Watch around."

At the next table, the handsome captain huffed another rueful laugh.

After a second of thought, Click nodded. "Okay."

"Click, this is important," Swindle emphasised. "And for the time being, you need to keep this to yourself. Not even Malian is to be informed, do you understand? When we're dealing with stakes this high, one can't ever know who to trust."

High stakes? Click thought. *Doesn't get much higher than one's own life in the balance!*

"Okay," he said again.

Chapter Five
Kathryn

Arlon sat beneath the shade of a yellowing chestnut tree, its wide-fingered leaves blown about by the frostiness of the autumnal winds that pushed down off the Choat Mountains in the east. Within days, this region could start to see the ground frost of winter setting in, and the snows would be close behind. Despite the early morning chill, the day was set to be fine and Arlon didn't feel the cold.

His cousin Carpion had departed the city two nights before, and Arlon had quickly found himself bored in the palace. The only aspect that kept him alert was the constant threat of bumping into Marta. Despite a growing mound of duties that he was ignoring—albeit minor ones—Arlon had taken week's end leave and ridden from the grounds of the palace, with no particular destination in mind. He had felt the need to cut loose of the city, plain and simple.

As was often the case, Arlon had ridden southeast of Shen Utah and wound his way into the low hills that overlooked both the Jow Valley to the east and the distant duchy of Mashtock in the north. After a tricky ascent, he had tethered his mount in a hilltop glade, where the horse had plenty of water.

Leaving his longsword stowed behind his saddle, Arlon set off into the woods on foot, seeking a comfortable place to sit for a while, still trying to convince himself that he was here by random happenstance. He wouldn't need the weapon; this region was peaceful and never suffered at the hands of bandits.

Historically, the region had been used as a game reserve for the de Hayne dynasty, and in the years since, it had been preserved just so, for hunting and for the training of Shen Utah scouts like the Wayfarers. Indeed, soldiers from the Wayfarer regiment were charged with protecting the game from poachers, increasing the security of the region even more.

And so he found himself sitting at the foot of the chestnut tree as a conker fell to the ground nearby, still encased in its green husk. As young children back in King's End, Arlon and his friends had used vinegar and sour cider to toughen the chestnut seeds before fixing string to them, making small weapons to fill the minutes of boredom between chores at the stables. Distractedly, Arlon retrieved the deadfall seed and started stripping the husk from the dark polished-wood centre.

A dog's bark sounded in the morning air from the familiar meadow below his position, and the song of the woodland birds was abruptly silenced. Arlon scanned the long, low wall a hundred yards away, down a short incline. He made out the bounding figure of a springer spaniel, eager to retrieve some thrown object and return it to his mistress.

The red springer's name was Sop, and his mistress was Princess Kathryn de Hayne, last known descendant of the usurped King Gerimond, daughter of the lone survivor who had been snuck out of the palace on the night of the revolution.

Officially, she didn't hold the title of princess, as there was no royalty in Shenmadock now, but those who knew her still referred to her that way.

Watching her follow Sop onto the grounds that surrounded her villa, Arlon figured it was because she acted with the grace and honour of a princess, more than in honour of any hereditary title. She simply radiated regal elegance.

He sat and watched the pair play for a while. Kathryn was alone in her garden with Sop, no maids or housecarls present. Rarely did Kathryn find such peace, and Arlon could see she revelled in it. Counterpoint to Sop's barks was the occasional gleeful laugh as the dog took a tumble or bounded gamely back, stick in mouth. The dog's entire body seemed to be wagging with the joy of the game.

As always, it didn't take long for Kathryn to look up and catch sight of Arlon reclining in the shadows of the tree. When Sop returned with his stick, Kathryn ignored the dog. Instead, she walked steadily forward to the stone wall, her eyes on Arlon. Perplexed, Sop carefully placed the stick on the ground.

The Knight Marshall rose to his feet and stepped out into the soft autumnal sunlight, tossing the conker aside on his way down to the wall. When he was halfway there, he put his fingers to his lips and blew two shrill whistles.

Sop's ears jumped, and the dog frantically scanned the hillside for the source of the familiar call. When the spaniel's eyes fixed on him, he barked loudly once and leaped into a gallop. The springer cleanly jumped the stone wall and surged the forty yards to Arlon, who stooped to gather up the dog. Sop jumped into him, the enthusiastic animal pitching him back, before he barked twice more and jumped away playfully as Arlon ruffled him behind the ears.

Returning to his feet, he walked to where Kathryn now stood at the stone wall of her gardens, smiling at the pair of them. "Sop is always so glad to see you," she said. "He misses having animals of his own intellectual level around the place."

Having completed two rapid loops round Arlon's feet, Sop reached the wall and put both forepaws atop it. He looked decidedly unimpressed with the slight.

"Not a problem, Sop," Arlon told him. "It's a compliment." Turning back to Kathryn, Arlon felt the welcome and familiar kick in the guts he experienced upon their every meeting. "I like your hair down," he told her without thought.

Although Princess Kathryn had never married, addressing any noble in such a manner was considered rude, but Arlon never felt the confines of proper conduct in Kathryn's presence—he had known her far too long for that. He had always felt he could speak freely. In fact, no other aspect of his life afforded him such a feeling of freedom as simply being in Kathryn's company.

"It needs cutting," she said, self-consciously touching the locks at her shoulder before turning away from the wall. She never accepted Arlon's compliments with anything other than deflection. But her hair shone like honey-touched mahogany as she walked, bringing to mind the colour of the chestnut seed. "The sun might be bright, but it's cold in the wind," she said. "Come into the shelter."

Arlon lifted Sop over the wall and then vaulted it himself. Sop's excitement seemed to get the better of him, and he galloped across the gardens, chasing invisible rabbits. Arlon fell into stride alongside Kathryn de Hayne, enjoying her nearness.

"So why are you here this time?"

The relative abruptness of her question caught him off guard, as familiar as he was with her confidence and directness. In her company, no matter what armour he wore, Arlon always felt bereft of defence. Kathryn, the gentlest person he knew, was—perhaps ironically—the only person to ever make him feel vulnerable. Knight Marshall Arlon, the Hero of Thes, Heathen-Bane, Lord Protector of Shenmadock, made vulnerable by this graceful, gracious woman. Carpion would laugh his ass off.

But it was precisely this directness that Arlon had come to tap. He trusted Kathryn's forthrightness, honesty, and integrity. And of course, because of her lineage, there were still those in the capital who—perhaps secretly—respected the old royal line. She had contacts in the city, and even within the government itself. "The Council of Lords is a nest of vipers," he complained. "I find the constant political manoeuvring is wearing me out."

"Has Lord Handee not yet returned from Unedar?" she asked.

"Something has delayed his return, although we have no reason to assume foul play."

Concern touched her brow. "You mean, not yet."

"Not yet," he conceded. "Look, I don't fear for his safety; Handee is a wily individual, and the members of his entourage are counted amongst our finest warriors. I've personally trained and fought alongside many of them."

"Then you're obviously worried about something else," she pressed.

"I've sent my cousin to seek out the relay messenger. I can't imagine he's going to be more than another week. But until he returns, I sense troubling undercurrents in the Council of Lords. Nothing I can put my finger on, but there's something going on."

"Lord Handee is a powerful figure who will never hold his own personal ambitions above those that benefit the nation," she told him. "The same cannot be said for the rest of the council, Arlon. You're right to be wary. As a result of Handee's delayed return, there will be pressure to push through legislation and to force the settlement of contentious articles that Handee would crush, were he here. Politicians hide their true goals in the rhetoric of governance. Often the secret behind learning a politician's true intentions is listening to what they're not saying, seeing what they're not doing."

"I don't mind admitting I don't know how I am to recognise these things. I'm no politician!" Arlon could barely abide the plaintive tone of his voice. He feared he sounded like a child.

"I think it best you try to delay all such machinations until you can be confident of a return date for Handee, instead of trying to make decisions or judgement calls on things you're not comfortable with. Stall until his return. As obvious a tactic as it might seem to the council, it is a language they understand, and I doubt they will fight you on it. And if they do, you might have a clearer idea of who it is you should keep a closer eye on."

The two stepped to a series of low wicker chairs shielded from the wind by wooden fences. Up a short rise was the villa that Princess Kathryn had inherited from the vast estate of her family—a low, sprawling, grand affair with tall windows and impressive stonemasonry. Upon the hillside descending from the far side of the villa stretched miles of apple orchards, and the cider the estate produced to this day was reputed to be some of the finest from the northlands. The de Haynes had, of course, owned thousands more acres and properties throughout the land, and all had been swallowed up and disseminated after the revolution. Only a clever piece of political chicanery had kept this villa in her family long enough for her to take ownership when she reached maturity. Ergun and his allies on the newly formed council—as a direct favour to him—ensured no one had known about it.

Arlon watched as Kathryn took her seat, and then he sat beside her. Sop skidded to a halt nearby and sat, watching the two humans impatiently.

"Councillor Fargil has already come to me to raise concerns about Handee's absence," Arlon confessed.

"You want to be careful about the use of that word *absence*, Arlon."

"I know."

"So, he was asking about Handee?"

Arlon nodded.

"What did he *really* want?"

Not for the first time, Arlon wished he had Kathryn nearby every day. As with every other instance of that longing, Arlon kidded himself this was purely for her candour and wisdom, not just for the want of her.

"I don't really know," he admitted. "Although he didn't divulge any details, he said he was concerned about any possible delay in mediation during the coming weeks."

"A mediation in what?"

"He didn't say. In fact, I didn't ask."

Kathryn laughed. "Probably a good thing."

He shook his head. "Obviously, I should have, because he was clearly concerned about something. But when he offered no details, I was actually glad!"

"The absence of information can often cause more worry. But you and Councillor Fargil are both showing concern for different reasons, Arlon." Kathryn turned toward him to emphasise her point, the low sun shining on her face. "He is an old fox, experienced and cunning when cornered, though a man devoid of true malice. But accompanying those long years are weariness, cynicism, and possibly a little rustiness. He may genuinely be seeking your help."

"He's a likeable old salt," said Arlon with a smile.

They were silent for a long moment, staring at each other. Something passed between them, some recognition as her eyes flicked back and forth almost imperceptibly. Then, as quickly as the moment had come, it fled. Kathryn turned in her seat and looked out at the tree line. "I like when you visit."

A million weighty replies flashed through Arlon's heart, but after a long delay, he simply said, "I like to visit. In fact, I don't do it anywhere near often enough." Unspoken was his belief that, were he to visit every day, it would still not be enough.

The following day, Arlon attended the latest council session and was surprised just how anxious Councillor Fargil had become. Normally a placid individual, Fargil now sat in the diffused light in the Council Chamber, the picture of nervous agitation. His eyes roamed around the room, taking in the expressions of his fellow councillors and lords as the council sat in session. He mashed his hands together until the knuckles were bone-white, and clearly found it difficult to remain still in his seat. Arlon took these traits in over the course of the first hour of the morning. Only because he knew Fargil quite well were they so apparent.

The opening exchanges of the council meetings were often filled with business of a most mundane nature at best. The single point of interest was the discussion of the monthly games to be held the following day, but other than that, it was—aside from Fargil's agitation—boring. At least two dozen councillors and lords were in attendance, with their various aides and administrators swelling the numbers further. Even with such a good attendance of various officers of the council, the chamber always looked half empty, and the tendency of the chamber to echo voices and carry them high only increased the sense of emptiness.

In Arlon's boredom, Fargil's state of agitation had seized his attention, particularly in comparison with the mood of the ambitious Lord Karl II of Jow. The duke of the nation's smallest yet historically most influential duchy paced up and down periodically at the rear of the chamber, taking little or no interest in the proceedings. His barely contained fury—whatever the reason for it—was quite openly apparent, perhaps even demonstrably so.

The duchies of Jow and Mashtock were tense neighbours, and the contrast in moods between the representatives of these duchies put Arlon on edge. Something was afoot; he could sense it.

It was nearer noon when the reason for the tension came to light, but it was not the bold Lord Karl who addressed the court first, as Arlon might have expected. When any remaining merchants and members of the public guilds had left the chamber, Councillor Ludovic—Senior Lord Handee's senior aide—invited the remaining council officials to present any other business. It was then that the apparently nerve-wracked Councillor Fargil raised a tentative hand.

Despite being a skilled politician, Fargil was never an aggressive public speaker, and so he waited a long time for the chamber to quiet enough for his words to be heard properly.

"My lords, we have a problem. Master Chairman, may I address the council?"

Ludovic, chairing the meeting in Handee's stead, indicated the Mashtock councillor could say on.

"As discussed in a previous session, I have concerns that I wish presided over in the presence of the most senior representatives of the five duchies, and especially Senior Lord Handee. As was revealed in previous sessions, and as is still the case now, Lord Handee is delayed in his return from Unedar. Today, in the presence of the Knight Marshall, I feel compelled once more to bring our concerns to light in order to receive the benefit of the council's collective wisdom and to perhaps seek mediation in this matter."

Fargil was talking around the subject, and some of his colleagues grew restless with it. "Get to the point,

Councillor," encouraged Councillor Ludovic sternly. There were murmurs of agreement.

"It falls to me to report that, for more than a week, residents along the banks of the River Jow have complained of marauding troops striking at villages, slaying cattle, burning crops, and killing villagers. According to our own magistrates in the towns near the affected region, the pattern of the tactics being employed and the specific locations of the attacks would suggest that the aggressors are originating from south of the river."

"Lies!" barked the rotund Lord Karl as he stormed to the centre of the chamber, full of righteous indignation. Arlon had figured Lord Karl would not sit still for such an accusation against his duchy. "How dare you present your duke's own unwillingness to quash the lawlessness of your indigenous bandits and renegades, and your inability to police the safety of your own citizens, as some imagined aggression by Jow! As was the case in previous sessions, you continue to present no hard facts regarding these incidents, let alone any proof that Jow troops are responsible!"

"Councillor Fargil," spoke Councillor Ludovic steadily. Ludovic was a fair mediator, a long-term servant of the Council of Lords and close ally of the absent Senior Lord. Indeed, many saw Ludovic as Handee's natural successor as Duke of Shen Utah. "Lord Karl is correct. You must have proof of your allegations."

"Our villagers lie in fresh graves in fields poisoned by the stench of rotting cattle and ashen crops. Come and see for yourselves. All along the river, and even further north, we are seeing the same tactics! These are uniform tactics, military tactics, not random banditry. These are organised assaults that speak of a coordinated and clandestine campaign! Our magistrate reports are unflinching in this assessment."

Karl harrumphed. "A councillor from Mashtock is pushing the boundaries of irony when he complains of bandit clans attacking his people. For decades, the rest of us have suffered at the hands of bandits roaming *from* Mashtock soil, wherein these brigands are largely unmolested by Mashtock's law-keepers, allowed to grow powerful by Mashtock's inaction. Now you seek to blame your neighbouring duchies when you suffer similar consequences!"

Fargil stood suddenly and jabbed an accusatory finger at Karl. "Seek not to hide behind conjecture and deflection, Lord Karl! It is clear that these attacks are coming from across your border! Long have you and your predecessors gazed across the river at our southern plains with envy!"

That much is true, thought Arlon. Most of southern Mashtock had once been opulent Jow territory, until a bloody war had established a tentative truce on the natural border of the River Jow. Jow itself—far smaller than any other duchy—had never been happy to settle for that, and considered Mashtock's hold on those lands to be nothing more than a longstanding occupation, one ratified by Shen Utah and Shenmadock itself. It was a touchy subject to say the least, despite the distance of time since those conflicts had been resolved.

"Stop this bickering, gentlemen," snapped Ludovic.

"I am compelled by my lord and duke to demand action!" pleaded Fargil regardless.

"What action could you possibly propose, when there is so little evidence for us to work from?" asked Lord Karl, still full of disdain.

Fargil looked up at Arlon, who sat mesmerised by the exchange. "I beseech the Knight Marshall to mediate a solution. Inaction when lives are being lost is a travesty! Something must be done!"

A hush descended. Lord Karl's swine-like eyes looked up to regard Arlon watchfully. All others in the chamber looked on with interest, for it was virtually unheard of for

Arlon to speak in the council. He normally liked it that way, and felt uncomfortable under such scrutiny.

A fist-match could usually sort out the type of dispute that Arlon was used to settling, but this posturing and bickering was alien to him. He remained seated as he spoke, trying to remember the myriad lessons he'd learned as a youngster. "Councillor Fargil, firstly, I do not doubt that you bring this matter before the council only after researching the accuracy of your magistrate reports, and so it is reasonable to assume that these attacks of which you speak are fact."

Lord Karl went to speak, but Arlon continued regardless, raising his voice to curtail any interruption.

"Nevertheless, you must have stronger proof with regards to the true agitators before making a direct accusation toward a neighbouring duchy. The opinion of some local magistrates, with all due respect, is not enough. You are experienced enough to know that, Councillor."

Fargil nodded once in open acknowledgement of the criticism.

"My suggestion is simple—a team shall be despatched to review these field reports with your magistrates. Once all the information has been gathered, we can take steps to curtail these incidents, protect our citizenry, and—should it be proven to warrant such—make any appropriate sanctions as the law so demands."

It was a delaying tactic, and everyone in the chamber knew it. Arlon wished to stall until Handee returned, to let the wemik manage this potentially volatile situation.

Arlon then addressed Councillor Ludovic. "Is this satisfactory?"

The chairman called for a vote, casting his own in Handee's stead. All five duchy representatives voted in favour, including Lord Karl of Jow. Still, judging by the general demeanour in the chamber, it was clear his decision had been sniffed out for what it was, even if no one was willing to challenge the Knight Marshall directly.

Fargil looked disappointed but quickly relented. "Of course, we submit to the council's wisdom."

Lord Karl stared with clear malevolence at Councillor Fargil before turning on his heel. "If there is nothing further for which I am required, I shall take my leave." He stalked from the chamber and left Fargil to quietly sit back in his chair.

Arlon thought he looked very old.

Chapter Six
Sage Council

"Agreed, it was a peculiar exchange, considering the length of time that peace has existed between Jow and Mashtock," mused Ergun over a cup of warmed wine once the council had adjourned.

Arlon sat across from his mentor in the old professor's chambers. Located on the lower floors of the ancient west wing of the palace, Ergun's room was modestly arranged, with little space wasted on frivolous decorations. Instead of long and expensive tapestries, his walls were hung with carefully preserved maps of the Land of the Lords and the southern lands beyond their borders. An arrangement of simple candles stood to the side, casting a soft light. The tomes on his shelves ranged from the overtly studious to the artistic, with no small number of volumes that most scholars would consider fanciful to a fault, and others that some religions might find dangerous. Dark smudges of soot on the low ceiling above the collection of candles were testimony to long hours of study. There was but one shuttered window, which now held firm against a buffeting storm that had blown in through the afternoon. It was, in short, a good night to be indoors, and even better to have a chance to share some time with Ergun.

The professor had taken Arlon under his wing when he had first arrived in the unpredictable world of Shen Utah, had been a vitally strong influence on his development as a teen, and had proven an invaluable advisor when Arlon had been elevated to the position of Knight Marshall.

Together with Kathryn de Hayne and Senior Lord Handee, Professor Ergun was one of Arlon's wisest and most trusted friends. His lined features and dark-grey eyes were steeped in wisdom.

"He seemed sincere, though," said Arlon, speaking of Fargil's conduct in the council session earlier that day. "I would find it difficult to suggest he was lying. Whether they are or not, I think he genuinely believes Jow is responsible for these attacks."

"Perhaps it is," suggested Ergun.

This stance did not surprise Arlon. "Really? You're not just siding with your brother, are you?"

"I know you know better than that. Don't forget that for many years, Fargil and I have not seen eye to eye on all things. What I mean is that the evidence we have at hand at the moment, circumstantial as it may be, would most likely support an argument that Jow was in some way responsible. Highly unlikely it is that a spike in banditry would carry identical tactics. We'd see sporadic strikes, varying numbers, some attacks by day and others at night. Fargil seems convinced that this isn't so."

Arlon tilted his head in surprise. "I suppose the tactics and patterns being described would not adhere to any tactic employed by small bandit clans, if those reports are ratified. It's even less likely that numerous clans would have banded together under a single leader without us knowing about it. The fact is, renegades, bandits, and brigands lack the discipline for large tactical organisation. But should we really entertain the idea that Jow is to blame?"

"Of course we should. Now, whether that blame is laid directly at their door is a whole other consideration," Ergun added carefully.

There it is.

"So we have to consider the possibility of some rogue element in Jow's leadership?"

Ergun nodded. "I would not put it past some ambitious people to employ bandit companies to cause unrest in Mashtock. If each bandit clan were given the same instructions, perhaps rogue generals from Jow's own regiments, that might explain the uniformity of these attacks. Even if Karl and his aides discovered such a plot, would it be in their interest to bring it to the attention of the council? Probably not at this early stage; they would seek to save face by quelling it themselves. Hence why Karl, despite his indignation at the accusations, did actually vote in favour of your solution."

"Well, if Karl was to blame, it wouldn't serve him to openly oppose such a toothless move on the council's part. Could you imagine the same tactic but with Lord Karl's complicity?"

"Not likely." Ergun shook his head. "Nowadays we have this forum for diplomacy to settle such disputes—in which Karl is a powerful figure. I am struggling to discern any motive Jow's duke would have for such a strong-handed tactic. If this was an aggressive move from Jow, they ultimately have nothing to gain but negative sanctions from Shen Utah. It would be folly; it is absolutely inevitable that you will find the truth behind these attacks. Even Karl wouldn't be so reckless without good reason. No, we must keep our minds open to other possibilities.

"I think your decision to send a team to investigate these claims was the most reasonable, under the circumstances. Handee shall return soon, and you can leave it to him to try and negotiate these stormy waters. If it *is* Jow rattling their sabres, then I imagine they will step into line very quickly on his return. We can only hope that the fact-finders you have sent will uncover nothing in those reports that is overly concerning. Lord Karl respects you almost as much as he does Senior Lord Handee."

"I am not so sure I agree with that," Arlon said. "True, he both reveres and respects the position of Knight Marshall, but I doubt greatly that he respects me personally. I think he actually resents me and my refusal to bend to his desire to have me wedded to Marta. I think he sees that stubbornness as me standing in his way."

Ergun nodded, but then said, "Lord Karl's resentment of you—if that is what it is—would be born out of his fear of your integrity, son, not your stubbornness. Mankind, much like the dwarves and the orcs, often fears that which it does not understand. Lord Karl, like any other successful politician, is a man beset by an ambition that knows no bounds. He could never understand a person who balks at the prospect of seizing power, for his life is underpinned by the desire for more and more of it, as well as a crushing fear of its loss. He is right to believe that a marriage between you and his daughter would strengthen both his position and yours in the echelons of power. He just can't fathom that you don't share his ambition."

They were silent for a moment, enjoying the warm berry-rich wine, the only sound in the room the odd spit from a burning wick.

"How are you?" Ergun asked quietly into the silence. Only then did Arlon realise the professor had been watching him closely.

"I'm tired," Arlon admitted, running a finger down his temple.

"More than that, I think."

Once again, Ergun had cut to the quick of it. "I'm tired of *this*, Ergun. I'm no politician. I'm not used to feeling stalked when I have no suitable weapon with which to defend myself. I'm wasting my time. No one lives forever."

"You want to settle and breed those horses of yours? I can see you being happy in such a setting." There was no fun-making in his words; Ergun was being sincere. After all, the old professor had known Arlon's father far better than he—the boy from King's End, tragically orphaned at an early age and robbed of that privilege. Looking into his pewter mug, the ageing man added, "How is Kathryn?"

At the mere mention of Princess de Hayne's name, Arlon's heart dropped in his chest. His eyes flicked to Ergun and then away just as quickly. The old man smiled knowingly.

"It is a shame that you're such a simple man, Arlon of King's End." Again, Ergun's tone was not mocking. He gave Arlon the title of his birthplace, not the moniker of legend that he'd earned over time. He still paid him the respect of not using his surname, though, and for that, Arlon was grateful. "I mean, of course, that these very qualities of simplicity are the virtues that keep you vital to this nation. You are the most trustworthy, capable Knight Marshall I have known in my tenure—and have grown into one of the best men I've known since your father. The very absence of political ambition and lust for power makes you the ideal officer for your current post. Cruel it is that you must continue to make such sacrifices after all you've already given." Arlon saw him glance at the terrible scars on his arms, hidden behind the colours of his tattoos—the colourful coverings a gift from the elven healers of Eladreen. "It is no wonder you're tired."

Arlon had no answer, only offering a nod of his head.

Sweat beaded on the archer's brow under a crop of sandy hair as he pulled the bowstring back beneath his chin. Even at this distance, Arlon could see the strain telling on the man's forearm, veins jutting like cords. He watched closely as he exhaled, settled, and then loosed his arrow. The shaft whistled through the pale morning sunlight and thumped into the golden centre of the archery target. The gathered dignitaries gave an appreciative ripple of applause, but the archer seemed not to notice.

The day following the testing exchange in the Council Chamber between Mashtock and Jow had begun cloudy, the remnants of the previous night's storm still lingering, but now the skies above were clear, the colour of cold blue steel. The grounds of the palace near the main gateworks were adorned with bunting and an intimidating variety of floral arrangements. Standing out above all other decorations, the emblems of the Shenmadock armed forces shone in the distant sunlight, which already cast deep shadows across the well-kept lawns, causing some spectators to shield their eyes as the next competitor stepped to the mark to compose himself.

Arlon stood at the stone wall of a raised walkway that surrounded the old royal gardens. The far side of the walkway across the grounds was covered by a series of lattice awnings bedecked by still-resplendent flowers. Beneath these sat many of the dignitaries in attendance, from lords of the land to the more affluent merchants of the city. Looking around at the gathered ladies and gentlemen, Arlon's breath caught as a pair of deep-brown eyes fixed on his own. Princess Kathryn stood behind the main ranks of seating, in the shadows, with a lady in waiting beside her. A quick smile passed between them before her maid passed some comment or other regarding the archery competition, causing Kathryn to turn back to her and laugh.

He wondered why she had come. A golden vein of hope burned within him that she might have come to see him.

Another round of applause echoed round the royal gardens. The second archer had sent an arrow to land alongside the first, their coloured fletchings intertwined. Arlon recognised this archer as one of Carpion's younger Wayfarers. Even at this early point in his training, he would be a skilled hunter, as well as a talented scout and fearsome warrior. At any age, Carpion's Wayfarers were a force to be reckoned with, often forged in battle on the outer regions of Shenmadock to the wild northlands, and even beyond the borders to the south. Arlon struggled for a moment but couldn't recall the archer's name.

Elsewhere on the grounds of the palace, other games would be afoot, with money silently changing hands on the success or failure of each event. Gambling on the regular games wasn't officially illegal, but it was certainly frowned upon as being base and unsavoury—especially where the temples were concerned. After all, anyone who was anyone in Shen society would be here, and not just to turn a profit on a warrior's victory or defeat. This was to be the last such competition before the games were suspended for the winter.

The local garrisons used the events to compete for trophies and bragging rights, and the Shen Utah courtiers took the opportunity to mingle and gossip amongst those with whom they might not have reason to converse under usual circumstances. Many minor deals and alliances were brokered and broken in such innocuous settings.

The impressive palace grounds, surrounded by botanical gardens and grand walkways, were also a place for the young ladies of the court to flirt with potential suitors—often under the watchful eyes of ambitious fathers constantly on the lookout for a marriage of opportunity to further their own gains. Despite the collapse of the monarchy, this was still an effective way for ambitious people to bolster any bid for power in the young republic. Some things never changed.

Just as Arlon resolved to leave his elevated position to try to engineer a chance meeting with Kathryn, a movement glimpsed out of the corner of his eye caught his attention. Standing in the doorway to the spiral staircase off the balcony was Lord Karl II, Duke of Jow. The rotund politician and landowner rarely missed the monthly morning sport in the old royal grounds of the palace. However, he was not alone, speaking closely with another man.

Arlon wanted nothing more than to turn and leave the balcony by another staircase, but in that moment, Lord Karl glanced his way and immediately held aloft a ring-bedecked hand to catch his attention. Reluctantly, Arlon acknowledged the sign and remained where he was, awaiting the duke's pleasure. After the last few words were exchanged between the duke and the other man, they parted ways, Karl administering an uncharacteristically friendly pat on the other's arm. Then they parted and Karl approached, smoothing his greying hair as he stepped out into the breeze. He stepped to Arlon's side, affording the Knight Marshall the shallowest of bows before he placed his hands on the parapet, his chubby bejewelled fingers laced in a show of nonchalance. The action made his clasped hands look like an uncooked meat pie.

"Good morning, Lord Karl," Arlon greeted him.

"Indeed it is, Arlon. I hope you don't mind me taking a few minutes of peace with you?"

"Of course not," Arlon lied. He knew Karl would have a good reason for approaching him—and it was sure to have nothing to do with peace. Loathing himself for asking but knowing that courtesy demanded it, Arlon enquired, "How is Lady Marta?"

Karl huffed. It was a strange sound. It might have even been a fart had it come from the other end. "She has grown into a capable and intelligent woman. It feels like only yesterday she was still a child. I struggle with the passing of time. It feels so fleeting, and I so old." He shook his head, his pink jowls wobbling.

Arlon had heard Karl speak this way before. The lord was given to striking the posture of wistful contemplation on occasion. But Arlon understood that a politician never spoke wistfully; there was always an agenda.

"As she grows into young womanhood, it becomes more pertinent for me to choose from among her many admirable suitors. Only recently has the impressive Failton of Breen requested my permission to court her."

Karl's tone suggested he was bragging about such a development, but the name meant nothing to Arlon.

"I don't envy you in having to choose a suitor for your daughter, my lord; there are many fine young men in the city." Arlon said this despite the fact he didn't know Failton of Breen either in person or by reputation. He could only assume he was not particularly highborn. It was unlikely Karl would entertain an approach by anyone who didn't afford him some kind of advantage.

Breen. He might not know the person, but he knew the town; it was an old farming community in central Unedar. Then something occurred to him, and he couldn't help but show the dawning realisation on his face.

"Do you know of Baronet Failton?" Karl asked, seeing his expression change.

"No," Arlon admitted, "I'm afraid I don't think I do. His home of Breen, though. Its mention has given me a prompt to recognise the chap on the stairs just then, that is all. Councillor Horvarth."

"Indeed," Karl said amiably. "Horvarth and I are old friends."

Arlon made a noise to indicate his understanding, though he struggled to keep the pitch of confusion from it. Breen, in the heart of Unedar. Unedar, the boundary duchy with Shenmadock's oldest enemy, Ipsica. Historically there had been little love lost between inland Jow and the boundary duchies of both Unedar and Choat, as Jow had long lamented the draw on national resources that the defences in both eastern duchies represented. During the monarchy, they had suffered in silence as ample funds were spent in the upkeep of those defences, and since the inception of the republic, Jow had indeed been able to regularly reduce those allocations—a little bit at a time, but enough to ensure tensions always ran high between Jow and the eastern duchies.

I wonder that there are any duchies at all who remain on good terms with Jow, Arlon thought.

Karl changed the subject back to less comfortable ground. "Perhaps it is my traditional bent or the memory of my own time in the armed service of this nation, but I would prefer a suitor of strength and integrity to help guide my lovely Marta in the coming years. Failton is a well-mannered young man and his family has great wealth, but . . ." He let the thought hang like a noose.

Here it was. Arlon knew Karl's "own time in the armed service of this nation" had never placed him in harm's way, for he had served two meagre seasons—a matter of months—in the Jow Household Guard, training as a cavalry commander, and Arlon remained convinced that this had been purely for the pleasure of exerting his will upon others. As for the mention of integrity, for goodness' sake, the man was a politician!

Arlon took a breath. He was being uncharitable and allowing his feelings about Marta and their history to cloud his view of the girl's father. Karl was an ambitious politician, but that didn't make him a bad man.

When it was clear Arlon wasn't going to spring his trap, Karl continued. "It comes close to breaking my heart to fear that you and Marta may miss the opportunity at such happiness. Will you not court her? Since you were both young, I have never seen her as happy as when in your company. Nor you in hers."

That was another pitch built upon something of a fallacy. Arlon had known Marta as a teenager, when he had been both studying at the college and training at the garrison. She had developed a crush on him then, and for a time, their relationship had become quite passionate, but then he had left for the south, and the rest was history. They had never truly been close, not in the way Arlon now knew people could be. Not in the way he dreamed of being. He resisted the urge to glance down at the princess.

Karl had not been in the city for the short period that he and Marta had been close. There was no way he could have possibly seen Marta and Arlon happy together, even had that been true.

As much frustrated at himself for allowing his mind to wander back to times he had fought hard to repress, Arlon embraced his chagrin and deliberately dropped Lord Karl's title in his reply. "Karl, we have already spoken of this at length."

"Of course," Karl conceded carefully. "But these are changing times, and Marta has grown into a capable ambassador. She would be a considerable asset to our nation's leadership. I fear there may be stormy times ahead."

Before Arlon could ask what he meant, Karl changed tack again.

"Won't you join us for the recital tonight? I know Marta would prefer your company to that of her fusty old father." He placed a self-deprecating hand on his chest, hidden beneath layers of fur-lined coats and fine regalia.

But that mention of future conflict struck a chord in Arlon. *Something about the way he said it, perhaps?* "I'm truly sorry, Lord Karl, but while I serve Shen Utah, Shenmadock, and the Land of Lords as Knight Marshall, I cannot entertain the idea of romantic affiliations," Arlon told him a little too sternly.

"But that is not true, Arlon." A true politician, Karl never missed the opportunity to argue semantics. "The nation imposes no such restrictions on the Knight Marshall, and never has. You are free to make your own choices, unlike us nobles." Arlon did not miss the suggestion that his own lineage was comparatively ignoble. "And such a union would only benefit those involved."

Arlon saw Karl glance down at Princess Kathryn de Hayne.

"All the better to guide this nation on its current course of freedom from oppression, thus ensuring we don't slip back to the trappings of a forgotten age of servitude and superstition. You must realise that it would be impossible for you to entertain the idea of marrying one of the fallen line. The council could ill afford such a thing. Marriage should be a unifying undertaking, Knight Marshall, not a fragmenting one."

Karl's reference to the royal bloodline of the de Haynes, and his reference to Arlon's relationship with Kathryn in particular, suddenly angered him.

Even through that anger, though, he could see the real truth was in Karl's own wording. What he suggested wasn't a marriage and had absolutely nothing to do with love or happiness; he sought that union for Jow and the position of Knight Marshall, which equated to a union between himself and the capital—an angle from which to strengthen his ambition in the Council of Lords, perhaps bringing himself closer to the position of Senior Lord. Ergun had been quite correct in his thoughts on Lord Karl.

"When I said I cannot marry during my tenure, I meant to say that this is a personal decision. I do not intend to marry, and that is for my own reasons. I feel to do so would be to jeopardise that very integrity which you have so gracefully complimented."

Despite the flowery wording, Arlon knew he had gone too far. He had snapped and had fully intended to suggest that a marriage to Marta would be to risk corruption. He shouldn't have said it, and he could see that Karl had registered the slight.

Too late, Arlon tried to lighten the mood. Turning back to the archery competition, he said, "The Wayfarers make fine archers, do they not?"

Lord Karl was silent for a long moment, his eyes on Arlon, before he replied, "They certainly do, Knight Marshall. Our nation is well protected. Regardless of what you might think of me—regardless of what others may whisper in darkened rooms—I am not your enemy. Nor am I an enemy of this nation. I am a patriot. Everything I do is for the nation of Shenmadock above all, including my own ambition."

Before Arlon could summon an apology, Karl said, "I will take my leave. I have just remembered I have many duties I am neglecting that require my attention before I return to Jow."

"Of course. Have a pleasant day," Arlon tried, but it was to no avail. Karl turned without reply and strode calmly away. This had been an unfortunate exchange.

Chapter Seven

The Harbour Master

Click moved like a shadow within shadows, passing silently along the foot of a high wall. In the near distance, the lamps of the harbour shone in the darkness and the lonely sounds of the river at night washed through the air. Other than those natural sounds, the harbour and quayside of the King's Docks were silent. It was perhaps four of the clock in the early morning, and Click was finally going about his work.

The city rarely fell to complete silence, for there was always work to be done. Somewhere to the south, a baker would be firing his ovens, rangers would be waking to leave the city for the day's hunt, and some wheelhouses of The Lows would still be plying a late trade. Even the harbour would soon be brimming with activity, for of all portions of Shen Utah, the harbour kept unsociable hours. However, the palace games had just taken place, and many members of the soldiery would be abed by now, including any auxiliaries tasked with patrolling the docks. He had waited for the perfect night to take action, but in truth, Click ran a great risk in what he was about to do. If he was caught, he'd have far too much explaining to do to far too many people.

And then he'd be dead.

By way of protection, he carried only his new dirk, relying on the darkness of the predawn night to shield him from harm.

High above, a square of dull brown light upon the blackness of the wall indicated a shuttered window into the customs building of the harbourmaster's complex, which all seemed deserted. In the few days since speaking with Swindle, he had spent long hours casing the premises and tracking the movements of the administrators within, patiently awaiting this small window of quiet and darkness to make his move.

It still twisted in his stomach that he had to mislead Malian, his Guildmaster, in almost everything he was doing at present. He disliked the man, yes, but he had pledged his loyalty to him and their guild. Yet the leader of the Sinecure had left him in no doubt as to both the importance and the secrecy of their current investigation. That suited him, for while Swindle knew Click had been involved in the sinking of the treasure ship, so far Malian clearly didn't. And at this moment, Malian was looking after his client's interests, while Swindle was seeking to protect his own. Click had to figure that the latter of these two gave him the better chance of survival.

The thing that had him worried about that was his longstanding arrangement with Carpion to gather information on the presence of Black Snake Venom in the city, for the Captain of the Watch had also made it clear that he was to keep any mention of that to himself. That had obviously been intended to include keeping it from Swindle. He had no way of knowing how the crimelord would feel about that, or Malian for that matter!

Click was treading a fine path between three deadly swamps.

Peering through the darkness, Click found the downspout he was looking for and slowly began climbing. Once atop the slated roof, he secured one end of a short length of rope to the far guttering, ensuring it would hold his weight at least for the short time he required, and then moved gingerly to the front of the customs building and inched forward on his belly. He stared down upon the front yard of the building littered with crates and discarded packaging. An easily climbed wooden fence surrounded the entire property, but within the grounds slept a dog with huge shoulders and wicked-looking teeth. They called him Snap, and Click could understand why. So far, Snap hadn't noticed his presence, but that could change at any moment.

He dropped the remainder of the rope over the edge and lowered himself silently down the front of the building toward the open window that led to the front office. His muscles protested and strained, the rope biting into his hands, but Click turned his mind away from the pain, as Acaelian had taught him.

Once at the opening, he rested both sets of toes on the sill and arched his spine forward to wriggle in through the narrow gap at the top of the cheaply installed window. He was forced to perform an uncomfortable handstand upon a wooden cabinet while he brought his legs through behind him. A short forward roll dropped him to the floor with only a small thump.

For agonising seconds, he remained still, listening for sounds that Snap had reacted, but he heard only the occasional canine snore. If Snap started barking, Click would have no time to extricate himself from the building and make good his escape. He was neck deep in an unsprung trap; one wrong move would be the end of him.

As anticipated, the building seemed deserted. Reaching up, he pulled the short length of rope in through the window to make it harder to spot and then turned his attention to his search.

It took him a few minutes to locate the file room. Even in the gloom, he could see the décor was spartan and the items on the walls were limited to work-related charts and record sheets.

One of these charts detailed the ships that were currently in port. Upon that list, scored through in angry slashes, was a vessel that had been removed from the port list with no departure date. Interestingly, the entry bore no ship's name, only a date reference. Click noted the consignment batch numbers entered against the ship.

Next, he located the rows of swing files that contained the bills of lading for each consignment into and out of Shen Utah, relieved to find that each folder was meticulously filed in consignment number order. There was something pleasant about the care that had been taken in the organisation of those files. Without disturbing the fastidiously arranged files, Click moved along the wall and located the consignment batch number from the destroyed vessel.

There was just one consignment file.

His hand hovered over it unsteadily as he considered his options. He took a nervous glance around the customs room and then removed the file, opening the folder to reveal a series of documents.

Some were dog-eared and others a little creased. The name of the sending party was one he recognised, although at first, he didn't know where from.

Then it came to him. Mr. Justin Dowling was a merchant and trader in Shen Utah, and a successful one at that. He kept his nose clean, by and large. The late Grimlaw had burgled his establishment once or twice before Click and Acaelian had arranged Grimlaw's permanent retirement. The consignment note listed the contents of the destroyed vessel as being Luxury Items.

No shit! Click thought. *Doesn't get much more luxurious than a king's ransom in gold and gems . . . not to mention a tonne of naphtha!*

Checking his details, Click scanned the document again, immediately concerned.

No, he'd been absolutely correct—the thing that had piqued his curiosity was the absence of any mention of naphtha on the consignment. Half the ship's hold had been filled with barrels and casks of the stuff, which was what had made it so easy to destroy. No way they could have passed that off as luxury goods. Expensive liquor, perhaps—but even that would be subject to excise duty and would appear on the manifest.

Swindle had been right—there must have been an inside connection for this vessel. That much explosive material in a single ship's hold would have surely caused concern for the customs people and the harbour master himself. If an inspection of the hold had been made, that would have resulted in penalties and perhaps seizure. Unless the inspection was carried out by someone in the loop.

There were legal exemptions from inspection, but that would be noted too—probably on the original list. There had been no such note. This bill of lading showed a ratified customs inspection; no mention of naphtha or barrels of any kind.

Click shook his head. He had expected to find proof of some evasion—perhaps a missing customs note, or one partially destroyed—but this? He *knew* there had been naphtha on that ship; he'd seen it with his own eyes. The breadth of influence, the number of payoffs, the power required to pull off this level of subterfuge was . . . terrifying.

He stared into the darkness of the office, suddenly feeling terribly small. A distant sound made him flinch. He turned his head to look at the dark doorway, straining to listen more closely to the now-silent building.

Had that been outside?

He returned his attention to the file. He looked overleaf on the bill of lading at the delivery details, but the destination name meant nothing to him—Du Lacigny Holdings, Choat.

Du Lacigny. Stupid name.

Nervous at the amount of time his search was taking and concerned about that noise he thought he'd heard, Click returned the documents to the folder and made to replace it in the rack. Then something peculiar caught his attention, and he hesitated.

He opened the file again and looked at the slightly creased pages, the dog-eared corner, the uneven filing.

Quickly shutting and replacing the file, he grabbed up the next one along. Its pages were perfectly flat, impeccably neat, meticulously filed in that same fastidious, perpendicular order he'd discerned before.

He checked several more and found them all to be arranged the same. He returned all the files to their rightful place and stepped back, regarding them from a distance, a finger of concern tapping his lower lip.

Someone else has been at that file, Click realised, *someone other than the ridiculously neat filing clerk who runs this customs office.* Someone else had to have discovered the same information. None of it was missing; everything was as it should be, so nothing obvious had been stolen to hide the illegal imports. *Have they been replaced? Are these creased pages forgeries? Surely not, for forgeries would not have borne the harbour master's seal of inspection. But what of the customs inspector?*

Becoming increasingly concerned, Click rushed to the duty register and leafed through the record of customs inspectors and found the date of the sinking. He noted the names of the inspectors on duty on the days preceding, too, when the ship would have come alongside and been due for inspection. There was just one name for that week.

Then he took to his heels. He raced back to his infiltration point and jumped atop the cabinet, curling himself through the window. His legs collided noisily with the sill below.

This time, Snap awoke, his rock-like head swinging up in a sleepy manner. Eyes like pits locked on Click's scurrying form, and a growl rumbled in Snap's throat.

The spy pulled the rope loose and spun about carefully on the sill.

Snap began barking, and Click could hear the scratch of claws upon stone as he rushed over. Panic surged through him, and he hauled himself up with a speed and power he hadn't known he possessed.

He heard Snap jump at his feet, but managed to pull them up in time, avoiding that toothy maw. The dog's lumpy head crashed against the glass of the window, which shattered on impact.

The dog recoiled and fell back to the yard, a small shard still stuck in the thick skin of his head as the rest of the broken glass rained down with an alarming volume. The dog began howling, much of his enthusiasm gone, allowing Click to reach the roof, scramble to the far side, remove the rope, and traverse the downspout.

In seconds, he had vaulted the fence and was rushing down dark streets, once more a shadow amongst shadows as Snap's howls rose mournfully on the chill night air.

He now had three names to investigate, although only two were within his reach—Justin Dowling, the shipping agent, and Paldron Ward, the customs inspector for that week. Each one would be difficult to investigate, but both were a damn sight easier than going all the way to Choat to investigate the mysterious cargo's intended recipient, du Lacigny Holdings. For the time being, whoever Du Lacigny was would have to remain a mystery.

Chapter Eight

Guy du Lacigny

Far to the east of Shen Utah, following the River Jow upstream into the Choat Mountain ranges that marked the ducal border with Shen Utah, deep into the plunging bowl at the heart of the Choat duchy, two men moved in the shadow of a bridge on the banks of a shallow stream. The first crouched at the water's edge, while the other stood aside, knowing all too well the anger the other felt. The city bustled all around them, unmindful of their reverie.

Despite the comparative warmth of the preceding summer, the first man knew that water had flowed beneath the bridge consistently all season, for this river never ran dry. Now, on the cusp of winter, the water was chill and quick. The glacial winds from the northern mountains often brought frost, sleet, and snow, but today, the air was only clear and bitter.

The crouching figure's thoughts were similarly clear, and even more desperately bitter.

At Stefon's feet, caught on the riverbank, were the mortal remains of his friend. He had only known Susu-Van for a matter of weeks, but her loss deeply affected him—perhaps more so than he had anticipated. He and his group had all been strangers to her, yet she had helped them when they needed it most, despite having no reason to do so.

But perhaps it was the nature of her death that compounded the emotions that flowed through him, chill and unrelenting as the stream at his feet. Her throat had been cut so severely that only her neckbone and the elasticity of the spinal cord kept her from being fully decapitated. No blood flowed from the wound now; her body had obviously been washed some way downstream. Her purple tongue protruded from her mouth in a grotesque, bloated, and final expression of defiance.

Stefon stood, drew his arms close to his chest to embattle the chill elements, and turned away from Susu-Van's corpse.

He nodded once to the constable who stood beside the body, attempting to strike an air of condolence when all Stefon sensed was boredom. "That's her," he told the young constable, and then he turned away.

As he climbed to the towpath above, his comrade left the shadows and fell into stride beside him. "It's confirmed, then," Stefon said through gritted teeth, "Susu-Van is dead."

"Murdered," corrected Rish darkly. Like Stefon, Rish was still in his twenties, and they were more like brothers than friends. His hair, a sandy brown, was always in need of a cut, and his vivid green eyes, slender frame, and athletic gait all served to highlight how catlike he was, albeit a feral cat.

Stefon, Rish, and the rest of their retinue had met Susu-Van on the road northwest from Wahib City. Just days before their chance meeting, Stefon and his friends had barely escaped the city of Wahib with their lives after a most desperate struggle.

Wahib had been under a quarantine following the outbreak of a deadly virus. As far as Stefon and his friends knew, it probably still was. His mercenary group had been tasked with uncovering the truth behind the quarantine, and their investigations had led to some unwanted attention from a religious sect called The Light. Stefon had barely escaped with his life after being attacked by zealots possessing strange powers and unimaginable strength.

The true nature of the virus itself had seemed to defy all reason. It finally transpired that, using corrupt local officials, the religious order of The Light had, at some point in the recent past, begun deliberately poisoning the populace, infecting them with a disease that brought about swift and certain death. There never had been a plague. It had been mass murder.

Stefon's investigations had revealed that no corpses had ever reached the funeral furnaces of the hospital. No bodies had ever been buried. Instead, they had simply disappeared. By luck, Stefon had discovered one such body, a recent victim of the plague, in the morgue of the hospital—not yet concealed or removed by the religious zealots. And under Stefon's inspection, the cadaver had . . . moved. No post-mortem twitch, no death throw; it had simply moved of its own accord.

It had been about that time that Stefon decided to leave Wahib City for good. So they had fled, Stefon leading the remaining members of his mercenary band through a secret exit in the bowels of the ancient city.

Rish, a wily scoundrel and Stefon's closest friend, had joined him in the escape, also leading with them a creative young engineer called Brooss, a moody and unpredictable dwarf named Jewl, and the towering warrior Pryn. Before the quarantine, Stefon had considered them professional contemporaries. Now the five had been galvanised into a single unit. They were inseparable following the horrific things they had witnessed within the locked city of Wahib.

Once free of the city, they had made for the inland duchy of Choat, known for its comparatively neutral stance in most things political—despite officially flying the flag of

Shenmadock. Fleeing from Ipsica, Stefon and his friends might not always be afforded a warm welcome in some parts of Shenmadock, but as the languages were barely different and each of the group was adept at disguising their accents, they chose to risk it. After all, it had been a long time since war had been waged between Ipsica and Shenmadock, and even then, such battles had mostly been fought along the Ipsica-Unedar border to the south. Choat benefitted defensively from the circular range of mountains that formed its border.

Once free of Wahib City, they found themselves in a land that seemed oblivious to the goings-on behind those walls. Worried about the distance to the Shenmadock border, Stefon's group had been lucky enough to meet a caravan heading into the mountains to make the dangerous journey through one of the old steep passes into the Choat Basin—a caravan willing to employ more guards for that crossing, as it was a route often plagued by bandits. They had helped escort the caravan train in exchange for food during their travel and a meagre sum upon safe arrival at their destination.

The caravan leader had been Susu-Van.

She owned an independent importer trading company in the southern portion of Choat City, running supplies in and out of the duchy for various merchants. The day of their arrival, over a glass of excellent wine, Susu-Van and her friend Coral had explained the full reason that the former had employed Stefon and his crew.

"I don't know what you're running from, Stefon," she had said candidly, "but it's pretty obvious to me that you five are highly skilled individuals, particularly in areas that might be of use to me. Specialist skills, let's say."

He had simply nodded, remaining guarded. His trust level in general had plunged since the summer, and being a mercenary captain, it hadn't been particularly high in the first place. The important fact was, agents of The Light and their enigmatic leader, Druid Lesjac, might still be hunting Stefon and his friends. One couldn't be too cautious.

"Those mountain passes we just came through can be trying," Susu-Van continued, "but they hardly warrant a dozen guards. There are more worrying things afoot, and I'm under pressure to retain my contracts. I don't want to lose my father's business. He always wanted a son, but as his only daughter, I refuse to disappoint his memory by losing control of his business."

The tall trader's friend Coral had gone on to explain Susu-Van's dilemma. It seemed pretty straightforward to Stefon—though he had little knowledge of, or interest in, such business contests.

One by one, the growing du Lacigny Incorporated Trading House was absorbing other local traders in the area. By undercutting the contract prices, Guy du Lacigny had been able to draw business from the hands of the smaller traders. Once that happened, it was only a matter of time before the trader was forced to quit or join Guy du Lacigny's franchise. Du Lacigny would pay a fee for the company far below the true valuation, buy control of the smaller trading house, and then farm the previously owned contracts *back* to the trader, with a commission removed from the contract price for every delivery. Making matters worse, no wealthy investors were willing to help the smaller traders, apparently fearing taking on the growing might of Guy's organisation.

Susu-Van had little interest in selling up, and had spent all her time trying to protect her contracts—hence her presence in the caravan train that had employed Stefon's retinue. Ordinarily she wouldn't have been away from the city, but important contracts needed to be nursed. But such tactics on her part had drawn her attention away from other matters, and "accidents" had begun to plague the company. As her resistance held against the pressure from du Lacigny, and as it became more apparent that her business savvy and social influence were cementing her contracts, her trading wagons had begun to suffer more bandit attacks and a few "transport mishaps". She had even lost her best driver to a plunge from a hillside road he had travelled every month of his life. It smacked of what Coral called industrial sabotage.

And so—somewhat in desperation—Susu-Van had turned to Stefon and his friends to try to stabilise the company and secure it from these tactics. The fact that they were outsiders to Choat was an advantage she had hoped to levy, an unknown quantity. But the move had been too late; Susu-Van had clearly underestimated just how far her competitors were willing to go to secure her "cooperation". And she had paid the ultimate price.

The two friends walked aimlessly through the eastern portion of the city for an hour or so. The buildings were mostly squat granite constructions with little gilding or adornment, functional at best. The early architects of the region had been dwarves, made rich from the export of stone and gems mined in the mountains surrounding Choat. They had constructed their home on the original site of Dwey-Dorma Kordaal, the stronghold of legendary dwarven warmonger Bannan Kehl. Ancient ruins at the centre of the current city were tourist attractions now, as were the tunnels beneath the ground that Bannan Kehl's descendants had constructed.

Through the centuries, the city had grown around the ruins, and all construction had taken on the same motif of function over form. There were broad plazas and sweeping concourses that snaked throughout the city, linking distant districts that otherwise would take hours to reach through the winding streets. The masonry skill of the dwarven people was in evidence everywhere. It might not have been attractive, but it was nonetheless impressive.

As they walked, Stefon said, as much to himself as to Rish, "We seem to hop from frying pan to frying pan. I'd thought this offer from Susu-Van a blessing for her as much as for us—Soriana taking steps in our favour, for once."

"You should know better than that, Stefon. She's called Soriana the Bitch for a reason, remember."

"Good point. Still, just when we needed help getting the hell out of Ipsica, with only our feet to carry us, we found the perfect solution. And Susu-Van found—or so she thought—the perfect solution to her own problems."

"It seems we were too late."

"And that rankles, if I'm honest," Stefon said testily. "I hate the feeling of a job going incomplete, and Susu-Van was a good woman. There's no justice in any of this."

"There rarely is, Stefon. And you've always been work-proud. We might do as well to leave this be, considering our employer lies in ruin."

Back in Wahib, work hadn't been hard to come by. They had commanded a good, discreet reputation in the right circles, but in Choat, no one knew them. To have found work so quickly had seemed a blessing from Soriana. But now that things were getting serious and their employer lay dead, Stefon couldn't help feeling that the goddess of luck had it in for him.

He felt the urge to exact retribution. He felt a great wrong had been committed, and he had the power to restore the balance. But there was conflict in Stefon, too, because his entire life up until this autumn had been ruled by a general apathy toward the welfare of others. The dice of fate fell where they may, and nothing could alter destiny. Since fighting for his life and the lives of those who had placed their trust in him, somehow his perspective had skewed. Altruism was an unfamiliar and invisible yoke around his neck.

At least I still have a neck, he thought bitterly.

What was in it for him to pursue Susu-Van's killer? They could just as easily walk away from the situation. Someone else would pick up the running of Susu-Van's enterprise; either someone in the organisation or this du Lacigny character—as unpalatable as that might seem. And yet he wanted to stay, to ferret them out—but why? Why stay?

What's in it for me?

A question that had been his lifelong mantra. Now it felt like something abstract, ludicrous. Things had changed. He had no choice but to seek justice for Susu-Van. He owed her that much; they all did.

They were almost at Susu-Van's compound when Rish pointed out, "It's not going to be an easy thing, telling her employees."

"I suppose not." There were a few capable individuals in Susu-Van's company, but precious few leaders. For the moment, it would fall to them to pick up the pieces if the trading was to continue. "Almost as hard will be to tell Pryn and the others that I want to stay and find her killer."

Rish glanced his way but didn't respond immediately. He waited a breath and then said, "I think they'll understand."

They paused outside the compound, the chill Stefon felt probably more than just the weather. "If we're going to stay and get involved in this, we're going to have to do it properly; no mistakes."

"When have we ever done things any other way?"

"We need to consider what little we know. We're well aware of a motive, but it's going to be impossible to tie the murder to du Lacigny. Looking at the body for as short a time as I did, it seems clear that it was a clean job. I saw no signs of a struggle on her body, apart from the deep cleave in her neck, of course. There were no ligature marks or bruising from bindings, and I saw nothing under her fingernails. On the face of it, it could have been an accident."

"Is that what the City Watch was saying when they asked us to identify the remains?"

"Of course," he muttered. "They're blaming fishing wire, I believe. In the cold water, she probably struggled to swim and quickly succumbed to the chill, becoming entangled in the wire beneath the surface. It's not an unreasonable explanation."

"Yeah, but I don't buy it," Rish said.

"Nor I. It was wire all right, but looks more like the clean slice of a garrotte than the tangle of fishing wire. And as for the speed of the request for us to confirm the body's identity? Ordinarily they'd have waited until the body had at least been removed to a morgue or temple. Susu-Van was definitely murdered, in my opinion, and they wanted us to see the body in the water. The City Watch were probably bribed to get an identification done swiftly. I doubt we're dealing with an inside job, but we must be wary. We can't trust anyone but ourselves."

"Again, when was it ever any other way? I hate to say it, boy, but I think we're in it up to our necks again. Want to bet on how long it'll take before we receive the next 'offer' from Guy du Lacigny's lot?"

Stefon spat on the ground as though ridding some foul taste from his mouth. "By sundown, I imagine."

Later, after Stefon had given the sad news to the employees in the warehouses, Rish impatiently paced the loading bay. He looked at Stefon and then shook his head. "I agree with the dwarf," he said. "It's a little frustrating that we can't seem to catch a single piece of good fortune. I was hoping for a nice quiet winter here, keeping our heads down, drinking and gambling . . ."

"Romancing," Stefon interrupted.

"Haven't found a brothel in this stony crap hole that I like yet," he parried somewhat defensively. "Haven't had the time."

"Indeed," Stefon replied with a knowing tone. Rish knew full well that Stefon recognised his response to be naught but bluster, although at one time, it might have been accurate enough, for Rish had seemingly found love, though he'd never openly admit that to anyone else. He was a private man, and such feelings were alien to him.

Inside the loading bay, the rest of their small group were having a spot of breakfast seated upon sealed crates containing all sorts, from carefully packaged gemstones and soft metals to fully laden silos of refined mineral ore. All the crates were destined for foreign fields. Choat still made the bulk of its income from exporting the minerals, precious metals, and gems mined from the mountains that dominated the extremities of the duchy, and gold prospectors still flocked to the area with dreams of fortune foremost in their minds. The vast majority of the mines had been emptied centuries before by the dwarves, but a few still yielded commodities in decent numbers, and there were always industrious types excavating new shafts.

The old mines from the dwarves were largely empty now, though a few contained bandits and many more were rumoured to be haunted—if one believed in such things, which Rish did not.

He took a seat upon an upturned crate. Stefon hovered nearby, seemingly lost in his own thoughts, as was increasingly the case since they had fled Wahib.

Rish had his own concerns regarding Stefon's "condition"—as they had come to call it—but it was nothing he was willing to talk about in front of the rest of the crew. They were a tight-knit bunch, almost as close as siblings, but the young scoundrel realised the need for a leader, and the need for that leader to have the confidence of the entire group. It wouldn't do for Rish to call that into question by raising concerns about Stefon's health, or even sanity. Stefon was changing—they could probably all see that—but it served nothing to address it now.

Pryn coughed and said, "Just to add my penny to the pool, for what it might be worth, I happen to agree with Jewl too, we appear to have run bang out of luck. We're struggling to find out anything of interest about your sword, Stefon." Perhaps as tall as seven feet, with midnight-black skin and strangely blue-black hair that cascaded down his back, Pryn was a man who stood out in any group. His aquamarine eyes, always so difficult to look at unflinchingly, turned upon their dwarven friend Jewl as they discussed the sword Stefon had stolen from a cleric of The Light before they'd fled Wahib.

"I've been to every blacksmith nearby," said Jewl through his voluminous beard. "I've asked about minerals and metal-folding treatments and everything I can think of, but they all just looked at me like I was some kind of lunatic. These smiths, whether human, dwarven, or otherwise begat, are all pretty much descendants of dwarven-trained smiths. If they don't know what could create something like that, then we're at a loss."

"Similar story to the sellers," agreed Pryn. "The fact is, this sword should not *be*. It's just not possible. And all we've asked these people about so far is to try to work out how it glows! We haven't even broached the subject of its incredibly light weight or the fact it cuts through people as easily as melting butter."

Rish looked at the weapon, which currently sat upon a crate on the side. It was still in its scabbard. Were he to draw the sword, it would reveal an impossible glow from the metal that varied in colour every time it was drawn, it seemed. This was actually the least alarming "strange" element with regards to the sword's properties, but it had seemed a good place to start in their research.

"The only help I was given was rather derisive remarks about wizards," confirmed Jewl.

"If that's supposed to be help, it's no help at all. There's no such thing as wizards or magic," said Stefon steadily.

"Not anymore, there isn't," agreed Jewl.

"I'll stop you there, Jewl," said Rish. "We've all heard the stories and fables; we've all been afeared as children by tales of the dark arts. But I remember reading about dragons and werewolves and all sorts of other guff too. It's not real. *Something* makes that sword do what it can do—something traceable or identifiable lends those properties. Wing of bat and spleen of emu has nothing to do with it."

"Then you find an explanation!" challenged the dwarf. "You explain how it can slice through tempered steel as easily as suet!"

"I can't," snapped Rish. Jewl got on his nerves sometimes—the dwarf was so quick to anger, so inconstant in his moods.

"We can't know everything about the universe," said Stefon quietly, staring at his feet. "There will be an answer somewhere. We just have to be patient."

No one had a response.

"Anyway, forget about my bloody sword for a moment and let us focus on more immediate concerns. Things are going to get very complicated soon, and we're bound to be in the thick of it. We're going to have to start working up contacts, opening up avenues of communication. We need to dovetail with whatever networks exist in this city—especially those Susu-Van trusted—and it's best we do it sooner rather than later.

"Pryn, I know you're not too happy about people enquiring into your past, but I'm afraid I'm going to have to.

It seems clear to me that you know your way around Choat City, if not the entire duchy. Have you been here before?"

The dark-skinned giant stared at Stefon hard. Finally, he said, "I've been here before, yes."

"I'm not interested in why," said Stefon. "What is important is that we can use your knowledge. If you've been here before, you must know more than we do about how this place works, who the big movers and shakers are, who holds the influence."

Again, Pryn held a level gaze with his captain and leader, and then finally nodded. "Probably."

"Ask around a bit; see what names you can gather in. Once we have some leads, we'll see if we can't get to the heart of what's going on here. We can't rely on the authorities because we have no evidence. We have to learn who else we can trust."

Moody as ever, Jewl huffed his discontent.

"Something to add, Jewl?"

Ruffling his massive beard in a show of something close to annoyance, the dwarf said, "It's not too late to just walk away. This argument isn't ours; this isn't our fight. If we upped sticks, went further west or something, nothing would be different. No one knows us; we could just disappear. Seems to me you're courting disaster."

"Susu-Van took us under her wing when she had little reason to do so, Jewl."

"Not strictly true," the dwarf grumbled. "She knew what she was getting when she recruited us. It wasn't an act of charity. She knew she was getting us into hot water."

Rish shifted uncomfortably as he found himself agreeing with Jewl. But Stefon levelled a gaze at the dwarf and said, "I couldn't walk away now, even if I wanted to . . . and regardless of your bluster, I don't think you could, either."

Jewl huffed again, his small eyes blinking angrily, but he didn't argue.

Chapter Nine

Acting with Purpose

A day after the discovery of Susu-Van's body, Stefon and Rish sat in the sheltered awning of a taverna on the edge of ancient Choat Square, sipping sweet liquor and enjoying the early evening air. Choatian weather was a far cry from where Stefon had grown up. The rain and the wind—warm as it often was—would be dominating the weather in Ipsica this deep into autumn. By contrast, Choat was protected by high mountain ranges at every compass point. The wooded ranges created a trap for thermals, keeping the temperatures high right to the turn of winter, when the cold snap promised to be harsh and abrupt. Snows would come to the north, and with them, a ground frost that decimated crops and threatened exposed cattle. The talk was that such a snap was not far away. Still, as warm as the locals considered the weather to be, for a lifelong resident of Ipsica, it was cold.

Choat Square was usually a throng in the morning hours with the huge markets that dominated the city centre, quieting to a hum of activity through the afternoon. By the time evening came, the marketers had drifted back to their homes or inns, surrendering the square to travelling troupes and the various entertainers that plied their trade in the area. On the cusp of the winter season, the variety of entertainers was less impressive than at the height of summer and spring, when many bards, troubadours, players, jugglers, and jesters would travel far and wide to benefit from the affluent but rustic Choat people.

"No matter what Pryn unearths in the way of contacts in this city, Stefon, you know that sooner or later, we're going to have to turn our attention to Guy, and when we do, we're going to be awfully exposed here," Rish said, his feral features etched with concern.

Since falling for Brooss, Rish had come to display a greater level of maturity and responsibility. Following Susu-Van's death, especially during those critical hours in the immediate aftermath, Rish had virtually run the wagon yard. Furthermore, since their first arrival in Choat, the resident engineers had quickly come around to the idea of taking advice from Brooss, despite the fact that she was both young and female.

The group's impact on Susu-Van's trading company had been remarkable in such a short period, so much so that the tactics employed to disrupt the wagon yard—especially Susu-Van's murder—had not had the impact Stefon imagined du Lacigny had intended, and the company continued to operate without a hiccup. It was early days still, but both he and Rish knew they would have to address the du Lacigny situation sooner rather than later. They were just at a loss as to precisely how to do that. Pryn was investigating the local independent traders to gauge what allies, if any, there were in the community, but there was no telling how long that would take.

For the time being, they were waiting in Choat Square for some unknown representative from du Lacigny's organisation to meet with one of their number. As had been anticipated, the next offer to purchase Susu-Van's small organisation had indeed quickly followed the discovery of her body, and the two friends intended to hear the offer first-hand, and see it rejected in similar fashion. Their intention was clear; they wanted du Lacigny to know that it was business as usual. They needed more information, too, and the easiest way was to watch while their enemy—if indeed that was what du Lacigny's organisation constituted—sought to play what they believed would be their winning hand.

And if Guy chose to deal with them as he had dealt with Susu-Van? Well, then Guy and his henchmen would find the lads from Ipsica a harder proposition.

The trap was set thus—Stefon and Rish were outwardly enjoying a sip of liquor and a moment of relaxation, awaiting the arrival of du Lacigny's man. Behind them, under the awning of the alehouse, was Dorwin, one of the teamsters from Susu-Van's crew. He was an old character, difficult to fluster and confident in his role. It was he who would meet with whoever showed up and—calmly but firmly—reject the latest offer, whilst letting slip some of his own carefully planned information. Dorwin was following a meticulously developed script provided to him by Rish. Stefon and the latter were there to observe.

As confident as they were in Dorwin, they had to recognise that this was a risk. Hence Rish and Stefon had positioned themselves within earshot of the planned exchange. It was likely that, if du Lacigny was as careful as they thought him, they would be marked as members of Susu-Van's entourage, but that was okay too. Du Lacigny had no way of knowing what these newcomers were capable of yet. It was perfectly reasonable for hired muscle to be nearby. Now all they had to do was await this mysterious representative's arrival—perhaps then they might start getting some answers.

"Are you still having the dreams?" Rish asked out of the blue.

Stefon nodded. "I thought they were just nightmares at first. Something to do with the pressure I was under when we were running from Wahib. But it's almost every night now, unless I get well pickled."

"A plan with no drawbacks," quipped Rish.

"I wish I could make light of it." Stefon noticed that his hand had dropped to rest on the hilt of his sword, as though taking comfort in its presence. The sword he had taken from a fallen cleric of The Light.

Known for being ferocious combatants, the clerics of The Light were only that in name, for while they were primarily religious zealots, those in Wahib were more ostensibly soldiers operating at the command of The Light, a religious order that had declared Stefon an abomination—the last remaining member of a long-extinct species capable of strange powers. A *Seer*, they had called him—whatever that was.

Stefon had fervently refuted this accusation during the quarantine, until the powers and abilities that myth had long ago attributed to that strange species slowly began to manifest in him. In moments of extreme pressure, when his life—and the lives of those around him—had been on the line, Stefon had exhibited feats of great speed, agility, and strength, defying reason and nature.

In one incident, he had slain two clerics in self-defence, a feat unheard of. At another point, he had rescued Rish from certain death by jumping from the top balcony of a tower more than thirty stories high. In those stressful moments, he found he could leap four times his own height, lift ten times his own weight, or even command objects to move by thought alone. There was no sane explanation for any of this.

No explanation, that was, until Stefon had been brought before the mercurial leader of that strange religious order—Druid Lesjac. There had been a strange fervency about his demeanour—an energised, manic quality to his speech—as he described the religious purge of the ancient race he called the Seers, of which Lesjac accused Stefon of being a member. The purge, centuries in the past and culminating in The Briadranon Massacre, had seen the full and certain extermination of the last remaining Seers at the hands of The Light.

Or so Lesjac and his predecessors had believed. Stefon's emergence as an apparent legatee obviously had Lesjac a little worried, resulting in a city-wide manhunt for Stefon and his confederates. They had barely escaped with their lives, and still had no way of knowing the fate of those citizens who had remained behind the quarantine walls of Wahib.

The fact that The Light had been behind everything seemed clear now. It also seemed obvious that the outside world had no idea what occurred behind those walls, for no one spoke of the disease on the outside.

Despite the feeling of responsibility Stefon struggled with, he had not revealed the fate of Wahib to anyone for fear that The Light would learn of their disclosure and hunt them once more. In keeping mum, it was entirely possible Stefon had consigned the entire Wahib populace to death, and a feeling of guilt stained his waking hours, despite knowing he had had little option.

The hardest thing to deal with was the knowledge that he had left friends behind. Quinly Bunnelshut was one such friend, who had risked his life to allow them to flee—and they had left him behind.

And when he did find sleep, Stefon's dreams had been plagued by visions. In some, he witnessed the dreadful massacre at Briadranon, depicted in a painting inside the Tower of Light in Wahib City. And yet, the dreams were always so much more vivid than that painting. In other dreams, he saw himself as an old man commanding great powers, bending the universe to his will; in another, he saw the rise and return of a terrible race of towering, bearded beings who enslaved the world. But worst of all, in his latest dreams, he watched the fall of the civilised world—the world he knew, the world he lived in—to an unstoppable plague army, spreading pestilence and death beneath their marching feet.

And still he could not chase from his mind a vivid memory, a memory of the strangest sensation. The feeling as a solitary corpse in a hospital morgue had moved beneath his hand . . . and the question of just where all the other corpses of Wahib City had gone, for the funeral pyres had not been fired for months. *And just how far-reaching is the influence of The Light and its leader, Lesjac?*

Even if Stefon hadn't been suffering visions or struggling from beneath the mantel of guilt, he would not have slept soundly for the unanswered questions surging through his mind.

And now he had more answers to find—who had ordered Susu-Van's death, and what else were they capable of next?

"You know what might help you sleep?" asked Rish, bringing him abruptly out of his introspection.

"What's that?" Stefon asked, knowing instinctively that nothing helpful was to follow.

By way of an answer, Rish inclined his head.

Looking over, Stefon spied the object of his joke and looked quickly away. Across the square, walking slowly among the few performers, was Coral—tall, alluring, slender, confident, soft-spoken, intelligent Coral. Hair the colour of wet sand was pulled back in a ponytail, accentuating her strong northern features. Even in that single glance and from this distance, Stefon imagined he could see the blueness of her eyes.

Quickly he threw back the remainder of his liquor and held up his empty glass to the serving staff to indicate a refill. Now that Rish had discovered love, it seemed he was on a mission to force others down a similar path. Stefon couldn't even think on that level at the moment, and it annoyed him that Rish could so easily allow his mind to slip to topics that were comparatively trivial at best. They had far more pressing things to consider than thinking about some mercurial gambler whom neither knew well—romantically or otherwise.

"Really?" Stefon snapped as the serving girl came over to refill their glasses. "That's what you're thinking about when we've got all of *this* on our plates?"

"Hey, come on!" Rish's own voice rose a touch. "Remember when we lived life? You know, actually *lived* life, instead of flinching at shadows?"

"Things have changed, Rish." He glanced around but saw that no one was taking an interest in their argument. "We can't afford to be reckless—not right now."

His friend's angry reaction seemed to abate somewhat, much to Stefon's relief. "Okay, I know," said Rish. "It just frustrates me that things have changed so much so quickly. We're only young still, and it seems we've completely lost control of our fates. I feel like a twig being swept along a river."

"I know what you mean," agreed Stefon. "But I promise you, things will be different."

"Once you've avenged Susu-Van? But then there'll be something else, and something else after that. Stefon, you're reaching for something, and I don't think even you know what it is."

He didn't reply.

Downing his own drink, Rish jabbed a finger across the square in Coral's direction and hissed, "*That's* life, Stefon. *That's* living, not this moral crusade you're yearning for!"

"I'm on no crusade! But you don't know—"

"The dreams again?" Rish interrupted. "The guilt?"

"All those people," Stefon said in quiet earnest, conscious now that Dorwin was giving them an odd look somewhere between concern and annoyance. They were abandoning their roles and noisily so. "All those lives, and we left them behind. We did nothing; we've said nothing. Perhaps something could have been done."

"What, Stefon? What do you imagine they'd have done? Had we gone to someone in Ipsica, in the capital, they'd have just as likely locked us up to keep us from telling anyone else, even if they weren't in on it. They couldn't allow knowledge of something like that to seep out. Stefon, you're just one man! Those people we left behind, their fate was never your burden to bear. We did the right thing in running, but you can't run forever, or you may as well have stayed and died with the rest of them, because that's no life!

"If you're not careful, one day you'll find you've run out of causes to fight and friends to avenge, and you'll discover you're completely alone!"

Rish made to stand, forcing Stefon to reach across their table. "Rish, wait!"

Dorwin looked concerned. Even the bargirl seemed to have noticed the angry exchange. His friend stopped, looking away from him.

"You can't just storm off!"

Rish heaved a sigh and slumped heavily in the seat. After a moment, Rish turned a dark glare at Stefon, but he could see that most of the fury had fled. Finally, his friend said, "You're paying our bar bill, then." And waved for yet another round to be brought over.

The pair sat in uncomfortable silence until Stefon sensed a man approach the taverna from the nearby lane and step to the table behind them. A glance Rish's way communicated all he needed to know.

The new arrival's breathing was heavy, and his gait audibly ungainly. With shuffling steps, he took a seat next to Dorwin and introduced himself politely. "My name's Morgan. I work for du Lacigny Holdings. We appreciate you sparing the time to meet with us . . ." He left a long pause, waiting for Dorwin to respond.

"Dorwin," he said finally, and not kindly.

Play it cool, thought Stefon, glancing at Rish. From his friend's expression, he could tell he shared the concern.

Ignoring the comparative rudeness of the response, the man called Morgan said, "We're excited about the chance to work together in the future."

Dorwin just hummed.

"We had hoped to be able to discuss the proposal directly with the owner; is she not available?"

Dorwin laughed bitterly. "Not exactly."

"Oh. So, can we confirm, then, that you speak in her stead and with her authority?"

"Difficult to say, considering she's dead."

This was a deviation from the script, but Stefon didn't mind. Dorwin was doing fine, so long as he didn't openly accuse anyone of anything; Rish had been very firm about that.

"I . . . oh my! I'm . . . my condolences, Dorwin. Please, convey our respects to her family." Unless Stefon was very much mistaken, the uncomfortable hesitation and stammered reply sounded genuine.

"She ain't got any, really," Dorwin said.

"Well, listen. This is clearly a poorly timed meeting. Please excuse our crassness. I shall leave you to grieve in peace." They heard Morgan rise from the table and take a step away. "If there is anything we can do, you only have to ask. Anything at all, whether it is assistance with vehicles, storage, staff, anything."

"Okay," Dorwin said almost quizzically. This was not an expected turn for the conversation to take.

"Please also pass on Mr. du Lacigny's personal condolences, as I am sure he will wish." Then Morgan added wistfully, "When you get to our age, you and I both know accidents are all too frequent, but Susu-Van was still so young. This is such a tragedy."

"Thank you," replied Dorwin, and then they heard Morgan departing. Stefon chanced a glance over his shoulder and saw the shuffling gait and shaking head of a man embarrassed by the exchange.

Once he left, Stefon and Rish turned in their seats. "That was . . . unexpected," admitted Dorwin. "He looked genuinely surprised by the news."

"Sounded it too," agreed Rish. "We might be getting a little hasty here. It might be that we've hung the noose around the wrong neck in du Lacigny."

"I don't think so," argued Stefon, his mind working over the conversation they'd overheard.

"Well, I think we must at least consider that this man didn't know anything about Susu-Van's death. That could mean one of two things," said Rish.

Dorwin nodded. "The first being that du Lacigny is keeping his own people out of the loop, for whatever reason?"

Rish nodded. "It would give his representatives more plausible deniability."

Stefon shook his head. "If du Lacigny was cautious enough to be worried about plausible deniability, he'd hardly be rash enough to murder Susu-Van in the first place, let alone leave the body to be discovered. That murder was a message, and not a subtle one."

"Then it must be the second possibility," said Rish, "that she might not have been murdered by du Lacigny's people at all. We might be facing a third player here."

Although Dorwin nodded his agreement, Stefon said, "You're forgetting option three: that your friend Morgan there is an expert liar. I think he just played his role in our little puppet show better than us; no offence, Dorwin." The old man shrugged.

"How do you know he lied?" Rish asked. "Seemed pretty genuine to me."

"Didn't he? Very genuine, and even surprised. But as he was leaving, he said that 'accidents are all too frequent' in your line of work."

"It's true," confirmed Dorwin.

"No doubt, but at no point did you actually mention how Susu-Van died. Might have been a mugging, a brawl, a suicide, food poisoning, slip in the bathhouse—anything. But we both know it was made to appear an accident, a drowning of a woman caught in fishing wire. Morgan *knew* that."

"It's a bit of a reach," said Rish, "but it seems to stack up. What do you think this means for us?"

"It means du Lacigny is even smarter than we thought, and he's far more patient. I think he's done this heinous thing, and now he plans to let the chaos reign at Susu-Van's place until he comes with an offer even lower than before. I think he's utterly ruthless, but he's smarter than we thought."

"Okay." Rish nodded as though all of that meant very little in the grand scheme of things. "So, what do *we* do now?"

Stefon stared at him a moment and then nodded once, firmly. "Now we step it up a notch."

Chapter Ten

Stirring the Nest

They stepped into the warehouse just after dawn of the following day. The autumnal heat and humidity, to which Stefon was unfamiliar, had formed a film of sweat on Pryn's brow when he met them just inside the tall and usually empty facility, causing his black forehead to shine like polished jet. Despite their hushed tones, the voices of those gathered inside carried eerily into the eaves high above.

The warehouse sat in a quiet eastern portion of town and was only used for storage, so their meeting was unlikely to be spotted and remarked upon as curious. Such were the precautions Stefon and his friends felt they needed to employ. They had all agreed it was safest to assume that—despite Morgan's show of allowing them room to grieve—whoever was responsible for the murder would surely have an eye on the company to see what they did next, a question they were struggling to answer themselves.

All they had sought to do so far was avoid allowing the everyday function of the business to fall into chaos. This had been achieved through a combination of Brooss's leadership in the workshops and Rish's sound administrative skills—the latter of which no one could have anticipated.

As requested, the imposing Pryn had gone out into the trader community of Choat to see which independent traders he could convince to attend a meeting regarding the pressure being exerted upon them all by, it was widely assumed, du Lacigny and his goons. Although it seemed a long time since Pryn had spent time in the city, Stefon could tell from his expression that his efforts had produced results.

"How did you get on?" Stefon asked his huge friend.

"It wasn't easy," Pryn replied, the muscles in his jaws working with poorly concealed tension. "There is a lot of nervousness in the local traders. They took some persuading."

Taking into account Pryn's impressive physique and generally intimidating demeanour, Stefon could well imagine the reaction many of the traders and privateers in Choat would have had to his approach—which was often beyond direct. And that was fine. If these people showed a trend for reacting to a little intimidation, Stefon didn't mind exerting a little of his own for their collective good. They would all benefit in the long run. A show of strength was precisely what these people needed, and Pryn was nothing if not the embodiment of strength.

"How many do you think have shown?" he asked both Pryn and Rish, glad that the latter had shown up. They hadn't mentioned the argument in Choat Square—such was the way amongst friends—but it meant a lot to him that Rish still stood by them all.

"I would say no fewer than eighty percent of those we think are open to our approach," said Pryn. "A couple dozen, perhaps. They may have required a little convincing, but in general, they seem to know what is going on in this place. Susu-Van's death has escalated things. They are scared of du Lacigny and what his monopoly might mean for them. Once I suggested that any one of them might next pay the same price, they seemed keen to hear what we've got to say."

"Good."

It makes sense, thought Stefon. *These people aren't stupid. They might not trust us yet, but they damn well know they can't trust Guy du Lacigny. They already know the nature of that particular devil, so it makes sense to gauge this new devil. Curiosity will have brought most of the rest.*

What he needed to do now was decide what the hell he was going to say to them. Stepping up onto the impromptu stage, Stefon held his hands in the air to quiet the gathered traders and freebooters. The sun had risen an hour before, and most of the trading houses would be in full flow by now, so most of these owners would want to be done with this meeting and away from the packed warehouse as soon as possible.

"My friends, please settle," he called. "I will not keep you long, but what I have to say is important."

They quietened a little, though there still remained a buzz of anticipation. He was pleased to see Coral's fine features somewhere near the front, for Susu-Van's loss must have hit her as hard as anyone, for they had been friends. Though she hadn't worked at the trading house since her death, Coral was still spoken about with affection by those who did. A traveller and gambler at heart, she was obviously an influential figure in the city, especially so amongst the trading community.

"A small number of you I already know personally, others by reputation alone. However, the time has come where circumstances may make strange bedfellows of us all. Those you stand beside today may have been competitors for a long time; others may be considered erstwhile colleagues or maybe even infrequent partners, but recent events have brought us all to this current unavoidable predicament.

"Most of you knew Susu-Van, owner of the trading wagon yard that came to employ us. Even more of you will have known her father." There were a few nods from the elder patrons. "All of you know she has perished, but what you might not know is that it is our strong belief she was murdered."

Stefon's voice filled the cavernous warehouse as easily as if he was shouting down a well. The gathered traders began speaking in earnest. Stefon had simply spoken what was widely suspected, but it was still shocking for these people to hear that speculation uttered with such conviction.

"Though we have no proof, it seems clear that her openly vocal opposition to du Lacigny Holdings has resulted in her being silenced . . . permanently. Susu-Van's company and its employees will undoubtedly be further pressured into accepting Guy du Lacigny's franchise arrangements." He knew that was a reach, virtually slanderous, but he was equally certain that it would come to pass. "Only our timely presence, which could not have been foreseen by Susu-Van's enemies, has forestalled a takeover."

A voice at the middle said, "Convenient timing, some might say." A few voices murmured in agreement at the faceless man's observation.

"Whatever you might suspect of us, we have nonetheless managed to arrest the chaos that Susu-Van's murder was intended to create. But it won't last. Long-term stability for all of us means facing this threat that existed long before we showed up. How many of you have witnessed similar firm-handed tactics by Guy and his representatives?" There was a long pause, during which no one moved, so Stefon said, "Know that you speak here in confidence. After all, if you truly don't believe what I am saying, then you equally should believe that you have nothing to fear."

At that, many in the crowd raised their hands in affirmation. Easily more than half indicated they had suffered similar intimidation tactics. That caused another ripple of concerned chatter.

"This cannot continue. If you fear for your livelihoods—as well you should—I implore you to consider our proposal."

There was a smattering of sceptical murmuring.

"If you are to survive as independent traders, you cannot risk remaining independent from one another. If you stand divided, you shall fall; only united do we have a chance of withstanding this pressure. We must act in concert to repel du Lacigny's aggression. Rely on each other. Speak with your neighbours. Try where possible to combine wagon trains leaving the city. The larger the caravan train, the more difficult it will be for saboteurs to target. Check each other's equipment and your own. Double and triple check. If you receive visits from du Lacigny's men, ensure you always have witnesses or conduct those conversations in public. Try not to travel alone, even around the streets of Choat. Watch each other's backs.

"But most of all, remain resolute! Do not give in to Guy's demands. He will try to tempt you, intimidate you, coerce you, undermine you, and ultimately try to remove you. Take care of one another, and we shall remain safe."

"What good will all of that do in the long run?" demanded a trader Stefon knew to be called Cayden. He was young enough to be possessed of youthful bravado, but regardless, his question was pertinent.

"We have examined du Lacigny's tactics, and something doesn't add up. Literally speaking. I appreciate du Lacigny might be a wealthy man, but raw wealth only gets you so far. To achieve what they have in such a short time, his holdings company must have conducted some shady dealings—dealings that will be hard to explain and even harder to hide, especially from people like us.

"Something is afoot at du Lacigny Holdings, and my team and I intend to find out precisely what that might be."

"What can *you* do?" Cayden asked.

"We're somewhat experienced in this type of business." Stefon flashed a knowing glance at Rish, who smirked. "When we uncover these irregularities—which we certainly will—and when we find evidence of Susu-Van's murder, then Guy can be brought before the authorities.

"We can be contacted at all times at the yard. Please keep the information flowing amongst those you trust so we can coordinate our defence against this threat. I am sure once Guy du Lacigny learns of our collaboration—and you can be sure that he will—his tactics will worsen before we see an end to this. We must be brave. We must be vigilant. An open show of solidarity is nothing to cause an innocent competitor any concern. Good luck."

The crowd began to disperse as the traders started to drift away in little groups, all in close discussion. Stefon could only hope that the response would be positive.

As Rish approached, Pryn stepped up to the pair of them, his eyes still scanning the crowd watchfully.

"So?" Stefon prompted him.

"A few strangers," Pryn said softly. "I couldn't say for sure that they'd not have a genuine reason for being here, but they weren't invited."

Stefon nodded. While it was more than likely that someone in the group would try to sell the information about their meeting to Guy, it was even more likely that the corporate tyrant would have learned of the meeting ahead of time and had his own spies in attendance. It mattered little. They had decided one of the payoffs of convening the meeting would be to see who showed up uninvited. It tempted a tip of du Lacigny's hand. And the fact that Stefon had voiced his suspicions of du Lacigny being involved in Susu-Van's murder might draw the man into attacking Stefon and his team directly in order to silence them. They were more than ready for that.

They stepped down from the platform and made their way to where a select few independent traders waited for them. Rish's eyes gleamed as he asked, "What was that last bit about this being an open show of solidarity? Nothing illegal? Us?"

Stefon only shrugged. "Just because I said it doesn't mean we'll follow through with it. The authorities are just as likely to be in his pocket as not, but if it reaches him that we're willing to play by the rules, then all the better."

"Because we never do?"

"Indeed."

Pryn introduced him to those gathered. He had asked for these traders to be held back after his speech, for they were known to be both influential and successful in Choat, and renowned for being supporters of independent trade. From what he knew of this town, Stefon considered this handful of people integral to ensuring this venture succeeded. And again, this time somewhat to his surprise, Coral was present too.

After she came up during their argument, Rish had seen fit to feed him titbits of information about her whenever they spoke, like a teenager baiting a lovesick fool—which he was not. To a certain extent, she was still a mystery, and Stefon wasn't sure he liked that.

Once the formalities had been dealt with, a burly gent of lengthening years who went by the name of Greel was first to speak. "I agree with you strangers in principle, but I am having trouble working out precisely what you intend to achieve. It wouldn't surprise me if many who were here tonight felt the same. If Guy du Lacigny has done his homework, he will be untouchable. What can you people do about it?"

"You'd be surprised," said Rish. "Even if du Lacigny feels he has a handle on you all, Stefon, Pryn, and our friends are unknowns. That gives us an edge. He doesn't know what we're capable of." The last sentence carried clear undertones.

The younger trader Cayden shifted his weight uneasily. "Is that supposed to make us feel better?"

Before Rish could answer, Greel continued. "Perhaps this is simply a sign of the times and we must move with it. I must warn you, though, I am not sure you will receive much support if you plan to rule this coalition of independent traders. After all, what would be the difference between your coalition and du Lacigny's franchise? Either way, each independent trader loses the options and freedoms afforded by being independent."

"Meet the new king, same as the other new king," quipped Cayden.

"We don't intend to rule anything, Greel," Stefon told him with as much gravitas as he could muster. "We're not proposing any financial collaboration, just a cooperative arrangement. A circling of our wagons, if you 'scuse the pun."

"There's something I don't understand," said Cayden. "We're assuming that du Lacigny is attempting to secure a monopoly on trade in Choat City, right? And from what you said, you think he is overspending to achieve that."

"It seems apparent," nodded Stefon.

Greel seemed to agree. "There's no way this isn't costing him a tidy penny and he won't be earning back enough to cover the outlay yet."

"You mentioned irregularities in your speech. What did you mean? What were you alluding to?"

"I'm not sure his own personal wealth is substantial enough to cover what is being spent," said Stefon. "That means the money must be coming from somewhere, and that place can't be legitimate. There will be a connection somewhere that, once identified, will help us both understand du Lacigny's motivations as well as giving us the evidence we need to bring him before the authorities."

"Why would they care?" Cayden asked. "If he's secured an investor, why would they care?"

Greel answered before Stefon could. "In my experience, such connections usually carry political complications, Cayden." Stefon's eyes narrowed. He'd sensed something from the older man, felt a ripple of something unseen. He couldn't put his finger on it, but it was almost like Stefon took a glimpse behind Greel's mask of aged cynicism.

"That's why you're not going to support this movement," Stefon gave voice to his uncertainty.

Greel, somewhat piqued at the accusation, said, "It's *one* of the reasons, yes. I've seen this kind of conflict before, sir. It rarely ends well for the smaller players."

"All the more reason to ensure you're a player on a bigger team, Greel."

"What else is holding you back, Greel?" Cayden asked. Again, Stefon got the sense that Cayden himself was wavering at seeing Greel's reluctance. The emotions, thoughts, feelings of these people were suddenly like coloured fibres in Stefon's mind. He could almost see the strands pulling taut as Greel responded.

"I'm not clear on their angle," he nodded at Stefon and his friends.

"My own motivation is entirely personal," Stefon said flatly. "As for my friends, I can't speak for their motivation, but they have always had my back."

Greel and the rest were quiet for a moment.

"Revenge isn't healthy," Coral told him. They were her first words of the exchange and her smile had vanished, replaced by a look of something akin to concern or even alarm.

For some reason, his frustration with the group began to rise in his chest. He could feel the hot itch of an anger rash dappling his throat.

"Be that as it may," he said firmly, "any reasons I have for following through with this action will not have an ongoing effect on the traders involved here. The fact that we are working toward the same goal with different motives should be beside the point. I mean, all we're actually doing is encouraging you all to look out for one another."

Arms folded, Greel stared hard at him. "I'm long enough in the tooth to know that's not how things will transpire. What if, in time, your personal motivations come to contradict what we are trying to achieve?" he asked. "Moreover, once you achieve your goals, do you really expect us to believe you shall wilfully lay down your position of power and influence?"

Something in the invisible strands, in the tension they held, told Stefon that Greel was a linchpin, a keystone in their plan. If he was unable to get Greel onboard, Cayden would falter too. Then the others would follow, and their task would be virtually impossible.

"Greel, the more you get to know me, the more you'll come to see that I have no desire to be trapped in a position of responsibility. I am telling you, as one man to another, you have my word that I will not betray you or your interests."

As Stefon spoke, he could feel the ripples his emotional response sent down the coloured strands between those gathered, especially between himself and Greel.

Is this another unnatural ability? He thought.

Abruptly, the strands between himself and Greel became rigid, solid, a thing unbreakable.

Greel nodded, his gaze like steel. "OK then. Count me in."

"Me too," confirmed Cayden.

And in such simple ways are rebellions begun, Stefon thought bitterly.

They began to disperse from the warehouse, each leaving by separate doors. All the while, Stefon tried to convince himself that Susu-Van's murder had placed them upon a road from which they could not deviate, but it was a lie as clear as day. He tried to convince himself that they had to see it through, not least of all to ensure a profit, but he knew there would be none to be had. And as he watched Coral's lithe form move out into the dawn's early light, he also pondered whether his motives were perhaps even more selfish than he'd thought.

She glanced behind, and he was too slow to remove his gaze. Her brow furrowed and she hurried off into the streets of Choat, as though she had something very important to do.

Rish was right, he realised. There was something unique about the woman, something compelling, but it wasn't as simple as some physical attraction. He had no way of knowing if he could trust her, despite how much the other traders in the city clearly did.

And as he followed Rish and Pryn to their own trader yard, he struggled to shake the growing disquiet at what had occurred with the strands of sense and emotion he had seen—now gone as quickly as they had appeared. What did it mean . . . and why had there been not a single strand between he and Coral?

Chapter Eleven

The Inside Man

Click shifted uncomfortably in the shadows of the workshop awning, trying to alleviate the cramp in his legs. He had sat for a long time in the grime of the narrow street, slumped against the wet stone wall of the sailmender's building, waiting.

Acaelian had always told him patience was the most powerful weapon in the armoury of a spy or a thief. And he'd been patient.

Since leaving the harbourmaster's office a few days before, Click had mulled over his next move with the same painstaking patience, considering the scant information at hand to decide his best course of action. For he had to act—he had to do something.

The intended receiving agent in Choat, du Lacigny Holdings, was an unknown outfit in the capital, with all ties seeming to stem from the eastern duchy of Choat. There was no doubt in Click's mind that this agency would know who had been responsible for the ship's illegal cargo, but they were beyond Click's reach. He couldn't ever imagine leaving the city to follow a thread so far removed from Shen Utah.

Aside from du Lacigny, he had two names.

The first was Justin Dowling, a shipping agent and somewhat elusive man. His business was widespread, with the majority of his holdings being in the capital, but Click simply didn't have the time to search all of them.

That left Paldron Ward, the customs man. The inside man. Click had been reticent to start his search with Paldron, despite it being the next logical step, because members of the customs house were famous for being incorruptible. It demanded the question, how had their unknown smuggling mastermind coerced an inspector of the customs house?

Well, in truth, it really demanded an answer to *who* could have that power. The *how* was largely inconsequential. Something in Paldron's life had weakened his morals enough to allow him to be bribed or blackmailed into betraying the customs house.

Click had followed Paldron for the best part of a day, watching as he arrived at the harbourmaster's office for duty before dawn, following his movements through a spyglass from the rooftop of a warehouse as he went about his inspection duties, and skulking through the streets of Trouton as Paldron found a place for lunch.

Paldron seemed to be a cool customer. Perhaps in his later thirties, he was stockily built, with thinning black hair, a bushy woodsman's beard, and mean eyes, watchful and suspicious.

But throughout the morning, Click thought he got more of the measure of Paldron, and he saw someone who was working hard not to constantly look over his shoulder. His gaze was watchful, but in a hunted way. The wary look of the prey.

You're worried, was Click's first thought. *You might even be scared.*

It convinced him that he was onto the right man. And in any case, Paldron had been the only inspector on duty at that mooring during the week the treasure ship was alongside . . . before Click sank it.

Having finished his duty and his lunch, Paldron had wandered the seafood markets of Trouton with apparent aimlessness. As the short late-autumn afternoon crept toward early evening, Paldron found a hole to crawl into—a watering hole. The Thankful Cooper was an unremarkable place, positioned well enough in the city to take advantage of the large number of visiting sailors during the high trade season. It sat across from the sailmender's warehouse, near a series of other such businesses that were necessary in such an active port, so even late in the season, it was fairly busy.

Busy enough that one more beggar lying on the filthy cobbles went almost entirely unnoticed. *Only almost,* Click thought. *This slimy-feeling drunk cretin I'm leaning against will start to think something's up soon. Does wonders for my cover, though.*

Thankfully, Click was in luck. After what couldn't have been more than a few drinks, Paldron Ward re-emerged into the rain that had swept in that afternoon. On first impression, he didn't seem too drunk—aware enough at least of the conditions to lift his jacket over his head against the thickening drizzle as he set off up the street.

Click counted to ten as he watched the retreating figure move up the hill, slipping once on the wet cobbles.

Patience . . .

With his eyes still on his mark, Click rose on numb legs and moved off after Paldron, keeping to the additional cover of the warehouse awnings and moving with practiced efficiency. The itch of pins and needles plagued his legs, but he put it out of mind. He needed to be focused.

As he followed the customs inspector, Click thought on his intentions. Did he have the ability to question the man? He certainly wasn't strong enough to coerce him should it come to a physical confrontation. No, he had to be smart about it. But what leverage did he have? He felt certain that this man had been involved in the smuggling effort. But he had no proof. If Click tried to blackmail the man, it could very easily go wrong and Paldron could be pushed into an attack. Click didn't want that.

Nor was he interested in bringing Paldron to justice; the man was just a stepping stone to a bigger target. All Click needed was a name. Perhaps he could get that without saying a word.

At the top of the rise, Paldron turned right and headed off along the road west toward The Lows. Resisting the urge to speed up, Click crossed the cobbled road as other city dwellers rushed to get in out of the rain.

When he reached the corner, Click stumbled round it as though drunk or faint from hunger. His beggar's cloak and hood obscured his features, giving him the freedom to glance down the street ahead. Paldron was farther away now—he'd quickened his pace.

Have I been spotted? he wondered. *Surely not.*

He pressed on, trusting to the greyness of the winding street to protect him. He had to be patient! Yet still, he found his pace quickening, his soft-soled shoes padding across the cobbles, the rising wind pulling at his hood.

Paldron glanced over his shoulder and kept moving with increasing urgency. But he didn't glance at Click. *You're just nervous*, he thought. *Why would you be nervous, Inspector Ward?*

Still, such nerves were infectious. Even Click began to feel watched.

After a few hundred yards through the winding streets, Paldron slowed before appearing to consider his next turn. Click had closed the gap between himself and the customs inspector, but he was still too far away to judge the expression on his face. There was no mistaking the care the man was taking, though.

Just beyond him was a row of houses clustered together on the left of the street. Across from those stood a large tavern familiar to Click, something of a competitor to the Thankful Cooper when it came to attracting visiting sailors.

With one more glance over his shoulder, Paldron lurched to the left and rushed down a narrow alley. Click hurried to follow, forced to let drop his hooded cloak. When he reached the mouth of the alley, he stopped and risked a quick glimpse around the corner. He spotted Paldron moving quickly away from him, feet splashing in the gathering rainwater.

Click waited until Paldron turned another corner, halfway along the lane, to give further chase. He kept his boots to either side of the narrow alley, where the rainwater was not so deep, to avoid making much noise. At the corner, he was rewarded with the sight of Paldron stopping at a door partway along, which opened onto a yard at the rear of one of the properties they'd previously passed. Click could hear the locking bolt sliding into place from the inside.

You're home, Click thought. *Why are you using the back gate? And for that matter, why travel so far from your home to drink in The Thankful Cooper when you have a tavern on your doorstep with largely the same brand of punter? Who are you avoiding? And if you're that keen to avoid them, why go outside at all?*

If this is your home at all . . .

Click paused, suddenly unsure. The patter of rain on the grime of the alley made the world sound an empty, lonely place. He wanted to turn from the alley and return to The Lows, but curiosity drove him onward. He was seeing too much in the way of odd behaviour from Paldron Ward to ignore his apparent plight.

So, he crept forward in the shadow of the alley wall and stopped a dozen yards short of Ward's gate. There he carefully climbed the poorly constructed wall to its top and edged his right leg up and over, squashing his body to the rough stone. He edged forward, desperately trying to stay out of sight from anyone who might chance a look out onto the alley. As uncomfortable as the rain was—and as treacherous as it made most surfaces—its din helped disguise the sound of his movements and the clouds foiled the moonlight's betrayal.

Paldron was in his yard, hesitating somewhere between the back door to the property and the midden in the rear of the yard. He was staring at the ground before the back door, although Click doubted he was really seeing much at all. *Something on your mind, Ward? On your conscience, perhaps?*

Then the inspector shrugged, turned to the midden, and began unbuckling his jakes.

Oh, right.

Click shook his head, stifling a laugh as Paldron moved to relieve himself in the tiny wooden shack. All humour was cut short when the door to the midden was thrown open and a shadowy figure burst from within. There was the flash of steel and then a wet thud as the assassin slammed the blade deep into Paldron Ward's throat.

The pair stumbled away from the midden as the door slammed shut behind them. After a few steps of their morbid dance, the assassin yanked the dagger free of his victim's jugular and pushed the body to the ground, where Paldron's skull cracked against his back step.

Click was dumbstruck, mesmerised, terrified.

It was at that point that Ward's corpulent wife emerged from the property's small larder and called out, "Who the bloody hell is making all this racket?" She brandished a rolling pin. It didn't save her.

The assassin, acting faster than Click could have imagined, lunged forward and stabbed Mrs Ward right in the heart, driving her back into the larder where the soft candlelight revealed the masked face of her killer.

All Click could make out was a pair of malevolent eyes that stared at the woman's dying form with palpable fury, as though annoyed that her death had marred an otherwise perfect murder.

Click clung hard to the wall as the rain continued to fall, slowly lifting his legs so that he lay like a plank along its length.

He lay that way for what felt an hour as he prayed the assassin had missed his presence. He waited for the punch of a blade in his ribs or the pull of grasping hands . . . but none came.

No hue and cry went up; no further sounds echoed through the night. The Wards' bodies would lie undiscovered until morning, or perhaps beyond that. The assassin had fled.

Paldron Ward had been ruthlessly silenced.

Click felt like fleeing, and not just from the rain-soaked wall. Acaelian was gone from the city, to Soriana only knew where. Claudia was increasingly preoccupied. Martin Galvan and Delgado were good men, for scoundrels, but were they friends? For the first time, Click thought seriously about leaving the city of his birth, his home, for the enormity of the challenges set before him—seemingly all around him—was becoming too much to bear. The city streets now seemed to hold an ever-present threat, like being stalked through the night by a pack of wolves.

And yet, where could he go? He knew nothing of the rest of the world. The thought of trying to make his way anywhere but Shen Utah was even more terrifying than anything that could befall him if he stayed.

The unknown mastermind had silenced their inside man, and not subtly. The murder of a customs inspector? Strong questions would be asked. It was an act of desperation.

Click waited as long as he dared and then climbed down from the alley wall and fled into the night on stiff legs. He had to plan his next move, and carefully.

Part Two

On Turning Tides

"The golden moments in the stream of life rush past us and we see nothing but sand; the angels come to visit us, and we only know them when they are gone."

George Eliot

Chapter Twelve

The Coming Storm

The ship's prow cut through the afternoon waves as the tall clipper named *The Moistened Barnacle* took advantage of the building winds to make even swifter progress than they had since leaving Hightower. Andi stood at the portside railing of the forecastle, staring at the bank of clouds on the horizon.

"A storm," Eidos stated simply as he came to stand next to her.

"I can see that," Andi snapped. Eidos seemed either oblivious or impervious to the venom in her curt retort, just nodding thoughtfully.

"Still, we've made good time since leaving port, and Captain Bophamel seems a capable commander."

Andi only nodded, suddenly feeling contrite. She found herself increasingly short of temper with her friends without real cause, and especially so with Eidos. Perhaps it was being in such close quarters with the same people day after day, something she'd not had to be comfortable with for some time.

By contrast, Eidos was rarely quick to anger; a man who committed quickly to action when it was necessary. In the few conversations they'd had below decks on their journey so far, Andi had learned that he was well read, probably as a result of having grown up in the court of Hightower under the guidance of a few capable tutors. He was no stranger to the politics of the Hightower Court either, and spoke at length about the varied reasoning behind courtly decree, but his own moral compass had just two polar-opposite points—right and wrong. He seemed oblivious to the subtle nuances of the real world.

No, she amended, *he wasn't oblivious to them. That wasn't fair; he simply chose to ignore them. He existed in a world of absolutes. He was as simple a man as one could hope to meet. The world needed such men.*

In other times, or perhaps in other company, Eidos might even be considered a hero. His actions were certainly easily characterised as heroic. Andi had seen Eidos wilfully put himself in harm's way on numerous occasions. The first time, he had raced to rescue a mother from illegal slavers when a young child sought his help. They had succeeded in finding the slavers, though not the mother.

Something occurred to her then that she had not previously thought about.

"Eidos, do you have family back in Unedar somewhere?"

The big man nodded. "A mother and an older brother, no father. Why do you ask?"

"I was just thinking about that little girl in the village; the one whose mother had been taken by slavers."

Eidos nodded again, but didn't respond.

"I wonder what will come of her."

"She'll probably be taken into one of the estates around Hightower as a maid, I should imagine. There is always work to be found."

"Work for pay, though?"

"No, work for board. A skilled path is rare for a human female even with a family to pay for her training. Tends only to be dwarves who train both sexes." Eidos's brow furrowed and he asked again, "What has this to do with my family?"

"I just realised I know very little about you."

"I suppose we hardly joined forces under ordinary circumstances. Well, as you asked, my mother lives in our family estates near Blue Gate in the duchy of Choat. My brother, a boorish man in the mould of our father, still runs the estates. They keep cattle and sheep mostly, turning a decent profit in fair seasons."

"Don't see them often then?"

"Obviously not. As the second born, I am of little use, and I never found the farming life to my taste."

"I thought you'd spent your formative years at Hightower, training in the navy."

"I did. It didn't take long to realise I was no farmer."

"Were you a farmer, you'd not be in this mess now."

"If our assumptions are correct about a spring invasion from Ipsica, and I wasn't here to do something about it, *this mess* would find me wherever I was in Shenmadock, no?"

"Fair point. How well did you know Magistrate Jakrat?"

"Only as well as any other officer of Reinhart's court," he answered. "I knew *of* him, and what I learned from listening to others was not pleasant. By all accounts, he was a cruel and ambitious man, although apparently quite fair in his dealings with the peasantry. Why?"

"I was just thinking back to the first time I saw one of those hooded figures." She recalled the mysterious men who seemed the faceless protagonists of the town's subversion. "It was when Manic and I were dragged before the gallows in Hightower; the magistrate seemed quite keen to have us hanged and done with."

"Hasty justice," commented Eidos.

"Well, the thing that stopped the hangman stretching our necks was the intervention of one of those cowled figures. Reinhart called them clerics."

Eidos hummed. "They were unlike any cleric I've ever seen."

Eidos himself was considered a cleric of the Hightower Court—a cleric of the court, not a religious cleric. "He spoke in Jakrat's ear, and then we were spared," Andi said, "at least long enough to go and retrieve that damn jewel from the old dungeons beneath Hightower itself."

"*The Baerv*."

"Yes," Andi confirmed. "I can't help but think that we had been sent after that thing not because Jakrat wanted it, but because that cowled figure wanted it. No, he *needed* it."

Eidos nodded. "If you remember, Reinhart's arrogance certainly seemed to suggest so when we confronted him in his tower. He seemed to care about little else, so long as that jewel was in his possession. Unfortunately, I don't know much about such things," he said apologetically. "I was little more than a navigator and erstwhile military advisor—and the latter of those in peacetime."

"It was curious, though. At our execution, the cowled figure seemed to hide from Reinhart, as though the duke—at that time—had no knowledge of their presence in the keep."

"Are you suggesting Magistrate Jakrat introduced them to the keep?"

Andi shrugged. "Well, perhaps not, but it certainly seems Jakrat had been turned before his cousin the duke, doesn't it?"

"I don't remember seeing any cowled figures when in court with Reinhart," Eidos said. "And before you ask, as far as I know, *the Baerv* is a worthless gem. I wouldn't have the first clue why Jakrat or his confederates wanted it."

"Jakrat told me it was without value but far from worthless," Andi said. "Cryptic. . . but what if that gem had some kind of power or significance? What if it had given him the power to return the dead to life, for example? Could that be the evil weapon Barabel mentioned?"

"That doesn't make any sense," said Eidos. "Those people we saw who were reanimated in Jakrat's manor house before we burned it to the ground, they were dead, gone, and reanimated long before you retrieved the gem for them." Eidos shrugged. "What's more, we'd have seen its use employed in the manor house somewhere, yet all we saw were pentagrams, ancient books, and such. No, I doubt necromancy was the gem's purpose, although I do agree that it likely does *have* a purpose."

Andi nodded, her fears somewhat allayed. The last thing she wanted was to be implicated in the plan by retrieving that gem for their enemies, whatever the plan was! Still, her mind wandered back to the moment she and Manic had retrieved *the Baerv*, and the discovery of the other gem—by contrast seemingly of immense worth—that they had uncovered in the same location. Jakrat had made clear, dismissively, that any other treasure was theirs for the keeping. The dwarf had hidden it from Jakrat, and indeed still had possession of it. She had to make sure she got her half of whatever they sold it for, should they ever get the chance.

Andi glanced around the deck of *The Moistened Barnacle* and asked, "Do you think we're doing the right thing?"

Eidos heaved a heavy sigh and obviously pondered his response. Andi knew he would be conflicted about their plan. After all, she, Manic and Finhead were all foreigners to Shenmadock, but the place was Eidos's home. Hell, he was employed by the Duke of Hightower! His loyalty would have to be to his nation, and yet their plan was dragging them south, away from any potential conflict come the spring thaw.

"I am not sure there are many more paths left open to us."

Andi held her hands out to show she agreed. "The Senior Lord of Shenmadock is dead at Reinhart's hands and the duke's own cousin Jakrat is in league with necromancers who are apparently subverting the leadership of the land. It leaves us with few options."

"Well, yes. But I was talking about the fact that you killed Duke Reinhart during our escape. Pretty difficult to have open dialogue with a nation once you've murdered one of their ruling council."

"You and I both know that Reinhart's mind and position had both been usurped, along with most of his court."

"Yes, *we* know; but how would we be able to convince anyone else of that fact before they tie the knot around our necks? And regardless, how would we know who to trust? Who is left to tell?"

"The corruption can't be that widespread," Andi said. She'd thought on this topic a lot since they had fled Hightower. "If they could just take over the minds of anyone they liked, they would have no need of an invasion force."

"Yes, there must be a limit to what is possible."

"I think we're all coming to terms with a new understanding of what is possible. Why else would we be undertaking this nonsense? Heading to the desert cities of Peena in search of some relic sceptre? What do we think we're going to achieve with it? I'm caught between being worried that we're on some fool's errand into the middle of nowhere and being relieved that we might avoid the calamity that is about to befall those we've left behind."

"I'm not intending to leave my nation without hope," Eidos said with an edge of pride. Again, almost heroic.

"And yet you're here. You're not back home trying to make a difference by employing more . . ." she struggled for the right word.

"Mundane methods?"

"Precisely!"

"You of all people must know that our meeting with Barabel and what we saw thereafter in Jakrat's manor house changed everything. It was you who convinced the others that this was the right path. Are you now changing your mind?"

"Absolutely not," she said. "I'm just conflicted. I don't believe in destiny, never have. Faith, hope, destiny, belief—it's all just a way of excusing one's actions or lack thereof." Andi didn't like to deal in *somehow* and *perhaps*. They were vagaries of life with no definable anchor in reality, regardless of how curious and disquieting Barabel's impossible knowledge of her had been. The old man had called her *lady*, and a lady she had been born. But Andi had come to think that her mysterious heritage was now known only to her, for she had gone to great lengths to hide her past.

But Finhead's intuitive questioning of her when leaving Shenmadock now meant that her three companions knew she was a rare kind of half-elf, born of a human mother. Eidos, Finhead and Manic knew more about her than anyone else alive, apart from perhaps the mysterious Babarel. She had to learn to trust them. That in itself posed her a problem, as trust was something that didn't come naturally or easily to her.

Before Eidos could bring her past up, Andi said of the storm clouds ahead of them, "I think the captain intends to sail right through the storm."

"It would be a long way around it. I think it favours our cause to take the storm on. We would not be best served by a delay in our journey."

"Agreed." Andi nodded. "But our cause would be served even less were we to sink to the bottom of the sea for the sake of trying to save two days' travel, when realistically, we probably have all winter to sail there and back."

"I'm not sure I agree. We need to be swift in our mission. If the threat we perceived on the border of Ipsica is real, then we must return long before the spring thaw. And without a clear and precise search location for this relic to hand—or even a detailed description of what it is we're actually searching for—we're going to be fumbling for a needle in a haystack down in Peena. Two days spent on this ship are two days we don't spend searching.

"Winter is already upon us," Eidos added as the ship pitched beneath them, the storm ahead growing in intensity. "This has been a short autumn. We can only hope that it leads into a longer winter." He stamped warmth into his feet, boots booming on the wooden decking, and Andi noticed he had his thick arms clutched around his chest. His gambeson flapped in the sea breeze.

"At least it's cold," Andi said. "If this winter had proven to be as mild as last, it might have been possible to march an army through the eastern passes even now. With a harsh winter, no sane army will risk it, and that gives us time."

Eidos nodded his agreement. After a long moment, he said, "To answer your question more directly, Andi: Yes, I believe we are doing the right thing. I know enough about this world to know I don't know everything about everything. Is it unlikely that a single relic will somehow forestall our destruction? Yes. Is it impossible? No. Anything is possible. I don't think you lack faith, Andi. From what little I have learned about you in our time together, I think you must be the most inclined to believe the impossible."

With a wry smile she said, "Believing something and believing *in* something are two very different things." She looked toward the coming storm, the saltwater spray stinging her face and soaking her dark hair. A storm was definitely coming.

The sun had dropped beyond the horizon, and the storm was in full force. Towering waves slammed into the wooden hull, bullish winds whistling and howling through the rigging. Below decks, Andi and the rest struggled to deal with the effects of the storm on their landlubber stomachs. Manic the dwarf, already proven to be the least comfortable in such an environment, was having the hardest time handling the constant motion and terrifying creaks of the hull. He had finally stopped vomiting, but for how long was anyone's guess.

Eidos stood with his arms braced between two bunks, his face grim. "I think we should do something to help," he said.

Fin shook his lizard head, which seemed only to make him greener. "Eidos, our presence would only complicate things. The crew is used to working as a team. We should not interfere."

Andi smiled. The reptile had no desire to move, she could tell.

"But I have experience." As Eidos spoke, the vessel pitched violently and there was a resonating crack from above, followed by shouts of concern from members of the crew.

"That didn't sound good," Fin conceded.

"That does it," Eidos barked, and turned for the cabin door. Suddenly Manic started vomiting again. That did it for Andi too.

"I'll help," she said, rising with some difficulty from her bunk. The degree of pitch and roll in the vessel was more evident when on her feet, and with the amount of water washing down from the decks above, it was hard going to reach the door to the waist of the ship. Without falling over more than twice, they reached the door and opened the latch.

Saltwater lashed their faces as the wind ripped the opened door from Eidos's grip. It crashed open, splintering the wood around the hinges. They were beneath the overhang of the aftcastle, looking at the waist of the vessel. Crew members were scattered all across the deck, trying to keep the ship in sailable condition, highlighted in the staccato blue flashes of lightning that streaked across the cloudy night sky. The sails had been fully reefed, but the storm winds were still tossing the ship with the recklessness of a child with a toy.

The night sky flashed again. Thunder boomed all around them, shaking the very timbers beneath their unsteady feet. Another wave crashed against the side of the vessel, white seawater raining down on the crew. From somewhere above—upon the aftcastle—they heard the ship's captain bellowing orders, incoherent from their position.

It was immediately obvious that they could do little to help. A nearby sailor slipped on the wet decking and fell to his rump, but quickly scrambled to his feet and helped pull taut a rope that had come loose in the rigging. Andi recognised the expression of a man galvanised by the fear of impending doom, his actions guided accordingly—do his job or drown.

"What can we do?" Andi screamed at Eidos over the howling winds.

"I don't know," he admitted.

Andi spotted a flapping rope used to secure some cargo on deck. The knot was coming loose. Eidos saw it sooner and scrambled across the decking to secure the fastening.

"Crewman, I told you to cut that rigging!" the captain shouted from above at someone out of sight. Andi saw a man rush into view to undo a heavily tied rope, at the end of which dangled a mid-sized anchor used to stabilise the vessel. He pulled the knot loose, and the kedge dropped into the water, the rope unravelling fast.

The crewman turned as another heavy wave thundered into the front of the ship, forcing the bow high into the air and pitching the deck beneath them.

Andi grabbed the frame of the door to steady herself. There was an almighty crash from above. The ship seemed suspended for an age, and then it suddenly plunged forward with a stomach-wrenching tilt into the storm waters, a massive wall of seawater spraying up in a roiling white V.

A shout went up. Suddenly, the ship's helm flew from the top of the wheelhouse above, the large wheel slamming amidships.

The crewman saw it too late. His legs were swept from beneath him. He tumbled to the deck.

The helm wheel flipped in the air over Eidos's head and slammed into another crewman's face. His severed head tumbled over the rail, and the helm disappeared into the blackness of the sea.

Near Eidos, the first crewman's foot had snagged in the unravelling kedge rope. He was being pulled overboard.

Eidos grabbed for the man's hand. He caught it firmly, but the weight was too great. They were both skidding toward the edge. Without conscious thought, Andi grabbed a broad-bladed knife from her belt and threw it at the rope. She got lucky and the blade thumped into the decking, severing the thick rope and freeing the kedge anchor. Eidos and the crewman crashed feet first into the gunwale railing. Only then did Eidos release the man and scramble back to where Andi stood, holding her hand out to him.

She pulled him back into the shelter of the doorway as they heard more shouts from above. The sailor Eidos had saved rushed on with his duties, unmindful of how close he had come to death.

Slamming the door shut with no small effort, the splintering hinges forcing her to jam it in place, Andi turned to Eidos. "Was that the steering wheel?"

"Looked like it," Eidos confirmed.

"Well, are we going to sink?"

"Not necessarily. They'll have a spare."

"Oh, that's comforting."

Morning finally came. The storm had blown itself out not much more than an hour before, but Andi and her companions had remained below decks, trying to rescue some sleep from what night remained. Manic looked drained—a literal possibility, considering the frequency of his bouts of vomiting—but insisted he could stomach no food yet. He had washed away what vomit had caught in his impressively broad moustache the night before. Thankfully he wore no beard, a rare thing for a dwarf, especially a male one. He remained on his bunk while the others went to see what damage had been done.

Stepping out onto the waist of the vessel once more, Andi could hardly believe she was looking at the same scene. There was substantial damage to the rigging and the railings, but most had been repaired as best the crew could manage. As the three comrades stepped into the morning sunshine, the crewman Eidos had saved came over and took the cleric's hand, pumping it in both of his own with vigorous gratitude.

The high winds of the night before still stirred the air, and Andi assumed they were still in the tail of the storm. Indeed, a glance behind them and to port showed imposing thunderheads on the horizon, dark columns proving that rain still fell there. The deck beneath her feet was sopping and treacherous still, and the air had a charged quality to it.

The crewman began enthusiastically regaling the tale of his rescue to Fin as the stout cleric stood by, looking decidedly uncomfortable.

Leaving the pair with the crewman, Andi moved off toward where a weary-looking captain was overseeing the installation of a replacement ship's wheel. She spared a glance at the railing, over which the first wheel had been blown the previous night. Eidos and the lucky seaman could easily have followed. She shuddered at the memory.

"Captain." She greeted the portly commander.

Amphibian by descent, Captain Bophamel was a curious being. He was clearly an able commander who seemed to shy away from asking too many questions, which was just how Andi liked it. Standing a little under six feet tall with a wide toad-like face and deep green skin, his species was just as rare as a wemik in the northlands, though she knew not where either beast originally hailed from.

"How do we fare?" she asked.

Stepping away from the work, he ushered her away from the wheel and then fell into stride alongside her, walking to the stern railing. With the heavy winds left over from the storm and the sails fully run out, they appeared to be making decent time again, to her untrained eye. "Pretty well, all things considered, m'lady," the captain responded. "We lost three crewmen, the main mast was cracked, the helm wheel went overboard, and there's a little damage below, but nothing that can't be replaced or repaired, albeit at a cost."

They watched the wake that the sturdy vessel left in the sea. It was obvious the captain had more to talk about than a broken steering wheel.

"You make for the Twin Cities," he said after a while. It was not a question, so being taciturn by nature at the best of times, Andi refrained from offering a response.

The nickname for their destination, Jrnak and its twin Mrnak, was an archaic thing. That the nickname had been specifically used by Barabel when charging them with their secret mission was surely telling, and it concerned Andi that the captain had employed the same strange moniker, especially when he seemed so careful in his approach. He was making an effort to be conversational, but his manner belied his nervousness at raising the subject.

The captain tipped a slight wry smile her way, his green features creasing. "I overheard the dwarf and the lizardman talking of our destination—Jrnak."

The little mercenary had a habit of shouting at Fin, knowing that Shen Common was not the lizard's native tongue, which made being overheard a fairly easy feat. "Jrnak is our destination, yes. But you know that already, Captain, for it is yours also."

"M'lady, you need not be evasive. In my experience, one can't kid a kidder."

Andi made a motion with open hands as if to claim she didn't know what he was talking about, but he interrupted her.

"I'm not intending to throw you and your friends overboard." She didn't know the species well enough to know if that had been a smile or not. "Listen, I saw that knife throw last night that saved my crewman's life. That was no idle toss of a blade. I've never seen such a well-executed strike. In the heat of the storm, there was no time to register it. But upon longer consideration, I'm afraid I can't accept that you're an everyday travelling noble, as your documents state. There's no way you're just a diplomatic envoy, and I'm afraid that while those forged documents you used to board my vessel might have fooled most captains, I'm slightly longer in the tooth."

He laughed, trying to seem relaxed, and his joke about teeth—being a toothless amphibian—was not lost on her. Still, she was too tense to afford him a laugh in response.

"There is more to this trip for you than cementing trade agreements or whatever else it is that envoys do, but that's none of my business. You're not the first passenger to whom I've had to turn a blind eye. But your situation, and you in particular, compel me to explain a little about the Twin Cities, before you blunder into an uncomfortable situation down there."

Andi nodded for him to go on, deciding that she was not in a position to argue that last remark.

She also doubted that her knife throw last night had been the first time Bophamel had suspected them to be travelling by deceit. When boarding, Andi and her companions had been forced to flee Hightower Port, and in the confusion, she had been pitched overboard. Her disguise—an ornate dress—had threatened to pull her to her doom, and she had been forced to cut it loose. While this had given her the excuse to wear her usual attire, the fact that Duke Reinhart's men had assaulted them at all had thrown her cover story as an envoy into doubt. Still, for the time being, the captain seemed more focused on their intended destination, so she played along.

"The southern lands are barbaric compared to the Land of the Lords," Bophamel continued. "And more superstitious too. While magic and sorcery are a long-forgotten myth in our heritage, some of the barbarian lands to the south still hold a belief in such powers. Most practitioners are considered journeymen and conjurors, there to please the crowds, much like the few charlatans we still see in Ipsican ports performing children's tricks in exchange for scraps of food or cheap whiskey. But there are others in the south who are looked upon as religious shamans or witch doctors. Just be wary about flippant remarks when you encounter these people. They tend to be held in higher regard.

"Furthermore, the Boyareen cities of the Inlet of Theed have long been a bone of contention between the nomads of Boyareen and the peoples of Peena to the south. The land has changed hands too many times to count. This means the social attitudes in Jrnak are different too . . ."

"Captain, I appreciate the concern, but I'm sure we will be fine. Softly does it. I get it."

"One more piece of advice, then," he said, turning away from the stern rail. "While you're being mindful of *what* you say to *whom*, also be wary about where you're travelling to. Jrnak is a sprawling, lively city, but her twin Mrnak is not to be travelled lightly—if at all. The road to Mrnak is one of abject misery, and the city itself contains only certain death."

Andi nodded. "We're nothing if not careful, but thank you for the kind warning. Obviously, we have no use for an abandoned city."

Bophamel seemed to measure her for a second, mulling something over. "Careful is one thing, but well informed is another. If you feel the need, I know a man who knows the world of both Boyareen and Peena inside out. No one alive knows more of the barbarian lands and their history than him. If for some reason you change your mind and feel compelled to visit the dead city, then seek him out. His name is Aal a Zass-al-amel."

"Easy to remember," she said drily, though she was increasingly concerned that the captain seemed convinced of their true destination—the Dead Twin.

"You'll find him in Jrnak. He's an old friend and will help you if you mention my name."

They walked back to the working crew, the sea air stirring Andi's hair. "Have we lost much time?" she asked, suddenly reluctant for this leg of their journey to end.

"Some," he admitted. "We won't be able to make such good time from here on in, I'm afraid."

"I thought you said we'd make better time being nearer to the coast?"

"Ordinarily that may be true. I know the reefs and rocks off the eastern Boyareen coast well enough that I'd have caught up some time driving close to the on-shore winds. But with the damage to the main mast and a little hull split, I'll not risk it. We've still got favourable northerlies to drive us on, though, while they last."

Andi stopped short of the helm. "Wait, there's a split in the hull?"

"We're shipping a little bit of water right now, but it'll be fine."

Only then did Andi notice the gentle list of the vessel to the starboard side. "We're sinking?" she asked.

"Not at all," Bophamel replied with a green smile. "More like . . . seeping."

Chapter Thirteen

Regrets

Arlon turned the broad page of the opulently bound tome and smoothed the expensive vellum to better examine the carefully drawn script in the candlelight of the library, the crisp sound of the vellum rippling through the high-ceilinged chamber like distant lightning. The librarian fixed him with a wary glance, obviously worried about leaving the tome in anyone else's care but her own. He ignored her, focusing as best he could on the wording before him. It was a challenge, for the language was archaic. Luckily Arlon had been afforded a classic education in Shen Utah's college, so he was able to follow the subject material closely.

It didn't help.

He was trawling through as many historical accounts as he could that—according to the ever-watchful librarian—mentioned an incident of the Senior Lord or reigning monarch being declared *in absentia*. So far, his search had yielded nothing useful. This account, for example, detailed the apparent fall of King Armand de Hayne in 621 during a campaign to bring the southern lands to heel. The declaration had lasted for a month, allowing the senior commander of the Shen infantry to take command of the nation and retain sovereign control of the barons and nobles. King Armand had been found in the field and returned to the capital, whereupon he made a full recovery, resuming command of the nation within five weeks of having been declared *in absentia*. But this account was from wartime.

Resisting the urge to slam the tome shut, Arlon carefully closed it and indicated to the librarian that it could be taken away. Rarely had he seen such open relief on someone's face.

Arlon rubbed his eyes with the heels of his hands. He was getting nowhere.

Deciding that time would be better spent on other duties, he stood from the table and gathered his cloak. As he moved quickly between empty chairs, heading for the exit, another figure emerged from an aisle to the left of him. A quick sidestep stopped them from colliding.

"My apologies," Arlon mumbled distractedly.

"My fault, Knight Marshall," said the other, "my fault entirely."

Arlon blinked at the man. "Oh, Councillor Horvarth. I didn't recognise you in my hurry." Horvarth stopped and turned fully to him, an expression on his face that betrayed his delight that Arlon had recognised him at all. "How are things in the East, Councillor?"

"Peaceful, Knight Marshall."

Arlon smiled at that. Horvarth was old enough to remember the times when that was as much as one could have wished for, in eastern Unedar especially.

"And how is your Lord Reinhart?"

"Last I heard, he was fighting fit and enjoying a good summer of hunting."

"Summer?" That surprised Arlon. "You've not heard from him since?"

"Oh, of course, there is constant communication," Horvarth said quickly. "He's simply not sent anything directly to me since the summer."

"I understand," Arlon said. Then, as Horvarth made to nod and take his leave, something sprang to Arlon's mind. "I didn't know Reinhart and Lord Karl of Jow were on such good terms these days."

Try as he might to hide the reaction, Horvarth's manner suddenly changed. "Knight Marshall?"

"Karl himself told me how he and yourself are old friends."

"Me? Not especially so, Knight Marshall. And as far as I understand, it has been some time since Lord Karl and my duke have had reason to converse directly on anything."

"Is that so? Must be my mistake, then. Ignore me." Smiling suddenly, Arlon said, "Don't let me keep you any longer, Councillor."

"Thank you, Knight Marshall." With that, Horvarth left Arlon in mild confusion. As he moved outside into the cold air of early evening, he pondered Horvarth's words and manner.

Why would Karl have lied to him about his friendship with Horvarth? Why mislead Arlon as to the nature of relations between Unedar and Jow? For that matter, who was the real liar? What if Karl and Horvarth *were* friends, and it was the latter who had just lied to Arlon in denying it. What would the Unedar councillor gain from such a denial?

The ghost of a question haunted his mind, and he shook his head to clear it; he did so loathe the machinations of politicians. What he loathed more was that it seemed he'd started sharing such paranoid anxieties himself.

He stepped down to the exterior grounds of the library and paused at the gate before deciding to take the long way back to the palace. He would take a quick lunch in the mess hall with the other palace guardsmen and then look for someone to train with for the afternoon. With Carpion away from the city, capable sparring opponents were few and far between.

He reached the main concourse to the north of Temple Link and turned south toward the palace before stopping outside the old training garrison that stood off the broad thoroughfare. A smattering of young recruits was still out, conducting drills in the parade behind the railings, and he stood for a moment to watch. People of the city still moved about in the crisp late-morning cold, their breath fogging on the air as they passed. None recognised him.

He couldn't help but afford a glance north at the statue that stood proudly at the doors of the Shen Utah College. He shook his head at the posture the sculptor had given him: sword held aloft, wind lifting his hair in rampant locks—hair he had long since decided suited him shorter. He hadn't worn his hair that long since Thes.

Suddenly he was aware of a presence approaching from his left, across the concourse. She moved gracefully between the others crossing her path and arrived at his side, her hood up and pulled forward to protect her identity. But Arlon didn't need to see her face to know her.

Kathryn turned to look up at him from within the confines of the hood. The hue of her complexion was made vibrant by the late-autumn colours. Both the hooded cloak and the gown beneath were of a soft crimson material. She gave him a stupefying smile in greeting.

Arlon was transfixed. He felt the knot of childish infatuation in the pit of his chest, like a pendulum upon his heart, and couldn't help but smile back like an excited child.

Kathryn indicated the statue across from them. "I can't imagine you're out here admiring yourself."

"Hardly," he said. "It could do with a scrub, though." In the daylight, it was easy to see the build-up of moss at the base of the statue and in the detail of his booted feet.

"The same could perhaps be said for its subject," she teased, pointing out the ink smudges on his hands. He hoped he hadn't smudged any of the more precious tomes in his fruitless search. The stains on his fingers were most likely from the more recent entries; still, it explained the librarian's attitude toward him!

"I've been in the library," he offered. "Even books don't help me understand this city." Those people who were passing by could not hear their conversation, he was certain, but still, he dropped his voice, for Shen Utah had a thousand unseen and all-seeing eyes. And the exchange with Councillor Horvarth still played upon his mind, enough to make him wary.

"It doesn't surprise me that you struggle to find answers that are wrought by pen and not sword," she told him, turning to regard him. He could see the playfulness in her expression.

"I've never beaten anyone with a pen before—or a book, for that matter, although some of the fat tomes and manuscripts in there would probably do some damage. Scholars do waste a lot of energy with many words in order to talk around the simplest of things, often to simply conclude that there are no satisfactory conclusions."

"Perhaps. Although I've never seen a piece of scripture, or the words of the wise, wound a man, either," she countered.

"Not directly, I suppose."

"You mean to suggest the written word has the power to wound *indirectly*?"

"Do you really think I'd have marched as many armies as I have, across as many different lands as I have, were it not for the decree of the supposedly wise put into writing, made law, and rendered irreversible? Take the barbarians, for example. There are books upon books in there"—Arlon jabbed a thumb over his shoulder—"about their heathen ways and ignorance. Volumes have been written about the struggle to civilise and educate these wild people. From the very first moment we encountered them, we've railed against their inability to agree with our own view of the world. When indoctrination failed and still they grew in numbers, we marched with swords and war engines to exert control over those peoples who our learned scholars would have us believe to be the collectively stupid.

"Not one book in that library describes the civilisations our ancestors marched to destroy, none offers an account of their own history, and none asks the question of whether the barbarians *asked* to be educated or civilised, or whether they ended up better off for it."

Kathryn nodded. "That's because history is written by the victors. Their motive will always be to present a truth that justifies their actions."

"Agreed. Moreover, there is no proof on those pages for the justification for war. There is no document that presents a salient explanation as to why our ancestors were right to wage war on those so-called heathens, because there is no proof that they *were* heathens. It is just as likely that our gods are equally as false as the gods we accused those barbarians of worshipping—from whom we rescued their souls!

"And now, in large portions of the population outside of Temple Link, we have a growing belief in the One True God—a philosophy that, if anything, mirrors that of the early Boyareen peoples. If that movement gains momentum and finally challenges the spiritual monopoly the polytheists in Shen Utah hold, will we have to march an army on ourselves? Is our faith so fragile that we must protect it against the merest shadow of proof? Will we have war just because of the difference in a number written down on some ancient parchment? A parchment that was probably only ever a set of instructions for building a dog's kennel—a parchment accidentally elevated while the true history of even our own people was burned generations before by equally terrified and angry men who coveted power, not knowledge, domination instead of peace."

Embarrassed by his own outburst, Arlon paused for breath. These were topics that the two of them had spoken of before and largely agreed upon. After all, Arlon knew full well that Kathryn was plenty smarter than him.

"Has anyone ever told you that you read too much?" Kathryn asked, laughing at the irony. "I miss seeing you so passionate about this kind of thing. What's happened to raise your hackles?"

Arlon heaved a sigh. "I was looking for inspiration. I've been trying to find some record of a situation similar to the one in which I now find myself, so that I might learn from the past and wriggle out of it."

"You anticipate Handee being declared *in absentia*?"

"I certainly do, yes. But there's nothing I can find that helps. There's no record of a Senior Lord or ruling monarch ever being declared *in absentia* during peacetime. Any time the law has been acted upon, there has been an immediate and existing threat to the sovereignty of the nation. Worse still, and probably predictably so, this law has never been instituted during the time of the republic. If I don't get good news from the east soon about Handee's location, it looks like I'm going to make history." He exhaled heavily.

"Again," Kathryn said softly. The weight and importance of that one word, the things to which it referred, was enough to crush any man. They both turned away from the statue and began walking toward the palace. After a moment, she showed her usual intuition by asking, "What else is afoot?"

"It's a concern that I might be called upon to take charge of the council if Handee is declared *in absentia*, but it's the reasons for such a requirement that have me really worried. Sod's law that this unrest in Mashtock should come when Handee is not here to mediate."

She seemed to ponder something for a moment, as though he'd said something profound, and then asked, "Do you think Handee would have gone about things any differently to how you've approached them?"

"Probably not, but then I suspect his very presence would probably have nipped most of the bickering in the bud in the first place."

Kathryn laughed at that, the sound like music.

"I don't like being lied to," he elaborated, "but I dislike more not knowing who is lying."

"All politicians lie, especially those who were once nobles too. Who do you suspect?"

"In the most recent instance? Either Councillor Horvarth or Lord Karl. Neither account tallies, so one must be lying."

"About anything serious?"

"Probably not, that's what rankles! I can't work out a reason for the lie, whoever told it." Quickly, he explained all that had happened with Karl and Horvarth, along with his suspicions.

"So, either Karl is lying about the improvement of relations, or Horvarth is lying that there's been no such thing. To discern the reason for the lie, you must ask the question, what would be the ramifications of an improvement in relations between Jow and Unedar, especially considering the unrest on Jow's border with Mashtock?"

"I have no idea," he confessed.

Kathryn nodded. "You're right not to trust any of these politicians. However, Karl's record of support for this council and Shenmadock as a whole is unrivalled. Don't forget, without Jow's support, we'd have lost Choat to the Ipsican infiltrators not so long ago."

"I know. I remember. It frustrates me to exist in a world where your enemy could just as easily slit your throat as share a meal with you."

"Or a bed," commented Kathryn. Arlon had never made a secret of the fact that Lord Karl, and Marta herself, had ambitions to corner him into a marriage he didn't want. Or at least, that they *had*, before Baronet Failton of Theed had thankfully drawn those attentions away.

Suddenly the weight of the world seemed to press down on Arlon. He felt small and inexplicably alone, standing at the edge of someone else's world, like a moth drumming his wings against a window in the dead of night, desperately yearning for the light of a distant candle within.

"I don't want to have to do this alone," he said.

Kathryn was silent, looking once more at the palace before them.

"I miss you," he told her riskily. She closed her eyes for a long moment. "I've tried to forget you," he went on. "For the longest time, I've tried to push what I feel down inside, where it can't affect me. I lost all hope for us a while ago, so I turned away. That's why you've heard so little from me. It wasn't meant to be hurtful. I've tried to focus on pretty much anything else, but I don't think I can do it any longer. And what's worse, I don't think I really want to."

He pressed on, desperate to say the things he'd kept bottled up and worried she might interrupt. "You're all I think about. You're my first thought in the morning, and my last before I go to sleep. You're the colour in my world. Without you in it, my life is just some washed-out, sepia-tone joyless dirge."

Although he had spoken earnestly and confidently, it still felt like the words had come out in a babbling rush, like a blade had slit his heart and the sentiments had spilled like blood from his chest. And now that he had stopped, the silence between them was deafening.

"Will you not tell me how you feel?" he asked.

"You know how I feel," she replied. "But it's not that simple—it never has been."

"It was once," he said with a soft laugh. "But I do understand." Although in truth, his feelings were so strong that his thinking was clouded by his longing for her, and by a profound loneliness. He didn't really understand at all. "As frustrating as it is, I still consider myself one of the luckiest men alive," he said.

"None of this feels lucky to me," Kathryn replied as they recommenced their journey, a despairing tone to her voice that simultaneously gave him hope and cast a shadow over him. Her eyes locked on his for a moment that seemed to stretch interminably, a held gaze that spoke more volumes than any words she'd ever shared with him. "If we were *lucky*, I would not be a de Hayne, and you would be just another soldier. But that's not the case, so how could we be lucky?"

"Because I found you," Arlon said simply. "Imagine the people who go through life without knowing feelings like this, without knowing the beauty of someone who is a perfect match for their soul. We would be unlucky had we never met. Despite the pain of not being with you, I could never wish we had never met.

"And we have no way of knowing what will happen in the future," he added.

Kathryn looked down at her clasped hands. "I'm sure everything will work out the way it is supposed to, in the end."

"I hope so. I think it's meant to be."

"As do I," she confessed without any hope at all.

Chapter Fourteen

Above and Below

Arlon's boots thundered on the marble floor as he stormed down the long hall toward the Council Chamber barely an hour after having taken his leave from Kathryn, their conversation still fraying his emotions. Ahead, he could see various minor councillors and administrators entering the old room, gathered in small, excited groups. In counterpoint to the Knight Marshall's furious footfalls came the patter of Professor Ergun's sandal-clad feet as the elderly advisor hurried along in Arlon's wake, showing a spryness that belied his age.

"Patience, Arlon," the wise old man implored.

"Easily said, Professor," Arlon growled, "but these politicians and their manoeuvrings are testing my restraint."

"It would profit us to listen to all the information before we react," Ergun tried once more.

Arlon stopped five yards short of the grand chamber entrance and turned to speak closely with Ergun, his anger leaching out despite himself. He cared little that those minor lords and councillors still entering the chamber for the hurriedly convened afternoon session could overhear them. "I will not be manipulated by these cowards," Arlon snapped. "I don't know what transpires here, but I will not put up with being asked the same question thrice!"

The old man took a careful step back and allowed Arlon a breath. It was not the first time Ergun had witnessed his fury, and he understood precisely how much effort it often took for Arlon to control it.

"Arlon, you are Knight Marshall, and this council will now look to you to make some difficult decisions in Handee's stead. We might have to accept that the time for delays has gone. It is a test for you, yes. Perhaps this is precisely the reason for these repeated calls for arbitration by the council—to test you. You must trust your own judgement. You are a capable leader and a sound judge of men. Senior Lord Handee trusts this. The only person who ever seems to have a doubt about that is you. Believe in yourself."

"I'm sorry that I snapped," Arlon apologised. Perhaps his exchange with Kathryn weighed more heavily upon him than he'd thought. He had bared his feelings openly, something completely unusual for him, and he had not walked away with a fairy-tale ending, only with a fistful of reality—that their situation was almost impossible, and yet his love was kept alive by the smallest, agonising kindling of hope. He forced himself to calm.

"It shows you still have integrity, son. And passion. Both should serve you well."

The councillors had scuttled away from the raised voices, and the hallway was empty. Arlon allowed Ergun to precede him as they entered the tall chamber, which was full and thronging. Arlon judged that almost every member of the court must be present—aside from those seemingly ever-absent dukes of Mashtock and Unedar. Even Duke Aaron of Choat was in attendance.

There was tension in the air, but it was a strange kind of electric tension that Arlon felt akin to excitement. The same morbid excitement he had sensed a dozen times up and down battle lines—the anticipation of a bloody clash.

Despite the late hour and the urgency with which the council had been convened, all those present—including councillors and aides—were regaled in brash and over-exuberant colours. They made Arlon think of sparring peacocks. He warned himself to remain wary, for this was no flock of fowl; these were people whose ambitions and desire for power made them dangerous.

In Arlon's opinion, the very desire to rule a nation should preclude one from being allowed to do so. Such a longing could surely never be for the benefit of others. Perhaps a young politician might set out with grandiose ideologies, but the very nature of the Politik was sure to corrupt those under its thrall.

He sensed eyes turn to regard him as he entered the chamber with long, controlled strides. Immediately Arlon spied Councillor Fargil, Ergun's brother, off to the right-hand side, talking to some minor officer. Further around the room, he saw many faces that had been present the other day, including—of course—Lord Karl II, Duke of Jow. Senior Lord Handee's lieutenant, Lord Ludovic, was also in attendance, and Arlon was concerned to see him sharing a word in passing with Councillor Horvarth. He was sure they had plenty of things to talk about, but it still struck him wrong.

Arlon stepped to the middle of the floor and snatched up an apple the colour of blood, taking a hearty bite and savouring the sharp sweetness. He then walked calmly to a seat nearby, a few rows up the auditorium, and sat patiently. He noticed that Ergun had remained at the entrance to the chamber to view the coming discussion from floor level.

Arlon's confident entrance had produced the desired effect, and the Council Chamber quieted to a hush. Lord Karl sat on the opposite side of the chamber to both Fargil and Horvarth, his elbows on his knees and his neatly bearded chin resting on steepled, chubby fingers. Arlon's seating position was carefully selected between the two potentially warring parties, though across the chamber from them. It was a bonus that this position also kept Horvarth in sight.

"Well?" Arlon asked into the burgeoning silence. "What news from Mashtock?"

A scribe stood at the side and looked in his direction. "Knight Marshall Arlon, an hour after noon, we received a messenger bird from one of our scouting parties. The message reads: 'Evidence of unrest exists in the previous disputed region north of Jow River. Heavy losses to local townsfolk as well as livestock. Attacks appear widespread and without discernible strategic pattern. No residual evidence found to suggest an aggressor's identity, but it is clear that these attacks are made without warning or apparent reason. Hit and fade tactics are being employed.' They request a reply for further instruction, sir."

During the scribe's oratory, the Council of Lords had turned on itself, various lords and aides slinging accusations and haranguing each other. More than a few suggested Jow was to blame; others countered with increasing vitriol.

Arlon refused to rise from his seat. Instead, Lord Ludovic—who himself had walked away from Horvarth's side—pounded his staff on the marble floor. His sharp-eyed expression demanded silence. It was slow to come.

"This is a disgrace!" shouted Lord Karl, standing up. "Once again, I refute the veiled accusation that Jow has any involvement in these crimes! The evidence itself strongly suggests a rash of banditry!"

Ludovic raised his hand. "You will note that no evidence has been found to implicate Jow at this time. But your protestations are duly noted."

"Predictable as they are," threw in a councillor on a higher tier.

"Enough!" shouted the normally meek Councillor Fargil. His features were ashen, and he looked dog-tired. Apparently, the confirmation of the unrest in his home duchy had unsettled him. "I demand action and satisfaction from this council. Such injustice cannot go unchecked. Lives are being lost!"

"First, we need to identify these aggressors," Ludovic interjected. "It is clear we need to investigate this further with a stronger presence."

This raised choruses of derision from some lords. Clearly most felt that "investigate" meant a weak response.

"Hold!" barked Arlon, unwilling to remain mute a second longer. The lords were silenced as quickly as a classroom. "The need to gain more information is a distant second to the safety of our citizens in Mashtock." Ludovic narrowed his eyes at the challenge, but spoke not. "Their safety and security is paramount. We must dispatch defensive units to secure villages on the northern banks of the River Jow."

Looking at Councillor Fargil, he said, "Direct your Lord Vale to do likewise with units from his own garrisons at Abnavil, Stroming Blod, and Cync, but make sure to inform him that we intend to support from here also. I want it made abundantly clear that the Shen Utah scouts already in the region are in complete command of all forces deployed in this action. Leadership must come from Shen Utah until peace is brought. The risk of misdirected revenge is too great, so I want no jurisdictional nonsense from Lord Vale. Do you understand?"

Fargil nodded.

Lord Karl had turned sharply in Arlon's direction, although there was no flare of anger to his features, only mild surprise. The commissioning of a Shen Utah force on that side of the River Jow, under the command of Shen Utah scouts, was perhaps too plain a suggestion that

Arlon suspected Jow could still be to blame for the attacks, whether directly, through malice, or indirectly by inactivity or mismanagement of his duchy. The direction that the Shen scouts already in situ would have command over even the locally garrisoned troops was also tantamount to a military occupation of the Mashtock duchy, although Fargil only seemed relieved at the prospect and eagerly acceded to Arlon's demands. Perhaps that two-edged approach had cooled Karl's response somewhat.

Even so, that would not sit well with many traditionalists, though it could not be helped. Fargil had asked for help, and he was going to get it.

Arlon faced down the many glares from around the chamber, including that of Councillor Horvarth. "I trust the council would have no objection, considering the importance of quelling these attacks and identifying the perpetrators? After all, none here has reason to believe we will find any member duchy of the republic to blame for these shameful attacks."

It was a risky gambit that might have tempted a whiplash reaction, from Jow especially, but Arlon would not be bullied.

Instead, Karl stood confidently and took a single breath before replying with a level tone, "On the contrary, my Knight Marshall. A threat to Mashtock can only be seen as a potential threat to Jow, and as such, we will stand beside our Shenmadock brothers."

Supporters of Mashtock, and those perhaps with reason to be suspicious of Jow in general, snorted with derision at such a statement. Fargil only sat and watched Karl closely, who continued regardless.

"In fact, I would even go as far as to suggest that this threat to our neighbours to the north is also a threat to Jow, and further represents a direct threat to the sovereignty of the Council of Lords and the republic of Shenmadock itself."

Arlon sensed Professor Ergun look up sharply in his direction.

Karl increased his volume as though speaking to the gods themselves. "In light of this threat, and with Senior Lord Handee yet to return from the East, I propose we declare *Senior Lord in absentia*." Arlon's heart thundered in his chest. *It was happening!* "The duchy of Jow calls on the Council of Lords to afford executive powers to the Knight Marshall, in order that he may lead a force of arms to settle the unrest in Mashtock and bring those to blame under the gaze of this council's justice. I call for Arlon to be voted Protector of the Realm."

The Council Chamber exploded with shouts. Lords jumped to their feet. Fists shook. Spittle flew. The chamber had been hurled into pandemonium.

Arlon simply sat, unable to comprehend what had just occurred. He might have anticipated such a plea from Fargil further down the line, but such a vehement proposal from Jow? And at such an early juncture? Suddenly Arlon was convinced that Kathryn was correct, and his suspicion of Jow's involvement in the unrest might have been entirely inaccurate, clouded by his own prejudices.

Above the heads of the arguing politicians, in the shadows of a small arched alcove high in the chamber's otherwise empty public balcony, Arlon caught sight of Kathryn de Hayne. She stood watching the verbal melee with a maroon wrap pulled closely about her, as though chilled to the bone.

Full autonomous power over an entire nation stood within Arlon's grasp. The lurch in his stomach, which some might find akin to excitement, only made his bile rise. He desired no such power.

Suddenly his resolve was steeled. He stood and called out, "Order!" It took a while for the voices to stop, such was the vehemence of the council's argument. "Damn it all, I'll have order! All of you, stop your childish bickering!" The noise abated. "Such behaviour is irrelevant, for I refuse the call—it is premature. The evidence at hand does *not* warrant such a decree at this time!"

Several voices expressed alarm. Karl of Jow turned on Arlon, and Fargil seemed equally agitated. Clearly, he felt abandonment was to follow, but Arlon would not allow that, either.

Karl jabbed a finger at the Knight Marshall. "You would abandon your duty?"

"Do not seek to lecture me on duty, politician!" Arlon's voice was dangerously close to a bellow now. "I will not stand for it! And I will not see the principals of this republic undermined by a panicked decision. There is no vote to be had. The Council of Lords will not declare *Senior Lord in Absentia* this day, for the case does not warrant it." Arlon glared at those before him, including Horvarth, who watched the exchange with a strange passivity. "I shall organise a defensive force to set out for Mashtock duchy in order to preserve the safety of the citizens from *any* threat they may perceive. But I shall not lead them myself, and I will not remove sovereign power from this chamber until we are left with no other course of action.

"Councillor Fargil, rest assured that the Council of Lords shall not abandon you and your lord, Duke Cordon Vale. Scribe, prepare messages to the expeditionary team in Mashtock that reinforcements are being sent to stabilise the area, leaving this evening. They are to continue their investigations, but citizen safety is of paramount concern."

"What of the identity of the perpetrators?" It was Fargil again, his voice quivering.

"They will show themselves in short order, for there will be nowhere for them to hide now. But until they do, we will have no unwarranted reprisals, no escalation. Do I make myself clear?"

Arlon stepped down to the centre of the chamber. There was a murmuring that spoke of the Knight Marshall's weakness. Arlon could feel their fear; it was like a cold grease on his soul, and it sickened him.

"If there is nothing else?" he challenged.

No one spoke.

Arlon took one more bite of his half-eaten apple and then hurled it onto the refreshment table, fruit and drink containers scattering noisily. He strode purposefully from the chamber, past the stern face of Ergun, and out into the echoing corridors of Shen Utah Palace.

He wasn't entirely sure what he had just done.

Ergun caught up with Arlon at the end of the main corridor leading to the central cloister of the palace. The day crawled toward a crisp, chill evening, but Arlon felt another, different cold growing in his core.

"Knight Marshall," the professor murmured. Arlon slowed at hearing his mentor's voice. He angled to the right and took a seat on a stone bench at the foot of an ancient fountain, the large courtyard unpopulated but for the two of them.

"Don't," Arlon warned him.

"Don't what?" Ergun said defensively. "I happen to agree with your decision and your judgement of the information at hand, although I'm not sure what the apple had to do with it."

Arlon glanced at Ergun to see if he was mocking him. It was clear he was . . . if only a little. Arlon laughed the tension away, his temper cooling.

"For Jow to have made such a proposal at that moment was unreasonably rash and dangerous," admitted Ergun. "I expected Fargil to press for stronger help, perhaps, but for

Jow to demand *Senior Lord in Absentia*—that was unforeseen. I think Karl was almost as surprised as anyone at his own demands. It seemed impulsive, not contrived."

"I know," Arlon agreed. "It makes me wary that perhaps I may be wrong about Jow being to blame for the unrest."

"So spaketh the soldier," Ergun said, this time without mockery. "A politician would suspect Jow even more after this."

Arlon shook his head as if clearing a fog. "What?"

"A soldier's life is a simple one. Your enemy on the battlefield is usually clear by their conduct—they're the ones holding swords, trying to kill you. But a politician sees smoke and mirrors, shadows and empty darkness. They say within the words that have *been* spoken that which cannot be said. I can't begin to explain why, but I wouldn't discount Jow's possible role in all of this. My greater worry surrounds what *else* is in Karl's brain. Perhaps it was something of a gamble, requesting you lead military aid for Mashtock. Perhaps he knew you would refuse. The question remains, what other machinations are hinted at by this latest move, as impulsive as it may have seemed. After all," Ergun thought out loud, "he must have known that the evidence would never really support the move for *in absentia*. You had to refuse. Yet, could it be some veiled cry for aid on Karl's part? Perhaps we were right before when we postulated that some unseen rogue elements in Jow's ruling court might have triggered this unrest. Maybe this call for your strong-handed intercession is some move on Karl's part to bring you to his aid. Perhaps he can't openly request it, for other parties in the council might be watching for such."

"The most unexpectedly calm reaction came from Horvarth. He seemed almost unmoved by the exchange."

"Those councillors of Unedar rarely care a jot what occurs between the western duchies."

"All in all, it amounts to a move we did not anticipate," Arlon agreed. "So how can we possibly anticipate what is really being planned, and by whom?

Ergun nodded sagely. "That's the fact of things. I sense political currents that we are only vaguely aware of."

Arlon leaned back on his hands and allowed his head to rest along the crest of the bench. Something Ergun had just said resonated with him, and he lifted his head again to look at Ergun. "So, what if it *is* Jow who is to blame, but not Karl himself, as you say?"

Ergun's eyes narrowed.

"Karl can come to me any time he likes for a private conversation; lord knows he's done so on many occasion to get me to marry his daughter. So why not now? Karl's prideful. What if he suspects someone in his retinue or within the duchy hierarchy is to blame for these attacks but isn't willing to acknowledge that openly?

"Is it possible that Karl is behaving in this defensive manner in order to deflect attention, and to give himself time to identify and deal with whoever *is* responsible on his own? Better that he wields that power than the capital."

Ergun nodded as Arlon spoke. "I suppose that might make a strange sort of sense. And it's his pride that stops him from admitting to such fears without proof?"

"And once he finds that proof, he can deal with it internally and the problem goes away," said Arlon. "I mean, if it is the case that it's someone in his circle of trust, it would make such a seasoned and ambitious politician look remarkably weak."

"Moreover, if Karl is able to identify and neutralise the culprits, he earns the plaudits for it, strengthening his position in pursuit of the Senior Lordship."

Arlon shook his head and ran a hand down his face. "Far too much conjecture; only half of that is suspicion, and we've not enough proof of either. But regardless, my decision not to agree to *Senior Lord in Absentia* was clearly the right one. And yet, I can't help feeling that it plays into an unknown enemy's hands. I feel like I've stepped upon a trap that's yet to spring."

"We must be careful," Ergun agreed, dropping the topic as Lord Ludovic approached. The Shen Utah politician looked a little flushed, as though the excitement of the exchange had raised his blood.

"Professor, Knight Marshall," he greeted them, taking a seat across the fountain square from them while they heard the greater press of councillors and lords dispersing from the chamber some distance away, many voices chattering excitedly. Not too tall but slightly angular, Ludovic had bright, intelligent eyes that creased to crow's feet as a lopsided smile crept across his face, skilfully avoiding smugness. "That exchange was unforeseen."

"And unfortunate," agreed Ergun.

"I for one, Arlon, agree with your position on this matter, but it will soon become a problem. Just the mere proposal of *Senior Lord in Absentia* will have the council stirred up to no end. In the coming days, they will probably speak of little else, and the more ambitious members of the council will start positioning themselves for change."

"I'm not sure I care," said Arlon, his tone still carrying the heat of his previous fury. "The important thing is that they keep those opinions out of official decree. The last thing this nation needs is dissolution of the young republic. Appointing me Protector of the Realm would be a mistake. I won't be made a pawn."

Ludovic inclined his head. "I believe the most important thing right now is to locate my Senior Lord Handee and fix a return date for him. Any word from your cousin Carpion's Wayfarers?"

Arlon watched Ludovic. Years ago, Ergun had told him that Lord Ludovic was a well-informed member of the council who would undoubtedly have a network of "people" feeding him information. Ergun had used the word "people" carefully enough for Arlon to understand the implication—spies and informants. Likewise, Senior Lord Handee had long ensured Ludovic was well secured within his own staff, and Handee treated his trust like the finest currency. If Handee valued Ludovic, Arlon had to trust that judgement.

Be that as it may, Arlon didn't want to know how the lord knew such details as the identity of the expedition's commander and the composition of the team he had sent to Adar. None of that was common knowledge. "I have not checked the dispatches yet, Lord Ludovic. Rest assured, the moment that good news is heard, I shall convey it to the council."

"Of course."

Arlon stood to take his leave of the two elder men, and then stopped. "Lord Ludovic, might I ask your thoughts on Councillor Horvarth of Unedar? Only, I've not had much dealing with him directly, and I noticed the two of you in conversation earlier."

"My thoughts on Horvarth are simple enough—he's a bureaucrat. He is as ambitious as one might expect of a member of the council, but nothing for Duke Reinhart to be alarmed about."

"Do you mind if I ask what the two of you spoke about?"

Ludovic levelled a gaze at Arlon, who forced himself to remain stoic. Finally, the man said, "I was hoping he would know why Handee has been so delayed. After all, if anyone was to know, it would surely be a member of the Hightower Court."

"And?"

"Alas, he knows less than nothing. It appears it has been quite some time since Horvarth has heard directly from Reinhart. His communications have come from the court magistrate, instead, Reinhart's cousin Jakrat."

"And what do you know of this Jakrat?"

It was Ergun who responded. "He's a different consideration altogether. He strikes me as a lazy young man, but one beset by a chilling ambition and lust for power. Reinhart always trusted the former to keep the latter in check."

Ludovic nodded. "I always thought he was jealous of Reinhart's position, but he never fancied working hard enough to achieve his own goals."

Arlon made an aggravated noise. "So where does that leave us? We have no way of knowing what Unedar knows of Handee's location, because neither Reinhart nor his cousin are on speaking terms with their own council representative! What am I dealing with here, a sodding nursery?"

Ergun suppressed a smile. "We do have the report from Hightower that mentions the departure of Senior Lord Handee's retinue," he said, "but nothing after that."

Arlon looked to Ludovic again. "Can I ask your opinion on a slightly subtler topic? Why would Karl of Jow profess to be friends with Councillor Horvarth, and yet the latter deny it?"

Ludovic frowned at that. "Jow and Unedar have no love for one another, that is certain. Perhaps Horvarth is considering his own position, fearing he is to be supplanted by one of Jakrat's puppets should there be a shift in power in Unedar."

"How do we know so little about what's going on in one of our own duchies?"

The other men simply shrugged. "We might do well to look on the bright side," said Ludovic lightly. "If we've heard little from Hightower because of a breakdown in communication in that duchy, at least that reduces the odds of something terrible having befallen Handee himself."

"All of this is giving me a headache," Arlon confessed. "I have tasks to attend to, sirs."

"As do we all," replied Ludovic.

He turned and set off for the barracks. For the third time in a week, he would be commissioning soldiers from the Shen Utah garrisons to travel to neighbouring duchies. As he rushed along, he wondered how his cousin Carpion fared. After all, that mission appeared increasingly certain to be their only chance of discovering Handee's fate.

It was fair to say he did not feel good about his lot at present.

Click missed Captain Carpion. Constable Foord never stopped eating; that was the only explanation for why every time Click had reason to seek the fat man out, he was stuffing himself. On this occasion, it was a sourdough barm cake filled to its own startling corpulence with greasy, slow-cooked pork and shredded cabbage. Some unknown brown sauce dribbled down his chin as he bit into the snack and replaced the remnants on his wooden platter. He didn't even bother to wipe his chin. Yes, he missed dealing with Carpion over this tub of lard.

"Like you were told before, boy," Foord said around a mashed mouthful of swine, "you can't just roll up and arrange a meeting with someone as important as our mutual friend."

"Normally I'd find Carpion, but he's nowhere to be seen at the moment."

"Again, like you were told previously, Captain Carpion is currently out of the city. Anything you have of importance, you can give to me; I'll take it where it needs to go."

"But I need information in return, Foord. It's not that simple anymore."

It wasn't just that Click didn't trust Foord, which he certainly didn't. He was being truthful—things had become far more complex since he had last spoken to Carpion and Swindle about the sinking of the treasure ship. A man had died.

"Your needs are not our concern."

Click looked around the taverna in aggravation. It was a small place, with a single service counter fronting a large cooking fire and spit. A giant chimney flue straddled the fire to draw away the smoke from the cooking meats, and drips of fat spat and sizzled on the hot coals below. There was a comfortable hum of conversation in the place, and no one was paying Click and Foord any heed at all. It was clearly a secure taverna. *Probably protected by the guilds*, he thought.

He drew his attention back to Foord as the man finished his dinner and regarded the young spy with amusement. The constable was being deliberately obstructive. Click had sent a message to Foord to arrange a meet for him with his grandfather. Even for a screaming idiot like Foord, that code wasn't hard to break. The fat git was just enjoying his moment of power.

"We're on the same side, Foord. Throw me a bone here. I need to know what my best course of action is, and Grandfather is going to want to hear what I've found out."

The corrupt constable didn't respond, only regarded Click with that same infuriating half-smile. It was the flicker of his eyes that gave Foord away—just the merest movement to look over Click's right shoulder that let him know that an attack was coming. And had they come from the other side, he might have stood a chance.

For the second time in recent days, Click reached across his waist to draw his dirk with his right hand. This time he suffered a painful blow to the funny bone that jarred right up his arm.

Then a cudgel crashed down on the side of his neck, and the world exploded in darkness.

He slowly came to. The sense of pitching to and fro on the deck of a storm-wracked ship made his bile rise. He could see nothing. His first panicked thought was that he had been blinded by the sneak attack in the taverna, but then—through the painful throbbing of his head—he could feel the cover of a hood that obscured his face.

Slowly his sense of balance returned and the sensation of unsteadiness subsided. The pain in his head did not.

Robbed of his vision, he reached out with his other senses to determine where he was. He could no longer hear the spit of burning animal fat or the dull chatter that would have meant he was still in the taverna. This chamber felt much cooler, perhaps even damp. In fact, he could hear intermittent drips of water on stone that echoed in the chamber, and immediately deduced he was underground somewhere, perhaps in a sewer or subterranean river.

How could I have been so stupid as to trust Foord? he thought. He shook his head in frustration, causing a crash of pain in his head and bringing dancing lights to his obscured vision. He hissed against the pain.

Then he heard laughter somewhere close by. He was not alone. He heard two moist steps as someone approached, and then the hood was ripped from his head. His vision was blinded by the brightness from a set of candles on a nearby table, but that didn't last. Finally, he could see his captor, and didn't know whether to feel relieved or even more terrified.

"Hello, Click," said Swindle merrily. He was dressed as an old southern sailor, a massive salt-and-pepper beard obscuring most of his face, and a woollen hat pulled down to his brow. A navy-coloured woollen sweater protected him from the cold of the dank chamber.

It looked like a disused sewerage overflow that had been turned to better use. A table and chairs sat in one corner, and a sleeping bunk was in another. A chest rested at the foot of the bunk, and a bookshelf, crammed to creaking with leather-bound books, dominated the left-hand wall. There was only one exit, currently filled with Foord's fat form.

"You didn't have to brain me, you knob," Click told him bitterly. He lifted a hand to his neck tenderly, pleasantly surprised to find that his wrists weren't bound.

I'm not a prisoner, then, he thought with relief.

"I know I didn't *have* to," Foord replied unkindly. "I wanted to."

"That's enough, you pair," Swindle admonished them both. "You can fight on your own time. Mine is more precious, so get on with it. What's so important you would risk reaching out to me specifically?"

"Things have become a little more complex."

Swindle only raised an eyebrow in response to that, so Click continued.

"I broke into the harbourmaster's office as you suggested, and I came away with some interesting information. There was no mention at all of the naphtha on the manifest, and what's more, there had been a fully ratified customs inspection of the vessel that day! It mentioned only luxury goods—no barrels of anything. And trust me, there were barrels upon barrels aboard. They might have gotten away with calling them alcohol or something, but to completely omit them and still pass a customs inspection?"

"Unlikely," agreed Foord.

"I don't know the going rate for bribing an official these days. You might know better than me," Click sniped at the constable, "but it would have to be pretty costly to coerce a customs inspector."

"Or something more subversive than mere bribery, perhaps," offered Swindle thoughtfully. "Blackmail?"

"Well, it passed inspection either way. The entire contents of the vessel were under the same consignment note number, so if we assume the naphtha was part of the same shipment, everything was to unload upriver, in Jow."

"Jow? So there was a recipient name in Jow, then?"

"No, the goods were marked as due for onward shipment to Choat. The recipient's name is a holdings company called du Lacigny Holdings."

"Never heard of it," Swindle admitted.

"There was a name on the shipping manifest, the name of the carrying company, I think—Justin Dowling."

"Dowling is a Shen Utah man, born and bred," Foord said.

Swindle nodded. "Dowling has been known to run small shipments of contraband, mostly for the guilds, but nothing even close to the volumes we're talking about here. If any of this was done with his knowledge or even say-so, he's dodging the Sinecure by taking this action. We would demand our cut, and then questions would be asked of what was going on. Such a huge shipment like that, the fewer people who know about it, the better."

"You knew," said Click without thinking.

Swindle looked amused by the slip, but Foord said, "Watch your tone, boy."

"All I'm saying is, you knew there was something illegal on that ship. You tasked Acaelian with ensuring it never left Shen Utah. You must have known something."

Swindle nodded sagely. "Quite right, of course. I knew there was something going on. I thought it was weapons and armour, to begin with—illegally imported from Boyareen or even Peena—but I was wrong. Where the naphtha came from, we'll probably never know. I can't even be sure the treasures on the ship weren't actually loaded here in Shen Utah!"

"Listen, I wasn't just being petulant when I pointed out that you knew about the vessel. When I was leafing through the harbour master's office, I noticed something odd. The filing system in there was precise and neat like you wouldn't believe; regimented, practically. All except for that one file. It was as though someone else had been at it before me."

"Another player?" Foord asked.

"Or a party of an existing player," Swindle threw in. "So now we know the ship was owned by Justin Dowling, but the cargo was being run for someone else. What we've learned from all this is that the owner of the cargo isn't just rich, they're influential too. I doubt even I could compel the customs supervisors to go against their code."

Click had to raise an eyebrow at that.

"What could the shipment have been for?" Click asked. "What is there in Choat that is worth such payment?"

Swindle hummed. "I have my suspicions, but nothing I'd like to verbalise yet."

"Well, ignoring the Choat link and this man Dowling, I followed the lead on the inspector, Paldron Ward. I tracked him down and followed him to see if I could learn more."

"Resouceful," said Swindle. "Very good."

"So, which was it?" asked Foord impatiently. "Bribery or blackmail?"

"We'll never know; he was assassinated."

Swindle just made a concerned hum, but Foord asked, "Not just killed? Are you certain it was an assassination?"

"It was professional, Foord. The killer had been hiding out and waiting for Ward to return home. Not only did he make short work of the inspector, but when Ward's wife stumbled upon the scene, he wasted no time killing her too."

"The double murder near the docks," said Foord in realisation. "The investigating constable had been lost for a motive."

"Really?" Click snapped. "You didn't put it together in your head? I go to investigate the harbourmaster, and within a couple days, a customs inspector and his wife are both killed; none of that struck you as a little more than coincidental?"

"Easy, Click," warned Swindle.

"No! I'm not having it! Carpion would have put it together. We're in a real pickle now, because I somehow doubt Ward's assassination was ratified by the Black Cats guild."

"Not that I know of." Swindle nodded.

"It seems clear that our unknown enemy is silencing his co-conspirators. Next in line might be the shipping agent, Justin Dowling."

Swindle said, "I'll make some inquiries about Dowling myself."

There was an uncomfortable silence as Swindle seemed to ponder something. Click remained rooted to his rickety chair, increasingly concerned that he might have outlived his usefulness. If that was the case, as pleasant as Swindle had been while it served his purposes, it was entirely possible Click was taking his last breaths. Swindle and the rest of the Sinecure tended toward ruthless efficiency when it came to those who knew too much.

Somehow, he had to make himself more useful. Due to Carpion's prolonged absence from the city, he'd already come to the conclusion that he'd have to gamble on betraying the captain's trust to do it.

"Sir, there might be another issue. I don't know if it's linked, but it might be."

"Spit it out, then."

"I've been working for Captain Carpion since the fall of the Shredder. It pertains to a consignment of poison that was brought into the city recently by an apothecary named Jorus."

"Okay," Swindle encouraged.

Click was aware he was probably signing Jorus's death warrant by revealing his betrayal of the Sinecure guilds.

But Jorus had brought that on himself. "Well, the poison is one that's long been banned by the guilds. Black Spider Venom." Swindle's eyes narrowed at the name. For whatever reason, Black Spider Venom had become a taboo poison in the city long ago. Even the assassins of the Black Cat guild refused to use it, despite its reputation for being swift and highly effective. "After recent developments—the other party who searched the harbourmaster's office before me and now the assassination of Paldron Ward—I am left wondering if the ramifications of the sinking of the treasure ship and now this poison might somehow be linked.

"Anyway, a week or so ago, I broke into the apothecary's workshop and recovered the vial of poison."

"Very good! And where is this vial now?"

"I handed it off to Carpion the other day, when you and I first met."

"Right. At least it's safe. We can't have a product like that in circulation, if you excuse the pun."

Click marvelled that Swindle trusted Carpion to such a degree. Of course, Click also trusted the tall ranger, but Swindle had much more to risk.

"So how do you suspect a link between the ship and the poison?"

"Well, if you look at what the two events have in common—that the shipment of naphtha and the consignment of Black Spider Venom were both in the city without the knowledge of the Sinecure—it stands to reason that they might be linked. What if the poison was requested when the vessel was sunk? What if the poison was intended to do away with those who sank the ship?"

"This unknown assassin?"

"Precisely."

"Does that prospect frighten you?"

"Of course. Whoever these people are, their influence is clearly far-reaching. Ending me would be as easy as reaching out and pinching a candle."

"You need protection? Perhaps think to disappear like your friend Acaelian?"

"No," he lied.

The response earned a raised eyebrow from Swindle. Even Foord huffed a laugh. "You've got balls, boy."

"The way I figure it, I'd not like to live the rest of my life looking over my shoulder. And anyway, there's only a small number of people who know I was involved in the plot to sink the ship."

"Very true." Swindle nodded. "Furthermore, if you are right in that assumption, we might use it to draw out those who would purchase such a poison, and also perhaps those who would ship a hold full of naphtha through the city right under our noses. If there is a connection, then this assassin may be the key."

"I'd like to help," said Click spiritedly. This was his best chance to survive this little meeting.

"Of course you would." Foord smirked knowingly.

Swindle, itching at his fake beard, pondered the situation for what felt like an age before saying, "If the assassin is a guild member operating outside of the Sinecure, then we need to keep this out of guild circles altogether. For that reason, your continued help would be beneficial. I need to look into Dowling's affairs, see what contacts he has in Choat, especially who this du Lacigny Holdings company belongs to and what they do. You can help by shadowing that apothecary."

"Because if the two are linked, then he's the best course to identify the buyer?"

"Yes. And the reasonable assumption is that the buyer will probably also be our smuggler."

"Do you think Jorus will be the next to be silenced?"

"Not likely. But now that you've stolen the poison, perhaps his customer will return demanding more, or demanding their money back. Either way, their identity might be revealed. When you learn something, get the info to Foord here. And learn to trust him with it; he knows what side his bread is buttered."

Foord nodded in emphasis.

"Fine."

Foord produced the hood again and walked slowly toward Click.

"I don't need to be unconscious again, do I?"

"No," Swindle said, clearly disappointing Foord. "I think we have an understanding. The hood, however, is for your own protection."

Yes, Click thought as the material of the hood was thrown over his head, *I do certainly miss Carpion. He has a calmer way about him.* Then the shroud descended, and he was cast once more into complete darkness.

Chapter Fifteen

Burden of the Past

The foothills of central Shen Utah gave way to the rolling meadows and farmland more characteristic of the duchy of Unedar, though the border still lay some miles ahead of them. Captain Carpion's mixed band of Wayfarers and Shen Utah City Guard were battered by westerly winds throughout the course of the day's travel. By the time they made evening camp, the sunlight had all but bled from the sky, and the cheeks of the travellers were rosy with the ferocity of the winds.

"My ass is killing me," grumbled Guardigan, rubbing gingerly at the seat of his pants. Dale shook his head and tossed his armour to the ground near their bedrolls. Carpion had afforded them no fire on the first few nights, as they were in a region dotted with abandoned strongholds and collapsed watchtowers that bandit groups and the like often used as hideouts, and the last thing they needed was for such distractions to slow their progress. But in the few evenings that had followed, they had enjoyed the opportunity to camp nearer to small hamlets, some with small tavernas at which Carpion had made subtle enquiries. None could offer any mention of Handee's messengers having passed through.

Since then, they had left such smaller dwellings behind and were now in open common land, and so Carpion had permitted a small fire, and three brace hares were roasted to help feed the travellers. The game cooking on the spit was certainly something to look forward to after another full day in the saddle.

Despite the gruelling nature of their travel, Dale's spirits were high, for the lands around him were becoming familiar. He had grown up in such surroundings, and the change from rolling hills and valleys to the sloping plains ahead was comforting.

"I'll end up with a rump like a horse myself if I spend many more days in that saddle," Guardigan continued. As his tirade melted into white noise, Dale recalled fond memories he had allowed to fade over the last few years. He got to wondering if his parents would be in the village when they arrived. Absently, he hoped they would have a chance to rest overnight near the village so he could seek them out. Surely there would be no rush once they discovered what was going wrong with the relay messengers.

After they'd begun to settle around the fire and had eaten their fill of game, he spied the captain near the hobbled horses, outside the reach of the firelight. Taking his leave of the still-grumbling Guardigan, he moved quietly over to the Wayfarer captain as he groomed his own mount. The young officer glimpsed Dale approaching and nodded a subtle greeting before returning his attention to the horse.

"Captain," said Dale, suddenly feeling foolish. He realised it would be wholly inappropriate for him to enquire as to how long they planned to remain in Adar once they reached the village, and even less appropriate for him to request a family visit. He found himself in an uncomfortable situation, unable to leave but with nothing to say.

"How did you find the ride today?" Carpion asked, rescuing Dale from his idiotic bind.

"It was easy enough. It's good to be returning home after this many years."

Carpion only hummed in reply.

"Captain, you're the Knight Marshall's cousin." It took Dale a moment of silence to realise he hadn't actually asked a question, and he could see the corner of Carpion's mouth turn up in a knowing, wry smile as he continued his slow and steady strokes with the grooming brush. "What's he like?" Dale asked finally.

"Taller than you think," Carpion replied simply. "Though not as tall as his cousin," he added with a wink. As Dale was about to return to the fire, figuring the captain didn't want to talk, Carpion continued. "Do you want to know what the warrior-turned-reluctant-politician is like? Or what he is like as a cousin? How about what it was like in Shen Utah, when we were boys? His time spent under the tutelage of the great college professors? Or perhaps you're interested in tales of the legendary Arlon, Hero of Thes?"

Dale tried his own pensive hum in reply, but thought he probably failed miserably. "The conflict of Thes does fascinate me," he admitted.

"There are plenty of ballads and epic poems about the legend. The Battle of Thes and Arlon the Heathen-bane is something that fascinates a lot of people who weren't there." There was something hollow in Carpion's voice, but Dale was unable to decipher the meaning. Carpion's brush had stopped mid-stroke. Shaking off his reverie, the captain looked over his shoulder at Dale. "Why don't you ask your friend Guardigan about it?"

Dale was taken aback. "Guardigan was there?"

"Of course he was there. That old warhorse has been a foot soldier so long, I almost feel guilty for making him ride out like this." And so, he returned to his grooming while Dale wended his way back to the fire, enjoying the growing warmth. Night-time on the plains in autumn was a cold time.

He sat by Guardigan again and looked his friend in the face, holding a questioning, level gaze.

"What?" the old soldier asked.

"You never told me you were at Thes."

"You never asked."

"What does that matter? Why have you never mentioned it?"

Guardigan just shrugged.

"I've so many questions!" Dale said excitedly.

"*That's* why," Guardigan replied drily.

"What was it like? Did you see any action?"

Guardigan stared into the fire for a while, and Dale thought, to his annoyance, that he wasn't going to answer. Then he nodded softly. "For a start, the Battle of Thes was a little more than just a battle; it was almost a war in its own right. The fighting in that region alone raged for more than five weeks, but our enemy had been on the march for years. For those of us in the thick of it, one day blended into the next, but we were in the field for more than a month.

"It was like a siege on open lands, an impossible fight. The village of Thes was of no true value to either side, but the bridge it laid claim to came to be absolutely vital. The only major crossing point left on the river, it was always going to be a strategic point once the bulk of our forces had repelled the barbarian attacks farther to the west. Thes became the pivotal point for a war we hadn't even expected. The horde's arrival was something of a surprise, and our southern garrisons had been caught cold.

"When the first elements struck us at Thes, we were almost overwhelmed by their ferocity and their numbers. They attacked like madmen, with little regard for their own lives. The Shen Utah line faltered for more than a full day, supported by what few reinforcements we had. The Royal 31st Mounted Infantry was one such unit, deployed to stopper any breech in the line.

"I was just a foot soldier, my brigade guarding the lands beyond the southern banks across the bridge. We were to hold our line for as long as we could, searching for sappers looking to cross the quick river. We were waiting until the main force could muster a counter charge. The western line was in disarray." He shook his head slightly. "Our religious commanders, safe on the hill, had prepared no formal battle plan. They considered it a waste of time without knowing what the disorganised rabble of the barbarian horde would do. The real leaders—the ones in the field with us—understood full well that we'd face the depths of hell on that riverbank, but the brigade commanders were clueless and arrogant."

He spat into the fire.

"Fat pigs! We lost a fifth of our standing force on an attack that lasted more than two whole days and nights. There on in, the fighting was brutal. In time, we were driven back to the river. With local commanders slow to react, we ended up heavily pressed, protecting the far bank until, finally, the horde fell back.

"The river and fields ran crimson; bodies floated downstream and littered the farmland south of the river. I remember one day, on a morning so silent it was like the eye of a storm, looking at the man next to me, and then the man next to him. In the morning sun, I saw that every face and suit of armour was awash with the blood of the fallen.

"When the sun had set on the longest day, near war's end—although we couldn't have known it then—I returned to my squad exhausted and badly wounded. I'd cut a man down as he rode over the palisade before me, but his crescent sword cut a groove in my thigh. It could have been serious, but it wasn't going to stop me from fighting."

Dale remembered that during the seriously cold nights, when walking the walls, Guardigan carried himself with a minor limp. He'd always imagined that it was simply age, but now he wasn't so sure.

"Our squad sergeant had also fallen, and we numbered less than half of our original complement, but our forces had held the bridge. Fighting on the frontline, fatigued and battered as we were, we had assumed it would not be long before reinforcements arrived . . . but they never did. The generals and colonels back at high command had assumed our regiments were of adequate size to repel the last of the barbarian army, but the local commanders had wasted soldiers at every turn, and the battalion commanders in the west—who had seen the first of the fighting—had been slow to heed the call to reinforce the eastern flank.

"I was given a field promotion to replace the squad sergeant, despite my injury. It's surprising how fast you can progress in the field when your army has just been decimated. Speaking of which, our captain had fallen leading a charge of reserves to hold the bank. His charge had saved the crossing, halting the enemy in their tracks, but he gave his life for it. A young soldier had been promoted to captain."

"Arlon?" asked Dale, as excited as a youngster listening to a fireside fable. Some of the Wayfarers around the improvised camp smiled wryly, previously stone-faced whilst listening to Guardigan's recount.

"The very same," Guardigan confirmed. "I remember him as clearly as if it were yesterday. He seemed to stand a full foot taller than anyone else. In truth, I was probably taller, but he had a presence about him. Even at such a young age, he commanded attention—demanded it, even. His light armour was clean and gleaming in the late-morning sun. A mop of dark brown hair, made black for want of a clean, was pushed back from his face, and despite all that time in the field, he was clean-shaven.

"I immediately assumed he had just joined the ranks, probably from a safe command tent on the rise two miles north. But as soon as he sat a handful of us sergeants down and spoke of his plans, it was clear he had seen plenty of action. He spoke of enemy war engines being brought up from the south, described the unfamiliar armour and arms of the enemy in detail, detailing the weak points for the less-experienced soldiers in our ranks. Even for a seasoned soldier like me, he was inspiring to listen to, clearly a student of warfare.

"And his comrades looked up to him. He had a small retinue with him." Guardigan inclined his head to where the Knight Marshall's cousin was almost lost beyond the firelight. "A taller, clean-shaven lad his own age and a huge bull of a man who had taken command of the standing defenders up to that point. I forget the second man's name now." Guardigan gave a regretful shake of his head. "Both those men trusted him, it was clear. They were like brethren, all those who stood with him. And there was a determination and drive about him that gave us hope—a belief that we could win through, vanquish the enemy. It was a single bright spark in the darkest of nights."

As though punctuating his words, a log on the fire snapped, and a shower of cinders danced on the breeze.

"But there was something missing in his eyes too—something I've come to know is vital in a man, and it was simply not there in that moment."

Dale felt a touch at his elbow and turned to find one of Carpion's Wayfarers, a young man with jet-black hair, was offering him a wineskin. All the others around the fire had since stopped their own conversations to listen closely to Guardigan's story. Dale accepted the skin and took a healthy draught before handing it on to Guardigan. The weathered soldier took a quick swig, wiped an errant dribble from his grey-stubbled chin, and continued.

"The commanders weren't all idiots; they were experienced and capable men. Unfortunately, in time, that experience had become prejudice and had cost innumerable lives. Arlon told us they had admitted underestimating the ability of the barbarian horde. Our spies had located several concentrations of the enemy forces, he told us, indicating that they were preparing various strategic attacks to break through our ranks. If nothing was done about it, he said, the battle would be over in hours, not days.

"While the senior-ranked officers marshalled forces to counteract these concentrations of the enemy, the newly appointed Captain Arlon had ideas of his own. He knew the commanders were doing the right thing, attempting to hold the line no matter what, but he had a more direct intention. He believed—quite rightly—that with our backs to the river, we would lose a war of attrition.

"As we dispersed toward the frontline, Arlon and his companions wandered the ranks. Carefully he selected the youngest members of each platoon and each squad and took them in tow. Soon, Arlon marched west along the riverbank with almost a hundred men in his charge, barely one of them above the age of nineteen. I heard tell that the further west he rode that morning, the more youngsters he drew to his banner."

As Guardigan passed the wineskin on to the next man, Dale shook his head in confusion. "Why did he seek to recruit the inexperienced?"

One of the Wayfarers around the fire answered, "The young are fleeter of foot. I'd say Arlon wanted a fast force."

"That he did," replied Guardigan, "at least for the sake of the history books. But more importantly, he split the battle-hardened warriors from the inexperienced youth. Toughened warriors, long in the tooth, were made to stand the river line. Youngsters were more likely to buckle under the pressure. If the line began to break, the threat of a rout was too great. He needed to leave the old veterans on the line. We *had* to hold that bridge, or all was lost. But even more important, Arlon wanted an inexperienced force—lightly armoured—who knew nothing of what they were to face *behind* the line.

"When he reached an abandoned crossing point far to the west, originally built and then abandoned by the enemy's foiled sappers, tales tell that the great Arlon of Thes led with him more than four hundred young soldiers. No one knows the truth of that number. Those lads followed the charismatic, determined young officer in his gleaming armour. He took them because they were expendable. He took them on a mission that I doubt he had any thought of surviving."

There was a beat of silence around the fire.

"I can't believe the legend that is the Battle of Thes was just a mindless suicidal charge," Dale argued.

"It wasn't a suicidal charge!" Guardigan told him earnestly, his voice rising. "It was a mission without a plan for what would happen when it was done. There is a difference. He understood precisely what needed to be done in order to protect the futures of those the army had been sworn to protect. There was no other consideration—certainly not for the lives of those who rode with him, or his own. That's not suicide. The first time you see battle, you'll understand—though I pray you never have to learn the distinction.

"There was no *heroism* involved in the decision-making that morning. I saw it in his face. Arlon cared nothing for living or dying. The issue for me was that he had no care for whether those boys lived or died, either. He recognised a necessity and acted upon it, callously, dispassionately. He saw something that had to be done"—the old soldier flicked a hand in the night air as though discarding something distasteful—"and he threw hundreds of young soldiers upon Death's path in order to achieve it." The disgust was palpable in his tone as he stared intently into the fire. "Amongst that number was my only son."

Dale was struck dumb. Guardigan had never once spoken of any family at all, let alone a son. All he knew of Guardigan's heritage was that he was ironforged, descended from a proud warrior people, hailing from the clans of the frozen north. Though these men had since spread throughout the Shen Utah lands, most of their line held firmly to their warrior code. Every man's son served his time with sword in hand, whether soldier or mercenary, always fathering children at a young age. There was no sense waiting until middle age to begin a family when there was no guarantee one would reach middle age in one piece. Such was the ironforge mentality. As a result, men like Guardigan were not often particularly family-oriented. But for him to have never mentioned a family at all was odd. Dale thought he was getting a glimpse as to why.

Guardigan's tone was growing in bitterness, though the volume had lowered. Every man around the fire listened intently. "I led my men back to the riverbanks the following morning, fed but not well rested. The barbarians came with the dawn once more, the fighting lasting beyond dusk. The enemy was growing impatient, or so we thought. Our crossbowmen were brought to the banks, and many barbarians fell in the first onslaught. But it was clear we might be overrun before dawn. The frontline was being cut off from command, and we were beginning to falter. We had fought through the night without realising it.

"As the first rays of sun painted the valley floor, we were on our last legs, exhausted from hours of furious combat. All at once, the enemy catapults stopped. Messengers rushed back and forth, desperately trying to re-establish communication with the command tent. The barbarians had taken the bridge, overtaken the river itself, and were advancing up the bank. While we held the high ground above the northern riverbank, we were able to retreat in a controlled line, but we had lost the river. We had failed. The war was lost. Once we reached the plains beyond, we would be finished; that much was clear. It was simply a matter of time before the barbarians rolled over us like a typhoon of blades.

"The fact that each of us, to a man, was a seasoned warrior helped us hold firm. The youngsters Arlon had taken from our ranks would have broken much sooner, creating panic—and panic on a battlefield spreads like burning pitch. But we held. As we neared inevitable defeat, the command point at Thes having already begun their retreat, the barbarian line inexplicably broke.

"Suddenly I saw him—standing on the crest of the bridge we had lost an hour before, his armour shining in the morning sun. He wielded two swords, one long and one short, barbarian blood spraying all around. The enemy could get nowhere near him. The way he moved was like nothing I've seen, with a fluid grace and a terrible power, cleaving a path of destruction through the enemy ranks. He was unstoppable. Untouchable. And pouring across the bridge behind Arlon—flanking the enemy—came more armed men of Shen Utah. What remained of our youngsters.

"Cut off from their support lines and stranded on the north bank between our retreating line and the marauding Arlon, the barbarians collapsed. His impossible charge behind their lines had already broken the enemy's back.

"Crossbowmen from our reserves rushed to the fore and turned the northern riverbank into a killing zone. Every one of the trapped enemy was dead before the sun had fully risen. By the time we had turned about, our mounted infantry and cavalry had already crossed the bridge and overrun the barbarian positions south of the River Thes. It was a massacre."

"Incredible!" exclaimed Dale, looking around the fireside—but few reflected his excitement. Instead, each face wore an expression he couldn't identify, as though everyone else had heard another story. "I mean, the legend is true! With the Shen Utah forces drawing their last breath, Arlon brought the barbarians to their knees."

"Were you not listening?" snapped Guardigan. "There was no heroism! Arlon ignored our orders and abandoned his lines. An inhuman and dispassionate fury led his actions, and he took hundreds of young, impressionable soldiers to their deaths because of it. Yes, on the pages of a history book, it appears a brilliant manoeuvre. He and his men drove through the flanks of the barbarians like a hot knife. For every one of our young soldiers who fell, more than a dozen barbarian lives were forfeit.

"Once he found himself behind their lines, Arlon moved swiftly on the trebuchet emplacements *because they were the most dangerous option*. He pressed for the strongest concentration of men every time, driving harder for the deepest level of hell. Yet he survived and singlehandedly turned the flow of the battle. Many questions have been asked about what really happened behind the line, but they've never been answered. I'll tell you this, though—I've never seen such crestfallen victors. They looked as though their souls had been stolen.

"I'll never forget watching Arlon's face as the truth of what he had done dawned on him. Hundreds of young soldiers had died to satiate his unquenchable fury, and only he and two dozen more survived. Two dozen from a force of more than four hundred! Boys!

"The idea of legend meant *nothing* to him then. I doubt if it does now. The cost of that victory will follow him to the grave."

The fireside was suddenly silent. As quiet as a chastised schoolboy, Dale looked from face to face. He glanced over to where Carpion still stood by his horse, perhaps expecting to see a look of anger on Arlon's cousin's face at the account. But there was no anger. Carpion's grooming brush was still, his face turned to the ground, eyes closed.

Looking back at his friend, Dale didn't need to ask if Guardigan's own son had survived Arlon's charge. Reflecting the red of the flames in the night, unshed tears of grief and anger brimmed in his eyes.

Guardigan said nothing further all night, and a melancholic veil descended over the campfire, a silence that remained into the following morning.

Chapter Sixteen

Tracks of the Dead

It was common for travellers to give a good-sized troop of mounted soldiers a wide berth, and it happened a couple of times during the following morning as Carpion's men rode on toward Adar. They could see small groups of people, possibly families, travelling west—certainly nobody who was a threat.

They were deep into the plains of Shen Utah now, still some distance northwest of Eladreen's Heart, and Dale recognised small rivers and the odd ridge of rock. A couple of times they rode past small settlements, including a few that had made good use of the abandoned forts and strongholds that still littered this portion of the country. The old walled forts were often sizeable enough to house a good few families, and most villages had built considerable foulbergs around them. They worked the lands that surrounded each fortification, and for the most part, the old strongholds—testament to a long-forgotten age of civil conflict—were almost unrecognisable. The colouring of the land, the smell of the air, everything about the region drew the music of memory from Dale, like a bow running across the violin strings of his childhood.

Since the revelations regarding Guardigan's family and the death of his son, Dale wouldn't exactly describe the mood between the two friends—or the group as a whole—as tense, but conversation had certainly been restricted to topics that were considered safe ground. And yet, surrounded by sights that were so resonant with his own childhood, Dale could control his curiosity no longer.

"I grew up in lands such as these. I've spoken nonstop for almost a day now about the times I spent growing up here, about the different colours of the seasons, about living in the valley of Adar, the summer fetes and long evenings of cider and pies, about my father and his disapproval of my choice to come to Shen Utah, about my mother and her mutton stew and rock-like dumplings. You could write a story about it!"

"A boring one," Guardigan said, perhaps trying to keep the tone light.

"Without doubt. But I can't help wondering, after how long we've known each other, why you've never spoken of a family until now. What about a wife? Daughters?" Dale was very careful to remember that Guardigan had said the son he lost at the Battle of Thes had been his *only* son.

On his right-hand side, Dale's friend was quiet for just a moment, looking away to the south. "My wife's name is Ana. She, too, is from Unedar." Guardigan turned to look at Dale. "You're not the only man who finds these places familiar. I've ridden these paths before. Except back then, the road I travelled was farther south, and I had been riding toward Boyareen, my son beside me."

"I'm sorry," Dale said quickly. "I didn't want to pry about your son."

Guardigan waved a hand in dismissal. "In Unedar tradition, some lucky career soldiers serve their sixteenth and seventeenth years—the last of their training—at Hightower Point."

"I've heard of it," said Dale. "It's a secret training facility, right?"

Guardigan smiled sadly. "Not very secret. The Point is a tall spit of land peculiar on the southern coast, as it is pretty much the only natural berthing spot on that whole coast. The trick is, because of the formations of rock that cover it, the beach is hidden to ships that might search for it, unless you already know of its location. From the sea, one would struggle to see the inlet even up close."

Dale knew the city of Hightower itself had a complex structural array to descend the cliffs to a massive pontoon port, allowing a good amount of trade to come from the southern and eastern seas into Unedar.

"Hightower Point recruits are drilled and exercised mercilessly," Guardigan continued. "Some soldiers quit before their time is up, and those who graduate often have their choice of assignments across the land. In antiquity, it was rumoured that there was only one way to quit the Point—death. Thankfully, it's a little more forgiving now."

Dale had certainly heard of Hightower Point. No soldier in the employ of Shenmadock could avoid hearing of the ruthless establishment. The only surprising element of the Point—in Dale's opinion—was that Arlon of Thes had never served there, unlike his cousin Carpion.

"I married Ana when we were still young, the summer before I was sent to the Point. Ana was already pregnant with my son. She travelled with me and stayed in a village nearby. When I graduated, I chose to stay on at the village and took a commission at the Point as a trainee instructor. Two years later, I travelled to Shen Utah with Ana and my boy. I served in the army, marching out from Shen Utah and fighting in Mashtock mostly, during the renegade uprising. For ten years, we were happy, as happy as the family of a soldier can be. In time, I might have earned an officer commission, but that wasn't to be.

"Being of the Northern Clans and in keeping with the traditions of my ancestors, when my boy had entered his sixteenth year, he sought to follow in my footsteps, so we returned to Unedar and he enrolled in the Point. I had to call in favours for his enrolment, but it was what he wanted, so I made sure he got in. Ana settled into the same village, along with our two daughters, then eight and ten.

"By that time, Mashtock was in a fragile peace; Lord Cordon Vale had assumed the position of duke and put down the renegades, but rumours of trouble in the south were already growing—so I left my family and returned to Shen Utah alone and was sent to Boyareen with the bulk of our armed forces. That was the cusp of the Barbarian War.

"When the opening skirmishes escalated, we started calling in auxiliary regiments, including new recruits from the Point. I made sure that I was among those who travelled to Hightower Point when my boy graduated. I took him from his mother and returned to the Boyareen border, ensuring he was given a foot soldier berth in a strong regiment not affiliated with my own—one where he would fight alongside experienced men and under a competent command, for I did not want to be accused of keeping him close. By then, he was well into his late teens, and a warrior in his own right."

Dale shook his head. "No one would have blamed you for keeping him close, Guardigan."

"I would have. He had earned his rank. He was a warrior like his ancestors. He deserved his freedom and room to flourish. He died with that freedom."

They rode on in silence over the next bluff, the noon sun high in the southern sky. Now that Dale was learning about his friend's past, a lot of things were beginning to make sense.

"You never returned to Unedar after the Battle of Thes, did you?" Dale's question didn't need an answer. "You never went back to Ana."

Guardigan was suddenly angry again. "How could I! How could I possibly return, knowing I had escorted my only son to his death? She would despise me. And rightly so! It was wrong that he should die and I survive! No parent should outlive their child; it's arse-about-face!"

Dale did the arithmetic in his head as they rode on, Guardigan's face dark and brooding. Knowing that he was in danger of continuing to raise Guardigan's hackles, Dale said, "So your daughters would be ten and twelve when . . . at the time of the Battle of Thes? That would mean they are twenty and twenty-two now?"

"Yes. It's almost a decade to the day that I lost my son."

During his account, Guardigan had not once used his son's name. And the old soldier's focus was more closely fixed on his dead son than his living daughters or his estranged wife. Dale knew it was most probably linked to the warrior lineage of his clan ancestors, which dictated a firm link between father and son. A heritage. A continuity. But Guardigan's anger hinted to Dale that he was hiding feelings further enraged by his own guilt.

"You know what occurs to me?" Dale said. "Once we reach Adar and find Lord Handee's messenger drunk underneath a tavern table, I'm sure Captain Carpion would allow us leave to go and find your family's village near Hightower Point. We could go and visit them."

"No," Guardigan replied.

It had been a dangerous suggestion, and Dale had expected an angry reaction—or even to have to dodge a blow—but the flat, emotionless tone of his reply, a single word, left Dale with no recourse. The conversation was over. They rode on in silence.

They found the burnt-out campsite an hour later.

Carpion knelt in the damp grass, his eyes tracing the ground. Dale saw him reach into the reedy grass and produce something that glinted in the sun. Standing, Carpion tossed it to one of the Wayfarers who stood nearby. He then passed the item to Guardigan, who stood at Dale's side.

"What do you make of that?" Carpion asked as they turned back to the rest of the troop. Dale saw Guardigan turning the trinket over in his hands, but could make out no detail.

Instead, he watched the rest of the troop as they worked the clearing, gathering what information they could from what remained of the destroyed encampment they had stumbled across.

They had spotted the wispy column of smoke first, a short time after Dale's poorly judged conversation with Guardigan. A quick gallop brought them upon a scene of an ambush, from the looks of things. Bodies were badly blackened from having fallen into the encampment fire, which had burned out of control. The sweet stench of charred flesh still filled the air.

Dale marvelled at the manner in which the Wayfarers had immediately gone about their business of scouting the area for evidence of precisely what had occurred. Following their lead, the members of the City Guard who made up the unit confirmed the area was secure and there weren't nefarious elements hanging around, ready to cause a problem. It didn't take long to realise that whatever had occurred in that clearing, they had missed it.

The clearing itself was in the lee of a copse of cypress trees that would have protected the campers from being easily spotted from the distant road.

"Aleks, report," ordered Captain Carpion. One of the Wayfarers came away from the centre of the clearing, brushing soot and dust from his hands.

"Looks like an ambush, sir. The cinders are still hot, and the bodies there are barely cooked." Dale made a face at that. "Whoever they were, they probably hit them at dawn or a little before, I'd say. Came at them from the north and struck fast."

"Who were the victims?" Carpion asked.

"Judging by their belongings and attire and some of the odd tracks leading here, I'd say they were cattle thieves. They arrived at site yesterday and built the fire, roasting a goat they'd probably stolen. You can see where they slaughtered it—pretty clean job. I'd say there were perhaps half a dozen or so wranglers here when they were hit. You can see footmen took the single sentry down quietly, and then the rest of the attackers stormed the camp. A bit of a botch job, though, because the defenders fought back."

"A failed surprise attack, then?"

"Maybe left it too late." Aleks shrugged. "Half the camp was already up and had weapons close to hand. They should have hit them an hour before."

"What of the attackers?" asked Carpion. "What do we know about them?"

"Not much from the camp, sir. Their tactics were sound and they were well coordinated, even if you forget the mistake of timing. I think they're well known to each other, but they're not military. Also, there are tracks leading back east from here that suggest whoever hit this location went that way and had heavier horses than when they arrived."

"They took the survivors prisoner?"

"Looks likely," Aleks confirmed.

Carpion hummed thoughtfully before taking the item he'd found off Guardigan and handing it back to Aleks, finally affording Dale a glimpse of it. It was a cloak pin with a coat of arms or emblem on the front—two sickles crossed to form an open circle, with a goat's head at the centre.

"Don't recognise it," Aleks said, "but it looks like a clan or house emblem to me."

"It's a house emblem," interjected Dale. "A coat of arms, if you like. One of the larger family ranches north of Adar, though I forget the name. They have a lot of grazing land, lots of cattle. It made them a target for wranglers when I was a lad, so I don't see why it would be any different these days. I heard the sons of the family started their own private militia when the old man grew tired of having to alert the town guard every time."

"That all makes sense, then," said Aleks.

Dale liked the Wayfarer. He was usually quiet and reserved, much like the rest of his brethren, but there was a quick humour to him too. Not tall, perhaps three inches short of Dale's own six foot, Aleks had lank brown hair that he kept tied back with a headband made from a thin strip of leather. He was as slender as he was short, in keeping with the typical build of his regiment.

"So," said Carpion, "we're assuming the ranchmen tracked the wranglers here and hit them before noon yesterday, not catching them quite as off guard as they might have liked. The fight was tough, with five men dying." He pointed at the bodies.

"Captain!" interrupted another of the scouts from over near the bodies, which they had arranged away from the smouldering fireside. "I'd say only four of the five bodies are brigands. This one here was dressed quite different, and his boots are finer than those of the others. He's got expensive-looking spurs on 'em too."

The captain nodded. "Right. So, four wranglers and a rancher died, but the horses that left the area were heavier than when they arrived, so they certainly took prisoners."

The captain thought for a while, his eyes wandering the destroyed camp and occasionally looking up to measure the sky.

"The fact is, there's no reason to assume this has anything whatsoever to do with either Senior Lord Handee's column or any Shen messenger, so it's not our primary concern. I'm not too happy about the possibility of vigilantism, though. Wranglers or not, if these thieves killed a member of the ranch household, there's no telling what they might do to the prisoners." He shook his head, his mouth made thin by frustration.

"If I may, sir?" Dale asked. Carpion nodded, apparently impatient that Dale asked for permission to speak. "It seems clear to me that if the rancher they'd killed had been a member of the family, they would be unlikely to leave his body behind in favour of taking prisoners. If they intended to kill the prisoners in answer to the death to a family member, they'd have done the deed here, set a pyre and spent the horses to bring the body of their comrade back instead."

Carpion nodded. "Makes sense. Still, I'm not happy about this." He looked at Dale. "How far to Adar, local boy?"

"Almost a full day's ride now, following that trail." He pointed back to the road they'd been travelling.

"Excellent. So, we stand a good chance of being there before dusk." He then pointed at Aleks. "You and one other Wayfarer follow those tracks and see where they go. If they end up going to the ranch, then that's all well and good—come and find us in Adar. If they go someplace else, I want to know about it. Investigate as safely as you can and then meet us at the village." He jabbed a finger at Dale and Guardigan. "Take this pair with you. The rest of us will ride on in to Adar and see if we can find any sign of the relay messengers. We can sort this wrangling mess out once you four meet us there. Everyone clear?"

"Sir!" Aleks turned to go. Guardigan caught Dale's gaze, rolling his eyes heavenward.

Chapter Seventeen
Arrivals

The prow of the ship cut through the waves like a blade. Since punching through the stormfronts many days ago and having to endure slower speeds as a result of the damage to the hull and main mast, the *Moistened Barnacle* had finally limped into the Inlet of Theed and was making for the port of Jrnak. Andi and her group had made good use of that time, weapons drilling in the hold or on the waist of the ship. They had offered to assist in some of the lighter duties on the vessel, but the offer had always been declined. The crew seemed both efficient and proficient, and reticent, perhaps understandably, to allow her to be worked by strangers. Sailors were a superstitious lot. The most tumultuous portion of their voyage suddenly seemed an age ago, now that the ship was within a few miles of their destination.

Travelling south had caused them to chase the seasons, and now the sky above was clear and blue, with a raging sun and a soft, dry wind. It was more reflective of a Shenmadockian late summer than any winter Andi had seen, though Bophamel insisted this *was* winter by Boyareen standards. "Of course," he'd said, "Peena is an entirely different kettle of fish. Hot as holy hell all year round. Terrifyingly hot." Andi hoped they wouldn't have to travel too deep into Peena, the country to the south of their inlet, for it didn't sound pleasant. They had sailed around the large Boyareen Peninsular and were following the inlet that divided the eastern portions of both Peena and Boyareen.

Looking out from the starboard gunwales of the ship, Andi and her three companions stood in pairs and watched the alien coastline, that of Boyareen—Peena's northern coastline to the south wasn't close enough to see even on such a bright day. Golden beaches, often crowded with people either fishing from the sands or simply enjoying the glorious weather, were separated by green-topped, rocky headlands. As they neared the outer buoys surrounding the port of Jrnak, they could see many small fishing vessels out in the calmer waters, seeking to fill their holds with the small fish that so opulently populated the waters. Each little boat made sure to steer clear of the larger *Moistened Barnacle* as she slowly lurched for the Jrnak quayside.

Out of earshot, Andi watched Fin and Eidos talking together. They were certainly an odd pair for her to have thrown her hand in with. And a glance at the dwarf standing next to her did nothing to dissuade her from that conclusion. Through the decades of her unnaturally long life, Andi had fallen in with various nefarious types, often getting herself in some fairly tight scrapes, but none of those people had come close to rivalling these three for strange company.

"Manic," she said, drawing the dwarf's attention away from the passing coastline, seabirds high above them following the ship. "Can I ask you something?"

"You just did."

"Very clever." Andi noticed that his wit had returned with the settling of the pitching seas, and now he was his ordinary, gregarious self again.

"What is it, lass?"

"Why were you in Hightower the night we got arrested?" That night felt a century ago—the night before the pair had first met.

"I told you, I was looking for work."

"I know you said that at the time, but we know each other better now, dwarf. You don't strike me as the lone sell-sword type. When we went into the catacombs under Hightower, you really seemed at home in that surrounding." In Shenmadock, there was still a large mining community of dwarves, and while it was common enough to find one living in an overground town or village, it was not so common to find them wandering the land. "I can't help the feeling you'd be more at home back in the Choat dwarven mines, not getting arrested in drunken brawls or slopping about on some boat with me. So tell me, what's the right of it? Why were you there then, and therefore here now?"

Manic was quiet a moment as the ship cut through the beautiful green-blue waters toward port. Finally, he said, "You first; why were *you* really there?"

The question caught her off guard, although she should really have expected it. "Okay, fair enough. You're right; I wasn't just passing through. I was running."

"From whom?"

"I've committed my fair share of misdemeanours, Manic. I'll never hide that from you. I've committed some fairly hair-raising crimes, in fact. But some time ago, I realised such a life wasn't going to keep me alive for long, so I decided to get out. Turns out it's never that easy to walk away from that kind of life. The people I was involved with didn't want to lose such a weapon as I represented. It all got very messy. A few people died. I had to do some things to make that right, things I'm not necessarily proud of—and a few things I'm bloody proud of. That brought me to Hightower with a mess in my wake and no course for my future. I remember that night of the riot, probably after the first bottle of wine,

I was contemplating taking this very voyage and making a life for myself down here, if you can believe that."

"Irony, they call that," Manic told her.

"So that's that," she finished. "I've not always turned in such auspicious circles as I do now."

Manic laughed at that. "Okay, fair's fair," he said with clear reluctance. "I'm not a sell-sword. At least, that's not what I'm made for. I was made for frostfinding."

Andi gave him a blank look.

"Frostfinding is the name that the dwarves give to the dangerous practice of seeking the biggest gem veins in the mines. Most of the best gems were found in the hardest-to-reach caverns where few—if any—had ever tread before. I was the best frostfinder in our clan. I found the largest gems in the deepest caverns for years. I was famous, and my children doted over me."

"Whoa! Children?"

"Yep, two boys. They thought I was some kind of hero. I spent longer and longer in the depths of the mountains, finding larger and larger gems, like I was competing with myself. As my boys got older, they wanted the same." Manic took a deep breath, and Andi suddenly realised how difficult this seemed for the dwarf. "The pair of them ran off from the clan one day and climbed down into the depths to find me. I'd been gone for days, which wasn't unusual. None of the other members of the clan were worried, but the boys came looking. They were never seen again. I came back with the biggest haul ever, but the clan was in uproar. My wife blamed me . . . hell, I blamed me.

"Straight away, I organised another search crew—there had been two already—and we scoured the depths for weeks. That was the hardest thing—dwarves don't lose things underground, especially family. After the rest of the clan were forced to give up, I continued searching for months after . . . but there was no sign."

"I'm sorry, Manic. I didn't mean to pry."

"Not your fault, lass. Anyway, that was when I shaved my beard off—to wear my shame." He touched his bare chin. "I fled the caves I'd grown up in because every day reminded me of what had happened. I made my way in the world as best I could. This was more than twenty years ago now. I don't miss that life, and I don't like to think about it."

"I'm sorry I brought it up," she said.

"I'm not," he replied, patting her hand on the ship railing reassuringly. The friendly gesture, so innocuous amongst regular folk, was entirely alien to her. She never ordinarily allowed people to touch her, even kindly. Oddly, this beardless, moustachioed dwarf was as close to a friend as she had known in more than a decade. It came as something of a surprise to her to find that made her sad.

The pair fell into silence. No one else on the ship had overheard the conversation, and Andi vowed to never mention it again, out of respect to Manic. Friends kept such confidences, she reminded herself.

Allowing Manic a moment to compose himself, Andi returned her attention to the passing coastline. The nearer they got to the port, the more populated the lands became, with many settlements surrounding the beaches now, villages scattered upon the low headland. Likewise, the vessels travelling in these waters were far larger, clearly trade and mercantile traffic as opposed to provincial fishermen. The *Moistened Barnacle* looked to fit right in.

The vessel was made to wait only a short time at the buoys. Even from this distance, Andi could make out the frenetic activity at the quayside, festooned as it was with myriad imports from the trading ships at anchor. Shortly a pilot vessel came out to them, and the impressive, if storm-battered, *Moistened Barnacle* limped into port. They were moored at an outer arm of the eastern quay, and the four travellers gathered their belongings patiently while the portmaster verified their dubious documentation.

The process caused a few butterflies to pass through Andi's stomach, for Captain Bophamel had seen through their ruse back in Hightower after just a short time, even before the skirmish at the portside removed any question of their legitimacy as ambassadors.

Andi still had a few reservations about Bophamel, for she knew next to nothing about the amphibian captain, other than he seemed both helpful and well informed. Sure, it was fortunate for them that he had helped out, but at what cost? In her experience, people rarely did anything for nothing. And then there was the question of the murder he had witnessed. While most others on deck had been hunkering down as they had fled Hightower, unlikely to have seen her remarkable arrow strike, the captain certainly had.

Despite her concerns, there were no difficult questions at this latest inspection as their forged papers passed muster without incident.

Eidos had done a good job forging them, and Manic told him such as they descended the gangway to the broad stone quay. "Impressive work, Eidos," he said as they passed between traders and merchants bartering for higher value on imports all along the jetty. They passed in pairs, ensuring they didn't lose one another. A quick glance over her shoulder as they left the quayside revealed to Andi a glimpse of Captain Bophamel, a curious expression on his unreadable green face. She tried to put it out of mind as they melted into the crowd.

The indigenous people of Jrnak were olive-skinned and hard of complexion, due to the arid quality of the air and the salty sea breeze. Interspersed with these locals were the fairer-skinned types from further afield, and the variety of languages and accents was dizzying.

Once they were off the quay, the travellers pushed through the thronging markets that surrounded the port promenade. Clear of those, they were able to breathe more easily—the markets and portside were liable to be rife with pickpockets and cutpurses.

They took a stroll along the beachside west of the port, enjoying the sensation of being able to stretch their legs after days on end cooped up onboard. They listened to local musicians playing traditional tunes on foreign instruments and passed many small shacks that were selling sweet pale ales or watered fruit juices. A few even sought to peddle overpriced attire to the unsuspecting. The group ignored them, sticking to the seaward side. Andi took her valuable travelling boots off and enjoyed the sensation of the sun-heated sand burning between her toes.

"It's like paradise," said Eidos dreamily, his feet splashing in the waters of the beach.

"Rarely do summers at home get this warm," agreed Manic with relish, "and this beach is stunning. The sand is so fine, the waters so clear."

Following Eidos's example, Andi washed her feet in the warm sea, marvelling at the pleasant temperature. Once they left the beach, her feet were dry in no time, and she replaced her socks and boots before they reluctantly left the beach area behind and climbed a steep road that led to the upper town overlooking the entire bay.

Fin hadn't spoken since leaving the ship, and Andi noticed he now seemed markedly more relaxed than before. She threw him a questioning glance.

"I can't abide thieves," the reptilian told her. "I wouldn't have hesitated to cut them open if they'd tried anything funny."

Normally a fairly light-hearted individual, this reaction seemed out of character for Fin, but that kind of pleased Andi. She was beginning to get concerned that nothing at all angered the stranger from the East. He stood a little under six foot tall and was covered in a reptilian green skin. His large eyes were golden and watchful, while a muscular tail often did more to reveal his moods than his alien visage. If it wagged, usually he was happy—or off balance. That made him especially difficult to read when he was drunk.

Back at the port, it hadn't been wagging.

Andi had never met a being of his kind, but she felt it easy to like him. Bumping into more rarefied species like Fin and Captain Bophamel reminded her that there was plenty about the world she had yet to learn.

As they neared the top of the rise, Fin said, "I think it might benefit us to seek out a library of some description—see if we can decipher something of what it is we are here to accomplish."

Andi couldn't disagree. "Fin's right. As beautiful as this place might be, we're here for a reason. While this might feel like a stunning spring day, back home, winter comes. And when that winter thaws, there will be nothing to stop that army crossing the southern range and invading Unedar."

"If they haven't done so already," warned Eidos. "The southern ranges have a small number of passes that are accessible year-round. If they have capable scouts, the enemy—whoever they might be—could already have small squads on our lands."

"Small squads I'm sure Unedar can handle—despite Jakrat and Reinhart interfering as they are. But that staging area was designed to outfit an army." Andi nodded. "In either circumstance, we're not here to enjoy ourselves; we're here to find Barabel's relic. And it's not going to be easy."

The upper town was composed of far larger buildings—tall stone-made structures with white-painted walls and grand entrances. More people were abroad, and it seemed more likely they'd find what they were looking for in this area, as much as Andi would have liked to have remained on the beach.

Splitting into pairs, they set about looking for a library.

It proved harder than they'd anticipated.

Of all the lands of the known world, Andi knew Shenmadock and the rest of the Land of the Lords was one of the most open regions regarding its treatment of the many species it encountered. That cosmopolitan approach was even more prevalent in Ipsica, where elf and dwarf lived alongside human, half-orc, and many other species. Oddly enough, with that approach came a mix of shifting attitudes. Ipsicans, for example, were distrustful of elves in the main part. And a dwarf would do well to find a friendly face in the Free Cities of Briadranon—particularly in the city of Krasital.

However, down in the barren lands of Boyareen, it seemed that if one's face was anything but human—human male, she clarified—it just didn't fit. Only Eidos seemed to be welcomed by the local people, and even then, the welcome was a little stifled, for it was clear from Eidos's pale complexion and the mixed company he kept that he was not of Boyareen. Being female, Andi received short shrift everywhere—regardless of her efforts to conceal her mixed elven heritage.

This behaviour obviously sat uncomfortably with Manic and Fin. Manic in particular was a proud dwarf, almost to the point of belligerent jingoism, and he returned looks of distaste with equally powerful stares of derision, made slightly comical by the fact that they were usually upward, for every adult in Boyareen seemed to tower over him.

But as they searched the upper town of Jrnak for libraries, Andi's plight got worse. Away from the port, the only females they encountered were hard at work and well hidden from the lancing heat of the southern sun, still difficult to endure despite the winter season. Women were clearly considered to be a lesser species here, regardless of their *actual* species. Andi felt herself growing annoyed. It seemed ironic that she worked so hard to conceal her race, and yet it was her gender that set her apart here.

And so, once they found the Jrnak library within a polytheist temple, it had fallen to Eidos to enter—it had been made clear she was not welcome within. Sitting at the northern perimeter of a souq—a local name for an outdoor market—the temple library was the only collection of writings in the city, for it seemed that modern education beyond one's specific trade was deemed unnecessary here, and the level of literacy amongst the populace was limited. She had to suppose the Land of the Lords was not so different in that. Few people would bother learning their numbers or letters if they didn't need to.

Near noon, as the number of people packed into the thronging market began to thin, Eidos left the temple at the north end of the square accompanied by a swarthy-skinned man of middling years. He wore the robes of a priest, as well as wooden sandals that were tied to his feet with uncomfortable-looking rope. Despite that overly harsh raiment, he also wore a golden chain around his neck, covered in ornate runes.

Eidos was still speaking with the man, an expression of exacerbation on his face. Andi couldn't understand what language they were speaking, but she could tell it wasn't going well.

"Eidos," Andi interrupted as they reached the bottom step of the temple.

"Oh, hello, Andi. This is Prelate Khazri." Despite the introduction, the priest said nothing to her.

"A pleasure, I'm sure," she said sarcastically, her patience exhausted.

"Where are the others?" Eidos asked her.

"Over there." She waved a hand down the side of the market to where Fin and Manic were wandering from street vendor to market stall. "They're trying to find something even vaguely palatable for lunch."

Before Eidos could say more, Prelate Khazri said something to him and indicated Andi. Eidos responded in a curious tone. Not being able to understand the exchange was really grating on her.

"Eidos," she said with quiet annoyance. "What did he say?"

"Well, it's frustrating, but it would appear that what scriptures are held in this temple's library are restricted to relatively modern studies. There is little reference to history here. The few tomes I managed to find that looked into the local history simply don't go back far enough. It seems they have expunged all written knowledge of anything that predates the current religio-cultural governance. It's like the slate was wiped clean at that point.

"I tried at length to question the prelate here about the dead twin, and got nowhere. The only thing that sparked interest was when I used the twin city's actual name. It was at that point that Prelate Khazri led me outside. Apparently, my search is over."

Trying to remain calm, Andi said, "No. Not that. What did he *just* say? Just now, when he pointed at me."

"Oh! My apologies. He was offering to buy you from me."

"What!"

The prelate flinched at her outburst, but before Eidos could elaborate, a cry went up from the souq.

A glance to her right showed Manic with a startled expression and some kind of flour tortilla stuffed with grilled meat held to his mouth. Beside him, the green form of Fin was gesticulating furiously with his arms, his own meal dropped to the dusty stone floor.

Andi looked to where he was indicating and spied a skinny boy darting between stall owners, Fin's coin purse clutched in his grubby fist.

"Oh, for the love of . . ." Without finishing the curse, Andi set off at a sprint directly away from the temple, Eidos, and the inappropriate prelate. She cut a path down the centre of the souq, where the going was slightly easier, while Fin tried to give direct pursuit. His greater bulk struggled to part the vendors, most of whom were clueless as to the theft and simply thought Fin was trying to cause some kind of riot. His reptilian shuffling gait didn't help, either.

Very soon, it would all get quite out of control.

The thief was making for the far corner of the souq, where an intersection of narrow lanes would provide the perfect getaway, and at his current rate, Fin stood no chance of catching him.

As Andi ignored the grabbing hands of the street vendors seeking to halt her progress—perhaps suspecting *her* of being a thief—she saw the real pickpocket knock over a stack of wicker baskets as he lunged between stalls.

Too desperate in his pursuit and too slow to react, Fin stumbled over the baskets and their contents and crashed noisily into a stall, bringing loud curses from the vendor as his wares crashed to the ground.

Near the far end of the souq, Andi saw a stall of curiosities and snatched up a flat, curved wooden stick, causing even more uproar. Now at a full sprint, she threw herself into a crouched slide and then hurled the flattened stick to her left.

The escaping thief—so near to the narrow alley now—had no time to react as the thrown stick spun low to the ground and bit into his right ankle. There was a sickening sound as Andi's impromptu weapon and the thief's Achilles tendon both snapped. With a scream, the thief slammed into the dirt floor, the wind blasting from his lungs.

Fin rid himself of the angry stall owner's grasping hands and reached the whimpering thief, pinning him to the floor with a clawed foot and retrieving his stolen purse. As the boy was dragged away by a band of vendors, Fin dug in his purse and handed over a few coins to the basket vendor, then he set off back toward Manic.

Andi dusted herself down and followed Fin's example, tossing a copper coin to the vendor from whom she'd stolen her wooden weapon. He seemed surprised and grateful in equal measure.

The souq was still in a state of excitement at the commotion, and on her walk back, no one tried to grab at her.

"I told you I hate thieves," hissed Fin. He looked visibly abashed at having reacted in such a way, but Andi couldn't blame him.

"Clearly," she said. "How did he even sneak up on you? You were being so vigilant."

Fin looked even more embarrassed, the hue of his green skin deepening a shade. "It was a very tasty kebab." *He can blush!* Andi thought in amusement.

She clapped him on the back in consolation. "I'll buy you another one."

They arrived at Eidos's side as he appeared to be taking his leave of the prelate, who continued to gesticulate toward her as all three walked away to re-join Manic.

"I assume my behaviour discouraged the prelate?" she asked Eidos.

"On the contrary." He laughed. "He doubled his offer!"

Chapter Eighteen

Aal a Zass-al-amel

And so they found themselves at a quiet beach to the west of the port and availed themselves of some of the refreshments there. Sitting in the sand, soaking up the arid heat of the afternoon sun, they thought about their limited options.

"These superstitious creeps have managed to redact all written knowledge of Mrnak—but to what end?" Andi asked.

"To stop people going there would seem the logical conclusion," replied Eidos.

"It makes you wonder what they lost," said Manic.

"There are such wonders in the desert lands to the south," agreed Fin. "Our tribe possesses writings from previous explorers that mention evidence of ancient civilizations that far outdate anything in the known lands. Brilliant civilizations—the birth of modern culture. There is a real depth of history in lands like these, and more modern societies seem to have taken it upon themselves to attempt to destroy that."

"Like it or not, we're at an impasse," said Andi. "If the legends are true, then this weapon we seek is stuck out in the sands of the south somewhere." She indicated across the narrow body of water to where they knew Peena lay. "But that's the biggest country in the known lands. We can try to just set off into the desert and see what we can find, or we can find this twin city and see what it reveals. If they've emptied the libraries here, maybe they've neglected to empty them in Mrnak."

"Wherever Mrnak is," said Manic.

"I can't imagine it's hard to find, but time is of the essence, and we can't waste it in additional searches. We should use Bophamel's contact."

Eidos nodded. "This contact might help us reach Mrnak, but what then?"

"I guess all we can hope is that he'll set us on the right road. That old idiot Barabel sent us to find the sunken city of Aquilla San. He said the greatest knowledge of its whereabouts was to be found in the Dead Twin of Boyareen, which we've established is the city of Mrnak. If this Aal a Zass-al-amel can help us find that city, we might find a map or some directions leading to Aquilla San's sunken city, and then hopefully Barabel's magic candlestick—"

"Sceptre," corrected Manic needlessly.

"Whatever. Either way, when we meet this man, we know nothing of the legend, okay? We're simply looking for the dead city. We're adventurers or plunderers at worst; nothing about magic weapons. We'll get locked up."

"We hardly know anything as it is," agreed Eidos.

"I know. But the less we show of our hand, the better it will be for us, of that I am sure," she said.

After they finished their beverages, and with that same reluctance to leave the beachside as they'd felt before, they asked the vendors on the beach for directions to the address Bophamel had given Andi. They followed a small road up from the beach to the west, which steadily rose up through citrus fruit trees and along a secluded ridge path to an impressive villa that overlooked the bay below.

The summer sun was well beyond the noon zenith, and the quality of the light was gradually turning a syrupy golden as the group reached the gates of the villa grounds. White walls made stark by the surrounding greenery enclosed the property and gardens, from the top of which rose blackened steel spikes. The double gates were of the same blackened metal, and an impressive lock dominated the centre, embellished with engraved steel work and patterning. Despite the intimidating level of security, they were afforded entry to the grounds without question upon mention of Captain Bophamel's name, just as the old toad had promised.

Once admitted, the grandness of the place was overwhelming. A three-storey white-walled villa that was quite obviously ancient but equally well looked after dominated the centre of the grounds. The rest swarmed with complex botanical arrangements of dazzling variation, most of which seemed alien to the landscape outside the walls. The greenery, dotted with myriad bright colours, was refreshing, although the sheer humidity was stifling, and the constant *rickety-thrum* of cicadas confounded their ears.

A tall, dark-skinned manservant with eyes like ivory welcomed them at the door. Again, merely mentioning Captain Bophamel's name gained them an audience with Aal a Zass-al-amel. As they were led into the grand hall at the centre of the opulent villa, Andi saw Manic's eyes flitter from relic to artefact to tapestry in appreciation. There was obscene wealth in Zass-al-amel's collection.

The manservant led them up the main stairwell and along a grand balcony. A set of double doors opened onto an even more impressive room, the far-right corner of which was open to the elements through broad windows. It boggled Andi's mind to fathom how the huge glass sheets had been installed.

Andi saw whom she presumed to be Aal a Zass-al-amel sitting on one of the low couches and chairs before those windows. At the doorway, their care was passed to a young handmaiden, who escorted them to the chairs and bade them sit as the dark-skinned Zass-al-amel continued to admire the view. The overlook was grander still than anything they had seen inside the villa, affording a wide panorama of the harbour and bay. To the left, golden dunes and lustrous green plains stretched beyond the bounds of the city to the northeast horizon, while the royal blue of the sky looked like the deepest of oceans.

After a few moments, Aal a Zass-al-amel turned to greet them—Eidos first, and then the non-humans, and Andi last. It was clearly the way of things, so she struggled not to let her hackles rise. His skin appeared soft as a girl's, and his brown hair was gathered in a complex topknot, the plaid left to hang down his back. Cotton clothing did little to hide a strong physique, and his eyes were sharp.

"Well met, friends of Captain Bophamel, you are welcome in my home. Refreshments?" His voice was deep, rich, and heavily accented. His piercing eyes regarded them calmly from beneath a heavy brow.

Another handmaiden provided them chilled fruit drinks of a sweet flavour. Two more young women, fairly pale by Boyareen standards, were draped upon futons nearby, and all of them were scantily clad, the sheer material openly revealing in a way that would cause a scandal in Shenmadock.

The golden light of the day streamed in through the tall windows. Fixed to the ceiling was a wide propeller connected to a series of fine ropes. The ropes in turn ran through pulleys to a water-filled contraption. The fluid was allowed to fall steadily through a wide funnel into a paddle wheel, which, when pushed by the falling water, pulled on the rope, turning the broad propeller. In this way, the room was kept, if not cool, at least comfortable.

Aal a Zass-al-amel noticed Andi regarding the women. "Does their attire upset you, woman?" The term "woman" was not bitten off in a rude manner; it was simply what Zass-al-amel chose to call her, despite having been introduced. She tried not to take offence.

"It is not how *I* would choose to dress," Andi admitted.

"That is a shame, for if I am a sound judge of such things, I believe that—beneath your traveller's attire—you possess a most alluring figure."

That did offend her, but they needed this man, so she bit down her bile, which only seemed to amuse Zass-al-amel.

"The weather in Boyareen and beyond is not conducive to covering oneself up entirely all the time. One would die of heat exhaustion in a single morning."

"Didn't seem to stop the women of the city hiding away under thick cloaks," she muttered.

To Aal a Zass-al-amel's credit, he didn't take the bait. "I tend not to bother journeying into the city," he said evasively.

Andi said, "I suppose if your serving girls died of heat exhaustion, you would quickly run out of *hired* help."

"On the contrary," Zass-al-amel said, "these are four of my wives."

There was the briefest moment's pause before anyone responded, and Aal a Zass-al-amel seemed to enjoy their discomfort. Finally, Manic said, "More than four wives? You're braver than me."

Their host laughed aloud. Then, apparently finished teasing them, he dismissed his wives—every one of them at least two decades his junior. "So, to business," he said, pulling his attention away from the view. "I owe Bophamel much, but our friendship is one of mutual understanding and accommodation, so for him to have given you my name must mean you are in great need. How can I help?"

"Information," said Andi, wondering what history existed between this man and Bophamel. Aal a Zass-al-amel's eyes betrayed only a spark of surprise that it was Andi who continued to address him, not Eidos or even

Manic. He didn't even look at Fin, who seemed decidedly uncomfortable. Recalling their instructions delivered by the mercurial Barabel some weeks ago, back in Shenmadock, Andi said, "We must travel to Mrnak, but know of no sound means of doing so." After a pause, she finished, "Or even an inkling of exactly where it is."

"Oh. Then my assistance to you is very simple. Do not go. No matter what reason you might conjure up for visiting that loathsome place, it is not a sane undertaking."

"We have no choice; we must go to Mrnak."

"Why? Why *must* you visit the dead city?" His question carried an undertone of warning.

Andi took a breath and then decided that nothing was ever gained without risk. "We seek the halls of Aquilla San," she said, "in the deserts of Peena."

"You are tomb raiders, then? Seeking the sunken treasure city?"

"Something like that, yes."

Aal a Zass-al-amel regarded her for a moment, and then broke out in a gleeful laugh. "That's a legend!" he said. "There is no sunken city, and the risen deserts at the heart of Peena are almost entirely inaccessible."

"Still, it is important that we try. To that end, we mean to travel to Mrnak."

The dark man's grin disappeared. "I sense you mean no jest," he said. Andi nodded. "And no matter what I or anyone else might say, you will not be dissuaded?" Again, she nodded. "Then there are things you must know. I now understand why Bophamel sent you here, for if you travel to Mrnak without my advice, you would surely die. All who travel there die. It is not just a dead city; it is a murderous one.

"What I said is true—Aquilla San and his sunken city are the stuff of legend," he told them. "It seems certain that the man himself existed, but a sunken city of treasure?

Unlikely. Still, you are not the only people to have set foot upon this path, and I will tell you what I told them.

"Many hundreds of years ago, a hero of war sought to hang up his blade and settle in his home, Peena. He believed his battles were fought, his struggle was over, and that the fighting was to be left for younger men. He had attracted many followers and admirers in his time, as is often the case with people of great power and charisma, and many powerful men were indebted to him. This warrior's name was Aquilla San, Child of the Sun.

"Aquilla San was offered all the lands and titles any ambitious man could ever want, but each offer was tainted with the caveat that the mighty Aquilla San would stand and defend his benefactor's lands. So Aquilla San turned his back on the toadying, creeping chieftains and left the city of Mrnak for good.

"He headed into the desert and was lost for decades, thought dead. One day, a traveller returned to Mrnak with word of Aquilla San's fate. Having set out on a desperate attempt to follow San's old trail, he told of wandering through the massive desert, upon the verge of death, and stumbling across an oasis far from settlements of any kind.

"Standing at the crest of that oasis, having slaked his deadly thirst at the spring, he saw on the horizon mighty towers stretching into the westering sun, glorious, white, and pure in the burning desert heat. The traveller rode hard through the freezing night and arrived at dawn at the gates of a mighty palace.

"The traveller spent a season with the people of Aquilla San before he chose to leave the palace, journeying back to Mrnak, that he might speak of his discovery. His songs and scriptures tell of the most beautiful gardens and grounds ever seen—more a city than a palace. The inhabitants lived a perfect, peaceful existence.

"He spoke of a treasure room in the depths of the palace so huge that one could stand at its centre and see no walls. Every type of treasure and trinket was stored here. Many hundreds of kings had sent emissaries out in search of Aquilla San, their mission to bring the recluse back to civilisation, but every messenger chose to stay at Aquilla San's palace, the tributes passing into that massive chamber to remain forever. For Aquilla had no desire for wealth or gain. This way, the location of Aquilla San's palace and the fact of his continuing survival remained unreported.

"When the traveller's stories spread, more and more men of power came to seek out the great, and now venerable, Aquilla San to draw him once more to their banner—for it was widely regarded that Aquilla San was immortal. And of course, such a talisman in the time of Boyareen's tribal invasion would be a beacon; an army marching with Aquilla San at its head would be seen as invincible. To those people, the man was a god incarnate.

"And so more treasures and artefacts found their way to Aquilla's door, tributes of staggering wealth and supposed power. But still he remained in isolation.

"The Peenian tribal leaders marched on the Boyareen invaders—and each other!—for almost a decade without Aquilla San's influence. At the culmination of the tribal wars, a man had come to power who claimed to be a prophet of the gods. Believing he was empowered by the heavens, this man no longer desired Aquilla's help; he coveted his treasure trove, and some of his followers sought vengeance for what they perceived to be the slight of Aquilla's solitude. But all desired what was undeniably the greatest gathering of gold, jewels, and priceless artefacts the world had ever seen.

"This prophet, who had brought more than half the barbarian lands to his banner, attacked Aquilla San's palace day and night for more than a year, but the unforgiving elements cost every besieging battalion their lives. But this apparently godly man was obsessed, utterly seduced by the treasures that the palace promised, proclaiming that the gods intended them for him and him alone.

"Soon Aquilla, ancient as he was, grew weary of the endless sieges. He yearned for the sweet and peaceful embrace of eternity, but still his pride refused to accept defeat.

"His fury brought about the destruction of his city-palace. The sheer arcane power of the artefacts at his control, coupled with his immense fury, pulled the city beneath the sands, dragging the inhabitants and all the besieging armies into the deepest heart of the desert. Tens of thousands lost their lives in an instant.

"But regardless, as I said before, no one has ever managed to find any trace of Aquilla San's palace, or even a plausible location. It's all allegory. None of it can be real."

Worrying that Aal a Zass-al-amel enjoyed the sound of his own voice too much, Andi asked, "So, what you're saying is you can't help us?"

He sighed deeply, obviously frustrated that his warnings were falling on deaf ears. "I didn't say that. There exists only one reference to the mythical location, and that is in a library built by the traveller who originally left Aquilla San's palace and brought news of his existence to the known lands."

"Let me guess," said Andi drily.

He nodded. "That library is in the heart of Mrnak."

Manic asked, "So is this *reference* you speak of a map?"

"Absolutely not, my dwarven friend. It is the oldest riddle of our time. If it was something as mundane as a map, Aquilla San's palace would have been found long ago. No, if there exists a location reference in that library, then it will be both difficult to read and perhaps even impossible to recognise for what it truly is. Such is the way with riddles."

Andi laughed. "It'd be too easy!"

"Indeed," Zass-al-amel agreed. "Furthermore, this library is rumoured only to contain details of the location of the oasis, the point where the traveller laid eyes on Aquilla San's palace for the first time. Not the palace location itself."

Manic harrumphed deep in his chest. "You propose that, if we manage to find our way to the dead city of Mrnak, somehow locate the traveller's library, and miraculously divine where this oasis is, we *might* be able to travel directly west at precisely sundown in order to stand hundreds of feet above an unreachable palace that probably never even exist in the first place?"

Zass-al-amel grinned. "Eloquently summarised."

"Listen," said Andi, "about the palace—you mentioned that the treasure trove of Aquilla San contained more than just gold and jewels. It had lots of *magic* things, right? You called them artefacts. These godlike powers San wrought were fed by powerful relics, weren't they?"

"Correct," Zass-al-amel confirmed.

"Tell me, seeing as you seem to know plenty about this legend, was one of these rumoured artefacts a sceptre? Perhaps a couple of feet long, made of solid gold with a rose encased in a glass globe at the top?"

Zass-al-amel's eyes narrowed. "Perhaps."

"Perfect," she muttered.

"It is well documented that Aquilla's most prized gift had been a sceptre of some legend. He called it Tor Dewald, and it was rarely far from his side. One book describes it as a gift directly from the heavens. Most treasure hunters have sought out Aquilla San's palace just for this one artefact. In fact, one of my writings claims the power of this one sceptre was enough to cause the destruction of the palace-city.

"According to the traveller, Aquilla San kept complete records of his treasures—wherefrom they were given in tribute or 'donated' and their description. Tor Dewald had a description in his records but was the only artefact without an origin. There is no evidence from whence it came. It is this fact that lifts that relic above all others in mythology. It is described as being topped by an impossibly spherical crystal the size of a fist, at the centre of which is a perfect red rose. The traveller claimed Tor Dewald translated in ancient Peenian as Hammer of the Gods."

Andi looked at each of her companions in turn. It was too late to try to hide their true purpose; it seemed Zass-al-amel had sussed them out. "Sounds like what we're looking for," she mumbled.

"Do you really want my advice?" asked Aal a Zass-al-amel.

"Of course," said Andi, "that's why we're here."

"No, you are here for information, which I have freely given because of what I owe Master Bophamel. What I offer now is true advice."

"Is that free too?" Manic asked, earning a laugh from the man.

"Of course. If you do intend to seek out the library of the traveller, I can help you get to Mrnak safely, but the best *advice* I can give you is as it was before—turn back. The prizes in Aquilla San's collection would be of such value as to make my own collection seem like a box of toothpicks, but as sure as anything in this world, they are legend only. Scores have died seeking the palace, and none have succeeded. Worse still, the malice at the heart of the dead city of Mrnak makes it the most dangerous place in the world. You might not survive long enough to find the library, even if I gave you the address."

"Does that mean you're going to give us the address?" Manic asked cheekily.

Zass-al-amel's shoulders slumped in resignation. "Of course."

Seeing the man's reluctance, and judging that reluctance to be borne from genuine concern, Andi told him, "Friend Aal a Zass-al-amel, this is a path from which we cannot deviate, despite your advice—well meant as I judge it to be. We are set upon this journey, whether we like it or not, and we shall succeed where others have fallen, for the simple fact that we must, because if we don't succeed, then nothing matters anyway." Andi finished her drink and rose from her comfortable couch. "Now I am afraid we must take our leave, for we have a long journey ahead of us and time is a factor."

"Ever is it thus." Aal a Zass-al-amel stood with them and showed them toward the door. "You are not on this most terrible path for monetary gain?"

"No."

"Do you truly believe, then, that the stakes associated with your success are higher than riches?"

Andi thought for a moment, balancing her possible responses, for until this point, she had not admitted to herself that she completely believed everything Barabel had told them. She thought about the old man's warning, the burning animated corpses outside Jakrat's manor house, the cowled figures that haunted Hightower Court, the heavily armed staging area in the southern mountains, and an unseen invading army awaiting the spring thaw. Finally, she said, "We don't believe the stakes could ever be higher."

"Then let me set you on your path and give you what information I can. It might help keep you alive, at least for a little while."

Chapter Nineteen
Adar

Dale reined in and turned his mount away from the tracks they had been following. The trail met a narrow pass between monstrous gorse bushes. The familiar scent of exotic fruits wafted off the thorny bushes despite the dampness of the day, but Dale ignored the childhood memories it evoked. It was no time for sentimentality.

To their left, dominating the northern skyline, were a series of jutting, craggy rock formations. To the south was a long line of smaller, undulating hills that Dale knew rolled almost all the way to the Southern Sea. More of the ancient forts and strongholds dotted that landscape, but almost all of them had gone to ruin.

Stepping from the gorse came the Wayfarer Aleks. Corn, the second Wayfarer in their number, held his horse by the reins.

"The tracks continue through here," confirmed Aleks. "Whoever these horsemen are, they're making no attempt to hide their passing."

"Nor should they bother," said Dale. "This trail drops down across a gully and into the northern meadows, where their home ranch sits. They're almost home."

Aleks nodded, removing his headband to shake his hair out before replacing the strapping and pushing his hair behind his ears.

It had been a tough day following the discovery of the wrangler attack site. The afternoon was running long when they found the tracks that led through the gorse, and Dale was keen to be done with the investigation and to get to Adar. Now that he was so close, he yearned to see his home.

"There is something curious here, though," Aleks said, as though reticent to mention it. "Unless I'm losing my touch, a number of people made a real mess of the gorse back there yesterday. Looks like they might have been hiding. Would that make sense?" Aleks asked Dale. "Would people hereabouts want to hide from the passing ranchmen?"

"Only more wranglers," Dale shrugged.

Aleks hummed and looked at the edge of the gorse running north. "Once the horses of the ranchmen had passed, whoever was hiding in the gorse made their way out and headed north on foot.

"North?" asked Dale, slightly confused.

"What's north?" Guardigan asked him.

Dale wracked his brain. "Not much, if memory serves. It's craggy and unpleasant as a whole. There are lots of small caves, goat paths, and no small number of precipices that sneak up on you. Dangerous terrain if you're unfamiliar with it. Those jagged crags overlook the Adar valley. Beyond them is Unedar's ducal border with Jow, and the Fendale Woods, but no large settlements or anything."

He sensed Guardigan shiver in his saddle. The day was ending poorly, with a blasting southerly wind and the first signs of sleet-laden rain, both of which declared that they were now well into winter. With every passing day, their job of tracking on the sodden ground would be made all the more difficult. Soon the rains would be replaced by snowdrifts, even this far south.

"Damn it," cursed Aleks. "We've got to assume the ranchmen are heading home," he said dismissively, "but these new tracks are what we need to be concerned about now."

"Do we?" Guardigan asked unhappily. "Why?"

"Because there's no explanation for them. We've no way of knowing who made them, or why. They might have some impact on our mission. What if this unknown party was Senior Lord Handee's retinue or his messenger?"

"That's quite a conclusion you've jumped to there, Aleks," Corn put in. "Why would they need to hide in gorse? It all seems a little unlikely," Corn grumbled.

"But not impossible. We've got to follow the evidence to its source before we dismiss it."

"We could be in these hills all bloody night," Corn complained. "And it's probably just children. Why would a Shen messenger hide in a hedge and then go running north? The reasonable assumption to make is that it's nothing to do with Senior Lord Handee, so it's nothing to do with us, either. There—I've followed the evidence and dismissed it. Can we go?"

"You know as well as I do that's not going to be good enough for Captain Carpion."

Corn—a pinch-faced and pale northerner—asked, "Why would you even waste his time telling him about it?"

"Because lying to the captain is more dangerous than letting him down. You know that. Now come on." With that, Aleks jumped into the saddle of his horse and took his reins.

The rain had begun again by the time they reached a shift in the tracks. They took a turn at the foot of a hidden switchback path that led northeast up the nearest jutting ascent. The clouds above were almost black, and the slanting rain hammering on their leather armour and the ground all around them was a constant din. The rain made the rising shingle paths even more treacherous, but the experienced horses never shied. Nonetheless, they made the sensible decision to stake out their mounts in the rain and to continue up on foot. There would be ample grazing for the horses, and all agreed they didn't intend to be in the crags for long.

Still, the thunderheads in the sky and the distant winter sun made for a dark, foreboding evening as the switchback levelled out and began circling the bluff, not much wider than a goat path. They were two-thirds of the way up the full height of the angular formation and had long since lost sight of the tracks they were supposed to be following, and yet there was nowhere else these mystery people could have gone, other than over the edge to their doom. It was a disconcerting thought, for they had climbed into the passing heavy mists some time ago. Dale constantly scanned the ground ahead of them, looking for signs of the unexpected ledges and drops he'd spoken of, though the clinging mist made that difficult.

"For all we know, the people who made those tracks have probably long ago fallen to their deaths," Corn argued. "We've passed plenty of sections they might have turned off, and even more from which they could have fallen. We've lost the trail, face it."

Aleks shook his head. "Just a little further."

Corn the Complainer simply shrugged.

Dale turned to look at Guardigan behind him on the narrow track, amused that even a Wayfarer could express such discontent.

But Guardigan's face was set in an expression that suggested he wasn't listening, at least not to the conversation ahead of them. His brow was knitted, and his head tilted slightly to the air.

"Guardigan?" Dale asked, concerned.

"Shush," his friend told him.

"Hey, I was only going to—"

"I said shut it!" Guardigan hissed. "And you pair!" The two Wayfarers immediately silenced. The four had come to a halt as they waited for Guardigan to start making some sense.

"There," he finally said. "Did you hear that?"

"Hear what?" asked Corn.

"Shut up and you might hear it, fool!" Aleks snapped. Turning to Guardigan, he whispered, "I heard it. A baby's cry."

"Correct," confirmed Guardigan, though it was clear from Corn's expression that he had heard the same as Dale—nothing.

"We move forward in silence," Aleks whispered, beckoning them onward through the eerie mist.

They proceeded round the bluff, rolling their feet from heel to toe, all of them listening for the sound. To their right-hand side, the mist cleared, and Dale could see for the first time that steep, deadly drop to the jagged rocks far below. Rain lashed their faces as the clouds began to lift, and Dale's stomach protested at not having eaten since their light lunch. He sought to put it out of his mind as their tension rose.

Suddenly he heard it, carried on the driving rain—the sound of a baby's muffled cries. It was made unnatural by the mists and rain, seeming to come from every direction at once. Dale halted his advance, his blood freezing in his veins. His sword felt heavy in his hand. The shifting mists around them, swirling and lifting with the fall of the rain, disorientated him, upsetting his balance. He put his left hand out to the rock face to steady himself.

It came once more, this time more muffled. Dale glanced over his shoulder at Guardigan and pointed over the edge of the path. It had come from below them, over the edge.

Dale stooped to stare down through the scrub brush. Less than ten feet below their own path was a second, narrower path, until then unseen in the mists. He waved a hand to Guardigan and silently indicated his find.

A sharp nod. Guardigan produced a coiled rope. He passed the end to Corn at the head of the line, who set about securing it to a particularly stubborn tree nearby, while Dale took the other end from Guardigan and ensured it was wound tightly around his forearm and behind his waist. His sword was back in his scabbard.

Once secure, he set off over the edge backward, passing carefully and quietly between scattered shrubs and sharp rocks, steadily letting out the rope behind himself to allow a slow descent. The rope made a thrumming sound as it passed over the leathers of his right bracer and his armoured back plate, but he hoped only he could hear it.

Just above the lower path, he allowed himself to drop the final few feet and landed in a crouch. He immediately grabbed for his weapon, but left the blade in the scabbard, hand on hilt. Then he shook loose the coiled rope and allowed it to fall behind him.

Ahead was the entrance to a small cave. He stepped forward to look inside, and immediately saw a dozen or more villagers cowering at his sudden arrival. One brave boy, holding a short sword in two small hands, took a tentative step toward him, but hesitated at Dale's reluctance to draw his own weapon. The short sword looked like a claymore in the boy's grip. He stole glances left and right as someone else began descending the rope above. There was no one else outside the cave waiting to pounce.

"Easy, boy," Dale instructed the youngster. "Don't do anything rash with that old sword. We're here to help. See this emblem?" He tapped the Shen Utah City Guard emblem carved into the leather of his armour. "This means I'm sworn to protect you." Although, that wasn't strictly true. Either way, the boy didn't look convinced. Dale had to assume these were bandit captives. "Tell me, son, where are the men who brought you to this place?"

Dale stole another few glances either side, but no one approached. The rest of the villagers continued to cower. He could see no captors. *Perhaps they have already fled?*

Corn dropped to the path and immediately drew his weapon. Dale waved him off as the Wayfarer stared in surprise at the find. "Secure the path," Dale told him quietly. Corn did so, moving out of sight of the youngster with the sword and the others secreted in the cave behind him.

"Come, boy, tell me who brought you here."

Increasingly confused, the boy looked around for help from the others. A young blonde woman cradling the infant whose cries had attracted Guardigan's attention in the first place stared hard at the Shen soldier for a beat and then said, "Dale?"

He didn't recognise the woman immediately, but something familiar in her face lifted a memory from the depths of his mind. Though he could not recall her name, he remembered her as being the daughter of one of the smallhold farmers in Adar.

"Dale, what are you doing here? How many are with you?"

"We number just four; no need to worry."

"Only four?" The despair in her voice was visceral. "You need to leave!" she insisted. "Get away from here!"

"No! We can help. Just tell me what you're doing up here!" he repeated, increasingly worried. It seemed obvious that there was no threat inside the cave with them—no captors, and none of them were tied up. "Who brought you here? Are they close by?"

"No," she told him, "we came here voluntarily. It's our safe place."

That threw Dale. *Safe place?* Quickly he glanced around the cave. These were definitely not hostages; these were villagers in hiding. They resembled refugees. But that made even less sense than his original assumption.

Guardigan dropped to the path next to Dale, his breath wheezing out as he landed heavily, jarring his knees. Above, Dale could see Aleks looking over the edge at them, awaiting instructions while the mists continued to lift. The rains continued to hammer down, making the narrower ledge a treacherous place to tarry. "Stay there," Dale told Aleks, who nodded once. "Secure the top path and holler if you see any strife."

Aleks's head nodded once more and disappeared.

"Miss, listen," Dale said to the woman, feeling bad for forgetting her name, "I don't understand what's afoot. Why are you up here? What are you hiding from?"

Her only reply was a look of terror in her eyes that Dale couldn't interpret. Anything else she might have said died in her throat as she was interrupted by a terrible howling on the wind.

She turned pale. "It's okay," Dale told her. "That's our captain's signalling horn." The familiar sound had come from deep in the valley behind them—the sound of Captain Carpion's mustering horn.

"By the gods!" Dale heard Guardigan exclaim.

He turned to see what the single blast signal could have meant.

The two friends rose to their feet, coming to stand shoulder to shoulder, staring through the driving rain at the village of Adar nestled at the centre of the valley floor below them. The thick mists parted, hounded across the sky by northerly winds. The rain fell in grey sheets, washing the farmlands that surrounded the huddled village.

A broad bank of trees marked the rise on the opposite side of the shallow valley. A small force of mounted soldiers had emerged from those trees, bearing down on the village of Adar with swords drawn, held aloft in the dwindling light.

A second blast of their captain's horn drew Dale's eyes to the fields on the far side of the village, between Adar and the mounted attackers. Carpion's men were positioned to meet those strange attackers, forming a triangle of armed men. A small number of what appeared to be militia augmented their numbers, but they were still outnumbered. Still, that would never worry a Wayfarer. Such skilled fighters were worth two in the field.

Dale drew in a breath to tell Guardigan that they should hurry down to add their force of arms to the fray. Before he could speak the words, he heard a gasp from above. Aleks had returned to the ledge outcropping above. The Wayfarer pointed a finger at the eastern horizon, his mouth agape. "See the rise?" he asked them, awe in his voice.

Dale's eyes narrowed as he searched the horizon through the rain.

Suddenly his blood ran cold.

Beyond the tree line, an army approached. Hundreds of soldiers were cresting the rise and marching down into the Adar Valley.

But beyond *them*, for as far as the eye could see and stretching for miles to either side, Dale saw a mass of marching soldiers.

There's tens of thousands! Dale thought, panic rising. It seemed impossible.

Carpion's Wayfarers and the remainder of their City Guard were utterly doomed, as was the village of Adar. Small clusters of villagers could still be seen fleeing the settlement, but they would not get far before being overrun. The most massive force of arms Dale had ever seen was descending on the valley and would wash over them all as easily as the waters of a burst dam.

And soon after that, this impossible enemy would be upon Dale and Guardigan . . . and the refugees in the cave.

He looked over his shoulder.

"Where in holy hell did that army come from!" Corn stammered, returning along the ledge. "There must be thousands of them! Are they ours?"

"Of course they're not ours!" Guardigan blasted. "And it's more like tens of thousands! Get back up that rope! You"—the old sergeant jabbed a finger at Dale— "get the women and children up there too!"

Guardigan was right. Carpion had sounded his horn to warn them. He had to have known they were too far away to reach the village in time, and probably had an inkling they might stand a chance of hearing the warning blast. It wouldn't have been to bring them nearer—the captain was trying to give them a chance to flee.

Someone had to be told that an enemy army stood on Shenmadock soil, only a month's march from the walls of Shen Utah.

Someone had to give the capital a chance. And if it was possible to rescue these refugees at the same time, they had to at least try.

They watched dumbfounded as the forward elements of the army rode down on Captain Carpion's Wayfarers. Even from up here, Dale and Guardigan could see several riders taken from their saddles by Wayfarer arrows, but the mounts hit the defensive line hard. Wayfarers scattered from under hoof, some firing point-blank with their bows, others using longswords to try to unseat their enemy. Even so, the enemy trampled over them and surged toward the village.

Dale was sick to his stomach. The enemy rode into the heart of Adar. His home. Fighting down vomit, he set about his tasks.

It took more than five minutes to get the refugees organised and up the rope, by which time the village of Adar was already aflame, the first wisps of smoke curling into the drab grey sky despite the evening rain. They reached the horses safely, losing no one over the edge, but it was clear that the entire group was rocked by what they had seen—soldiers and refugees both.

The refugees themselves numbered twenty-seven, including five mothers with eight young children, who they were doing their best to carry. Dale carried one solid toddler with bones of lead, but the boy didn't complain once, even as they slid a little down the rain-soaked scree paths. Three boys and five girls just short of apprentice age were helping the elderly along—three venerable couples who proceeded without a grumble, though the journey must have been arduous on their arthritic joints. Some faces were familiar to Dale, but most were not.

At the foot of the hill, Guardigan pulled Aleks, Corn, and Dale aside as the refugees rested in the relentless rain. The young soldier's mind was spinning now, shock of what they had just witnessed dulling his senses, but a well of grief in his soul threatening to spill over into open despair. His family, all those he had grown up with . . . they were being slaughtered, scythed down like so much grain in a field. He'd not even had the chance to see them once more.

Determinedly, Dale shook his head to rid it of those thoughts. He willed himself to the present; there was no time for grief or despair yet.

The tattoo of the rain on their armour and the sodden ground around them served to hide their voices from the gathered refugees. "How in the hell are we going to get away from that army?" Dale asked, embarrassed at the desperation in his voice. "The marching line is far too wide for us to avoid by running north, and those horsemen will have us overrun by nightfall with all these refugees on foot!"

"Quiet, boy!" Guardigan said.

"He's right, Guardigan," Corn agreed. "We stand a better chance alone. We should leave them somewhere hidden. Hell, we should have left them up in those caves! They'd have stood a chance there. And we'd have a chance of riding away now!"

Due to his raised voice, some of the Adar remnant could hear his tirade. It was hard to argue with the Wayfarer's logic, but Guardigan did nonetheless, seizing him by his cuirass and pulling him close enough for spit to hit Corn in the face as he hissed, "Listen, you dog! No one gets left behind. We'll die protecting these people, if that's what it takes!"

"Carpion's men died on their feet," added Aleks.

"Exactly! And so shall we, if it comes to that!" barked Guardigan, shoving Corn away roughly.

"An admirable sentiment," said Aleks. "But that's not what I meant. Carpion's squad were on their feet. When they crested the rise south of here, they'd have had a sightline on the valley that we were denied by the clouds. What if they hobbled their mounts outside the valley? What if Carpion saw that Adar would soon be under attack and left their horses where we could reach them? Then he blew the horn to signal us to flee. He had to gamble we were in earshot."

"It's the kind of empty-headed, grandiose, heroic nonsense Carpion would think of." Corn nodded. His words were harsh, but Dale could hear the bitterness of loss in the Wayfarer's voice.

Aleks said, "If we can get to those and saddle up before Adar is fully overrun, we can get the more infirm refugees onto horseback. We might just stand a chance. A small party as we are will always move faster than an army that big. It will only be their scouts and advance elements we'll need to worry about."

"Aleks, by Akamon, you're a bloody genius!" Guardigan said excitedly, moving back over to the refugees. "Take Dale and get to those horses as fast as you can. Lead them to the clearing of the wrangler skirmish. Corn and I will take this lot and meet you there. Maybe we can get gone from this place before that mess of whoreson soldiers across the valley falls on us like a thundercloud."

Chapter Twenty

The Fallen

"I've said it before, and I'm sure I will annoy everyone by saying it again, but I've got a very bad feeling about this." Manic hoisted his sword belt on his considerable waist and looked at the gates of Mrnak with clear distrust, as though the very portal might be planning something deadly for the new arrivals.

The city was not a welcoming place.

They had wandered along the abandoned ancient path between the twin cities of Jrnak and Mrnak for the length of the day after departing Aal a Zass-al-amel's villa, stopping once to take refreshment in the shade of a copse of short trees. Despite Boyareen having the reputation of a barren land, the regions nearest the coast were remarkably verdant, which brought its own issues. The humidity was alarmingly high, and Eidos had taken to carrying his extensive armour rather than wearing it. Andi noted that his arms were heavily muscled, the forearms matted with fine hair. Despite the heat of the day, he toiled without complaint. Even Manic found it too uncomfortable to bother wasting energy on voicing any discontent.

As the sun dropped toward the horizon before them, they crested a rise to find the foreboding city of Mrnak in the valley below them, precisely according to Zass-al-amel's directions. The two cities were so close, within a day's walk of one another, and yet from the histories of Jrnak, one would think its twin had never existed.

Mrnak stretched to their left, toward the same inlet of water on which they'd sailed in. Even from that vantage point, though, it was clear that no ships were alongside, and the entire area was devoid of life. Given they shared the same coastline, Andi had wondered how hard it could possibly be to find Mrnak. But she reminded herself that it was fear and superstition that kept people from visiting the city, not lack of knowledge.

Looking upon the dead city, she had noticed even the birds seemed to avoid the area, for the skies overhead were clear.

And so they came to stand before the eastern gate near dusk. Towering above them, the rough-hewn rock of the ancient entrance glowed with archaic wonder. The wall of the city spread to either side of them, and even the sea was now out of sight. The wrought-iron gate that would have stood guard at this entrance had long since abandoned its post; only the hinges remained, and they were numerable and deep-set enough to suggest that Mrnak had once boasted an impressive gate.

The sun was rapidly descending, as though the very countenance of Mrnak was enough to chase it away. Soon it would be night. Back home in Shenmadock, it would be creeping toward the depths of winter.

They were running out of time.

Eidos was the first to shrug his shoulders and then, without a word, step confidently through the open gatework and into the city of Mrnak.

They moved through narrow streets between tall abandoned buildings, careful not to stray too close to the dark alleyways on either side. At the end of the first street was a gutted ruin that Andi could tell had once been a large tavern. The simple reminder that this place had once thronged with the mundanity of everyday existence discomforted her more than the complete emptiness, for it still carried an echo of life, a whisper of the souls who had once thrived in this city.

Every building was empty and in some varying state of ruin—as were the streets—but the place still seemed to be alive to Andi. She had no better way of describing it. She'd been in ghost towns and abandoned villages before, and she'd experienced the abandonment of a dwelling, and this place simply didn't feel like those had. And yet Mrnak was utterly devoid of life.

"It's as dead as a crypt," murmured Manic, echoing her thoughts.

"Even a crypt can teem with vermin," Fin replied in ominous tones.

They wended their way deeper into the city, hands on weapons, not a word spoken, as though to verbalise their unease would magnify its effect. Under their feet, the paving stones and innumerable cobbled walkways had long since gone to the dogs, with rampant weeds growing up through the groundworks and splitting the cobbling. It resembled more a wilderness path than a city thoroughfare.

Not one building had been saved from the looting over the ages, and many had suffered structural decay, with plenty of taller buildings having lost the walls of upper tiers, perhaps even a roof here and there. A confusion of smells wafted from each empty dwelling, testament to the rot of decaying matter within. Something about that smell of decay alarmed Andi even more. *Even in death, there is life*, she remembered being told once. In this place, those words felt like a blade of ice.

And yet, more than anything, it was the silence that unnerved her. Even at this late hour, they might have expected some birds or rats to be scurrying round, perhaps even feeding upon what was still rotting, but there was nothing. She would have expected bats to start taking to the skies, but her sharper-than-human eyesight could pick out none.

"This place is *spooky*," complained Manic, but his last word trailed off to a whisper as his voice seemed to echo through the streets. "No wonder it has no visitors anymore. Just a few minutes here and I've already decided I'm never coming back!"

Andi nodded but declined to reply. Obviously, it hadn't occurred to the dwarf that most of the previous visitors to this city had never returned because they'd never actually left.

Emerging from a short street, they found themselves standing at the corner of a small market square, the north face of which opened onto a wide concourse that led uphill, lined with many tall and stately buildings in various conditions. Two paved roads marked the concourse, each wide enough for three wagons to travel side by side. Between these roads, on raised platforms, stood many statues and monoliths depicting angels, warriors, artists, and great animals, again in various states of disrepair.

In the distance, at the top of that grand and impressive roadway, stood a once-splendid walled building, a tall glass dome rising from its heart. In the late evening light, the setting sun cut shafts of amber through the domed windows and across the stonework.

A large metal sign on the wall of the market square nearby told them the broad road was named Krigaresstig. Andi had no idea what that word meant, and she didn't care. Unless, of course, Krigaresstig meant *Road that people walk up just before they die horribly*. She would want to know that.

"That's an old dwarven word," said Manic. "Well, two words, really. It means Warrior's Path."

Eidos said, "Perhaps these statues once depicted great warriors. It would make a kind of sense that the traveller would settle here after having met the mighty Aquilla San, arguably the greatest Warrior King the plains and the sands had ever seen."

"Don't see many dwarf statues, though," Andi pointed out.

"Why would you expect to see a dwarven statue?" Eidos asked. "Aquilla San wasn't dwarven."

"I didn't say he was, but why would they use an ancient dwarven word for warrior to name a road with no dwarven warrior tributes on it?" Eidos shrugged as though the entire question was nonsense. "Manic, when you say this word is old, how old is old?" she asked Manic.

"It would be almost nonsensical if used in conversation today," Manic said. "*Krigaresstig* is certainly older than the foundations of most of these buildings—and certainly older than the statues."

Andi looked toward the building in the distance, trying to gauge how long it would take to reach it. By the time they got to the far end of Krigaresstig, it would be full night.

They forged on.

Despite wanting to feel brave, all four travellers stayed in the rapidly lengthening shadows of the right-hand buildings as they made their way up the broad thoroughfare. No one wanted to be out in the open. The roadway was marked by several footpaths and departures that led off the main strip. All were dark and made to look strangely closed off and foreboding by the comparative openness of Krigaresstig.

But it was something other than the darkness that caused Andi to hurry her steps when passing the first junction. A sound, half heard on the movement of air through that alley, pushed her on—an indistinct chittering, like that which a child's marble might make when rolling down a washboard. It was so subtle, Andi couldn't be confident she had even heard it at all. Still, she had an increasing feeling of being watched, and that nigh-on inaudible sound did nothing to assuage her sudden fears that they were not alone.

At each of the subsequent turnings, Andi stopped and listened before stepping out, but only a small handful of times did she suspect a repeat of that first sound, though it was so faint that she couldn't be certain she'd heard it at all. The others looked at her quizzically each time she stopped, and she could only shrug. They had obviously heard nothing.

And so it was, all the way up that strange broad roadway. Not a soul in sight. Not a soul speaking. But always that half-heard infrequent chittering. And the sense of being watched.

They arrived in the shadow of the grand building just as the sun disappeared beyond the horizon. Everything was shrouded in darkness, the residual heat of the sun-baked stonework still giving off decent warmth.

The building before them was surrounded by yet another stone wall, over ten feet high, which easily obscured close inspection of the building. It was an impressive effort to achieve just a little privacy, and that added to Andi's disquiet, especially since some effort had also been made at some point to wall up the only gate to the property. Thankfully those efforts had failed, and it took little time to break a hole through the crumbling masonry big enough to squeeze through—even for Eidos, who was now once more secured inside his gleaming armour.

"Isn't that odd?" Fin whispered, his lizard tongue flicking out at the air nervously as they prepared to breach the fallen barricade. "Someone didn't want anyone getting in." His sibilant voice was little more than a breath on the silent breeze.

Manic looked up at the reptile. "What happens if they blocked it up not to keep things from getting *in,* but to keep things from getting *out*?"

Andi laughed, though she knew the gesture was like whistling in the dark. They were all scared; there was no hiding that. She stooped to climb through the hole, but Manic's hairy-knuckled hand stopped her.

"What makes you think you're going first?" he asked. "There could be anything in there!"

She gave him what she hoped was a rakish grin and—with more bravado than she really felt—said, "I can handle myself."

Once through, she saw that the gardens and footpaths between the outer wall and the building were winding and sparse. The vegetation had grown wildly enough to make a mockery of the term the Dead Twin City. Looming over her across the main path stood the largest building they'd seen so far. Judging from the description Aal a Zass-al-amel had given them, this could only be the traveller's residence.

It was a monster of a building, with climbing columns, gothic pointed arches, and baroque relief work, and it resembled a cathedral more than a residence. Many extra wings and annexes had clearly been added throughout history, and the story of architectural evolution was clear in the sprawling development. It was not at all what Andi had expected to find.

Through the gloom, she could see that the entrance to the building itself, at the top of a flight of marble steps, was not walled up. That was a bonus, she supposed.

Once the rest of their number were through, they moved to the steps and ascended two at a time, Andi with her bow drawn and an arrow notched. At the top of the steps was a tall, grand doorway, ordinarily barred by two massive bronze doors. Each of the doors stood slightly ajar. Both Eidos and Fin stepped up to push them open.

The hinges protested loudly with age and rust, the grating shrieks of the ancient mechanisms echoing into the night sky. It was possible to imagine hearing the echoes resonating throughout the whole city.

Manic winced.

Andi expected a wave of bats to burst from within the mansion, but nothing was forthcoming. She even half expected a ghostly wail, but the place was as silent as a corpse.

"Slowly and carefully, lads," she told them. "Watch your step. We don't want to have to fish you out of any cellars that might have been exposed beneath weakened floorboards or cracked flagstones."

Fin and Manic moved forward, weapons at the ready. Andi followed them into a huge central hallway dominated by a grand stairway at the far end, which split in two before sweeping up to the higher floors.

Barred doors and open entrances peppered the ground floor, but a glance as they passed revealed nothing but reception rooms and a large dining hall. Two long corridors filtered off in either direction, too, and Andi's warning regarding the floor might as well have fallen on deaf ears, for the flagstones were solid.

Andi nodded her head in the direction of the staircase directly ahead. Where the staircase split in two, there was a mezzanine, and opening off this was another massive and ornate double doorway, this time of varnished oak. It was the most impressive thing inside the building so far.

Manic spent a few moments striking sparks into oil-soaked rags he had brought with him, and they used the tapers to light a couple of torches Eidos had purchased in Jrnak. They crossed the darkness of the hall in silence. While they disturbed wisps of cobwebs, no other evidence was left of their passing. Even the ancient dust on the floor was thick enough not to betray them.

Her uneasiness increasing, Andi pulled her bowstring even tighter, her eyes ever watchful of the gloom around them. The strain of the string bit through her leather finger protector and into her flesh.

Ascending the stairs, they passed through that massive doorway and into a tall, square room furnished with plenty of tables and chairs in each corner. They quickly fitted the torches into several of the many empty sconces on the walls.

Off to the right rose a steel spiral staircase, which ascended to an upper balcony level that covered one quarter of the floor space below. Although the majority of that floor was covered in a badly moth-eaten carpet, the centre was dominated by a circular flagstone design from which the colour had long-since faded.

More impressive than any of that was the sheer number of books lining three of the four walls. The ceiling was easily fifty feet high and, when occupied, would have been impressively illuminated by the massive chandelier still suspended from the ceiling.

"Is that chandelier . . . gold?" Manic asked in awe.

Andi looked hard at the fitting. The precious metal appeared heavily tarnished, but she suspected he was right. "I think so."

"Why has no one pinched that?"

Andi released the tension on her bowstring and replaced the arrow in the quiver at her back. She slung her bow about her torso to free up her hands while she regarded the massive chandelier appraisingly. "Would *you* like to carry that out of here?"

Eidos nodded. "For that matter, would you like to be the one to catch it when it falls? It is a chain that keeps it suspended, not a rope. A rope would have perished long ago." He was correct, and the pulley in the ceiling led the chain across to the balcony of the upper level. "It's a beast, though. I'm surprised *someone* hasn't tried to steal at least a part of it yet."

Who says they haven't? Andi thought, the hairs at the nape of her neck bristling. "Keep your eyes peeled for traps and your weapons to hand; this place might not be as abandoned as it looks."

But despite a thorough search, they revealed nothing malicious and could concentrate on searching for what they had come to find.

The majority of the books were works of epic fiction, some so old that their language was hard to follow. Others were research tomes regarding explorations to all the lands Andi could name, and plenty that were alien to her. Even the artistic works that they found were explorative in nature, concerning themselves with distant lands in long-lost eras. They found an entire section devoted to Fin's home across the seas to the southwest, and by his own admission, he could have sat for days and read those books. But that was not what they were here for.

Despite the apparent safety, Andi's hackles remained up. She felt no comfort in the place. That sense of being watched was growing worse.

"This is all fascinating," admitted Fin, displaying the excited explorer in him. "There's a book here full of map sketches that seems innocent enough, but if it's accurate, it rewrites the entire globe! Most assumptions place the hottest part of the world across this very region, but this book plots more continents to the south, and even another landmass to the west, beyond my home! They reposition the equator upon the waist of Peena, much further south than current convention dictates. That's amazing enough in itself, but when you look at *this* book, it suggests that the ground we stand upon is not as stable as we believe. It postulates—"

"What does postulate mean?" asked Manic. Andi saw Eidos shrug with a smile.

"—that the ground is made up of a series of huge slabs that are constantly shifting minute distances, and it's this momentum that causes earthquakes and volcanoes, even forming mountain ranges and seas!"

"I don't get it," admitted Manic.

"Well, my own lands are beset by innumerable volcanoes, both dormant and active. That ever-shifting topography that some might call hellish is what keeps our peoples tribal. *This* book suggests these volcanoes are the creative force in the world—not some mystic group of deities carving out valleys and lifting mountains on command."

"That's not very encouraging, considering we're here looking for evidence of a magically sunken city and a weapon of God," said Andi.

"Well, actually, it *is* encouraging. What if Aquilla San's city fell beneath the ground, not because of some magical event but because of an earthquake or fissure in the ground? It would lend the entire story more credibility, no matter how those events are then interpreted.

"This book claims the legendary risen deserts of Peena actually form the northern ridge of one of these ground slabs that has been pushed up against the slab beside it, the one we're standing upon. As the pressure has built over the centuries, one slab has pushed up and the other sunk beneath it."

"How is this helping us?" interrupted Manic. "I mean, I've found a book here that speaks of an ancient all-knowing race of beings who once walked the lands commanding fearsome powers. They disappeared in an instant. But who cares? It's not going to help us!"

Andi turned away as her own frustration began to mirror the dwarf's. She glanced around again, thinking about what Fin had said. Underneath the upper landing, the wall was lined with map upon map, some detailing the same lands but with quite staggering differences. Everywhere she looked, there was reference to lands both recognisable and confounding. How were they to discern what was helpful and what was not?

"How do we even know we're in the right place?" she asked. "If all this crap is true, then the world of Aquilla San's day might be completely unrecognisable to ours! Even if we found a map, would its references still be relevant?"

She cast her eyes heavenward.

On the opposite wall to that which was covered in maps rose the most impressive tapestry Andi had ever seen. Age and light had taken their toll, but the imagery was still fairly clear. The others saw what she was looking so closely at and came to stand beside her.

It was a mural of the traveller's oasis, from which he had first sighted the palace of Aquilla San. The depiction was undeniable.

"Okay, then," Eidos muttered. "At least now we know we're in the right library."

An hour of searching and further reading passed before Andi heard that curious chittering sound again. They had looked through shelf upon shelf of books, but there was no way of discerning if any of them held a clue to the location of the oasis depicted on the tapestry. Fin had spent a few minutes expressing his excitement at some find or other, but that had quickly abated.

And then Andi heard it again, seemingly inside and outside the building at once—within the walls and beyond the confines of the building simultaneously. That staccato, resonant sound. It crept through her bones like a thief.

"This is no use!" bellowed Manic from the upper level, where he was sifting through more shelves hidden in the eaves.

They still can't hear it, she thought. It made her question whether she was imagining it.

"I could read every damn page," Manic complained. "How would I even know if I came across the clue?"

"He's right," agreed Eidos.

"I'm open to suggestions!" Andi snapped, throwing down the large atlas she had been leafing through.

"Well," offered Fin quietly, "perhaps we should be thinking more laterally about this."

Disappearing into the aisles above to continue his search, Manic shouted, "I'm all for lying down on the job, lizardman, but how is that going to help?"

"I mean lateral thinking, dwarf! What if the secret to the location has something to do with this tapestry, for example? I mean the tapestry itself."

Eidos clicked his fingers. "Or these maps!"

"I've reviewed all the maps, and there are no mysterious markings or clues," Andi told them both.

The torches they had lit burned quietly in the sconces, giving them all light enough to read, but the fire cast eerie shadows on the walls as they moved about.

Eidos stood in the centre of the room to gain perspective. He looked pensively at the large tapestry and then at the maps behind him. Then at the tapestry again. And back at the maps.

And all the time, that almost inaudible, tantalizingly distant chittering got louder. Soon they must all be able to hear it, surely!

Just as that thought ran through Andi's mind, Fin locked eyes with her. He could hear the same sound; she could see it in his alien eyes.

"Something's coming," he warned the others. "Something . . . strange." He seemed a little miffed at her for not mentioning it, but didn't say anything.

"He's right," Andi agreed. "We need to find this information and leave *now*."

"I don't know whether you've been keeping up, skinny, but that's proving to be easier said than done!" shouted Manic.

Andi moved quickly to the open doors of the library. She looked down from the mezzanine and through the hall of shadows toward the main building entrance. The giant glass dome that sat above the long hallway shone with the silvery blueness of moonlight.

They were not alone.

Silhouetted in the bronzework doorway at the far end of the hall was a stooped figure. With a strange jerking stance, it regarded her as she stood in the light from their torches. From this distance, she was pretty sure it was armed with a sword, or perhaps a thin-headed axe. She could see moonlight glinting off a domed helmet.

With that same rickety gait, it slowly moved toward them, taking short, punching strides in the silence of the hall.

"So much for this place being dead," she muttered to herself before shouting to the others. "We've got a visitor!"

She looked around. If they shut and somehow barred the doors, they could hole up in the library, but then they would be trapped there. Andi could see narrow windows above the shelving at the top of the library walls, just at the point where the walls met the ceiling. They might afford an escape route, if they could be reached. They would have to do.

Unless they stood and faced the new arrival? Something in its manner dissuaded her from trying.

"Fin, come to me!" She tried to push the library doors closed, but the hinges were old and damaged by time. Even when the Finhead leant his strength to the effort, they moved only a short distance, and noisily so.

They narrowed the gap to one shoulder width.

Andi glanced down the hall. The building was echoing with that teeth-itching, chittering sound, and suddenly the doorway at the end of the hall was filled with more figures running toward the library, catching up with the leader. There were dozens.

Reclaiming her bow, she started firing arrows down the length of the hall, felling several attackers in her first volley. The shafts of her arrows seemed to glow in the moonlight as they thumped into each target.

Even from such a distance, Andi could see that there was something not quite right about these men. They moved without grace, their actions clumsy but rapid. They were all armed and armoured, but Andi could see the gleam of polished white on some limbs. And if she wasn't very much mistaken, the leader's helmet wasn't a helmet at all—it was exposed skull.

Giving up any hope of closing the knackered old doors, Fin drew his own bow and shouted out to Eidos and Manic, "We're in big trouble, my friends! Hasten your lateral thinking!"

Manic had never been a big thinker. He was quick with a jape and had a good memory for places, but he was never one for riddles or cryptic nonsense. And suddenly he was being called upon to help by using his brain instead of his broadsword. He'd have much preferred to be down at the door, facing whatever enemy was abroad, than up in the rafters looking at books! He ran to the balcony railing and looked down at Eidos, who had drawn his axe. The big human stood behind Andi and Fin, who were at the door, unleashing hell with their bows. The two archers didn't seem to be slowing down, so whatever they faced was clearly still coming.

"How are we supposed to get out of this?" Manic shouted down.

"It has to be something in the tapestry!" insisted Eidos, his eyes fixed on the doorway. "Can you see anything obvious from up there? Something about the palace, the desert, or even the sceptre itself?"

Manic stared across at the tapestry. It was just a picture! There was nothing!

He glanced below. Andi had slung her bow and drawn her sword, stepping back to ensure the unseen enemy could only come at them one at a time.

He looked back at the tapestry, and something caught his eye. There was no sun in the picture. There were golden rays of sunlight, but no sun.

Suddenly there was the sound of breaking glass above him. Dark skeletal figures began tumbling into the library from the narrow windows in the ceiling. Eidos spun to face them.

Lumps of decayed flesh flecked from their limbs as they scurried toward Eidos, who began laying about himself with his axe, sending chunks of mort flesh and decaying limbs flying. Fin stepped up to help as Andi fought alone to hold the narrow gap of the door.

Manic looked around for a picture of a golden sun, but there was none.

Sun. Golden sun.

Gold . . . the chandelier!

He looked at the solid-gold monstrosity at eye level from his elevated position on the balcony. The tapestry was on the eastern wall. The chandelier was west of it, where the sun would set.

But they already knew the palace lay west of the oasis! That was nothing new!

More scurrying figures dropped from the ceiling; his friends were going to be overrun. The armour-clad decaying bodies were fighting like devils. Lumps of muscle and sinew hung from impossibly animated skeletons.

He had to help!

Manic looked once more at the chandelier.

The sun . . . but more than just a sun. There, at the centre of the chandelier, *what was that?*

Suspended from the ceiling—forming the centre of the chandelier—was a hammer. Only from this angle could the dwarf finally make it out. The central chandelier column was a golden hammer with the head pointing down.

Tor Dewald . . . the Hammer of the Gods!

There was a scream from below, and a bellow of rage from Eidos.

Manic looked over the railing to see Eidos doused in blood and flesh, surrounded by the undead. Near him, Fin was trying to fight his way back to the door. There, in the light of a torch, Manic could see Andi.

His heart dropped.

A rusty spear had punctured her ribs. Her face was slack and pale. Fin reached her side and scooped her body up, swinging his axe wildly at the foes still pouring through the now-undefended door. Manic's eyes raced across the room, seeking an escape, but they were trapped.

They were doomed.

Beneath him, in the centre of the flagstone floor directly beneath the chandelier, he could make out a faded symbol.

A sun, at the centre of the stonework.

A sun, to the west of the tapestry.

Beneath the Hammer of the Gods.

The western sun, the sunset . . . a falling sun.

Manic grabbed his broadsword and ran the length of the balcony as undead soldiers climbed over the railing, swarming toward him. He slashed out at a couple, lopping off a head or two.

But instead of running for the stairs, his pounding feet took him to the southern wall, where he slammed his sword into the chain that kept the chandelier suspended. His mighty strike didn't even score the chain, but it did dislodge the anchor bolt from the stone.

With a deafening groan that filled the library, the chandelier dropped to the floor, smashing through the flagstones and filling the chamber with a cacophony of thunder and an explosion of dust and stone. The floor of the library roiled with unseen power, as though an earthquake shook the very foundations of the world.

In the clamouring, Manic could suddenly hear a chorus of angelic voices singing high. The hole he had created in the floor burst with golden light, and shafts of brilliant sun shone through the dust and carnage, lancing the bodies of the undead. The ghoulish enemy soldiers were felled to a one, and the group was left alone as the shafts of light dissipated to nothingness. The rumbling of the floor faded to silence as the sound of the choir reached a crescendo. Then was nothing but a memory of an echo half heard.

Through the swirling dust of destroyed flagstones and masonry, Manic saw Eidos clutching his axe. His tabard and armour was awash with rank stale blood and gore, his eyes shining from behind a mask of horror. Behind him, Fin stepped forward, carrying Andi's body in his arms. The spearhead still jutted from her lung, the shaft broken at the head.

She was dead.

Fin and Eidos both stood on the ledge of a mighty chasm in the floor. At the edge of their vision, they could make out an ornate doorway in the ground, identical to that which

Aal a Zass-al-amel had described as fronting the palace of Aquilla San.

"The palace is beneath Mrnak itself," Eidos said, his voice profoundly empty.

No one could bring themselves to respond.

Part Three

From the Shadows

"The difference between treason and patriotism
is only a matter of dates."
Alexander Dumas

Chapter Twenty-One

Death's Fool

The three survivors of the library attack sat huddled around the solitary burning torch they had been able to salvage. Darkness wrapped them on all sides, and silence permeated their very bones.

But none more so than their fallen comrade.

They had collected what belongings they could from the destroyed library, prepared a rope down to the strange, sunken doorway, and then Eidos had lifted Andi's body onto his shoulder and climbed down into the depths, bearing her weight without complaint. All of this had been done in sullen silence, the bodies of the maniacal zombie soldiers littered all about them as the first rays of the morning sun shone through the smashed windows in the ceiling.

Despite the ghoulish arrangement, the group's discomfort had fled immediately with the ignition of that strange burst of light from the ground. Something about that sunlight eruption had dispelled the tar-like sense of seeping evil that had characterised the chamber in the hours prior to the enemy attack—a sense of evil they had not been fully aware of until it had been chased away.

"I think we need to look at things rationally," Eidos said. "This whole area is ancient and has been abandoned for a long time. Especially this building. Whatever those apparitions were, it was probably an automated trap we sprung by being in the building. When the floor was broken by the chandelier, there were gases that escaped from down here that were ignited by our torches. That's what destroyed the trap's apparitions and freed us from the trap itself."

Manic saw Fin watching Eidos as he spoke, the lizardman showing no emotion—so far as one could tell with a reptilian face. When Eidos mentioned the escaping gases, Fin's head tilted. "Apologies, Friend Eidos, but that makes no sense. If the gases had escaped and ignited, we'd be just as badly burned as those creatures up there. Also, the point of ignition would have been from the torches themselves. This fire came from the ground. And make no mistake, they were creatures, not apparitions or trap devices; they were walking skeletal zombies. Imagined things don't kill people. I think it more likely that the light that burst from down here was the trap. A trap designed specifically to destroy those creatures whilst leaving us unharmed.

"Something else occurs to me too," the lizard pressed. "Those weren't flames that erupted from the hole; they were shafts of light. Not only did we remain unharmed, I for one felt a pleasant warmth. But when they touched the creatures, they dropped like lifeless dolls. All of them."

"Master dwarf." Eidos turned to Manic, obviously seeking at least one ally in his quest to explain the unexplainable. "You must have seen some strange things caused by escaping gas in your time in the mines. Have you ever seen anything like tonight? Some methane compound or other?"

Manic looked at the two of them. It seemed suddenly to be an unnatural collection of travellers, and certainly not one that could achieve what they had set out to achieve. All three of them resembled ill-fitting pieces in a puzzle. He wondered if the others felt the same thing, and that was why Eidos was suddenly so talkative.

"No," he said simply. "Never." Then he added, with no small pinch of sarcasm, "Certainly no gas that comes supplied with a choir of angels singing from the ground."

As the other two ignored that last comment and continued their pointless debate, Manic's eyes wandered around the chamber that the falling chandelier had uncovered beneath the floor.

It seemed to have been a grandiose reception room of some kind. The floor was marble—now badly cracked and spoiled—and the ceiling was tall. A series of corridors had once run off in three directions, but two had long since collapsed. The general assumption was that, having dropped the chandelier onto the flagstone floor and broken through to the subterranean chambers, they had somehow stumbled upon Aquilla San's palace, hidden beneath Mrnak instead of the deserts of Peena all this time. Of course, this entire region had once been under Peenian control, so the legends did make a kind of sense.

If anything, the discovery that they needn't travel any further south should have come as a pleasant surprise, because Manic bloody hated sand. But he couldn't bring himself to see the joy in that fact.

Eidos changed the subject. "It occurs to me that it makes sense that the traveller's library was built atop the ruins of the sunken palace, for he had surely been the last survivor to know their true location."

"And then there was Zass-al-amel's assistance." Fin nodded. "He'd made it very clear that he didn't believe any of the myths of desert palaces, and had specifically called the tales allegory. And yet, once convinced to help us, he had still gone to great detail to feed us the tales in all their glory.

What if he meant the tales he fed us were actually allegorical too, and that he was giving us the clues we needed to work out this puzzle? Without us really knowing."

Manic nodded, but he couldn't raise that same enthusiasm for problem solving, not with Andi's corpse so close by, growing ever colder by the hour.

Once the group had opened the giant doors in the bottom of that sunken depression, they had lowered themselves down to the far wall and settled for a short rest near a torch brazier that would have once stood out from a wall, but now rose from the ground. Into that, they had secured their last torch, intending to search for additional material with which to make new torches once they decided what to do next.

Andi's body lay a short distance away, wrapped in a tent tarpaulin from Manic's pack. The dwarf looked upon her unmoving form for a short moment, but had to look away.

His friend was dead. It didn't seem possible.

No, that was wrong. Of course it was possible; it just somehow didn't seem *right.*

They were coming too fast. Andi slashed to either side of her as fast as she could, but she and Fin were being driven back at the library door. If the unreal zombified enemy got past the bottleneck they had sought to create at the library doorway, Andi and the rest were done for.

It was then that she looked over her shoulder and saw Eidos being surrounded by more of those baleful beings tumbling from the broken windows near the ceiling. Their escape route was blocked. They were trapped, surrounded, outnumbered, and soon to be overwhelmed.

"Get to Eidos!" Andi yelled at Fin. The lizard hesitated but retreated nonetheless. Andi lunged twice, severing a gnarled head from

decomposing shoulders, and then was forced to abandon the door, retreating toward the centre.

The creatures tumbled into the room through the doorway. Andi stepped forward, slashing left and right, decapitating one foe and crushing the skull of another.

As she hopped back toward Eidos and Fin, her foot caught on the ruined rucked-up rug, tripping her. She caught her balance mid-stumble, but then something thumped into her right side, the impact lifting her off her feet for a moment. A scream—her scream—echoed from somewhere distant. She lashed out with her short sword, breaking the wooden shaft of a spear and severing a mouldy arm. A flash of furious pain erupted through her flank.

Stumbling backward, she looked down. The spearhead was buried in her ribs, a cold swell pulsing through her chest. She took a breath, but her lungs gurgled with welling blood, causing her to retch and cough. A mist of red burst from her mouth, and blood spilled down her chin. She staggered back as Fin ran toward her. "Run!" she told him, but the words seemed so far away, she hardly heard them herself.

Her legs went weak, and she tumbled back. Blood poured from her wrapped tunic. Her vision twisted, swam nauseatingly, and turned to grey, and then all was darkness . . .

The pain rushed through her, each burst of her heartbeat marking her life ebbing away. She could no longer feel her body, and the senses of sight, touch, smell, and taste had left her. All she could do was hear. As the timpani of her heartbeat faded, the only sound was that of a waterfall cascading onto rocks, thundering through the absence.

And then that, too, ceased.

She tried to move, but the carbon construct of her body in which she had existed for almost a century was no more. She was abandoned, suspended in nothingness, swaddled tightly in a vacuum. Even the existence of "Andi" ceased to make any sense. Without her body and a world to exist in, Andi ceased to be.

Only her mind was left to struggle with the concept of nothingness. But even nothingness—being a concept, being something—was therefore not *nothingness at all. The sheer depth of that terrified her—nothing, inexistence, void. None of these words could put a name to the terror she sought to fathom, for the very act of naming it would be to give it existence and rob it of its terror.*

Yet she was terrified, and that was an emotion. A feeling. A concept. Something. The antithesis to nothingness.

Suddenly shadows were rushing all about her, brushing past like bats in the night, a dark wind churning through her soul. And then as abruptly as it had begun, it ceased.

"Welcome."

A deep, harmonic, androgynous voice spoke from the inky ether; although, it wasn't quite a voice. Instead, each word was like a thought infiltrating what little remained of her consciousness, put there as delicately as a mother placed her child in a cot.

A rush of panic surged through her.

"My apologies; this can't be comfortable for you." Immediately she became aware of a coalescence of form all around her. Those same shifting shadows began to converge like churning dark clouds, creating rational shapes where before there had been nothing . . . less than nothing. Her soul was wrapped and enveloped in melting shade that gradually formed into two legs, two arms, a torso, a head. She had a body again, albeit one formed entirely of shadow. Her feet touched down to a solid ground like shiny glass. Four walls solidified to create a chamber of reflected darkness.

"More comfortable?"

"Where am I?" was her petulant answer. "Where are you?" Andi asked next, her words folding into the dark chamber with a strange harmony of voices—as though she now spoke with every timbre she ever had when alive, now in hollow harmony.

"Of course, my apologies."

Suddenly a dark figure blinked into existence before her, not four steps away. No features were discernible other than the tall shape of a man. He seemed to be wearing a shifting crown, but there were no colours or textures other than shadows in shadows, despite the fact that there was no light to cast them.

"You are in a place no sentient being has ever knowingly entered. It is a place of inexistence. It is a place of shadow."

She felt a barely controlled anger replace the terror of a moment before. Andi wanted to scream at this figure that their words made no sense, but something stopped her outburst.

"You are angry." The figure seemed to read her thoughts. "You do well to control your emotions, for they will be to you here as the first emotions of a child. This is understandable, considering what it is you are truly feeling."

It was true; she felt something unfamiliar. After searching beyond her anger and frustration, Andi realised what was wrong. Her terror hadn't been replaced by the anger, only masked by it.

"You can tell what I'm feeling?" Andi embraced the anger in an attempt to avoid the fear swelling in her. "Tell me where I am, and stop talking in riddles!"

"A rusty spearhead has pulled you screaming from that world like a new-born baby. You would have already passed into nothingness but for the fact that I have brought you here. I have made this so, because I am not finished with you yet. You still have work to complete, and your death is something I consider . . . untimely."

"You won't find me arguing there," Andi mumbled.

So, it is true, *she thought. Lady Andrijanna de Krasital was no more. Andi had died. "Is this the afterlife, then?" she asked, but the figure did not respond. "Are you—"*

"You don't quite understand," the voice interrupted. "This is not the end. I have interceded prematurely in the natural sequence of events. There are powers that dwarf my own that shall not approve of my actions, and so I must be swift. The spear of the palace guardian pierced your heart and ended your life as you know it. If you continue on your natural path and travel beyond this realm of shadow, you shall pass on to the reckoning, where you shall be judged."

"So, you're not God, then?" Andi asked anyway, refusing to allow this strange thing to govern the conversation.

"What is God? There is good and there is evil, and your every deed shall be measured against that scale. Some God figure is merely a vessel for imparting those simple polar opposites."

Confused, Andi asked, "If there's no God, then who measures the soul? Who decides what's right and wrong?"

"That's irrelevant."

"God's irrelevant? Brave statement . . ."

"Long have I watched you, Andi. All the things you have done, when held to account, will unfortunately show a moral deficit. You owe a price for your actions. The root law of all existence is causality. Once the simple tenets of cause and causality become dogma and religion, they cease to be truths and are robbed of both meaning and power, becoming the crude tools of a cruder people.

"Only one factor exists that is directly linked to causality, and that is accountability. It matters not whose name you yell to the skies every seventh day before turning around three times and lashing yourself with palm leaves—or whatever it is that your religions force you to do in order to prove your faith. The only thing that matters is how you've lived your life. Were your actions more often good or evil?"

The voice fell silent, and Andi almost felt like her soul was being searched, a feeling like fingers being pulled through mud. "You know the difference," the voice told her. "You've always known the difference. All beings understand what they should or shouldn't do. It is up to the individual if they want to ignore these feelings or heed them; it is all a matter of choice. Your actions have greater consequences than your tiny soul's fate."

"That sounds ominous."

"Choices, Andi, decisions. One more awaits you, and that is why I have risked much to bring you here before you reach your own reckoning. Once you have been measured, there is no turning back.

"There are ethereal beings you might consider angels, and there are those you might consider daemons. They feed on the souls of those who are judged and draw their power from them in order to wage war upon each other in my realm. But while it is true that your direct choices and

actions may one day minutely influence the ethereal plane, the reflex is also true.

"For centuries, the balance has been shifting. The only reasonable conclusion is that more sentient beings are being found to have led a more evil existence than those who have led a good one. Daemons now outpower angels in this realm; we can call it heaven, if that helps."

"Thank you," Andi said without sincerity. "So, these angels and daemons—do they look after us and tempt us, as we're taught by the temples? Do they meddle? Do angels sit on our shoulders? Do daemons lay temptation at our feet?"

"In a way," the voice said infuriatingly. There was still that edge of impatience to his voice, simply an acknowledgement of time—if time truly existed in this realm. "Angels and daemons are able to affect sentient existence to a certain extent. A daemon or an angel may seek to compel a willing sentient being to perform deeds that forward their own ends, and can imbue that willing soul with some of their powers. The individual may even come to manifest supernatural powers, but their life is usually shortened as a result. In rare cases, the soul may even expire while the vessel continues to function under the control of the angel or daemon. This can last some time but is hard for the angel or daemon to maintain. Generally, only the most powerful beings can accomplish such a feat."

"If that's true, why isn't my world filled with the possessed?" Andi wished she could roll her eyes. "Although how would I be able to tell, right?"

"I told you, child, everything comes down to choice. Angels and daemons govern their own realm but are powerless to initiate anything in yours. They can only act using a voluntary vessel—for example, someone who yearns for guidance and inspiration and ultimately begs to be possessed by an angel, whether they understand it on those terms or not.

"A religious zealot sets out on a mission of mercy and asks for divine assistance to guide them; an angel may use this man's devotion to good in order to help the zealot in achieving his goals. The angel who helps such a man achieve his goals may succeed in turning the balance

of the war in this realm in their favour, for all those saved souls become his fuel upon the zealot's death.

"Likewise, a daemon may channel his influence through a power-hungry king whose heart is sick with ambition, turning his hand to evil deeds and conquest. Even though they may believe they are doing God's work, all the souls the king leads to evil are fuel for the war in this realm, strengthening that daemon and his brethren."

Andi's mind swelled with the thought.

"So, if my work is not yet done, why not have one of these angels find a conduit in my realm and get them to finish what I started?" she asked. "Why am I so important?" For a terrible moment, she felt she already knew. "I'm already a conduit, aren't I?"

The dark figure shook its head, a mane of shadowed hair shifting behind him. "No. Up until now, you remain without influence. No matter what your life has thrown at you, it has never compelled you to seek guidance from the heavens. Everything you have done, you have done for your own reasons and with a rare single-mindedness and focus. You have always relied on yourself; you've never trusted anyone else. At least, not for a long time."

A swell of emotion surged up in her chest at the memory, but she crushed it down swiftly, refusing to think of her distant youth.

"The balance in the heavens is being lost. I fear now that one powerful daemon has already found a way to influence your world. There are those who believe it is only a matter of time until this daemon is able to command the same powers there as he does here. He is a daemon of necromancy, a player of souls. We fear he intends to harvest your realm on an unprecedented level. Those souls will imbue him with enough power that ultimately all the inhabitants of your world will be slaves to his whim, and the heavens would be his for the taking."

"I have no idea who you're speaking about, but I think I've seen his handiwork," said Andi. "Necromancy has to do with reviving bodies and the like, right?"

"Yes, but much more than that."

"Okay, but what can I do if I'm trapped here?"

"I place before you now a choice. You can choose to take my assistance or you can choose not to. I have the power to repel you from this place, no matter what damage has occurred to your vessel."

"My vessel. You mean my body?"

"Yes. The course you and your allies are on may be the only hope we have left. For if your world falls to his will and those souls flood into this realm, there is a very real danger that the heavens may fall."

"That does sound like something I'd like to avoid." Something occurred to her. "If you have this power, does that mean you're one of these angels?"

"Something like that. I can return you, and I can repair your vessel, but more than that, you have already felt the touch of the shadows. A part of you will forever reside in this realm. Likewise, your time here will not have passed without leaving an impression on you. You shall have to live with certain . . . changes. Use these changes, use these abilities, but make the right choices. More than just your own soul will be held forfeit should you fail. Your realm and mine may depend on your success."

"So Barabel is right? All the tales that old man told us are true? Secret magical weapons and ultimate battles?"

"Possibly. The important thing is that he is right in his belief in you. Word for word, the prophecy he follows is nonsense. That he believes you to be something you are, in fact, not, does not mean that you cannot perform the function he believes you need to. And he is right to follow that course."

"You're going to have to start learning how to speak plainly!" she told the shadow testily. "I'm not sure I followed a word of that!"

"Continue on your path; do not be swayed from it. Trust your heart, for you are vital, as is your moral impartiality. That is so *vital!" His voice was insistent, impatient now.*

"I'll do what I can. You can send me back. I'm not ready to die yet. Just one more question, though. Can you tell me what this place is?"

This time when he answered, his words were underlined by a dark humour. "This place of shadows and darkness is your soul." The figure stepped toward her, the tendrils of his mane flaring out to both sides, threatening to envelope her. For a moment, she thought she saw a toothy smile in those dark shadows. "Barabel thinks he knows who and what you are, but he is mistaken," the voice echoed. "You shall become something amazing, the likes of which the people of your realm have never seen. You shall dance within the shadows of your world."

Chapter Twenty-Two

The Golem

Somehow Manic Frostfinder had managed to keep their group of three together, despite their differences of opinion regarding what to do next. He'd seen such fragmentation in people before, when a group was struck by such a setback and the unseen fragility of their makeup was tested. Eidos was the most vociferous objector in the end. His concern was understandable, considering he feared for the security of his duchy and wanted to journey back as soon as possible now that their mission seemed so dangerous.

"What sense is there in all of us dying in these strange catacombs when a nation is in peril?"

Fin's reaction had been largely ambivalence. He admitted to feeling sorry about the loss of Andi and to some underlying sense of duty to complete what they had started, but—like Eidos—he was equally worried about the dangers that might lie further below and their likelihood of survival with just three members of their party left.

What they lacked, all of a sudden, was some sense of belief in what they were doing. And the irony of that was, Andi had always seemed the most cynical of them.

Manic had argued long and hard that they should honour her passing by forging ahead, convincing Eidos that, even if he didn't believe the sceptre would help them in a war with Ipsica, perhaps it would help them stave off another attack like the one they'd already suffered in the library. It was clear that the palace beneath the city of Mrnak held some mystical power; they agreed upon that much at least.

And still, Manic had to confess to feeling that same sense of despair that was turning the others away. Climbing down into the depths of the catacombs was the very last thing he wanted to do, and he wondered if it was something to do with this place that was crumbling their resolve.

For the longest time, he had journeyed Shenmadock in solitude, refusing comradeship. And then Andi's company had been forced upon him—the kindest blessing, for only now did he realise how lonely he had been. Andi, Eidos, and Fin had become his friends. He was closer to Andi after what they had shared, but she was gone now. He was not about to let those who remained break apart like seeds in the wind.

In the end, Manic had told the other two, "If we turn back now, she died for nothing." It had been a gamble, for Manic knew he wouldn't go on alone. If they turned back, so would he.

But that statement had convinced them to forge ahead, leaving Andi's remains next to the fire hopefully awaiting their return. Then they had gathered the remainder of their belongings and moved into the confusing dungeon.

Their plan was simple—search for the Tor Dewald down in the sunken palace. Once they had it in hand or had exhausted all hope, they would return to the library doorway and collect Andi before resurfacing and returning home. They would think of somewhere to inter Andi's remains—somewhere far from Mrnak, that was for sure! *Perhaps near the sea*, Manic thought. *She'd seemed happy by the sea.*

The three were galvanised by the desire to ensure she hadn't died meaninglessly. Every time they came across something mysterious and alarming, it leant weight to Barabel's case for a mystic enemy; it behoved them to remember that.

Now that the decision had been made, they wasted no time in being about it. As though some enforced pallor had been lifted from them all, they pressed on with suddenly renewed vigour.

They had set off less than an hour ago, and already they were deep into the chasms and chimneys formed of crushed rooms, fallen ceilings, and collapsed corridors turned near vertical by the cataclysm that had occurred here long ago. Thus far, they had encountered no foes, but the place was unnaturally quiet and eerie. The air was stagnant and smelled of decay. And the very environment through which they walked, crawled, or climbed was deadly for its confusion.

In some chambers that hadn't been fully overturned when the city was brought low, it was possible to see where people had been interrupted going about daily tasks. And yet there were no mortal remains or skeletons.

They had come across an infirmary with sleeping pallets racked up against a far wall by gravity; each bed was empty. They had discovered a kitchen opening onto an outside courtyard, now filled with stone and rubble, compacted by centuries of packed earth above. Kitchen equipment was smashed and destroyed throughout the room, but no remains lay within. Whoever had died during this event had long since gone to dust.

They were now some distance deeper, walking along a plain, low corridor that had been turned on its corner. They struggled to keep their footing but proceeded down the almost diamond-shaped passage without a sound, torches held out to drive back the crypt-like gloom. Fin indicated that there was a chamber on the right wall ahead, thankfully upon the more upright side.

Keeping low, Fin scuttled forward and reached the doorway, which Manic could now see clearly. It was as unremarkable as any other doorway they had passed, except Manic could make out a series of complex hinges and lock plates on each doorjamb.

The lizardman stepped round the door, keeping hold on the doorjamb in case he lost his footing and slid deeper into the room. Down in these catacombs, every turning might result in a fall to certain death.

When Manic approached, more secure on his footing than the two lankier individuals, he saw a broad chamber with a broken floor. The area leading away from the door slanted down to where the great stone floor had been smashed to form a long crevice, spanning the chamber from left to right. A few feet beyond that fissure, the floor appeared to be perfectly level, so far as could be discerned.

That fact alone set Manic's nerves on edge.

Around the walls of the chamber were a series of strange large jewels or translucent rocks of uniform shape embedded in the stonework, illuminating the chamber with a dull golden light. Only one of these odd jewels was missing, the nearest on the right-hand wall. He noticed it, because it struck him as being the only sign of looting. *They only took one*, he thought, *must be worthless.*

The truly startling thing in the room, however, was what the strange shining jewels were designed to illuminate. Pile upon pile of treasure lay arrayed throughout the chamber—glittering gold and silver, myriad jewels and ornate artefacts, shiny suits of armour and elaborate weapons set upon display plinths. The spread of treasure was like a shining ocean. There was only one conclusion—they now stood in the fabled treasure chamber of Aquilla San.

"If there is going to be a trap anywhere in this wonky dungeon," whispered Manic, "it would be in here."

Fin hissed his doubt. "Is that because you believe this is the only treasure chamber? How can you be so sure this is where the Tor Dewald is even stored? *I* wouldn't keep it somewhere so obvious. If it was Aquilla San's favourite trinket, it might be in his private chambers, for all we know! Perhaps it was even lost and now lies in some unknown chamber, deeper underground than we could ever hope to reach." Despite his words, he wedged the single torch into a crack in the wall; they wouldn't need it down in the treasure room, such was the light supplied by the gems.

"That's a fair enough statement," whispered Manic, slightly annoyed. "I simply base my assumption that this place will be riddled with traps on the fact that this chamber, while pitched at a slight angle, is almost perfectly straight and flat—unlike the rest of this cursed place. This whole dungeon is ancient and in ruins. The traps we're likely to face will be no use if constructed from tension springs or even if they were wire-sprung. Any *active* traps left would need counterweights, and that would be easier in this chamber, if it is as well preserved as it looks."

"I'm not sure that's good news, dwarf."

Manic stepped into the chamber. "It's not," he told the pair of them, "but we'll find nothing by just standing up here." With that, he walked down toward the crevice and looked boldly over the edge. The side upon which they stood was steeper than the far side, he could now see; hence, the treasures hadn't slid away from them and remained fairly neatly piled.

He kicked some dust over the edge.

Behind him, Eidos whispered, "Is it deep?" Despite his low tones, his voice thundered round the chamber.

Manic cringed. He stepped back from the edge and rejoined his colleagues. "Bottomless," he confirmed.

"Well, like my old ma used to say, nothing ventured!" Eidos then turned and sprinted down to the edge, jumping clean across the gap to land heavily on the other side. The metallic sound of his armour was a clattering accompaniment to his landing as it echoed round the huge room.

Silence. No trap.

Still, something wasn't right.

Manic looked at Fin and said, "After you."

With a wicked, sharp-toothed grin, the big lizard broke into a run, his muscular tail whipping back and forth behind him, and then leapt across the gap without calamity. Manic's heart fluttered. "I hate running and jumping," he muttered to himself. "I'm much better at sitting and farting."

Suddenly, he missed Andi; she would have laughed at that. She always overheard when he was talking to himself. He felt a terrible plunge in his chest. He realised now how much her playful taunting had pushed him on at times like this. "Oh, lass," he muttered. Then he set off for the gap, his short legs punching the ground without grace, and leaped across the void.

His broad feet thumped against the ground as he landed, but already there had been a sound from above. A strange clattering somewhere deep in the rock.

Manic drew his sword and threw his hat to the ground as he came skidding to a halt. "Something happened!" he barked out. His eyes followed the line of the crevice, and he could now see careful furrows in the facia of each adjacent wall. *A counterweight!* "A trap!" he shouted. "All our weight being on this side instead of that must have set something off!"

A slab of stone burst from the ceiling and cascaded into the room in a cloud of dust and debris.

Behind them, the doorway to the chamber slammed shut under another huge stone slab. The floor beneath them lurched forward a few feet, expanding the crevice between them and the ramp to the now-sealed door. They were certainly trapped now, for that gap seemed impossible to jump. The room was filled with the broken-glass sound of the treasure mounds being disturbed.

Then from within the expanding dust cloud came an immense crash, as of something incredibly heavy and metal thumping down to the floor. The impact threw all three of them to the ground. Quickly regaining their feet, they readied for an attack.

The dust melted into darkness as the mess settled, and then they could hear the whine and clank of machine-work in the chamber. A deep, menacing inhuman voice growled from the dust, "Trade in treasure or trade in blows; return what you stole or relinquish your souls!"

The three spread out, trying to keep low and move away from the newly expanded fissure behind them. They were caught between this new presence and the crevice, not a good place to be. Slowly the dust began to settle and the array of glowing gems revealed their enemy—a gigantic mechanical figure made of bronze and steel. It stood upon two massive legs and easily reached ten feet tall. Within the confines of the limbs and torso, glimpsed through vents and slots in the exoskeleton, Manic could see whirling mechanics so complex that they confused even him—a dwarf! There were pulleys, cogs, chains, and ropes, all working furiously as the machine moved forward.

The chest and arms were equally impressive, with spinning and turning circles of serrated razor wire encompassing the upper arms and around the neck. At the end of each arm were long sword blades, thick as axe heads but as long as a person. The head of the construct was small in comparison, made to look pea-like upon the broad bronze shoulders. Inside the head were tiny white lights that served as eyes, blinking periodically from within an empty steel helmet.

Most impressive was the construct's chest, for this encased something fully alien to Manic. There seemed to be a suspended ball of steel or even gold enwrapped in caged lightning driving the machine's movement, like some impossible, fabricated heart. The tendrils of lightning coursed through the chest like blood.

The head turned to regard the new arrivals, and the little eyes blinked twice before the construct repeated its original challenge. "Trade in treasure or trade in blows; return what you stole or relinquish your souls!"

The three looked at each other.

"We haven't stolen anything yet," said Manic.

Eidos shrugged. "I don't think it cares. Should we throw money at it?" he asked.

Fin dug around in his hip pouch for a handful of gold coins and threw it in the face of the stationary construct, the coins ricocheting noisily off the armour, crackling when they caught in the skeletal bands of harnessed lightning. Nothing happened. The coins tinkled to the ground in a shower of treasure, ignored.

"Trade in treasure or trade in blows; return what you stole or relinquish your souls!" it bellowed one last time before rearing up and raising its arms.

"Oh crap!" Manic exclaimed.

The massive blades swung ominously above their heads before the construct shifted with unpredictable speed. The right sword cleaved the air at chest height in a massive circle. Fin and Eidos were hard-pressed to duck beneath the blow that whistled clean above Manic's head. He felt the wind of the strike ruffle his moustache.

The dwarf rushed forward, hoping to take advantage of the machine's slowness, but it stepped away from him with two huge, booming strides and aimed another strike at Eidos. The court cleric jumped back as the sword smashed into the floor at his feet.

Again, Manic lunged forward, jabbing his sword at the left knee section. The blow was inaccurate, and his blade crashed off the armour without even leaving a dent.

As Fin tried a similar attack, the construct swung his right foot. With horrific strength, the steel foot slammed into Manic's midriff. For a terrifying moment, the dwarf flew through the air and then crashed into the wall. He slumped to the floor, dazed by the kick.

Shaking his head clear, Manic looked up to see that Fin and Eidos seemed to have gotten the measure of the thing's pace and reach, now successfully evading its attacks—though the exertion of doing so was plain on their faces. There was no way they were ever going to beat it by just staying out of its reach. Sooner or later, they would run out of space and energy, and then they were doomed.

Manic scrambled to his feet.

Snatching up his dropped sword, Manic ran toward the construct's hindquarters, hoping to flank it while it chased his friends.

Eidos and Fin both saw him and feigned attacks from either side. The whirling, whining, straining sounds from the machine were deafening in the cavernous chamber.

Reaching its hindquarters, Manic swung his heavy blade at the hamstring area, only to be repelled by a sharp spike that lanced out from within one of the vents in the back of the thigh. From another vent, in the calf this time, a whirling circular blade slashed out at him, cutting deeply into Manic's shoulder. He screamed.

A sideways roll took him away from the construct's next step, which would have easily crushed the dwarf. Once out of reach, he scrambled backward, his sword still in his hand. Blood seeped from his deltoid muscle, though he did what he could to staunch the flow. He had little strength in his left hand. Looking up, he watched as the lizard and the human were left to fend for themselves.

The construct was an amazing machine, moving with a speed Manic could scarcely believe of something so big. As Eidos stepped round the extreme of its reach, Fin tried to lunge in at the torso. Time and again, myriad weaponry lashed out from the vents and gaps in the armour to deflect their attack. All the while, the great swords slashed down and across with startling purpose.

"We're going to die," Manic muttered to himself, trying to get to his feet. He'd be damned if he was going to die on his back. "Come on, you greedy beast!"

Manic could see Fin was trying to pierce the electrical chamber in the machine's chest, despite how well armoured it was. From the back, Manic could see four large vents, lightning rippling within. These also vented steam or smoke, like chimneys. Taking careful aim, Manic lobbed his sword over arm, hoping the blade would puncture the orb within.

Instead, the machine shifted, raising an arm to deflect the flying sword. The blade punched in through a gap in the thing's forearm, and Manic heard ropes snapping inside. Without warning, one of the construct's blades dropped from its left grip. For a moment, the machine stood and regarded the lost blade, as though confused.

Seemingly enraged, it redoubled its efforts, driving furiously at Eidos with its one remaining sword. Manic's thrown sword remained lodged in the machine's arm, but the missing weapon had obviously unbalanced it, and it now seemed clumsier, as though fighting upon the deck of a ship.

Manic looked about for a better weapon, and realised he was surrounded by treasure for as far as the eye could see. Searching desperately for one of those ornamental swords he'd noted earlier, Manic's eyes alighted on an ornate plinth just a short distance away, atop which was a carefully placed golden sceptre. At the head of the artefact was a large spherical crystal that encased a perfect red rose. The entire artefact was perhaps no more than a yard long.

The Tor Dewald!

Now they just had to find a way out of this trap.

Manic rushed over, snatched up the precious sceptre, and ran back toward his friends, struggling to shove the Tor Dewald into his shoulder bag. He'd kind of hoped that lifting the sceptre from the plinth would somehow stop this nightmare, but they weren't that lucky.

As he approached, he saw his friends were even more heavily under the cosh than before. He drew a shorter blade from his belt and rushed at the construct's back, hoping to sever another rope. Eidos took advantage of the missing sword and slammed the head of his axe into the left knee, but was rewarded only with the wrist-jarring clash of metal upon metal, and then a swiping back hand riposte across his chest. Blood sprayed from the cleric's face as razor wire gouged his jawline and cheek. His body thumped to the floor near the crevice.

Fin stood alone, dodging each deadly blow, slashing out with his own weapon when possible, but all without impact.

They were going to die!

Manic reached the rear quarter once more. He drove his short blade into where the construct's coccyx would be, hoping for a similar result as before, but his blade was snapped at the hilt by some unseen mechanics. The heel of the monster snapped up behind it with the whine of straining gears and caught Manic in the ribs. He was propelled across the room once more, landing heavily on his side.

The cumbersome Tor Dewald clanged dully against the stone floor through the material of his bag. Panicking, he checked to see if it was in one piece. It was.

His chest was constricted, causing his breath to come in ragged gasps, and his ribs ached where he had been struck—or was it where he had landed? Near the chasm, Eidos moved groggily.

Manic's fingers brushed something strange. *What was that?* He felt a massive lump beneath his tunic.

For a moment, he thought his lungs or guts had burst from his torso, but then his fingers wrapped around a solid, familiar form—the large, dull gem he and Andi had stolen from Reinhart's keep at Hightower, back when this whole nightmare started. The gem they had kept when they handed over what they had assumed was *the Baerv* Reinhart's cousin had sought.

The worthless gem the cowled figures had been so obsessed with obtaining.

He pulled it free of his tunic. The shape was identical to the hole in the wall above his head. This was what Manic had found so familiar in this chamber; all the illuminating gems were identical to it. *This* must have been what the twisted Jakrat had been after. He must have believed *the Baerv* was the jewel that would grant entrance to this chamber—but the fool had taken the wrong one! Reinhart, Jakrat, and those cowled figures had sought to secure the gem key to this chamber, to ensure it didn't fall into their enemy's hands. Manic's hands.

He got quickly to his feet.

Andi had killed Reinhart, they'd all murdered Jakrat by burning down his manor, and now Manic held the very jewel the enemy had been after.

Trade in treasure or trade in blows; return what you stole or relinquish your souls!

He regarded the jewel and then the hole he intended to fit it into . . . and immediately saw his problem.

"Eidos!" Manic called. "Get to your feet, you idiot! I think I know how to stop that thing!" Manic showed him the gem. "I'm just not sodding tall enough to put it in the damn hole!"

Eidos looked across at Fin, who had to roll forward between the construct's legs to avoid being cut in two. A defensive spear thumped down from within a vent in the machine's crotch area—which was normally something

Manic would have laughed at—and slammed into Fin's tail. With a sickening cry, the lizardman rolled painfully free of the spearhead, ripping the green flesh of his tail. He came up in a defensive stance, though the wound had clearly hurt him badly.

"I need to help Fin!" shouted Eidos.

"This might turn it off!"

The cleric was clearly torn, but chose to run to Manic, hand held out for the gem. The dwarf let him snatch it, and the huge human jumped high, arm swinging overhead, and thumped the jewel into the gap in the wall. It sank in perfectly and immediately bloomed with the same iridescence as the others.

Eidos snatched his hand away as though scolded. The two friends turned to see if the construct stopped its onslaught, but they hadn't even slowed it down.

What *did* happen was the trap reset. The floor beneath their feet retreated to shorten the size of the crevice, and the far entrance was opened once more as the giant boulder retreated into the ceiling.

As Manic looked away from the door, he could have sworn he glimpsed a dark figure moving through the gloom of the entrance, but when he checked again, he could see nothing.

"Bloody run!" shouted Eidos.

"What about Fin?" the dwarf asked.

"Yes," he answered, "he should bloody run too!"

But the lizardman was cut off from escape. It was plain to see he was doomed without them, for the construct was turning to face him. And Fin was limping, badly unbalanced by the grievous wound to his tail. Manic made to run to him.

Suddenly a black-clad humanoid stood before them, emerging from the shadows cast by the deadly construct. A black blade flashed into the vent beneath the hip of the machine. Manic heard a cord snap.

The construct turned to swipe at the new foe, and another blade jutted out of a vent. Both strikes were aimed to kill the shadowy assailant, but they only passed through air.

The figure had gone.

Only dusty darkness remained, like powdery smoke wafting away on the wind of the huge sword's passing. Then Manic saw the dark assassin reappear from the shadows beneath the construct's other arm and drive the black sword into the armpit. Another snap and twang echoed in the machine. Now only one leg was functioning, and the sword arm could not move above the shoulder. Time and again, the figure of chalky shadow reappeared, struck, and melted away before the machine's defensive blades could do their damage.

Fin stepped gingerly away from the machine, sword at his side. His tail hung at an odd angle, and deep-red blood poured from the wound. Fin put away his weapon and cradled his damaged tail for a moment before running for the crevice, which had returned to a jumpable size. He cleared it with one leap, as Eidos did in following. Manic made the jump too, and then all ran for the exit.

They had their prize, and the door was open, but still the dwarf stuttered to a halt at the exit, looking back at the strange struggle as the others fled. He watched the incorporeal figure leap up from within the shadow of the construct's back and land atop its shoulders. The dark stranger was little more than five and a half foot, and moved with deadly grace. Manic could see now that only a slit of skin was visible around the black pools of their eyes. They drove the short black blade deep into the bronze skull, sparks leaping in the darkness.

The machine uttered a strangled, ululating whine; oil and hot water squirted from vents throughout its body, steam bursting from others. It slumped to its knees as the shadow assassin jumped to the ground with the agility of a thrown cat. Dust plumed as the body of the guardian-machine slumped forward, dead as only a machine could be.

Just as Manic had, Eidos and Fin had stopped at the doorway to watch. Though the threat posed by the construct seemed over, Eidos still brandished his weapon warily. Manic stepped tentatively toward the stranger.

"Manic!" hissed Fin in warning. "We should leave!"

But he ignored the lizardman.

The shadowy figure stopped and regarded the steel and bronze carcass for a second before pulling Manic's sword free from the ruined arm. There was something terrifyingly familiar in the figure's feline gait as it stepped up to somersault, straight-legged, across the crevice, landing with perfect, silent poise.

"This can't be," Manic muttered.

The figure reached up and lifted the hood away by the back of the neck, revealing a familiar face and a roguish grin. Behind him, Manic heard two sharp intakes of breath. "Hi, shorty," Andi greeted Manic amiably.

It was undeniable. Andi was alive!

"How . . . I mean . . . *How?*" he stammered, still cradling his wounded arm.

"It's a long story." She hefted his sword and handed it to him handle first. "Lose something?"

He took the sword and quickly stowed it, wincing at the pain in his shoulder. "But . . . we saw you die. That spear went straight into your heart."

"It must have missed," she said simply.

Andi stepped past Manic, and the dwarf fell into step next to his miraculously revived friend. "But you were cold, and I could find no pulse, for an hour at least! You weren't breathing! Deader than dead!"

"We'll talk about it later," she insisted, and her tone brooked no further discussion on the matter, so reluctantly he dropped it. "The most important thing is that you found the treasure chamber safely."

Manic shrugged, regaining some of his own poise. "Of course we did. And what's more . . ." He reached into his pack and produced the Tor Dewald as they reached the others. They were all in poor condition, Manic decided—apart from Andi. Fin's tail had stopped pouring blood but would certainly need tending to, and Eidos's face was a mess from the razor wire that had raked it. "Now that we have what we came here to get, maybe we'll have time to get back before the spring thaw and this predicted invasion."

They all studied the artefact, the seemingly simple item that had caused them to risk so much. The gold of the sceptre was dull in the gloom of the cavern, but the vibrancy of the encased rose held just as much lustre as one still living, and they could clearly see the perfection of the cut gem. Now that no adrenaline coursed through Manic's veins, it was incredibly heavy in his grip.

Standing in its presence, Manic expected to feel the aura of something powerful, perhaps even the crackle of something holy. But he felt nothing other than the numbness in his arm from holding the thing out.

"It's pretty," said Fin without enthusiasm.

Chapter Twenty-Three

Escalation

"Things are getting out of hand, Stefon," Rish told him, like that was news. "We've got three reports from last night of separate attacks on independent trader convoys out of Choat. All of them were repelled successfully, and the convoys got away, but we lost a number of mercenaries, and Darkeni lost his son."

Stefon's shoulders slumped. Darkeni was a powerful and positive influence in this strange alliance of traders they had created. He was a proud father; the death of his son would hurt him. Stefon found it hard not to worry about what this might mean for their little collaboration as a whole. He knew it seemed selfish, but this was a time of strife, and as young as he was, he was also long enough in the tooth to be aware of the cost of freedom.

Stefon rubbed the space between his eyes. The pair sat in Susu-Van's trading house while the morning loading finished up and the few wagons going out that day headed off. "Did we retrieve any more intelligence from the dead attackers this time?" Stefon asked.

Rish gave him a long, measuring look before answering, as though he had glimpsed Stefon's thought process and didn't really like what he saw. "Actually, one of the attackers had a parchment list of convoys out of Choat that day. Twelve of the nineteen were intercepted by bandits. All convoys and shipments were owned by traders in our consortium."

"That's a pretty damning piece of evidence. It seems we've become dangerous enough to warrant an escalation. They're turning up the heat to try to divide us. We've rapidly become a threat, and du Lacigny's wasted no time recognising that. Shame we've got no real, tangible evidence yet to link it to him, or else we could go to the authorities."

Rish nodded. "Unless du Lacigny has them paid off already. You could always use the reports we got back about Guy's own shipments. I'm sure the Choatian authorities would be interested to hear that du Lacigny's companies are shipping huge volumes of weaponry out to the west."

That particular piece of alarming evidence did at least seem to be true, and Rish was right that *someone* would be interested to hear about it. "Shame they're not selling them to the east or even into Ipsica," he thought aloud. "At least then it would seem to indicate he was betraying Shenmadock to our homeland. For that, du Lacigny would face charges of treason. But selling weapons and armour across duchies? I don't know how illegal that actually is." Rumours of a civil war between the Shen duchies of Mashtock and Jow were rife, and the consignments Rish's teams had uncovered indicated du Lacigny was selling weapons and equipment to elements inside both Jow *and* Mashtock—and doing it without proper documentation.

To ship such a large quantity of weapons into another duchy required ducal authority. These shipments they'd spied leaving Choat did not bear the ducal seal. Guy seemed to be fanning the flames of civil war in neighbouring duchies, and no doubt reaping the rewards. The Shen authorities definitely frowned upon that; Stefon was confident of that! But could he prove anything properly illegal? Anything that couldn't easily be explained away as some administrative oversight?

For Stefon, things were escalating too. He hated du Lacigny without even having met the man. Not only had he arranged to have Susu-Van murdered, along with dozens of other private traders and couriers, but now he appeared to be profiting from the deaths of hundreds—potentially thousands, as would be the cost of civil war.

"This is going to come to a head," Rish said. "Sooner or later, du Lacigny will have to take care of the principals in this rebellion. That means us."

Stefon knew he was right. "It's not just us now. If he comes after this consortium of traders we've assembled"—Stefon disliked having it called a rebellion—"he'll go after *all* the principals. That means us, yes, but it also means senior traders like Greel, Cayden, Darkeni. . . the list goes on. We have a duty of care to those people."

"By Soriana, when did we ever earn a duty of care to anyone but ourselves? We're scoundrels, Stefon! We're scurrilous! We're mercenary!" Even as he said the words, Stefon knew Rish didn't believe them.

"We earned that duty when we got Susu-Van killed."

"That wasn't our f . . ." Rish's protestations trailed off as Stefon waved them away. "Stefon, there was nothing we could have done," he said anyway, and then paused before changing the subject. "Are you still having trouble sleeping?"

"Of course. It's the same every night." Stefon sat forward and took a sip of his bitter coffee. "It wouldn't be half as bad if I knew what the dreams meant."

"Dreams don't always have a meaning. You're starting to sound like a priest, with your obsession with discerning meaning where there is none."

"I want understanding, that's all. I get why I had those dreams about The Light. The things that happened behind the walls of Wahib City were enough to drive anyone crazy."

Rish looked at Stefon slyly. “Like you running up walls and moving so fast you become a blur?”

Stefon shook his head. “Precisely,” he agreed. “I don’t know what happened to me inside Wahib, but I’ve no desire to lose control like that again.”

“Lose control?” Rish asked. “Is that how it felt?”

Stefon shrugged, reticent to speak of it.

“It just occurs to me that we have a weapon in our arsenal that might turn the tide of this struggle with du Lacigny and his goons.”

“I’m not sure I like where you’re going with this.”

“Well we know now the wagons that they’re targeting. Why not place ourselves as mercenaries escorting one of these wagons. Then, when they ambush it, unleash you! You can use that sword and your abilities to deal with them all. That would send one hell of a message.”

“No.”

“Well, at least you considered it for a moment!" Rish said sarcastically. "Why not? Why wouldn’t you use what you have to save these people?”

“It would be one shipment, one wagon, one band of attackers. It could even be a bloodbath, and we might not be able to save anyone anyway.”

Rish knitted his brow. “Are you worried about tipping your hand?”

“No!” Stefon snapped. “I’m worried about what using those abilities might do to me!”

“You’re supressing them,” Rish guessed correctly. “They haven’t gone away, you haven’t lost them, you’re resisting them.”

“Yes,” he said. “And it was working, until the dreams worsened.” Stefon hadn’t spoken at length about the content of his most recent dreams, but he felt it was time to share. Rish could be intuitive when he wanted to be; despite their recent differences about their enterprise in Choat, they were still like brothers. "I don't dream about Wahib anymore. I don't have nightmares about a moving corpse or a headlong dive off a ten-storey balcony."

"I do," muttered Rish.

"I dream about Lesjac. I dream of his eyes burning into mine while he speaks of ancient civilisations. I dream of him standing on a mountain, fire springing from his fingertips. His flesh begins to seep a black fluid, bubbling from his mouth and nose and eyes. I float into the sky, away from the mountain, while a circle of fire radiates from his body and he is consumed by the blackness. All around him are fields and meadows filled with gravestones. Suddenly, the soil begins to bubble and surge, and I wake up in a cold sweat."

"Nice."

"Lesjac was up to something when we encountered him in Wahib; we know that much. That he was ultimately behind the quarantine of Wahib is evident, but to what end? Where were all those bodies going?"

"An especially worrying question when we consider The Light's ability to keep corpses moving! Seeking to kill the entire city through releasing a plague is one thing, but—ignoring for now the question of how—*why* are they reanimating them?" Rish said. "And let's not forget, we'd have been on that list of victims but for you."

"Us," Stefon corrected.

"Whatever you want to tell yourself. Anyway, that might explain the dreams of Lesjac, fear of what was going on back there, but you said these new dreams centre on *people*, not just *a* person."

"I . . . am having dreams about a woman." Stefon was incredibly reticent to speak of this.

In a typical Rish move, instead of showing discretion, his friend poked fun at him. "Don't tell me. Coral! I knew it! Didn't I tell you she was your type? And there you are, spinning tales of having no trust in her. You old dog!"

Rish started clapping his hands in a faux show of girlish excitement. "Oh! I'll have to buy a new hat!"

"Shut up. It's not Coral. I'd prefer that it was! At least then I would have an explanation."

"You tart."

"No, this woman is different. All I see in my dream is the silhouette of a short, slender woman stepping toward me, sunlight streaming out from behind her, almost blinding me. Her details are obscured to begin with, but as she gets closer, her face is revealed. Her features are sharp, almost elvish, but not unpleasant. She always has this strange, soft-mouthed smile. But her eyes . . . those eyes . . ."

"What?" asked Rish, rapt.

"In the dream last night, her eyes were black . . . *so* purely black."

"More black? Really? You're obsessed with the colour, like some crazed landscape artist. Black!"

"Black, yes, but differently so. They're deep, like potholes. It's not a flat black; it's a black with no end. Then suddenly they burst with a massive darkness that obscures the sunlight and casts me into inky night, and she becomes ghost-like—just half-seen images, a shadow dancing in shadows."

"That's a strange phrase," Rish said, at last showing some concern.

"And she reaches out to me . . ." Stefon extended his arms, stretching his fingers. "She reaches out for my shadow."

"And then you wake up?"

Stefon's hand dropped to the table. "Yep."

"And you don't recognise her?"

"Not at all. Except . . ."

Rish tilted his head. "Except what?"

"When she becomes enveloped in that darkness . . . she looks even more elvish than before. Not really human at all."

"They could just be dreams, you know."

Stefon shook his head. To him, they were much more than just dreams.

"Just now, you said you had been supressing your abilities—past tense. Does that mean you aren't any longer?"

"The other day in the meeting with Greel, Cayden and the others, something happened that I can't explain. I saw something."

"Waking dreams?"

"No, not this time. This was something different. I saw these strands, these ribbons of energy between us all. They rippled with emotions, sensations, feelings. I quickly felt attuned to them, as though I could read the feelings of those around me as easily as reading a book. And then, when it became a little tense, and I was trying to convince them to stick with the plan . . ."

"What?"

"I was able to affect them, disturb them, change them somehow. I think that's how I convinced Greel."

"You altered his mind?" Rish asked.

"No, just encouraged him to change it himself."

"Wait a second. Could you see my strands?"

"Of course."

"Did you pull on them?"

Stefon laughed and shook his head. "No, Rish."

Rish made a noncommittal hum in the back of his throat. Before he could give any further opinion, the door to the trading centre burst open and Brooss bustled in, followed closely by the huffing dwarf Jewl.

"We'll continue this later," Rish said quietly. Stefon could only scowl.

"Stefon, Rish—we've important news," garbled Jewl.

"It's Coral. She might have done something a little rash," explained Brooss calmly, her delicate features made harsh by her frown of concern. Even in such circumstances,

Stefon saw that Rish couldn't take his eyes off her. "Knowing we would probably need something to link du Lacigny to these attacks, she snuck into his headquarters. Pryn has word that she was discovered inside and has been locked up by Guy's goons."

Jewl nodded. "I hate to say it, but local snitches have confirmed it."

Stefon started gathering his weapons. Rish followed suit. "Well, that does it. The only reason for Guy not handing Coral over to the authorities immediately under charges of burglary is that they have something to hide from them."

"What happens if they kill her like they did Susu-Van?" asked Rish.

"Then I'll be even madder. But I don't think that'll happen. He'll want to keep her to use against us. Murder didn't work last time; he's not going to try something that subtle again."

"Murder's subtle now?" Jewl asked.

"What I mean is, he's going to be more direct."

"So murder is indirect . . ."

"Look! The important thing is that we can't afford to lose Coral," Stefon said. "With Darkeni's son dead last night, we're almost one leader down; we can't afford to lose another, especially Coral. She's new to this city, just like us, but we still can't be sure if she's to be trusted. It's just as plausible that she might be selling out the other members of our cooperative as we speak. Ultimately, if she and Darkeni are both lost to us, the rest will lose confidence, and all we've strived to achieve will fall apart."

"So, what do we do?" asked Jewl.

"Get your gear together, wear dark clothes, and don't bring anything that rattles. We're going to get that wily gambler back before word gets out of her capture."

Chapter Twenty-Four

Infiltration

Later that day, Stefon once again pulled out the stolen plans to Guy du Lacigny's establishment and pored over the drawings in frustration. It was a secure place built into the face of an inland cliff—on a plot that had once been a quarry—with clever sentry points well disguised within the original design of the structure so as not to resemble a fortress—which it effectively was. Without proper planning, it would be impossible to infiltrate the defences without detection or being easily repelled.

Making it even more difficult were the broad grounds and gardens surrounding the front of the building, which served purely to provide the sentries with a clear line of sight for approaching visitors. Along the exterior of these gardens was a pair of fences, one wooden slatted and the other wire mesh. A "welcoming platform" at the only entrance was clearly just a security control, designed to filter and appraise those entering and exiting the complex.

Stefon didn't doubt his team's ability to circumvent the security at some point, but it would take more equipment than they currently had, and time was not on their side. They needed to get cracking, or it was all for nothing. The traders would disband and du Lacigny would get away with Susu-Van's murder.

They were huddled in the larder of one of the local bakers, who held little sympathy toward Guy and his monopoly. Jewl and Brooss stood nearby while Rish and Stefon perused the diagrams, trying to decide on a plan. They had no time to locate Pryn. They had sent someone to find the big man, but only to inform him of what they were doing, not to bring him into it. The last thing they needed was for him to give the game away.

Developments had forced their hand. With the death of Darkeni's son, the trader had done what Stefon had feared he would—he had gone to ground. Darkeni had sent a note to Stefon stating that he would risk no more of his family and had lost the stomach for a fight. He wished them luck, but that small gesture left a sour taste in Stefon's mouth. Although the feeling sat uncomfortably with him, Stefon considered Darkeni's decision to be one of disrespect, for it meant his son had died for nothing.

Coupled with the capture of Coral, information was sifting through that one by one, the principals of their trade rebellion were considering going to ground or giving in to du Lacigny. A mild panic had begun to ripple through the consortium, and Stefon felt powerless to stop it while Coral was under lock and key. Her presence in the city would be a galvanising, unifying one, perhaps their only hope of forestalling the failure of their resistance—but it had to be now.

Perhaps more concerning still were the rumours that du Lacigny wasn't listening to those who wished to capitulate to his former pressure. That seemed a curious move on Guy's part too. He knew too little about what was going on, and that rankled.

"We've got one chance," Rish said. "We need to get in and get Coral freed tonight. Once we reappear in the market with Coral walking round free, telling her story, we can get around the other principals and impress upon them the fact that they still have a fight to win and a duty to stand up and complete what they started. And it will prove du Lacigny isn't all-powerful, that he can be beaten. And maybe Coral will have evidence we can finally present to the authorities."

"Easier said than done, but you're right. The problem is timing. Tonight is the perfect time for our allies to go to ground or to try and capitulate to Guy's demands. Ideally the perfect timing would be for us to go to the principals *now* and convince them to hold strong. We might be able to reach them, but I doubt many will follow through whilst Coral is still in Guy's custody."

"We're new to this city, but these traders have friends and family," agreed Rish. "They have roots here that du Lacigny can get at. They'll want to disassociate themselves from this rebellion."

Stefon nodded, looking again at the plans. "I wish I knew why Guy was suddenly being so coy. We've got a weak hand at a loaded table; not a great position."

"Unless . . ." Rish encouraged.

Stefon smiled his best wolfish grin. "Unless we cheat. We get in there"—he jabbed the plans—"and snatch Coral back before they know what's happening. We get back to the consortium principals before they disband, and then we all turn on Guy du Lacigny like a cobra and strike!"

"When he thinks he's strongest." Rish nodded.

Agreeing, Brooss said, "One is rarely so vulnerable or sloppy as when one feels all the hard work is already done and the day is won. There is a possibility we haven't yet considered. What if this is a trap?"

"Of course it's a trap," Jewl said. "It's really obviously a trap!"

"Easy, dwarf," Rish warned Jewl about his tone.

"What I mean is, what if Coral is more of a *willing* part of that trap. Not bait but a lure."

Rish said, "I hadn't considered that."

Stefon thought about the warehouse meeting and the complete absence of thought-strands he'd felt from Coral. He'd connected with everyone else, but not her. What, if anything, did that mean?

"Whether she's in it or not, we need to find out one way or the other," Stefon said finally. "Once we're in and the trap is sprung, they'll find we're not the sort of easy prey they've been dealing with until now."

Rish looked galvanised by his words. "As for getting into the building, it's clearly not going to be easy," he said, "but there's something they probably haven't thought of."

"Rish, we can always rely on you to have thought processes that are alien to those of normal people."

"Thanks, I think. Anyway, Guy relies on the fact that one side of his building is protected by rock, having been built into a disused quarry. Whilst this is undoubtedly a good idea, they didn't factor in the sewage issue when the place was built."

"How did I know this was going to come down to shit?" Jewl asked, not taking his eyes from the early-evening scene outside the bakery. It would soon be full night; in a couple hours, the baker would be in to start his daily routine, and they needed to be gone from the establishment before then.

"Sooner or later, my squat friend, it always comes down to shit."

"But I'm the one who always gets volunteered to wade through it!"

Rish grinned at Stefon. "This occasion is no different, dwarf. However, you won't be alone."

The silver disc of the moon winked from between grey clouds in the ink of the night sky, clouds pushed along by an intermittent wind that blew the smells of night and the scent of burning from somewhere distant and meaningless to those who stood atop the low cliffs overlooking the western portion of Choat City. Down the slope to the north of their position was the main road out of town, toward the interior of Shenmadock. There was a deep cold to the night.

Below them, in the silence of the bowl valley where the city resided, du Lacigny's facility sat as still as a flytrap. The compound surrounding it was poorly illuminated by tall lamps, with thuggish guards idling around the grounds. It all looked blasé and relaxed, but Stefon knew it to be anything but.

"Okay, Rish, we're all up here and it's nice and cold. How about you get on with whatever it is we're up here to do, before an eagle-eyed sentry spies us knocking about?"

The feral thief flashed a grin in the shadow of the wagon. Brooss picked up the reins again, and Stefon climbed back into the bay. "Drive west for two hundred yards or so," Rish told Brooss. "Stop when the grass gets thinner and the ground is hard under the wheel."

They bundled around in the back of the wagon as Brooss forced the team of horses into a fast walk, pulling the armoured vehicle west. The gradual change in terrain was easily evident, and the coach came to a halt. The team spilled out and collected their weapons. Each had brought their shortest, lightest weapons. This was fairly difficult for Jewl, who most often favoured his great axe that seemed bigger than he was. Instead, on this occasion, he carried a small selection of hand and throwing axes tucked into various pockets about his person, secured in place by dark cloth wraps.

Rish was armed with a short sword currently strapped to his back. Brooss would not be joining them, and she remained on the wagon, preparing to leave. Hopefully, Pryn had already gotten their message and was setting about trying to keep the remaining traders from disbanding. The big man had shown real familiarity with the city, though Stefon still hadn't found the time to quiz him on it. Still, that was probably for the best; Pryn didn't take kindly to too many questions, and he had the physique to back up that stubbornness.

Hopefully Pryn was turning that capacity for persuasion to good use!

Despite—at Rish's behest—issuing the order not to arm themselves heavily, Stefon had brought his mysterious sword with him. He had it strapped uncomfortably to his back and was beginning to worry about the cumbersome nature of it, now that he saw where they were going. He'd be damned if he was going to leave it behind, though. He had become quite attached to the strange sword.

Rish indicated a small depression, perhaps once a shallow gulley that marked the end of the taller grasses. "That's our way in."

"Rish, that's a dry riverbed."

"I know. But think about it; why is it dry?"

Jewl looked from one to the other. "Because there's no water in it?"

"Obviously." Rish shook his head. "The water has gone underground. There's a series of fissures beneath the surface here where the rock has become porously eroded, and an underground river leads south. Brooss told me she had heard about an entrance to the narrow catacombs hidden somewhere up here." He beamed proudly. "I found it."

"And this helps us how?" Stefon asked, as Brooss drove the horses and the wagon away with a noisy clattering. She would make her way down to the main road and wait within sight of du Lacigny's compound, in case they needed a quick getaway. Stefon tried not to let his mind wander back to the last time she'd provided such a getaway.

"The building below was built by Guy du Lacigny's predecessor," Rish explained, "an arrogant ass with no common sense. But he was a successful man and managed to earn enough to build that fortress down there.

"Unfortunately for him, over the years, the rock formations have shifted slightly as the rainwater—mildly acidic from the minerals of the bedrock—dissolved weaker portions of the escarpment made weaker still by the quarry work that once took place. It's a young region, and one subject to geological changes. It's possible that the entire Choat duchy is one massive dormant volcano, with a mixture of bedrock types, from volcanic to limestone."

"A volcano!" Jewl exclaimed.

"I know, it's hard to believe, but when you look at the maps, it makes a strange kind of sense. That makes the soils around here really fertile, but it also makes the bedrock more porous in places."

"Listen," Stefon interrupted him, "I know for a fact that you hardly understand any of what you just said, let alone discovered it yourself, so who have you and Brooss been talking to?"

"Does it matter?"

"Of course it matters! We already know we could be walking straight into a trap," barked Jewl.

"I know, but I really trust this information."

"Because *Brooss* trusts this information?"

"Look, it came from Coral, OK?"

"Oh, that's not ideal," muttered Stefon. "I mean, I know I said I didn't believe she was involved with du Lacigny, but I've been wrong before."

"Pryn did the rest of the research," Rish pressed. "The big guy knows a lot about this town, you know."

"Still, this is a risk we're taking."

"You said it yourself before, we need to find out either way. Triggering the trap is the best way to do that, so what difference does it make?"

"That makes good sense."

Rish made a gesture that he thought it was understood that he *always* made good sense, then continued, "The cliff face at du Lacigny's back, which protects one quarter of his building, has begun to slip inch by inch from the bottom. For now, the only issue this is causing is with the privy system, which was designed to dump human waste directly into a series of narrow tunnels and out into the river south of Choat."

"Nice!"

"I wouldn't swim in the river, no. But listen to this; the cliff subsidence . . ."

"What does subsidence mean?" Jewl asked, scratching an itch on his knee.

"Basically, subsidence is when the cliffs are moving really slight distances over time, apparently. Or something. I pretended like I knew what it meant, but you don't have to do that for me."

"Thanks, Rish."

"Anyway, the human waste has stopped flowing into the river. Brooss says Coral thought it unreasonable to assume they had stopped crapping, and that it was more likely the waste material was being diverted. It's now flowing down into a fissure somewhere, and out into the underground river beneath our feet."

Rish pulled back a tangled bush from inside the dry creek and revealed a narrow landfall. In the darkness, it was difficult to see just what they were looking at, but in a rare bright spot from the winter moon above, Stefon saw Rish had revealed a flat and broad passage leading down.

Rish looked proudly upon the find. "Here's my plan."

Stefon's dark eyes pierced the bleak blackness ahead, the tightness of the fissure crushing his shoulders together. His breaths came in short, silent huffs. All around him, the rock seemed to perspire, moisture running in milky rivulets near his face. He could hear Jewl forcing his way between the rock formations ahead, and somewhere beyond that was the sound of running water. Despite the almost complete blackness of the underground fissures, Stefon imagined he could see the dark shape of the dwarf scrambling over a short rise of rock.

All Stefon wanted was to stretch his arms out over his head, flex his knees, and take a long, cool lungful of mountain air. Instead, he remained cocooned hundreds of feet below the surface.

He pressed on, turning his shoulders to move through sideways. Small edges of both rock formations scratched at his cheeks and shoulder blades, and the uneven V shape of the ground beneath his feet put heavy pressure on his ankles. Several times, the blade of Stefon's sword, in his scabbard on his back, saved his spine from receiving a painful graze.

Somewhere behind him, Rish swore as he slipped once more against the same moist wall.

The going had been arduous, but they had been travelling down and forward for an hour now, and Stefon judged they must be nearing their destination. He was just glad the dwarf was leading the way, for it was widely held that they had an affinity with such surroundings and an innate sense of direction.

The sound of running water some way ahead was a welcome one. Perhaps soon they would be out of these tight confines.

After a short while, the fissure once again broadened as it had a few times during their journey, allowing for a little more freedom of movement, although still not enough to face forward. And yet, such moments had been the only thing to drive away the fear of becoming trapped down here forever. Several times, Stefon had doubted the accuracy of Rish's information, and that they were doomed to die in the darkness—but then the pressure had abated, the tunnel widened, and the spaces opened up. Most of the time, those chambers contained pools of stagnant water.

"Slow down," Jewl said from the darkness ahead. "The underground river is up ahead, and we don't want to fall in."

The other two gathered behind the dwarf, who led them out into a tall chamber. Jewl lit a tiny kerosene lamp and struggled to hang it from a nearby rock. The miniscule, easily concealed lamp was more than enough to illuminate the tunnels; such had been the absolute darkness through which they had crawled.

The lamp revealed a small, shallow decline to the quickly flowing river that sparkled across the rock in the kerosene glow. The river chamber was tall and had clearly been formed over centuries of erosion.

"We can leave this lamp here," whispered Jewl. "What we need to do now is find the leak. Somewhere up or down this river will be a crack in the rock wall on the far side. Hopefully this lamp will provide enough light to find it." He jabbed a thumb to the right. "I'll check downriver. You pair check upriver to the left."

Without a word, they did as the dwarf instructed.

It took them at least twenty minutes of slipping into the river, straddling the fissure, and fumbling over the sheer rock faces to find the crack they sought. It rested ten yards upriver from the lamp, and Stefon and Rish each missed it twice, for the broadest part of the crack lay beneath the surface of the running water.

"This will make things a little trickier," commented Jewl. "Try to make sure you don't have things jutting out from your clothing or loose laces dangling anywhere. You'd be surprised the manner of things that can get caught up in such a swim, and that would afford you a watery grave."

The crack started at the surface of the river, a small triangle of darkness lapping water noisily, but the depth of the river concealed a natural entrance no more than two feet across at the widest point. Stefon supposed he could fit through sideways, but with the water undoubtedly soiled with the bodily wastes leaking from du Lacigny's headquarters, it was hardly his idea of fun.

"Swim?" Rish blurted. "Through there?"

"Rish, this was *your* idea!" Stefon snapped.

"My idea was for the dwarf to swim through shit and then, I don't know, open a door from the inside or something."

"What door? We're underground! Now strap yourself up and get ready to follow Jewl."

Rish grumbled noisily. Jewl dropped beneath the water, and his figure, shimmering in the undulating waves and the light from the distant lantern, passed from view as he swam into the tunnel. They'd have to leave the lantern behind.

Stefon's best friend went next, his face pale in the cold air of the underground river. After counting to thirty, Rish looked up at Stefon, the anxiety clear on his face. With a nod, he took a huge breath and dropped under the water, kicking above the surface once and splashing Stefon with watery filth. Then he was gone too.

Alone in the dark, Stefon muttered, "Here goes nothing," before taking a few deep breaths of the musky, fetid air in through his nose and out through his mouth. He tried to ignore the malty stench as he dropped under the water.

The frigidity of the river slammed his chest and face. He pulled for the tunnel, kicking frantically to get forward into the crack. He turned sideways, and his fingers scrabbled into the smaller tunnel. Then he was wrapped in water and rock. The tightness of the tunnel meant he couldn't kick effectively, and the water rushed back and forth with the flow.

He pulled along the wall, grazing his knee and catching the back of his head once or twice. His lungs began to pulse and burn. Nameless detritus washed past him as he swam. His eyes throbbed with the pressure. His sword pommel caught on a rock outcrop and then released. Still, he pulled.

Fire burned in his chest.

He began to panic.

Suddenly his vision swam, and the visage of the woman of shadows punched into his mind like an arrow, her hand of darkness reaching out to him.

A feeling rushed through him as though his very soul was turning cold. His limbs went into spasm, but he held his mouth firmly shut.

I will not drown in shit!

As quickly as the fugue assailed him, it passed. He had lost momentum in the water and began kicking furiously, bashing his knees and heels on the rocks above and below him. His fingernails scratched over wet rocky ridges, one peeling painfully back.

Finally, his searching fingers met empty water. He turned flat and kicked for the surface, hand uplifted in case his skull met an underwater ceiling. He burst through the surface, gulping stale air and coughing out dirty water. The wretchedness of the air in this chamber almost made him vomit, but he managed to regain his composure and—despite the quality of it—savoured the next breath.

Rish was waiting for him. "Take your time!" he accused sarcastically. They were half submerged in a tiny rock chamber with no exits. "Jewl has already swum on. The next tunnel is a flooded crawlspace, should be easier than the last, but this chamber is full of bad air. Don't tarry!"

Rish was right; Stefon could taste the acidic nature of the poisonous air.

Without another word, Rish sank beneath the still water and kicked on. This time, Stefon didn't wait before he followed him. He kicked hard and pushed his hands forward into the flooded crawlspace. Turds and other filth were more frequent here. He could see light ahead through the brown and yellow water, silhouetting Rish as he swam. Stefon kicked harder, almost catching him up.

They both tumbled out of the flooded crawlspace and pulled for the surface, where they emerged into a small, disused storage chamber. A small ledge to the right was above the water level, and Jewl stood atop it, admiring the structural damage opposite. Rish and Stefon fished themselves out of the cesspit.

Stefon huffed deep breaths, slowly calming his racing heart. Rish looked at him. "You okay?"

"I'm fine; just got a bit tight down there."

"Well, you would insist on bringing your sodding longsword with you. Are you sure you're all right?"

"Yes," Stefon said too curtly. "Let's get on with it."

The dwarf indicated the broad crack in the far wall and the sections of plaster that had fallen away. "Do you see where the pressures from the shifting rock have caused the wall above us to split? That's ruptured their normal sewage flow and resulted in this waterfall of piss and faeces you see here. That then flows down the old crawlspace to the overflow chamber beyond. It filters back into the same pressure cracks, and ultimately into that underground river."

As Rish and Stefon both tried furiously to wring the filthy water from their clothes, Jewl turned toward the door that opened to their chamber—a door without so much as a slide bolt.

"This should lead out into the sub-basement sections of the facility. From there, we should be able to move to almost any section we need to."

Rish tipped them a lopsided, mirthless grin. "Told you it would work a treat."

Chapter Twenty-Five

A Hostile Takeover

Stefon, Rish, and Jewl waited in the stink of the cesspit for over an hour. One of the leaking fissures had proven to be pouring out clean water, not sewage, and so they had done their best to clean themselves and recover from the ordeal of getting this far. Once they freed themselves from the confines of the underground privy, they were relieved to discover that the water hadn't carried too much stench and their efforts to clean themselves had worked, somewhat.

At least they won't smell us coming, Stefon thought. His still damp clothing clung to him irritatingly, though.

It was an uncomfortable wait, but a necessary one. Stefon judged it to be just an hour before dawn, and now the guards on site would be at their slowest and least alert. Though it was unlikely they would run into many guards on the inside of the facility, the last thing they needed was for Soriana, Goddess of Luck, to turn her back on them and for the alarm to be triggered before they could find Coral.

On Stefon's signal, they vacated that uncomfortable room and ventured deep into the sub-basement complex of du Lacigny's monstrous facility. The subterranean chambers served mostly as storage for equipment and materials, along with old transport vehicles and wagons long disused. The entire floor was abandoned.

However, in the corner, they had uncovered a rickety old counter-lever lift mechanism that sat at the foot of a wide shaft. It had been nominated their best bet to ascend floors without being discovered, for it appeared as disused as the equipment surrounding them. Jewl set about securing climbing hooks, knowing better than to try the lift mechanism itself.

Four floors up, they abandoned the lift shaft and exited onto a floor dominated by small rooms, cupboards, and administrative chambers, all unmanned. However, at the end of one of the corridors, they found a servants' stairwell leading down. They took it quietly, weapons drawn. Disappointingly, they had not discovered any cells in the basement complex, and now had to proceed on a wing and a prayer.

The whole building had felt silent up higher, but descending the servants' stairwell to the floor below, they were able to discern faint sounds of work being conducted.

"Where are we going?" Rish asked at the exit of the stairwell.

"I've no idea," confessed Stefon. "I'm just following the noise. We can search from that."

Exiting the stairwell at what he assumed to be the first storey above ground level, they proceeded through a narrow doorway onto a short corridor, at the end of which stood a pair of oak doors. They approached silently, stepping carefully across the expensive pile carpet that topped the stone floor—an ostentatious luxury even for a manor house, let alone a business—and passed an adjoining corridor.

Pushing one of the oak doors open, Stefon could see it led to a lounge or meeting room, one that overlooked a loading area on the ground floor below. They entered and silently closed the door behind them.

The empty chamber only had three walls; the fourth—adjacent to the doors—had been replaced by a short railing that served as a balcony. Clearly the room was designed to oversee the loading of cargo from a position of comfort, for the room was furnished in a plush fashion.

There was activity in the loading bay below, explaining the sounds of labour they had heard. They could now clearly distinguish voices, together with the clatter of goods being loaded on wagons.

"Guard the door," Stefon whispered to Jewl. Then he and Rish crawled forward until they reached an area from which they could look down into the loading bay. From here, they would be hidden from sight in the darkness of the room, while below them, many torches illuminated the dozens of workers loading the day's wagons in preparation for departure. Apparently du Lacigny believed in an early start!

All the workers were dressed in dark-navy overalls and wore hard leather work boots. Below them, they could see a small group of men, the shortest of whom was dressed in a grand burgundy tunic and ruffled shirt. He sported shiny leather riding boots and wore a rapier at his side, probably more for show than action.

Guy du Lacigny.

He signed a consignment note for one of the workers before he shooed the man away. Guy then turned to an administrator nearby—a man who looked equally out of place—and spoke to him above the din of the loading bay. "That should be the last of the current shipment to Mashtock. You can tell your master that his orders are ahead of schedule, as I said they would be."

The sinewy conspirator nodded his pale face. He wore simple dark clothes and seemed uncomfortable in the environment below. Stefon didn't doubt that Guy had done this on purpose. Du Lacigny enjoyed the finer things in life just as much as the next despot, so the choice to meet here would be deliberate, making some point or other.

"We anticipate that the conflict shall not continue much longer, Master du Lacigny, but we are grateful for both your continued efficiency and candour." The stranger had a western accent.

"Your reasons for purchasing these . . . products are of no concern to me. My only concern is that you ensure we are paid in the particular currency I specified; that's very important."

"But still," the man said in oily tones, "you might have asked more pressing and discomforting questions, considering the rumours of civil unrest."

Stefon and Rish exchanged glances. If they needed confirmation that du Lacigny was somehow involved in fuelling civil war, they had just gotten it. Now all they would have to do was prove it! The special currency Guy had mentioned was no doubt untraceable.

"I'm a man of the world," Guy replied with plenty of pomposity. "Whenever a conflict takes place, it usually benefits someone. When I take an order to ship weapons and armour to Mashtock, I will fulfil that order. If I take another order for weapons and armour to Jow, I will meet that requirement also. I am a businessman. It means nothing to me that these orders might originate from the same requestor. It's all perfectly irrelevant to my bottom line."

The westerner nodded brusquely before turning on his heel, consignment notes gripped firmly in his hand.

Guy halted the man's departure with the words, "I do have one small concern."

The other man stopped short and looked over his shoulder at du Lacigny, an eyebrow raised.

"I am yet to see any sign of that payment. I had hoped to get something before now. Specifically, the naphtha I requested. Some things are harder to acquire hereabouts.

I have certain terrain problems with this building. It's not going to last forever, and I can't afford to sell it at a loss. I need the naphtha."

Stefon and Rish glanced at one another again. Naphtha was indeed hard to come by . . . legally. The explosive substance was mined in the north, and was often traded abroad illegally through the small ports in Mashtock. The only legal use was in certain quarries operated by the dwarves in the Choat Mountains.

"I understand," the other man said knowingly. "I am sure, should the worst come to pass, that you are adequately insured." Perhaps in response to Guy's expression, the westerner turned back to face du Lacigny, his manner more supplicating. "You are right, of course, to have concerns. It is my understanding that there was an unexpected delay with the vessel's departure. I believe that, due to the unrest upon the border of Mashtock and Jow, vessels leaving Shen Utah for the east have been delayed."

Guy laughed unkindly. "Seems a little odd that such a thing would be 'unforeseen' to your master."

"With all due respect, Master du Lacigny, you assume too much. But nevertheless, I am assured that your generous consignment shall be delivered to you in short order. Transiting the River Jow at the moment is obviously tricky, especially when transporting such . . . commodities. Getting the goods from the Jow quayside to your wagons may delay it further, but hopefully only by a day . . . two at the most."

He couldn't be sure at such a distance, but Stefon was sure the man was lying. *Why would Guy gamble on selling weapons and armour to someone without guaranteeing payment in some form or another?* He supposed it depended on who the customer was.

Guy nodded. "Just so long as you can ensure swift delivery. I am not known for my patience. Do you understand?"

The westerner paused and then said, "I shall enquire further of the vessel's projected arrival date in Jow. The onward transit will be your concern." With that, the stranger departed.

Du Lacigny stood on his own for a moment as the chaos of early loading took place around him, in the eye of a storm of crates and loading trolleys. People were clearly trying to remain busy in his presence, and Stefon wondered how quickly such behaviour would collapse into laziness once Guy left.

Rish elbowed him, and he nodded that they should continue their search elsewhere. They still had a fool-hardy friend to locate somewhere in the vast building.

But as they began to crawl back, another figure emerged at the back of the hanger and scuttled across the loading bay toward Guy. Stefon put a hand on Rish's arm to belay the retreat. Like tendrils of coloured smoke, the strands were back. Twisting and unravelling throughout the chamber, dim strands twisted and turned as though the loading bay itself was a water tank packed with squid.

Most formed a cat's cradle of confusion amongst the gathered workers, but plenty more fed straight to du Lacigny. They all carried the hue of unease, but the rigid strand that linked this new arrival to Guy du Lacigny was a deep and shimmering navy blue folded with a sickly mustard yellow.

The man hurried over, dark hair greasily slicked to his head and his clothing dishevelled. He had a film of sweat on his brow and the look of someone who had something important to say and no idea of how best to say it.

"Sir," the poor wretch simpered en route. "Sir, I have a message."

"Fitch!" Guy barked.

The greasy man skidded to a halt, his eyes darting from side to side. He approached more slowly, trying to control some of his nerves.

In quieter tones but no less threateningly, du Lacigny continued. "That's better. You know I dislike agitation."

"Yes, Mr. du Lacigny."

"What is so important to get you out of your pit so early in the morning, Fitch?"

"I've actually not been to bed y—" A level gaze of short-tempered disinterest cut Fitch off. "Sir, the prisoner has escaped," he finished miserably.

Guy's brow lifted in surprise, but before he could reply, Fitch continued his report.

"One of the evening guards reported seeing her door ajar before dawn this morning. He immediately reported it to his captain, who in turn came to me. He and I searched the cell and immediate area, but there was no sign. I sent word to the gate guard superintendent, but thought it would be best to report it to you, too, sir. Directly, as it were . . . sir."

Still, du Lacigny didn't respond. Stefon guessed he would be turning the new information over in his mind, but his face was a mask of concentration and calm.

From the same entrance at the far wall, another figure emerged—an imposing one this time, with a long, purposeful stride. He wore leather armour covered by a simple tabard, and a wicked sabre swung at his hip with every confident step. Another rigid strand of feeling linked this man to Fitch, similarly navy blue.

"Here's Superintendent Gerhard now," Guy said, only the merest hint of tension in his voice. "Let's see what's afoot, shall we?"

Stefon glanced at Rish, whose face belied the same emotion he was feeling. Coral had escaped? She had to be the prisoner they were referring to.

"Gerhard, Fitch here reports that our bird has flown her coop?"

"That's confirmed, Mr. du Lacigny. There's no sign of her on the premises or the surrounding grounds." The super's voice was gruff and authoritarian, but he didn't betray any worry; he was simply confirming the report as though it was the most mundane of things. Stefon was starting to get uncomfortable with how this was going. He would have expected a little more concern.

"Do you have any idea how she got past your guards?" Fitch snapped at the superintendent, who towered over him. "Were they even awake?"

The man's words were brave, but the same sickly yellow strand linked Fitch to Gerhard too. He feared both men.

"My guards followed orders to the tee, as they do every day. The question at the heart of this matter, *Fitch*, is how she managed to get out at all. Your officers on site had clear instructions that the room was to remain locked. How could that fail?"

Du Lacigny watched as Fitch took an almost imperceptible backward step as though blown by a gale. "Well, if you had deemed my men worthy of being informed as to *why* it was necessary to hold this person and who our esteemed guest was, then perhaps they might have halted her in the halls!"

"Don't bark at me, you little pup!"

Fitch shrank further.

Guy let out a sigh. "Gerhard, calm yourself."

The hairs on Stefon's neck stood up. Inexplicably, his heart began to pound in his chest.

"The important thing is not that your men were culpable enough to allow her to escape, Fitch. The fact that she *has* escaped has allowed us to identify a mole within our organisation."

"A mole?" Fitch said, stunned. "Here? Why?"

The strands rippled malevolently.

"Because some people in this town—nefarious types, you understand—might not necessarily want to see us become such a successful venture. It's the competitive market at play. Competition is a healthy thing, until our competitors are so poor at performing that they cease to be any real competition at all. Then we'll swallow them up like a Peenian rattlesnake and be richer than the gods.

"Such a situation makes people desperate, capable of anything. Unfortunately, it is also the case that some people may be a little susceptible to coercion, if they happen to have any underlying sympathies toward 'the underdog.'"

A chill swept through Stefon like an icy hand brushing down his spine.

Guy absently kicked a small block of wood as he ruminated. "I can't blame you really, Fitch. Did she flutter her eyelids? Perhaps even show you her curvaceous figure? She's a beautiful woman, in a strange kind of way. It would be easy to fall into her thrall."

Fitch made to stammer a denial, but Guy would not be swayed. Suddenly the dark navy strand flushed to black.

"The problem I have, Fitch"—Guy's voice grew in anger—"is that the one thing I demand above all else is *loyalty*!"

Guy du Lacigny drew his rapier and quickly punched it through Fitch's eye, which burst with a jet of clear fluid. A scream filled the large chamber. His greasy head flinched backward, and blood began to squirt from the ruined socket.

Fitch didn't die straight away. His screams continued to echo up through the eaves of the warehouse and loading bay for what seemed an age, resonating through the building. Every worker in the bay stopped to watch, struck dumb with fear.

The banshee wail of agony cut Stefon to his core. The desperation, the pain, and the fear all washed through him and seemed to go on forever.

A feeling of intense emotion slammed through his body like a wave, rocking him and causing his eyes to roll into his head. He shuddered as a terrible anguish flooded him.

Again, the vision of the woman of shadows flashed before his eyes, her hand reaching to him—not beckoning but imploring, demanding, threatening him. Bright light shone behind her, casting her features into hellish darkness.

Just as it had in the caverns below the building, the waking-dream-seizure passed as abruptly as it had come. Stefon's vision flickered back to reality. The strands were gone.

Fitch's skull slipped lewdly from the thin steel of Guy's sword and dropped to the floor, where his body continued to convulse and shudder.

Finally, the seizure-scream stopped as Gerhard stepped heavily on Fitch's throat, crushing his windpipe and breaking his neck with a sickening crunch. Nevertheless, his left leg continued to twitch.

"Fitch," Guy said to the twitching corpse, "I'm afraid you're fired."

Stefon could feel Rish pulling at his arm, but he couldn't move. His eyes were focused entirely on Guy du Lacigny. In that moment, Guy's loathsome form was Stefon's world.

"Gerhard, get this scum out of my sight. Have the rest of his staff who were on duty last night put to death too, just in case. We can't afford any mistakes."

"Yes, Mr. du Lacigny."

"I trust all our preparations have been made?"

"Yes, Mr. du Lacigny. It has already begun."

"Good. Better fetch a mop too."

Before Rish could even think to react, Stefon sprang to his feet, jumped up onto the balcony railing, and leaped out into the loading area.

He dropped the long distance to the floor with hardly a sound, taking the impact of the landing on his thighs. His strange sword was already in his hand, singing mysteriously in the darkness of the warehouse. The blade seemed to glow a fierce, angry red, as though fresh from the blacksmith's forge. The mysterious, guttural thrum filled the room like a growl.

Gerhard and du Lacigny recoiled in surprise. Gerhard recovered his composure first, drawing his wicked curved sabre and stepping between Guy du Lacigny and Stefon protectively, the weapon levelled at Stefon.

Above them, Rish turned away from the balcony and out of sight.

Ignoring the balcony, Guy said, "Ah, Stefon, what an annoying surprise. I don't believe we've been formally introduced." His smile was a cold lacquer of deceitful confidence, but Stefon could tell he was scared.

Stefon stayed low to the ground, his left hand touching the floor and the sword held out to the side, singing malevolently.

"Am I to deduce from your rather unexpected arrival here that you are launching a disturbing sideline in burglary? You are the second such thieving pest I have snared this week!"

Stefon remained low, mindful of his surroundings. The other workers in the bay were still watching, but none were running over to interfere. Instead, a few had moved to the exits. The majority remained where they were, caught like startled vermin, clearly worried but too fascinated to run.

"Or perhaps you have come to rescue your friend? Maybe to beg for her life? I can only assume you have overheard—or rather listened in on—our little discussion here and now know that your rescue attempt is futile. Coral has already fled."

As du Lacigny spoke, Stefon watched Gerhard closely; the bunched muscles in his arms, the racing pulse in his neck, the red flush of his cheeks. The way he held his sword levelled steadily at Stefon told him he faced a capable swordsman.

"But I am glad you're here, Stefon, despite how angry I might be about precisely *how* you managed to get this close to me without discovery." The barb—directed at the superintendent—made Gerhard's cheek twitch.

Guy stepped around his employee, his own sword now levelled at Stefon. Fitch's blood still dripped from the tip. He was no more than six feet away.

"Still, every cloud and all that! With you here, I don't have to go out and have you killed. I knew you and your friends were instrumental in galvanising the independent traders against me. Everything seemed to change when you turned up. I can't say I'm very happy about that. You have been meddlesome, indeed, for a Choat newcomer. The thing I didn't know was just precisely who it was that you managed to turn against me. Some of my competitors might just still be stubborn, and they hardly deserve to die for that, but I fear most have been coerced by both you and that bitch Coral to resist my conglomerate venture.

"However, her escape has helped me root out the mole in my operation . . ."—he nodded at Fitch's dead body, which had finally stopped twitching—"I've actually achieved much more than that. Coral is talented, for sure, but I *allowed* the mole to arrange her escape. Now, when she unknowingly leads Gerhard's men to her allies in Choat Market, I will have your little traders' rebellion put down for good."

So, thought Stefon, *Coral hasn't betrayed us, after all.*

"Don't think for one second that the City Guard or militia will help your friends, either; they know which side their bread is buttered. I imagine they are completely surrounded by now, and should be dead by noon.

"And to cap it all, you have found your way here, little hero, and I have the convenient opportunity to run you through myself."

Guy du Lacigny planned it all. Would Coral be naïve enough to go straight back to the market? Surely, she would know she could be followed?

But it would be reasonable for her to assume du Lacigny had no knowledge of her escape, let alone had arranged for it to occur. And Coral believed in this rebellion more than anyone else, perhaps even more than Stefon and his friend. She would know how much her abduction would have hurt her allies, might even suspect that it could cause the alliance to crumble. Stefon was sure Coral would rush back to the market and round them up. Hell, that had been their own plan!

And then du Lacigny's hired goons would decimate them. Pryn would probably be there, but he was just one man. It would be brutal and swift.

"I rule this city, you worm!" Guy snarled. "I'm the one with the power. I will decide who profits and who suffers! I will decide who stays and who goes! I will decide who lives and who dies!"

With two quick steps forward, Guy drove his rapier toward Stefon's heart.

Stefon drew his blade up in an arc, deflecting the attack high overhead. He had to step quickly to the right to evade Gerhard's coordinated jab at his guts, stopping the two from flanking him.

He circled them in a low stance, the pulsing blade held above his head, the point directed at Guy's throat. Gerhard stepped to Stefon's right, Guy to his left.

Without communicating, the two lunged forward in a coordinated attack. Stefon was forced to hop backward, deflecting a high rapier jab and a low swipe of the sabre. Sparks flew from the collisions.

With blinding speed, he lashed out twice to the left, making Guy block hastily. The little man's expression betrayed his surprise at Stefon's speed and power.

He struck again at Guy and then ducked low under Gerhard's sabre strike at his head.

Stefon rolled on the ball of his foot and twisted at the waist. Two quick kicks ploughed into Gerhard's chest and face, rocking the superintendent back.

Du Lacigny was no powerhouse, but he was clearly skilled with the rapier, a weapon of some finesse often favoured by nobles. Gerhard was a different consideration, though—strong as an ox, big as a house, and deceptively fast.

Again, the pair charged him, Guy feigning an attack as Gerhard struck at Stefon's midriff, tearing a rip in the cloth as the blade grazed Stefon's ribs. A little blood seeped into his damp tunic.

The pain only served to focus Stefon, who jumped forward unexpectedly, driving a kick and then a knee into Gerhard's ribs. The superintendent staggered back under the onslaught as Stefon caught Guy's next attack on his sword. He had to dodge sharply as Guy produced a hidden dagger and slashed at his stomach, adding another cut to the first.

Stefon should have been skewered by the attack. It was as though his reactions were not entirely his own. He moved to block the strike before the attack began, as though seeing it before it happened.

If he even had the slimmest chance to get to the market and help stop the attack on the others, then he had to end this quickly. Guy's brow was already stippled with the sweat of exertion, but Gerhard was hardly breathing heavily.

Stefon lunged forward and slammed his sword into Guy's hasty block, hacked at Gerhard, and then at Guy again, but their defence was too good.

And Stefon had made a mistake; he had insinuated himself between them.

He was flanked.

Hurriedly, he tried to extricate himself, but felt Gerhard's huge arm thump into his head with a backhand swipe. It dazed him, and he stumbled and then rolled into a nearby cart, sending a couple of bottles tumbling to the floor. One broke while the rest rolled noisily on the stone floor. Stefon dropped his sword by his side.

Approaching, Gerhard snatched up a bottle and threw it at Stefon, who ducked. The bottle smashed against the cart. Shards of broken glass showered over Stefon. Reflexively, he swept an open hand through the air above himself. He felt a rush in his hand, and the shower of shards was impossibly propelled away as though blown by a strong wind. No glass touched him.

Du Lacigny hesitated, perhaps unsure of what he'd seen, but Gerhard didn't even seem to notice. Instead, he jumped at Stefon, swinging the sabre blade at his head. Stefon lifted his left arm to block the attack, though the blade would surely sever his arm. But the blade struck him as though his limb was made of steel.

Stefon slammed his right palm into Gerhard's solar plexus, shouting as he tried to exert all the power of his being into the unarmed strike.

His right hand—palm open—thumped into an invisible barrier a mere inch from Gerhard's chest. There was an explosion of energy between them. The superintendent's body was hurled away high into the air, and he uttered a confused wail.

Instinctively, Stefon reached out with his left hand, grasping at the invisible fibres of existence between him and his victim. Gerhard's propulsion was stopped mid-flight. Stefon pulled the strands of reality toward himself as a child might pull a kite, and *willed* his sword to his right hand.

Gerhard shouted in panic as he spun back toward Stefon, held in his invisible grip. Guy watched aghast as Stefon sliced his sword clean through the tumbling superintendent, cutting him effortlessly in twain. The torso thumped heavily into the wheel of the wagon, and the hips and legs flipped over the top. Blood splashed across the floor, and Gerhard's guts tumbled from his rent carcass.

Stefon stepped away from the mess, twirling his sword, the strange thrumming echoing around him. Power coursed through his limbs as it never had before. He could feel an unnatural force burning through him like the sun—for the first time an unnatural but *controllable* force!

Guy du Lacigny took a step back as Rish and Jewl appeared at a nearby doorway, barging past the fleeing bay workers.

"How . . . how?" stammered Guy. "That's . . . It's not possible!"

Stefon refused to acknowledge his words, drawing his strange sword back behind him like a discus thrower before hurling it at Guy du Lacigny. His quarry tried to run, tried to duck, tried *anything*, but the blade seemed to follow him. Spinning in a colourful blur, the sword cleaved through his neck, cutting off a wail of terror.

As Rish and Jewl looked on, the blade whirled around in a graceful arc and returned to Stefon's waiting hand. Guy's headless corpse dropped to the floor.

Stefon didn't stand to admire or celebrate, walking toward his friends whilst putting his sword away. Not even a speck of blood stained the blade. The loading bay was thrown back to its former drab darkness.

"We've got a bit of a situation, lads," he said, his voice seeming to resonate throughout the chamber.

Chapter Twenty-Six

The Seers Return

Sunrise painted the sky over the Choatian Basin a deep crimson with the reflected glory of the coming day. Notwithstanding the promise of the rising sun, the air carried the bitter slice of an icy wind blowing down from the Northern Ranges. It would be a bright day, but a cold one. Winter was well and truly upon them.

Despite the chillness, Stefon, Rish, and Jewl were sweating like fell runners as their feet pounded the morning dew from the cobbles of Choat.

It was surprising how fast Guy du Lacigny's organisation had crumbled following his demise. The three had made quick their escape from the facility, but rumours of Guy's death and the presence of some avenging angel in the loading bay had spread faster than they could flee. Workers from the loading bay ran from the building, fearful for their own lives; any guards they encountered had no interest in trying to stop anyone, especially considering most had probably committed certain indiscretions at du Lacigny's orders, and now feared the blanket of protection afforded to them by that relationship had been pulled aside.

So, exiting the facility had proven much easier than getting in, yet Brooss was nowhere to be seen. They had scouted about for a few minutes, but neither the wagon nor Brooss had been in the agreed location.

With Rish's concern for Brooss painfully obvious, they had taken to their heels, pushing every sinew and muscle in their bodies to get to the market before du Lacigny's trap was sprung. They bustled past startled bakers, agile street urchins, and lacklustre City Watchmen, no one seeking to stop them.

As they neared the streets around the market quarter, their breath came in ragged gasps and they must have stunk like horses. On the morning air, caught on a chill breeze, they heard the sounds of conflict in the market ahead.

Stefon led them into a small alley, at the terminus of which they entered a tanner's, the new stench pinching their noses and making their eyes water. They pressed on, hurrying toward the sounds of battle.

They slammed through a door, the hinges protesting loudly, and were presented with a grim vision through the front window. The market was a maelstrom of flashing blades, buckling shields, impromptu clubs, and hastily turned market stalls, the latter being used as cover by innocent bystanders caught up in the conflict.

"My god," muttered Rish. "It's a battlefield."

Stefon glimpsed familiar faces throughout the market, all defending themselves against attack by innumerable thugs dressed in dark blue tabards and wielding wicked weapons.

"Quickly," urged Stefon. "It looks like most of the privateers mustered out of the safehouses before they were attacked. They're all over the marketplace!" They ran across the tanner's shop, slamming through an adjoining door and out onto a lane.

The abruptness of the crashing door elicited a chorus of screams. The lane was cluttered with cowering forms taking refuge from the battle. Stefon held the door open and started to usher the scared people inside. "Out the back," he told them as they passed. "Don't stop; keep running."

Just as the last few were filtering past, two armed figures blocked the dawn light from the end of the lane. It was Brooss, accompanied by Coral.

"Brooss!" shouted Rish, gathering the dark-haired engineer in a hug as Stefon completed the exodus of innocents. It took Rish a second to remember himself and step away from her, clearly embarrassed at having made such an open expression of relief and affection. Stefon wasn't surprised.

"You're alive, then," said Stefon to Coral with a lopsided grin, genuinely happy for it.

"I am," replied Coral. "No thanks to Guy and his goons."

Jewl pulled his axe free of his pack and brandished it, ready to launch into the fray. "All this is your fault! You led them straight here!"

Coral regarded the dwarf calmly. "Things had to come to a head in this city. The situation could not continue as it was, for Guy du Lacigny was winning. With each passing hour, our rebellion was weaker. This battle was always going to be unavoidable and is the only way we can wrestle control of shipping and trade back from du Lacigny."

Jewl was incredulous. "You got kidnapped on purpose? Just so you could lead Guy's men here?"

"Not entirely," she confessed. "But once Fitch released me, I realised I would most probably be followed. This was du Lacigny showing his hand. Fitch has been an ally to us from the start, but such men are often unreliable. With this trap having been sprung, I can only assume it is because Fitch has turned on us."

"Fitch is dead," Rish told her plainly. "Guy murdered him right in front of us, and not pleasantly. He had no idea you would be followed."

Coral was quiet for a moment. "You were there?"

"Yes, we went to rescue you," Rish said. He glanced at Stefon and then said to Coral, "You should have told us you had a man on the inside. Perhaps we could have used such a connection a little better."

Coral looked at Stefon and then quickly away. "In any event," she continued, "when I fled, I knew I would most probably be followed, so I had a decision to make. I knew leading them here would result in this battle, but had I led them away and sacrificed myself, our rebellion would have fallen anyway, my life would have been given for nothing, and du Lacigny would benefit from it all. I knew Pryn was with the others down here somewhere, although I had no idea where you were. And obviously, I couldn't have anticipated that Guy would set his entire force against us."

"Guy's dead too," Rish told her flatly. "We don't need a rebellion anymore. These goons are acting on orders from a man who no longer exists and a consortium that is busy tearing itself to pieces as we speak!"

Coral looked at Stefon, rightly deducing that it had been he who had slain du Lacigny. Stefon, for his part, remained silent. He could see Coral felt something at the mistakes she'd made, but so aloof was her natural demeanour that it was impossible to tell what it was. He got the sense that she still believed that what was occurring behind her was unavoidable, inevitable.

Stefon looked hard at the gambler. "You're a fatalist, aren't you?"

"To a certain extent, I believe choice is illusion, yes."

"What's a fatalist?" Jewl asked.

"You don't regret your actions because you don't believe there was any other way," said Stefon testily. "It's a rather convenient view of the world that gives the fatalist the freedom to shirk their responsibilities."

"Destiny is destiny, Stefon—preordained. You can't avoid it, try as you will. If you don't seek out your own, it will find you in the end."

Stefon somehow felt her words were loaded with subtext, but he had no time to consider it.

Apparently Rish felt a similar way. "The lives being lost out there"—Rish jabbed his short sword at the market—"are all being lost for nothing. Fate and destiny be damned; we need to retrieve our friends and flee the market. Once out of this cauldron, things will quickly dissipate."

"Agreed," said Coral firmly. "I had not foreseen Guy's death. It changes everything."

"That's the problem with fatalism," said Stefon. "You can't be wrong, even when you are. Destiny or not, no one can see the future."

Coral laughed at that, though there was no humour in it. "We'll speak of that later," she said. "Right now, we have a real challenge on, breaking up this riot."

"Can we raise the alarm with the city watch or whoever?" Jewl asked.

"They've sealed the market," she said. "Standard behaviour in situations of large scale civil unrest."

"What!" snapped Rish.

"It's how they manage riots, I assume?" Stefon asked, to which she nodded. "Contain it, starve it of interference, like starving a flame of oxygen. Where's Pryn?"

"He's out there trying to organise the defences," Coral told him. "We were here protecting those women and children."

"So only we can stop all our friends ending up dead in the street?" Rish said plaintively. "We're only three."

"Five," said Brooss bravely.

"It's still not likely to be enough," said Jewl.

And that was how it was—as simple and as black and white as anything in Stefon's world these days. He had a choice. One of two—he could turn and walk away, leaving these people to sort their own mess and fight for themselves; or, he could stand and fight with them . . . *for* them . . . and for his friends. Stefon had always been a rogue and a mercenary, but neither of the two choices available could ever present him with any kind of payoff. Just like Wahib all over again.

A true mercenary would walk away.

"There isn't even a choice to be made," he muttered as much to himself as anyone. "We can't stand idly by while the people we brought into this are wiped out."

"Look out there!" Jewl retorted. "It's a meat grinder!"

"That doesn't matter anymore," said Rish. "The fact is, we either stand and fight or run and hide, whether we number five or five hundred."

"But du Lacigny is dead. Who is there to hide from?" Jewl asked.

Stefon stepped between the arguing pair and headed for the entrance to the market. "If you walk away from this, you'll never be able to hide from yourself." He reached the end of the lane and drew his sword, now glowing a vibrant green in the morning light. With his back to the others, he said, "I'm sick of sleepless nights and poisoned dreams. I'm sick of sitting idly by while evil people get away with evil deeds. I won't let it end like this while there's still something I can do about it."

Rish stepped up next to his friend, Brooss following behind. "Then let's end it a different way. What are your orders?"

Stefon glanced at Rish as the rest fell into step behind him, Jewl included.

"Pryn and most of the marketers are trapped in the middle of the square itself," Coral told him, glancing at the mysterious sword. "They're using the broken stalls for defence and keeping the thugs at bay using ranged fire from the few bows they have, but it won't be long until they've run out of arrows.

"The attackers are preoccupied by a number of roaming bands outside of that defensive perimeter. We were tracking Cayden and his group when you arrived. They're moving about the outer market, trying to break up the attackers' coordination, but without help, they won't last long. There is a second group led by Greel on the far side. They are larger in number than Cayden's crew but are getting pinned down."

Stefon looked up to the sky. Dawn had fully broken now, the sun a blood red.

"Okay. We move in a tight formation, me at the lead. Move in pairs when you can; Jewl and Coral to the right, Rish and Brooss to the left." Rish nodded appreciatively. "We need to get to Cayden and then break through to the centre of the square."

Rish nodded. "We've just got to hope Pryn and the guys in the middle don't mistake us for baddies and shoot us first."

With a shrug, Stefon raised his strangely glowing sword pointedly. "Hopefully they should see us coming." Then he turned and ran out into the open.

As they moved out after him, Stefon heard Coral ask Jewl, "I thought he said to move in pairs. Shouldn't someone go with him?"

The dwarf just laughed.

Hopping down a short step, they all rushed into the disarray of the market, driving for the space Coral had said she had last seen Cayden. It took a moment for the enemy to realise that reinforcements had arrived, but when they did, the uniformed thugs converged on them.

Stefon vaulted a broken trestle table and slashed a man's throat with his sword, blood squirting from his ruined neck. With a spin, he ducked a second attack to plunge his blade deep into the stomach of the next assailant. The man's eyes bulged, and gore jetted from between clenched teeth.

Three more approached.

Stefon dragged the blade free of his second victim as he began to fall. Tensing every muscle and sinew in his body to draw on his strange power, he completed a full turn and then swept his off hand through the air before him.

A blast of invisible energy propelled the falling corpse into the advancing three. Shattered stalls and injured men scattered across the market as the body flew thirty yards, the debris hurled back by the same strange power Stefon now commanded.

It was fair to say the whole market would now know another threat had arrived.

Following in the wake of the maelstrom, Rish and Brooss forced other attackers back by more conventional means. Using their swords to block and parry close-hand attacks, the two were able to defend their flank. Coral and Jewl, on the right side, were causing decidedly more damage with their longer weapons, producing a few more bodies.

Ahead of their wedge formation, Stefon could make out Cayden and a few of his entourage pinned down by two thugs armed with crossbows. The attackers had their backs to Stefon. Beyond this pair, two more could be seen crawling between ruined stalls, sneaking toward Cayden's position. They were using the cover to avoid being picked off by trader arrows from the central square, but so far, Cayden hadn't seen them. A fallen wagon separated the two crossbowmen from Stefon.

Power surged through his limbs as he pumped his arms into a run, the sword light as air in his hand. He sprang for the wagon, landed with feline agility, and then propelled himself effortlessly into the air, impossibly high.

Rish looked up in time to see the two crossbowmen startled by the clattering of the now-empty wagon behind them. Stefon had disappeared from sight. The men glanced back and across at Rish and Brooss, immediately realising they were being flanked.

Suddenly Stefon dropped from an impossible leap, landing on one knee and slamming his sword clean through the first crossbowman from skull to tail. Blood sprayed into the air, and all nearby debris was cast asunder by the explosive force of his strike.

As Rish looked on, struck dumb with fascination, Stefon wasted no time in jabbing the glowing green blade into the second crossbowman's chest and then head in quick succession, ending his life without a sound.

The two crawling comrades of the fallen crossbowmen looked back in sudden terror and began scrambling out from under the stalls they were using as cover.

Too late.

Fury was etched across Stefon's face as he reached into the air with his left hand, fingers stretched out to the heavens, and then pulled his hand down toward the ground, balling his fingers into a shaking white fist.

With a splintering, terrifying wrench, the stalls shattered and collapsed down on the hapless men, as though crushed by a great and invisible weight. Hundreds of giant splinters skewered and impaled the pair. Their screams filled the air. The echoes of the crash reverberated around the market.

A blood-splattered murdering machine, Stefon jumped across the decimated bodies and engaged two more souls, who were dispatched with equally dispassionate, inhuman speed.

Rish hurried along behind his marauding friend, reaching Cayden in a bounding run as Stefon forged ahead of them. “Cayden, my friend, I’m glad you’re alive.”

“As am I!” He pulled his vest loose and threw it down, the material having become torn during the battle. “What took you so long? We had no idea where you lot were. Greel thought you’d abandoned us.”

They made to follow Stefon as Jewl and Coral coordinated the last of Cayden’s band. Rish shrugged. “We might be late, but we usually turn up in the end, and we try to make a difference when we do.”

“Lord of the Understatement,” Cayden said as he pointed at Stefon, who continued his devastating onslaught.

They reached the centre of the market square, the rebel traders trying desperately to remain in cover as the attackers peppered the hastily erected defensive earthworks with bolts and arrows. As Stefon and the rest rushed toward the enemy, the impromptu fortification gave under the pressure and the defenders were forced to skirmish backward, using their bows to defend themselves in hand-to-hand combat.

Stefon became a blur as he shot forward, passing two attackers who screamed when he sliced their hamstrings to the bone. Rish hardly even saw the blade move; it was just a swirling green dance, like the northern lights of spring.

With increased vigour, Jewl and Coral cleaved into the gap behind Stefon, cutting into the attackers when their backs were turned. Rish and Brooss made short work of the outer elements. Once inside the brattice work centre, Stefon slashed through the next opponent, his chest ripped open and his head lopped cleanly from his neck.

By the time Rish and Coral had entered the square, both could see Stefon’s rage flush in his cheeks as he crouched in the middle of the market, staring at the last of du Lacigny’s hired men. Their friend's demeanour reeked of murderous malevolence; bloody, steaming carcasses littered the whole market.

The last man standing was a tall captain with arms bigger than Rish's waist. He hefted a mighty war hammer and turned on Stefon, who must have seemed like a bothersome mosquito to him. Though outnumbered, the captain nonetheless raised the hammer to swat this new pest.

Stefon's left hand reached out toward him, and his fingers curled, forming an unnatural grip as though crushing a rotten fruit.

The man immediately dropped his massive hammer with a loud clatter, shattering flagstones. He grappled at his neck, straining to release some invisible grip around his throat.

Stefon's arm shook with exertion, the veins of his muscles bulging like cords as he raised his hand higher into the air, standing straight and elegant with his sword held at his side.

Coral and Rish stepped toward him but stopped short, for his body seemed superheated, the air around him quivering like a desert mirage. The pair exchanged a glance. Coral's eyes were wide with wonder . . . and something else.

The throttled man uttered desperate sounds of choking, spittle bubbling at his lips. His mouth opened and closed like a floundering trout as he was lifted into the air, held by an unseen fist. His eyes rolled into his head. They could see the larynx and spine crumbling. A muffled crunch of breaking bone and cartilage crackled from his neck, and his limbs dropped limply to his sides.

With disdain, Stefon whipped his left hand down, releasing his impossible grip. The suspended captain's dead body was thrown into the ground, more bones broken by the impact and blood spraying from his tattered throat. His head hung loosely from the ruins of his spine.

Stefon stood for a moment, shoulders hunched, breathing heavily. His huffing breath hung in clouds on the chill air of the morning.

They could hear the clash of weapons outside the defensive perimeter, but for now, there was calm in the central area as Brooss and Jewl reorganised the defenders. They could see Pryn nearby doing likewise.

Rish felt the need to take command. The look of fear on Cayden's face in particular worried the scoundrel. "Jewl!" he barked. "Sort out Cayden's band of ragamuffins. They need to get over that far wall and fight through to Greel's men. Take Pryn with you.

"Brooss, get these archers formed up into two teams, the first to cover Jewl's team and the second to repair that hole we just made."

Brooss nodded once, her pale face loaned a golden hue by the dawn light. She went about her business. Rish felt a surge of pride for her.

Jewl bustled past Stefon as their leader turned toward them, now holding a blood-speckled hand to his mouth and staring ahead as though seeing into the distance, a look of abject horror on his face. He replaced his sword in his scabbard, cutting off the fearsome thrumming sound, and stepped toward them like a broken puppet.

Rish pulled an upturned carton toward him for Stefon to sit on. He was clearly dazed. "Sit down," Rish told him softly. "You look knackered."

His friend took a seat. Coral and Rish knelt nearby and waited for Stefon to speak. When he didn't, Rish felt he needed to press his friend.

"It's getting worse," Rish said. It wasn't a question.

"I can't explain it," Stefon muttered quietly.

"Well, you'd better," insisted Coral. "I've never seen anyone leap fifty feet into the air and then thunder down on someone like that. Your strange sword cut a man clean in half. Do you draw these powers from that? I've never seen a sword that glows like that."

Rish could see his friend hesitate, and knew Stefon was considering a lie. He could see it in his face. Then the expression passed, and he clearly decided to gamble on the truth as the sounds of conflict continued around them.

"No, I don't think so. It's something else. I was recently accused of being something more than human; in fact, I was hunted for that belief. Religious zealots in Wahib tried to kill us all, mainly for interfering in their plans, but ultimately because they believed I was becoming something they called a Seer. I'd never heard the term before, but they were convinced of it."

Stefon paused, and Rish noticed that the sounds of conflict had begun to dissipate around the market, the cries of battle melting away to be replaced by the moans of the injured. Soon, the city watch would descend on the square and begin making hasty arrests—and they wouldn't bother to make sure they were actually arresting the guilty.

"I had already started to show certain abilities before picking up this sword, and having strange dreams. These Seers were supposed to be some cross-species anomaly that could perform amazing physical feats at will. There could have been Seer elves or Seer dwarves . . . All sentient beings were able to manifest these abilities. They're supposed to be extinct, but the leader of *The Light* in Wahib think I am one. The only one."

Rish watched as Coral's face changed from wonder and concern to a look of dawning realisation, as though suddenly hitting upon the solution to some infuriating puzzle. When she spoke next, her voice betrayed the fact that her thoughts were far away. "Seers were so-called because they were reputed to see the future. Legend says many were driven mad by visions."

"*You've* heard of them?" asked Rish.

"In passing," she admitted. "What I've read described them more as troublesome false prophets than a powerful race, but those were religious texts and prone to prejudice; it would not have been in their interests to present a balanced portrayal. It was written that these Seers died out centuries ago. There's even conjecture that they may not have existed at all."

Stefon coughed to interrupt. "Lesjac told me that The Light wiped them out at a battle called the Rout of the Dranon Seers. Whatever the truth, I'd hoped my visions were some side effect of the plague, but since we escaped Wahib, my powers have grown in strength, as have the visions. Lately I've even had waking dreams, like seizures. Just now, when I made the mess here in the market, I felt the world around me become something different, as if I can sense strands between everything—fibres of existence. And I can interact with those fibres, command them, control them. I felt control!"

"Control of your powers?" Coral asked, rapt.

"Control of everything."

"While I was aware of destroying those men, it was more like some remote view or projection. My vision was also swamped by waking dreams, images upon images. Like shadow puppets cast upon the world around me."

"What are the dreams of?" Coral asked.

Rish looked over the defensive perimeter as Stefon fought for an answer. He could see the fight was coming to an end. He saw Pryn striding purposefully toward them, Jewl at his side. The huge human was covered in gore. They were leading Cayden, Greel, and their men back to the market centre, and the city watch were starting to filter through the outer stalls. The fight was over. "We need to flee," he told them.

Quickly they gathered their weapons as Jewl came barrelling past them, shouting, "I hope you're all comfortable!"

"We're alive, dwarf!"

Jewl scowled at Rish as he led the survivors from the market. The skirmish had taken its toll on their numbers, but it would have been a massacre but for Stefon's intervention. That much was obvious. "Brooss, cover our retreat; we make for the tanner's!" She nodded once.

Rish, Stefon, and Coral hurried along the path to the tanner's shop. They could hear shouts of alarm at the sheer scale of death and destruction that had been caused by the riot.

They ran at their fastest into the lane, through the side door of the tanner's, and out the back of the shop, following the path the bystanders of the market had taken.

They slowed to a jog and then an exhausted walk through the back streets in the crisp dawn air until they came across a small square with a fountain. They gathered around the pool of water and began washing the blood from their hands and arms. As they did so, Coral pressed her unanswered question once more.

"What are the visions of, Stefon?"

"Why are you so interested?" asked Rish.

"Because I may know a thing or two, that's why!" she asserted. "I might be able to help."

"Rish, it's all right," Stefon told him.

Rish's heart still thundered from the fight, but by contrast, Stefon was now the picture of composure. Only that haunted shadow in his eyes belied the recent exertions.

"The earlier visions showed me standing atop a mountain in the middle of this continent, and the land is ravaged by pestilence and populated by an army of the undead. Sometimes that horde of warriors turned toward me as though the vision was real. More recently, I see a woman constructed of shadows who beckons to me. I don't know who she is. It's always variations on the same thing."

With renewed vigour, Coral seized Stefon's shoulders. "Stefon, I believe this Lesjac is right; you *are* a Seer, and I'm afraid that things are only going to get worse for you. I may be able to help you when that time comes, but there is more at stake than just you right now."

"You're not just a gambler and trader," said Stefon. It was an accusation, not a question. Rish's hand hovered near his sword handle. If the words *The Light* came out of her mouth, they would be her last.

Finally, Coral shook her head. "I am a student of philosophy, some might say. I trade as I travel to make a living, but it is not my calling. My teacher and I know of a prophecy, and I believe you may be destined to play a part. It's the very reason I was involved in Susu-Van's trading company at all. My master believes that a shadow grows in the east. An enemy known only as The Harbinger rises. He also believes that hope will likewise rise in the east, coming west in our hour of greatest need. We believe they will not know themselves to be blessed with such a destiny."

"Destiny again!" Stefon snapped. "Blessed! Prophecy! Enough!"

"Hang on," interrupted Rish. "If you really do believe that fate and destiny are predetermined, why do you even bother gambling?"

Coral ignored his facetious question. "My teacher and I never even imagined that a Seer could be involved in this prophecy. We never even considered it a feasible possibility. But if you are a Seer, and you are the hope we're searching for, then this could change everything."

Rish stepped into Coral's line of sight, forcing her to release her grip on Stefon's shoulders. "Who is your teacher? What is this prophecy?"

"Knowing or understanding the prophecy itself doesn't matter much right now. The fact that Stefon *sees* the lands here under the tread of the undead may mean that we're already lost, for Seers are famed for seeing the future."

"Hence their name?" Everyone ignored Jewl.

"You think I'm seeing the future? A world dominated by the undead?"

Coral never took her eyes from Stefon. "I believe it is one of many possible futures. That you see this future so strongly can only mean it is a future towards which we now rush. But we can change that future, if we act."

"I'm not sure that's how a fatalist is supposed to see the world," Rish threw in. "Destiny is destiny, no?"

"Of course it is! But one must find one's own destiny. It is the illusion of choice!"

"That doesn't make sense."

"Look! While you remain here, trying to avoid what you must come to terms with, this future you see will remain *our* future. You must leave Choat immediately. Head for the western duchies of Shenmadock. Follow your heart and your dark visions. Find this woman of shadow. I think she may hold the key to your destiny, and I get the feeling she will need your help. If you stay here, you will go slowly mad, a madness that will quickly consume you. You must act, Stefon. Follow your heart."

She looked around them and said, "We need to get off the street and somewhere safe while the aftermath of this riot blows over. There are things you both need to hear before you make plans to leave Choat."

"I'm tired of running," Stefon complained. "I've spent my whole life running from one thing or another."

"I know, Stefon. But for the first time in your life, you'll not be running away; you'll be chasing after your destiny."

Chapter Twenty-Seven
Miller's Folly

An icy chill rushed at Dale's back as the winter wind pushed across the plains behind him. He couldn't help the feeling that the spiders running up his spine were only half due to the weather. It had been barely four days since they had fled Adar, and their horses were all but exhausted.

Winter had slammed down upon them like a blanket of ice needles, the heavy clouds overhead blocking out the distant sun and hurling the horizon into a gloomy mist. Very quickly, mist and fog had obscured the land all about them, chilling the bones of the refugees and making the ground underfoot all the more treacherous. They had toyed with the idea of avoiding the roads in hope of hiding their trail, but had quickly deemed the effort to be futile. Speed was of the essence now.

When the wind at his back brought heavier sleet and the temperature plummeted, the soldiers had agreed to seek the shelter of Miller's Folly, an ancient stone watchtower that sat atop a craggy hill some distance south of the town of Miller's Brook. There were no nearby settlements, and the folly was known to be abandoned. It also marked the halfway point to the capital from Adar.

With visibility rapidly declining, they began their climb to the folly, walking alongside an old hand-built stone wall, the damp grasses around them a drab olive in the dull daylight. Passing through a fallen section of the wall, they were forced to hobble the horses and allow them to crop the wet grass in the inclement weather while the group continued up the steep rise on foot.

The fog altered the quality of the sounds of the day, lending the scene an eerie air. They could hear crows nearby but could see none. Here and there, hares or rats ran for cover as the booted humans made for the short summit.

Dale led the way, picking a stable path between crumbling rock and slippery grasses until finally, out of the fog above them, the dim shape of Miller's Folly emerged. Dale drew his sword; he couldn't help it. The sound of the metal ringing from the scabbard was resonant in the dankness.

He continued forward, his eyes scanning the nearby foliage for any threat, all the while periodically sparing glances up at the folly as it took on a sharper aspect. With every step, the incline became steeper, until finally, they had to help the weaker refugees up to the steps of the folly in a human chain.

Dale signalled a halt when he reached the old stone steps. Leaving the group huddling in the increasing cold, and with sword at the ready, he edged up the half-dozen steps to the narrow opening at the base of the old watchtower.

He moved through the doorway and allowed his eyes to adjust to the deeper gloom within. Easily standing above sixty feet tall at its base, the watchtower spanned an area of at least eighteen square yards. The building was in total disrepair, the shattered remnants of whatever furniture had once been used here scattered across the ground. Weak-looking stairs led up to the next floor, and he could hear more crows somewhere above—or maybe they were the same crows.

It was empty within.

Signalling the refugees and replacing his sword in his scabbard, Dale looked around at the somewhat familiar building. He knew the views, on a better day, would have been impressive, but with the thick fog, there was nothing to be seen save a shifting vista of grey.

"Did I hear you call this place a folly?" Aleks asked Dale, once the refugees were safely inside and eating rations. A heavy, sleet-filled rain had begun to fall.

Dale nodded. "It's a bit of a misnomer."

"Clearly. I can't imagine the place being used for anything fun or entertaining. More of a defensive watchtower. Looks like a while since it's been in use."

"It was originally built as a watchtower; you're right. This craggy little peak marks the highest point on a small string of hills that run northeast to southwest. The watchtower was the last of the strongholds we've passed along the way. When our duchies were all separate nations, or simply districts constantly at war, these strongholds were key to protecting the territory northwest of here. This ridge marked the northwest boundary of the lands populated by the early Un peoples—the ancestors of those who originally raised the nation of Unedar, which later ceded to Shenmadock and became the duchy of the same name."

"You sound like a history teacher."

"When I came to the city, I really missed my homeland," Dale admitted. "I ended up reading as much as I could about the history of Unedar. It helped me cope."

"That was my idea," offered Guardigan as he walked past the pair, carrying a spare blanket to an old couple shivering in the corner. "Surprisingly, I didn't have to teach the idiot how to read."

"*You* can read?" quipped Corn, following just a step behind Guardigan and carrying a sleeping infant.

Aleks laughed and then said, "Obviously I know plenty about the strongholds hereabouts—kind of have to, in our line of work. But why is it called a folly?"

"The village to the north, Miller's Brook, sprang up decades after the watchtower had fallen into disuse. There stood a large farmstead upon a small brook that was owned by—"

"Some millers?" interrupted the Wayfarer.

"A family of millers, really. They became the landlords, and generations later, the mayors of the town that grew up around the small brook. Sometime later, Mayor Thomas Miller, the last of his line, lost his wife and only son in a terrible accident. Thomas lost his mind and abandoned his position, retreating to the watchtower many miles south of Miller's Brook. Here he remained for the rest of his days, writing poetry and foraging for food. Ramblers discovered his body some years after his death, with page upon page of poetry, most of which was erased by exposure to the elements. The majority of what was rescued sold quite well, although we'll never know where his mind was wandering to, in his madness.

"The locals from Miller's Brook adopted the old watchtower and renamed it Miller's Folly in his memory."

"Folly referring to his wasted years more than the structure, I guess?" Aleks asked.

"I think so."

"Sad story."

"Pointless, more like," declared Guardigan. "We've more pressing matters, don't you think? We have a decision to make."

Dale sipped from his flask and handed it to Aleks, whose ice-chilled face expressed his worry. To his credit, Aleks didn't voice any of his concerns. His colleague Corn, standing near Guardigan, was not so sensible.

"It's impossible," he complained, stamping his feet against the cold. "These refugees are slowing us down. Not all of them, but definitely the old and sick. We should give them a weapon each and leave them here in the watchtower—"

Guardigan's fist clamping around Corn's throat ceased his complaining. "Bite your tongue, coward!".

They were all getting tired, Dale knew, and Guardigan's patience was wearing thinner than most.

It was a Wayfarer trait to be willing to trade the lives of a few to secure the lives of the many, all without denting their conscience. It often made them difficult to deal with, aloof.

Even with Guardigan's meaty fist clamped around his neck, Corn didn't display any anger. His grey eyes were fixed on Guardigan, as though simply watching what he would do next. It was a rare thing for anyone to manhandle a Wayfarer with impunity.

"Easy, Guardigan," warned Aleks softly. "Corn's no coward; he's just thinking out loud."

Corn allowed himself to be pushed away as Guardigan released his grip.

Aleks led them out of earshot of the refugees, over to the doorway that looked out on the southern vista. There wasn't much of a view on such a grey day. "We have two decisions to make and no time to waste. Like it or not, Corn's right. The frailer refugees are slowing us down; we must consider what to do with them for the greater good. Further, the road to the capital from Adar takes us past no settlements large enough to house a garrison. So even if we chose to leave them somewhere, the choices are slim to none.

"This leads me to the second question—what are we doing? When we fled Adar, our purpose was to put as much distance between ourselves and that army as we could; we've done that so far. But if they dispatched scouts, then—with our current composition—that gap will undoubtedly narrow. So now that we're at the halfway point, is there a better solution? Can we strike for Miller's Brook to the north, for example? It is a shorter ride than heading back to the capital, and it should have a garrison sizeable enough to defeat whatever scouts might be following us."

Corn spat on the floor, stretching his neck. "They should have messenger birds too. We could send a message to Shen Utah informing, them of this invasion."

Guardigan, though, was shaking his head. "It wouldn't make a difference. The ride to Miller's Brook is perhaps half the distance of that to the capital. If we all travel together at our slow pace and then attempt to send a messenger bird—assuming they even have any—word will reach Shen Utah at the same time as if we split up now and pushed hard for Shen Utah."

"Split up to what?"

"Well, how about we four beat a hasty path for the capital?"

"We can't leave the refugees here," Dale protested.

"I wasn't suggesting that! We arm them, give them the horses, and send them north to Miller's Brook."

The other three looked back at the old soldier for a moment until Aleks said, "That might work. We'd have to abandon the horses before entering the woods tomorrow, anyway; why not send them on, spiriting the survivors north? This way, if the worst should happen to us and we get overrun before we reach the capital, at least word will still reach Shen Utah from Miller's Brook."

"More of those people stand a chance of surviving if we split up," Dale agreed reluctantly.

Aleks nodded. "If that's decided, then our only other choice is which direction we four take. Corn?"

"We either return to Shen Utah the way we came some days ago, which is the more circuitous, easier route south around the bottom of the Greendale Woods, or we cut through them. But I've ridden the Greendale Woods. They're not easily travelled. It might be a more direct route, but the terrain is more difficult. If we were taking the refugees, I'd suggest the longer route. With just us four, the woods are our best bet."

Aleks said, "We've made remarkably good time, all things considered. No way an army of the size we saw could match that pace. But we're in a different position if there are indeed scouts after us. That must be our assumption," he continued. "Even though the Greendale Woods are difficult to traverse, our passing would not be so obvious there."

"And that which would slow our passing would surely hinder the enemy too," agreed Corn.

"What would be the easiest way to know if they are tracking us?" Dale asked, more in hope than expectation.

"Stop and wait to see if they turn up and kill us," mumbled Corn.

Aleks, ignoring him, said, "If that was my army out there, I'd not let a band of witnesses escape a village we'd sacked with key intel on our numbers and composition."

"But we don't really know any of that."

"*They* don't know that," Aleks reiterated testily.

Guardigan slipped his flask into his pack and nodded to his companions. "Right, then. The Greendale Woods it is."

"Excuse me," came a voice from behind them, making Dale jump. An older gent from Adar had separated himself from the others and approached unobserved. "I couldn't help but overhear the conversation and thought to add my thoughts."

Dale glanced at Aleks and saw he was ready to argue the case for splitting up. Before he could speak, though, the old man said, "I agree with the move to send some to Miller's

Brook. The weaker members are slowing us down, and that will only get worse when the horses fail."

Dale saw Guardigan looking the old man over, taking measure of him, before he asked, "Are you a soldier?"

"Former Pointman, sir." Dale could hear the pride in the man's voice. Looking at him, Dale could see an obvious strength in his movement, not the frailty that most his age suffered.

"What's your name?"

"Garrick, sir. My thoughts, for what they're worth, are that you four need not take the brunt of the run to Shen Utah alone. We have two or three able-bodied villagers—including me—who would like to volunteer to join you."

"If you're able-bodied, you'd be better deployed leading the remnant to Miller's Brook," argued Aleks.

"With all due respect, if the enemy falls upon us without you four in our number, we'd make no difference. But augmenting your numbers might just get you home in the long run."

Dale looked into Garrick's eyes as the man spoke. If he was a former soldier, he would know as well as anyone, the risks the refugees ran in heading for Miller's Brook without escort. If the pursuing elements chose to follow the remnant of Adar or even split their numbers to follow both parties, there was a better than evens chance that the remnant would be overrun and killed.

Garrick would know this. Dale wondered if the other's he spoke of were precious to him. Family, perhaps.

Either way, Aleks only hummed in response, though Guardigan said, "Sometimes all you can hope for out of life is a chance to make a difference. But if any of you slow us down, we'll have to leave you behind."

"Understood." The gratitude in Garrick's face was clear to see.

Yes, Dale thought, *definitely family*.

They rested at Miller's Folly for a small number of hours. The refugees, minus Garrick and the three other volunteers, had taken the horses and set out after midnight. They pushed north into the mist while the remaining company marched for the Greendale Woods, grim determination keeping them silent.

They now numbered eight. Aleks, Corn, Dale, and Guardigan had been joined by the old former Pointman Garrick, his teenage grandchildren, Jarn and his twin sister, Larissa, and another young man named Arrin—perhaps a couple of years Dale's junior. The three younger villagers moved quickly across the rolling hills west of Miller's Folly, but when they hit the Greendale Woods, their pace slowed. Still, they were making far better time without the weaker members of the party.

Every so often, as they all pushed further into the forest, Dale heard Garrick giving voice to the same thought echoing through his own mind. "We've done the right thing. They'll stand a better chance making for Miller's Brook." Garrick was speaking to the three younger Adar villagers, but Dale could tell he was really trying to convince himself. Garrick had left his wife in that number, Dale reminded himself. It took a brave man to do something like that, even if in-so-doing he was giving his grandchildren a better chance to survive.

They journeyed through the rest of the night after leaving the folly, only stopping for an hour near dawn to rest, eat, and recuperate.

The forest was hard going. Overnight, the temperature had plummeted six or seven degrees, and come dawn, through a gap in the tree canopy, Dale recognised the tall and dense clouds to the north that told of snow. He'd worried at that, for a fall of snow would have made the tracks left by the refugees going north more obvious, but he had to put it out of mind. There was nothing to be done.

It was late in the afternoon on the day after leaving the folly that they saw the first evidence of someone following them. As they were chewing ponderously over their rations, a flock of birds was startled into the sky to the southeast of their position.

Aleks clambered swiftly up the nearest tree and attempted to make out any sign of pursuit. He returned ashen-faced. "It's difficult to make out, what with the poor visibility and such, but I think we're being followed for sure."

"That's good news," said Dale. "That means the remnant are free. Why so worried?"

"Unless they separated. But I'm worried because they're perhaps a dozen miles behind us at best. Certainly over that small river we crossed near dawn."

Guardigan gathered his sword again and said, "We'd best keep moving then."

"How are they moving so fast?" Dale said, fear in his voice. "And tracking us through the forest too."

"We always knew it was a fair bet they would be able to track us," said Aleks as he pushed Dale on and up the nearest rise, using the trees to lever himself up. "Probably easy enough with the ground not yet hardened by the coming frost, and the pace we're setting giving us no time to hide our passing."

"But they seem so close. How could they be moving so fast? Do they not sleep?"

"If we keep moving, then they will do well to overtake us in time," said Aleks.

They were halfway up the western rise of the river valley and the gradient was making progress heavy work on the legs. The younger individuals were bounding up the ascent like spring lambs, but Guardigan and Garrick especially were suffering with the damp climb.

Dale pushed on with the younger elements, keen not to let them get out of sight and allow their group to fragment. All the while, he listened behind for the sounds of one of their number falling down. Particularly Garrick. A fall for a man of his age could be serious.

But it was a startled yelp from above him that cut through the sounds of the forest. It was followed by dislodged foliage, and suddenly Jarn tumbled down past him, too quick for Dale to react.

Dale spun to see Corn jump to the side, managing to halt the young boy's tumbling descent. Unfortunately, Corn himself slipped and fell a little further, thumped into a tree bole that turned him round, and then clattered into a second. The snapping of his leg bone could be heard throughout the forest.

Aleks's face turned pale as he ran up the rise to his companion, who was growling through his pain with gritted teeth. To his credit, he didn't yell. To do so in the comparative silence of the forest, even at this distance, would give their position away for certain.

After a quick assessment, Aleks declared, "He's fractured both bones of his lower right leg. He will be unable to continue unless we carry him. And even then, he is still likely to lose his leg. We could try and splint it, but the terrain in the middle of these woods is hard enough to traverse in able-bodied fashion."

Guardigan looked around their small group. Jarn, looking sick, knelt near the fallen Corn. Pointman Garrick had offered his hand for Corn to grip against the pain. The fallen scout's face was ashen, and perspiration covered his brow. He looked in immense pain.

"We could fashion a litter," Jarn said. "There's plenty of wood around. If we apply a splint, the litter would give him a chance."

Jarn's sister, Larissa, was already shaking her head. "How long would that take?"

"Depends how quickly we find branches of suitable length," Jarn replied. Dale could see the guilt etched across his face at having caused this calamity, however inadvertently.

"Don't be stupid," growled Corn. "Leave me behind, as you know you must! Even the time you're wasting talking about doing anything else is madness."

Aleks looked at his colleague for a long moment. Dale could see him weighing the facts, the sum of which was undeniable. "He's right."

There was a terrible leaden silence as Guardigan and Aleks both stared down at Corn, their minds obviously racing to think of a better solution.

Suddenly, Dale felt like such a fool. He'd yearned for important work; he'd yearned for excitement. He had travelled to Shen Utah to be part of the greatest army in the west. Like a child, he'd imagined that this kind of action was what he'd wanted, and yet, now that he was in the thick of it, he had come to realise far too late that there was no excitement to it. Fear for his own life was one thing, but the mind-numbing fear for those in his charge—those who were looking to him for protection—was something else entirely.

Finally, Guardigan said, "There's nothing to be done." He looked directly at Corn and said, "I'm sorry."

"Me too," Corn said quietly. "I've got my bow, though. If you help prop me up against this tree and give me a few spare arrows, I'll do what damage I can to those bastards who follow us. Maybe I can buy the rest of you some time."

"You can't stay alone," said Garrick, still gripping Corn's hand. "I'm staying too. Give me your bow, Wayfarer," he said to Aleks.

"Grampa, no!" Larissa pleaded.

"If you're staying, then so am I," said Jarn defiantly.

"The hell you are."

"But it's my fault this has happened!"

"Rubbish, boy!" By Jarn and Larissa's reactions, it was clear Garrick rarely raised his voice. "You're young. You're strong. You carry on to the capital, bring them word of the assault. It should be a voice of Adar that speaks those words."

Aleks had unslung his bow and handed it to Garrick, together with his quiver. However, he then removed his travel pack and threw it to the floor, too.

"What do you think you're doing?" asked Garrick.

"I'm staying too. If the plan is to slow the enemy scouts, then sitting here and firing arrows at them won't work. It'll have to be a skirmishing retreat. Either of you going to run around these trees and lay traps? Either of you going to fight them hand-to-hand in these tight woods? Well, then. Besides, I'd like to see any of you try to stop me."

"I want to stay too," said the teenager, Arrin. He already held a short sword that he'd brought from Adar.

"Oh, for goodness' sake," muttered Guardigan.

"If you make me come with you, I'll just run back here the first chance I get. I lost my whole family in Adar. I'll stay with Aleks, and he can lead us after you once we've beaten these scouts down."

His words were brave, but it was a hollow bravery.

"We're wasting time trying to talk sense," snarled Guardigan, but he took Aleks's handshake with a heartfelt fervency. Then he gave Arrin's shoulder a firm thump before striding up the hill, again snarling at Dale to follow him.

Dale grasped Aleks's arm in farewell. There wasn't even the merest hint of fear in the young scout's eyes. "Good luck, Aleks. We'll ensure your bravery is remembered."

"I don't care about that, Dale. Just get back to Shen Utah and tell Knight Marshall Arlon what approaches from the east. And tell him that Captain Carpion died bravely, saving our lives."

Dale nodded and then pointlessly bade good fortune to the hapless Corn, who had already turned on the rise to more easily face the coming enemy. Dale caught up with Guardigan, and he could see the shine of tears in his eyes. It would have been difficult for him, Dale realised, to leave a young lad like Arrin behind, knowing now, as he did, Guardigan's own tragic past.

When the twins had finished their tearful goodbyes, Guardigan led them all away from the site of Corn's fall, this time at a run through the increasing rain. No one spoke.

Somewhere through the tree canopy, high above the thick clouds, a distant sun watched over Shenmadock. Somewhere, safety reigned. To the northeast, the bulk of the Adar remnant would be working their way to Miller's Brook while Guardigan and Dale were racing northwest to the capital, and the only thing left in Aleks's life was the desire to ensure their safe passage. The very fact that the enemy scouts seemed to have taken their tracks away from Miller's Folly gave him hope that the frailer refugees heading north from that tower stood a good chance of escape.

Adjusting his grip on the handle of his sword, he moved slowly through the undergrowth, staying low to the ground. His breath hung in hollow clouds from the cold. Around him, the forest was alive with the sounds of life, while he and the rest awaited death. Though they continued to say otherwise, Aleks knew it was an inevitability that their bodies would fall, their lives would end, and then they would decompose here in the forest, left to rot in nameless graves.

Their bodies would provide nutrients to the earth and feed the growth of new life. And while such grand notions were scant comfort, it was all they had left.

There was so much he had wanted to do.

The rain continued to fall, pattering noisily on the leaves above.

Then he heard them. Many booted feet were thumping through the forest, approaching from his left. There was small hope to be had in the enemy's arrival, for they were almost six hours behind Dale, Guardigan, and the twins. They might have a chance to outrun this chasing force, but only if the little skirmish here delayed them. Every second this action gained would increase the likelihood of their survival.

Aleks listened hard to the sounds of the forest and the strangers within it. He hid in the undergrowth, concealed behind a thicket. The enemy scouts were moving quickly but not quietly, as if they feared no ambush. That was to his advantage.

He faced across their path, the enemy climbing up the hill to his left and Corn further up the rise to the right. The old man Garrick was positioned to Corn's left-hand side, both armed with their remaining bows. Behind them, the youngster Arrin was also hidden, short sword in hand, ready to protect the archery position should it become overrun. Aleks knew it was something of a token gesture, and indeed, Arrin had wanted to help Aleks on his own duty, but the Wayfarer knew he would work best alone. His sapping assault relied on stealth.

Garrick, a former Pointman, would have seen battle first-hand, but the sad truth of the matter was Arrin would witness the horror of conflict before he died. *There is something awful about that*, Aleks thought.

Still, it would be a burden not long in the carrying.

Then, between the tree trunks, he could suddenly glimpse the enemy moving methodically up the rise, weapons still in their scabbards and eyes trained on the ground ahead of them. At the head of the unit was a tall soldier dressed in black robes cinched about his waist by a brown sash. He was massive—easily seven feet tall—and the hood of the robe was pulled up over his head against the steady rain, obscuring his features.

Something curious struck Aleks about the way the rest of them moved, but he had no time to think about it, for their trap was about to be sprung.

As the tall leader stepped round a broad oak, half a dozen strangely moving figures in his wake, a small storm of arrows flashed through the trees from the rise ahead of them. They had fired too early! Aleks forced himself to remain still as another volley of arrows was fired down on the enemy.

Many of the enemy were hit by the fire from the hill, but none fell. As the arrowheads punched into their bodies, they staggered back, eyes flicking up to the rise ahead, and in chilling unison, they drew their weapons.

They showed no pain. They showed no recognition of the shafts still jutting from their flesh. Instead, they charged the hill in absolute silence.

Aleks sprang forward, shifting swiftly through the woods. As he moved, he lashed out at a rope tied around another oak tree. The blade thumped home, releasing a series of hefty branches that snapped back into position, whipping through the forest and hammering into the flank of the onrushing silent enemy. Two men were propelled back down the rise, one thumping into another oak, his neck breaking with a crack.

Aleks burst from cover and rushed the sundered flank. He was now behind the charging line. Because Corn and Garrick had fired too early, Arrin would have work to do.

He stabbed the second fallen man through the heart with his short sword and then moved on to the next soldier, the shorter weapon abandoned in favour of his longsword. He attacked overhand and bellowed a loud battle cry.

On the rise, Corn and Garrick continued to fire into the far side of the melee while the clash of weapons echoed through the forest. Aleks deflected a sword up into the air and stabbed the man through the chest before moving toward the next.

"Steels!" Aleks bellowed through the trees, encouraging Garrick to draw his own sword, for the huge leader would be upon their position soon. He and Arrin would have to be ready.

With three of the six scouts downed and the leader rushing the rise above, Aleks suddenly thought, *This might work! We're now four on four!*

But then the hooded scout crashed mercilessly into Corn's position. Aleks heard his friend's wail echo into the trees. *Back to the earth*, he thought.

Aleks had to get back to the top to protect Garrick and Arrin. He broke off his attack on the last three scouts and made to rush up the hill.

But somehow, two enemy soldiers blocked his path. *Behind me! How?* The first swung his sword at Aleks's face, but the Wayfarer ducked the blow.

Then he spotted the short sword jutting from the man's chest—a wound he himself had inflicted. A killing wound as sure as anything, and yet the man still stood, fighting on.

Aleks bull-rushed him, bashing him to the ground and then chopping his sword through his skull. This time, he stayed down, but the blade became trapped in his skull. Aleks had to let it go.

Aleks drew his last spare short sword and pushed himself into a run, leaden thighs pumping to drive him up the rise to Garrick's position.

As he topped the rise, the huge enemy leader lunged from the trees to his left. Behind the man, Aleks clearly saw the dismembered bodies of Garrick and Arrin.

He kept moving as a massive broadsword thrummed overhead, the blade appearing to glow a curious amber colour. Aleks sliced through another rope trap, releasing more bound branches toward the leader. With inhuman speed, his enemy ducked the trap, which slammed into the remaining soldiers behind him.

Turning with his blade raised, Aleks had enough time to look into the hood of the tall figure as he drove the enormous blade deep through his chest.

He expected pain but felt only a strange release.

He expected terror but felt only peace.

His breath rushed out, and his hands went limp, releasing his last short sword.

From within the hood, a pair of crimson eyes seemed to flash in the darkness. Then Aleks's world bled to nothingness.

Chapter Twenty-Eight

The Apothecary's Tale

Arlon stood upon the ancient city walls overlooking both the East End and High Wall districts of Shen Utah. The sun was rising. The sky across Trouton to the west, over the city and out across the ocean known as the Great Green, still carried the last remnants of night, but to the east, it was the colour of pooling blood. Above his head was a rich pink-purple where the stars could still be seen. He stared hard at the show of colour for a moment, remembering what his father had always said about such mornings.

Arlon's scarred and tattooed arms were folded against the frigid winter wind blowing downriver from Jow, his dark hair stirred by a sharp breeze that promised more rain, heavy sleet, and perhaps even snow. It was overdue, for the temperatures in the city had already plunged and there were reports of the usual vagrant deaths that characterised the season. The thought that such things occurred in his city confused and upset him—that so many could exist in style and comfort while others starved on the streets and died from exposure.

Below him to the west, beyond the High Wall district, the King's Docks were alive with activity as the overnight delivery vessels from upriver fought for dock space, pilot vessels running at maximum to ferry vessels to berth. In the wide expanse of the river, many fishing boats of varying sizes were already heading out toward the Great Green for the day.

Ashore, dockhands endeavoured to offload cargo from Jow in the east and the western coastal ports, but despite the obvious peak of activity, Arlon knew the importation of goods from the east had slackened since the unrest between Jow and Mashtock began. It was only natural.

Further north, he could see the idyllic little island that sat at the centre of the River Jow. A popular retreat with the rich of Shen Utah, Pearl Island offered beaches and inland spas for those wealthy enough to afford such comforts.

Behind him, Arlon heard his mentor approaching, the familiar shuffle of his sandals a dead giveaway on the stonework of the ramparts.

"Good morning, Knight Marshall," Ergun greeted him nervously.

Arlon looked over his shoulder and couldn't help but smile at the professor's bleak expression. He had never enjoyed heights, and was even less fond of the cold. But still, the smile slipped quickly. "My father always said such mornings only followed a night of violence. Blood has been spilled this night."

"With such unrest as we are seeing these days, it's a wonder we don't see such mornings every day," Ergun replied, sounding jaded. Then changing the topic, he grumbled, "I should have petitioned for these useless ancient walls to be knocked down decades ago!"

Arlon looked at Ergun and recognised something. "You're not just worried about the height and the cold; what's afoot?"

"I have strange news," Ergun said simply. "Despite the increasing tension between Jow and Mashtock, or perhaps because of that tension, both retinues remain in Shen Utah, including their most senior council representatives."

Arlon shared his mentor's surprise. "They have not returned home? Neither of them? It's no great surprise that Fargil and his colleagues remain, but Karl? The last time we spoke, he gave me the impression he had pressing matters to be about—matters outside the city. He must have a bloody good reason for staying."

"Indeed. Lord Karl continues to claim he knows nothing of the unrest on the border, so perhaps it's his desire to ensure the council does nothing against his wishes that keeps him here."

Arlon nodded. "Returning to Jow at this juncture might be interpreted in some quarters as a guilty move. Fleeing the scene, as it were."

"Quite so," Ergun agreed. "As for my brother, his next reasonable move would be to attempt to petition the council to ready a portion of the Armies of the West in order to march up the River Jow and end the unrest. I would expect him to do this in Lord Cordon Vale's name very soon."

"That will never happen," said Arlon gravely.

"He will petition regardless. Until we get to the nub of that issue, he will press for intercession."

Arlon looked out across the northern vista for another breath. "What of Councillor Horvarth? Does he remain in the city?"

"He does," Ergun confirmed. "Why?"

"I still don't know what's going on between Horvarth and Karl. Something is happening there. I can't shake the feeling it has something to do with Senior Lord Handee."

"We know Horvarth is having issues with Reinhart. Karl is looking for a suitor for his daughter, and it seems Failton of Theed is the chosen one to handle that fractious mare."

Arlon laughed.

"Perhaps there is nothing more sinister going on than that . . ."

Arlon tutted in frustration. "For Karl to be confident enough to remain in the city and to carry on pursuing marriage arrangements instead of diplomatic treaties would suggest he has an inkling that the unrest won't escalate."

"Which in turn would suggest he knows a little more than he's letting on?"

Arlon made an aggravated noise in the back of his throat. "Or perhaps all of this is bloody paranoia on our part! If he knew something was afoot, surely he'd want to be back in Jow, rooting out the culprit before they do more damage."

"Unless, of course, the culprit is here."

Arlon was surprised at the idea. "Here?"

"Indeed. It could be a member of his entourage, one of his senior aides, anyone."

"If this situation escalates to the point that blame is placed upon Jow's doorstep, Karl can kiss goodbye to any aspirations he might have of one day being Senior Lord."

"Good point," Ergun conceded. "In fact, he would risk execution."

Arlon turned sharply. "Execution?"

The old professor nodded. "I spoke with Lord Ludovic late into last night, and he suggests that should a member duchy be found to blame for the intrusion into Mashtock, the council would have to vote on whether such a move could be considered treasonous. If they are able to establish that the intent is to expand ducal boundaries, it is but a short step to charge the plotters with an attack on the realm itself."

"That's dangerous speculation."

"Speculation is a politician's pastime, Arlon."

"Politicians!" Arlon spat. "They really get my goat. They never imagine that the lives they throw at a problem for political gain are someone's sons or daughters, not just . . . pieces on a game board!"

Ergun looked long and hard at his student. The professor was one of the few men Arlon had ever confided in about anything; that included the true events at the Battle of Thes, when Arlon had marched a small battalion of young men on a suicide charge to break the enemy's back. Ergun knew the terrible truth of what had happened that night—what Arlon had done and what had been done to him.

Since that terrible day, Arlon didn't sleep a night without seeing at least one of those young faces he had taken from this world as surely as if he had run them through himself. The lives that had been lost would haunt him more than everything else that had happened.

Arlon was relieved when Ergun decided discretion to be the more salient course. "It may actually be to our advantage that Karl, Horvarth, and my brother remain in Shen Utah."

"Keep your friends close but your enemies closer?"

"If any of them do turn out to be an enemy of the nation. Either way, they will prove easier to monitor."

Looking past Arlon's shoulder, Ergun seemed to notice for the first time the irregular pattern of soldiers posted along the length of Shen Utah's walls. Arlon followed his gaze. Every few dozen yards, a pair of stationary figures could be seen standing to precise attention, stoic in the morning chill. They wore long flowing cloaks of olive drab and ornate, brass-coloured helms. Arlon knew the armoured headwear hid the lobeless, upswept ears of the Eldar race.

"Elves," mused Ergun.

"Druidale Rangers, to be exact," Arlon told him. Ergun looked back at him, his bushy grey eyebrows climbing in surprise. "I have posted them along the walls to watch for news of Lord Handee."

It was a half-truth. Arlon did want watchful, alert guards on the walls, and no race in the world had better natural vision than the elves. But he had an ulterior motive for posting the Druidale Rangers, and he was happy to keep that motive to himself for now. "This is . . . irregular," Ergun admitted.

"I know that."

"Have you ratified this with the council?"

"Of course not," Arlon admitted. "I don't trust the council at the moment—if I ever have. And before you start, it is perfectly legal. I have not replaced the City Guard; I have merely augmented it with the best spotters in the known lands."

"To what end, precisely?"

"If Lord Handee is to contact us, it shall probably be via carrier pigeon now, with winter upon us; especially if he has indeed been delayed. Any day now, these lands will be covered by snow, and the southeast will already be ravaged by storms. If Lord Handee sends word, I want the message to reach us as quickly and reliably as possible."

Ergun looked at Arlon, a knowing smile replacing his look of astonishment. "You are indeed my protégée. You want to be sure *you* hear about it first, and from what you believe to be an incorruptible source. The official history of Shenmadock may remember the Druidale betrayal in one unwavering light, but you and I both know there has never been a more loyal and trustworthy regiment than the Druidale Rangers, and especially loyal to *you*, my boy. Very clever—very clever, indeed."

Arlon afforded himself a small smile. "The Druidale Rangers have sent word throughout the land to seek sign of Handee's passing through their lands. I actually asked them to send out their messengers at the time of Karl's first request for *Senior Lord in Absentia.* If they know anything regarding Handee's delayed return, they shall send word to me, and me alone."

Ergun looked genuinely impressed. "You have the walls covered, then, but what of our three unknown entities—Fargil, Karl, and Horvarth? We could do with learning more of their intentions."

"That's a problem I need help with. Now that my cousin Carpion and his select few are in the East, and the balance of his Wayfarers are leading the investigations in Jow and Mashtock, I have few or no agents left in the city and palace to enlist. It may prove difficult for me to monitor them."

"Perhaps, perhaps," replied Ergun. "Leave that to me. There is another resource left to us that is as yet untapped."

Arlon raised an eyebrow in question.

"The Princess de Hayne is still in Shen Utah."

"I thought I had asked her to return to her estates in the Greendale Woods yesterday."

"I know."

"Will she ever do anything I ask!"

"Probably not. I know that with such political manoeuvrings occurring in the palace, you thought it unsafe for an ex-royal to remain here, but she refused to leave, though she keeps her presence clandestine. She believes you might still need her counsel, and it turns out she's probably right. She can help us in this."

"This is not the correct course," protested Arlon. "There must be someone else we can trust."

"They would be Lord Ludovic's agents. He's quite wily and has proven to be a good ally. We could trust his contacts to spy on Karl at least—goodness knows there is no love lost there—but they would report to Ludovic first and to us second. Kathryn is the only person I trust implicitly with a task of such subtlety, and no one knows the complexities of this city better than a de Hayne."

"Okay. But I want her properly protected."

"Fear not, Arlon, she shall be safe. I'll see to it personally, once I have put my own house in order."

"What do you mean?" Arlon asked.

"Never you mind, young man."

His ageing teacher's evasiveness often threatened to pique his temper, but Arlon was forced to relent; Ergun would never reveal something he wanted kept to himself. And if Ergun felt that Arlon needed to know? Well, he trusted the professor to tell him. "Just be careful, old man."

Ergun nodded, a look of indulgent humour on his face, and stepped forward to look out over the wall. The old professor recoiled from the tall drop beyond the defences and muttered, "For the love of the gods!" Then he beckoned Arlon to follow him back along the ramparts to the stairs. Brightening, he said, "Still, that other news you spoke of must come as a great relief. That Karl has chosen a suitor for Marta, I mean."

Arlon nodded. "At least that should finally get her off my back."

Ergun smiled wanly. "You don't know much about women, do you, son?"

A rickety cart rumbled noisily along the streets of Shen Utah, the morning sun doing nothing to lift the chill from the wintery air. Huddled in the corner of the cage upon the cart, the sole occupant shivered, though more from fear than the cold. Jorus the apothecary wept quietly to himself, the welts upon his face still bleeding from various beatings he'd taken.

The streets of Temple Link were busy, but Click had learned long ago that people rarely looked up. It was no surprise that no one noticed the black figure that dropped silently to the top of the cart as it passed a simple dwelling.

The driver of the cart, an old City Watchman tasked with such a mundane task due to his lengthening years, didn't notice the stowaway either. Even Jorus, encased in his own misery and self-pity, was oblivious to the new arrival until a whispering voice spoke into his cage.

"Jorus, what the hell have you done?"

The broken man in the cage sniffed back his tears and looked up through the roof of the cart. Click smiled down at the caged man with just the merest sliver of sympathy. *Finally, I've caught up with you, you slippery bastard.*

"Leave me be," Jorus blubbered, his jowly features creasing in self-remorse.

"Black Spider Venom is virulent stuff, apothecary. You must have known the guilds would not stand for it." Click's mind flashed back to the perilous escape he'd faced when Jorus's hired guards chased him through the streets, the stolen poison secreted in his jerkin.

Jorus looked up through his cloud of self-loathing. "What do you want from me? Is this not price enough to pay? I'm to live out my life in darkness!"

It had taken Click longer than he'd expected to track Jorus down. Having agreed with Swindle to investigate the apothecary further, he'd thought it would be nice and straight forward, but it had been anything but! Then word had reached him, through Martin Galvan, that Jorus had suddenly and surprisingly been snared by the City Watch.

They had come for him in the morning, not even breaking down the door. In fact, they hadn't even sent members of the City Watch to capture him! Instead, an officious-looking man, probably a magistrate, had apparently knocked on his door as though inviting Jorus out for breakfast. Then he had gone to the gaol, unreachable.

So, Click had waited, straining and striving to remain calm, for there was nothing to be done other than await his chance to talk to the old man before he was transferred to the hole from which he would never see the light of day again.

"I want to know everything you've already told that magistrate, Jorus—which didn't come easily, judging by the mess they've made of your face." Click kept himself pressed flat to the cart roof, ensuring his voice remained low.

"I told them nothing! I've no tolerance for pain, but I told them nothing important, I swear!"

"Tell me instead," Click encouraged.

Alone and condemned to a life without windows—short as the remainder of that life would be—Jorus's resolve and composure wilted. "Are you here to kill me?" he asked feebly.

"No," Click replied in confusion. Why would Jorus fear that? After all, whoever his dangerous customer was, they'd already betrayed him to the authorities . . .

Then it all clicked.

"You gave yourself up, didn't you!"

"I'll be safe in the dungeons," he said.

"I wouldn't be so sure about that. If someone wants you dead, they'll get to you eventually. Tell me who you were going to sell that poison to, Jorus. I have powerful friends; they might be able to protect you."

"But I didn't *make* the poison; I only bought it."

Click was running out of time. He glanced down the street and saw the open expanse of the market square ahead of them. He would have to disembark soon, lest he be discovered.

"She said she loved me," he muttered, his voice so low that it was almost inaudible above the rattle of the cartwheels on the cobbles. "How stupid does that sound? I knew it was a lie—deep down, I knew."

"Who loved you, Jorus?"

"She was a proper lady," he said. "I was married to my Gildamere for more than fifty years. She died last winter. Did you know that?" Click shook his head, but Jorus wasn't watching. "I've been so lonely. But when *she* came to me in the middle of the night, I thought I might have fallen asleep at my workbench and was dreaming. But she was real. Beautiful as an angel—but real!"

Click shushed Jorus as his voice began to grow in volume, dangerously close to being audible over the clatter of the cartwheels.

"She asked me time and again to make her a poison, but I refused. You have no idea how hard it was to say no to such a beautiful face when you've been alone for as long as I have. In the end, I relented, though I had no ingredients to make her venom. I agreed to import it instead, in exchange for her kiss. I've never felt such a delicate, sweet touch. It only lasted a moment, but I can still feel it now." Jorus touched a hand to the badly bruised flesh of his cheek.

"Shut it back there!" the cart driver bellowed without looking over his shoulder. "I'm tired of listening to your constant bloody mumbling!"

Click pressed himself closer to the cage for fear of being seen. After a moment of silence, he pressed, "Who was it?"

Tears ran down the moguls of Jorus's battered face. "Oh, my sweet lady. She's a lady, a God's honest lady."

Click needed a name!

"Who was it? Why were they looking for poison?" Then something occurred to him. "Wait, she gave you her kiss? Does that mean you supplied the poison? Jorus, did you have more of the venom that I stole?"

Jorus's only answer was a pitiful nod, for he had succumbed to his fear and grief, sobs wracking his ruined body. He would have nothing more of use to say, but Click knew the truth—Jorus had supplied the Black Spider

Venom in the end. Click hadn't stolen all he had . . . just what little he had left.

He glanced ahead and saw an alleyway approaching. He edged over to the side of the cage and made ready to drop to the street.

Suddenly there was a punching sound from below, followed immediately by a grating, high-pitched screech that echoed up the street. Poor Jorus sported a crossbow bolt in his chest, directly in his heart, judging by the colour of the blood pouring from the wound. He bleated a startled yell that petered out to an anguished sigh of despair as he wheezed out his last breath.

Click looked up and behind him and spied the assassin inching back from the peak of a roof. The killer's face was fully obscured by a black hood. For a terrible moment, Click thought he would be next, having witnessed the deed, but the killer only afforded him a little wave and then disappeared over the edge of the roof, their work done.

"What's this!" shouted the City Watchman from the front of the wagon. He reined the horses in sharply and then stood up in his seat.

"Crap!" Click cursed. It would look as though he'd killed Jorus! No wonder the assassin disappeared with a jaunty wave—he'd killed two birds with one bolt!

The cart was stopping, the horses protesting noisily. The guard threw the traces aside and started clambering over the back of his seat toward Click. He drew a short sword.

Damn it!

Click jumped to a crouch and then sprang into the air as the cart lurched to the side. He caught the underside of an old balcony awning and used what little momentum he had to try to flip onto the next balcony.

He failed.

On the street, a hue and cry was going up as Click dangled from the balcony by his hands.

Balancing precariously on the bars of the cage roof, the guard lunged at Click's stomach with his sword as he hung from the balcony.

Click twisted to avoid the strike, and then kicked out at the man's face. He missed but managed to catch his shoulder instead.

The guard tipped forward, off balance, and grabbed at Click's ankle.

There was a squeak as the guard's boot slipped from the metal cage rail. Click released his grip on the balcony and dropped onto his assailant, forcing the guard to his right side. As his leg dropped between the cage bars, Click's weight forced him the other way, and there was an almighty crack as the guard's left femur snapped in the middle.

His anguished cry silenced the street. The short sword fell into the locked cage blade first, piercing Jorus's stomach with a thump.

Click sprang away from the wagon once more, this time performing a backward somersault to the street below, where a well-meaning citizen tried to detain him. He ducked the grabbing arms easily and then disappeared down a nearby alley. In moments, he was gone.

He had to find Constable Foord. The ship and the poison *were* linked! The same assassin who had killed the customs inspector had just silenced Jorus too.

And what was worse, someone in the city had Black Spider Venom!

Chapter Twenty-Nine
Betrayal

Kathryn de Hayne stepped gently on the flagstones of the upper balcony in her soft shoes, careful not to make a sound. She lifted her light skirts out of the way and travelled up a short flight of stairs to a higher balcony, which followed a long, covered passageway connecting the main complex of the Shen Utah Palace to the south-eastern wing. It was a rarely travelled route, for most palace attendees adhered to the easier paths through the beautiful gardens.

Right now, Kathryn knew someone in particular was using the passage, and the atrium to which it led, and probably with dark intent.

At Professor Ergun's request, she'd had one of her own agents follow Lord Karl II of Jow while she herself tailed Horvarth of Unedar for the best part of the day.

The Unedar councillor was certainly shifty, attending meeting after shady meeting with members of the Shen government, most of whom he had little business meeting with at all—and certainly not so covertly.

And yet all of that fitted nicely with the image of a political aide cut adrift by his leader. If Kathryn had to wager money on it, she would bet Horvarth was an ambitious man, but was he a conspirator? It wouldn't take much to push ambition to such extremes.

And yet, the man had shown nothing that would give her conclusive proof that he was betraying his nation.

It was somewhat frustrating, then, when she received word from Alice that her lady-in-waiting, who had always been a little more than just that, needed to speak to her urgently. Still, Alice was no fool. She had known it would be important, and so it had proved.

Abandoning her own task, Kathryn had made directly for the palace larder, wherein Alice had informed her that while Lord Karl had spent much of his morning in his town estates, keeping to himself during this horrid weather, he had then received a note from a messenger at his estates. Alice had bribed the messenger to reveal the nature of the note; cheap messengers were always susceptible to bribery.

Taken at face value, the note had contained no exciting information; just a request for the Duke of Jow to meet with the nameless sender in the south-eastern passage atrium that afternoon. The only additional information Alice could glean was that Karl seemed angered by the request, but not surprised.

Kathryn's immediate thought had been, could this note have come from Horvarth? He had certainly had a busy day of clandestine meetings already, could this be another?

She had left the palace larder and hurried through the grounds via the old servants' passages, in so doing avoiding careless eyes. For such a simple and nameless note to light a fire under the unflappable Karl was impressive, and the location for the meeting was concerning too. She had no doubt this was a secret meeting and that she stood a fine chance of uncovering some of the mystery surrounding current events by overhearing what was said—especially should she finally make an incriminating connection between Karl and Horvarth!

From her hiding place in the atrium, Kathryn stepped up to the balcony edge and followed the stone banister to the left. The passage below her seemed silent and empty.

Halfway along the covered passage was the famous circular atrium with an opulent flowerbed at its centre. The colourful glass ceiling was one of the most beautiful sights in the palace grounds, if one of the least appreciated. On such a foul day, it would be highly unlikely for anyone to chance upon her, but still, she was careful to ensure she remained composed enough to lie her way out of any situation, should she be stumbled upon.

The atrium was encircled by a balcony, accessed by a short arch just ahead of her. Now that she neared the portal, she could hear hushed voices from the atrium floor. Approaching in the darkness of the covered balcony, Kathryn de Hayne peered through the gloom and down onto the atrium floor.

She could see but one figure, leaning against the wall of the flowerbed in a relaxed fashion. As expected, it was Lord Karl II, Duke of Jow. He stood with his burly arms folded atop his round belly, his florid, baggy jowls wobbling as he spoke. His voice and that of his companion were frustratingly distorted by the high glass ceiling.

"Of course my supplier can be trusted," Karl was saying. "I've dealt with him for a number of years now, albeit on smaller projects. He is the biggest trade supplier in Choat. He will ensure as many weapons cross the border into the hands of your 'bandits' as they demand." He chuckled as he said the word *bandits*, suggesting the lie. "I'm just furious with that idiot Dowling for failing to replace my payoff; now I have to think of another way to pay for this *venture*. I can't wait forever for an insurance pay out that might never come. Even then, who's to say it would be enough?"

"Is it wise to supply your men when they're already in Mashtock?" the stranger asked, outside her field of vision. "And what about the local militia; is it salient to arm them all from the same trader? Should someone stumble across—"

"Quiet yourself. It will not be a problem. Even if such information was discovered, our names appear nowhere. Perhaps du Lacigny would have some difficult questions to answer, but nothing links back to us. As for Mr. Dowling, as soon as he gets me my cut of the insurance payoff from the sunken vessel, he will have exhausted all usefulness and I shall have him disposed of too."

Too? Who else had been disposed of?

"Then I can settle accounts with Choat and all will be done."

"It's still a big 'if', Karl."

Laughing derisively at his conspirator, Karl said, "You must learn to control your anxieties. Let us move to more pressing issues, that being keeping Unedar in line. I have been forced to promise my daughter's hand in marriage to an Unedar noble of concerningly low birth. Much as it rankles me, for the time being, it is necessary for our deal with that worm Jakrat."

The stranger was silent for a moment. Kathryn strained to see who he was, but her view was completely obscured, for he stood beneath her balcony. If she leaned over to view the stranger, Lord Karl would *have* to see her, unless he was entirely blind.

These deals with Unedar, she thought, *could this be Horvarth?*

Finally, the stranger replied, "Surely Unedar is already securely in line. Reinhart and Jakrat will keep silent to save their own hides."

What is going on? Kathryn worried. *Karl is forming alliances with Unedar, double dealing in arms through Choat, creating unrest in Mashtock . . . but why? To what end?*

"Because, you idiot, there remains one more obstacle to our ambitions—this stubborn fool of a Knight Marshall."

Kathryn's heart sank in her chest. "Long has he resisted Marta's charms, standing in the way of my ambition through his stubborn obsession with the de Hayne line. Without being able to have Marta's influence over him, I had hoped he would answer the call to declare Handee *in absentia* by now, but he has not."

"I'm still confused as to what purpose that would have served."

Karl laughed nastily. "Sometimes, when the indirect approach has failed, one must become a little more direct. I had hoped the nation's hero would lead the investigative force into Mashtock himself. It would have been a simple job to have my silent assassin end him in the field. Far easier than trying to get into the palace, that's for sure!

"But no, he delays and delays, awaiting Handee's return, a return that will not come." Karl shook his head. "It keeps him in the safety of the city, and such a tactic throws our own venture into risky waters. The longer all of this goes on, the greater the chance we will be discovered."

"That's what has me worried," said the other. "Reinhart's murder of Handee was rash to say the least."

Handee, murdered!

"All that's worth doing carries risk, fool! While rash, Handee's demise serves us well. But only if we deal quickly with the Knight Marshall, for he remains our prime barrier to success.

"Still," the other man said reluctantly, "with such a development, it's hard not to see all this as treason."

Because that's what it is!

"The men of Unedar's court are no more traitors than you or me!" Karl snapped. "Is being a patriot to this nation considered treasonous? Is protecting this nation from the weak, treasonous? If it is, then hang us both! Lord Reinhart has had border issues with Ipsica for too long, and Shen Utah has too often ignored his pleas."

"When I take command of this nation, Hightower shall receive all the support it requests. Shenmadock shall become a visible power again. A power not to be trifled with!"

A power enforced by bigger armies, armies bearing weapons and armour produced and sold by the forges of Jow's world-famous blacksmiths, Kathryn thought. *Of which you own the majority!*

"At any rate, we must have intercession in the civil war in the north. We have to accelerate our plans."

"The man's a national hero," the other man said with a warning tone.

Karl heaved out an exhausted sigh, as though tired of suffering fools. "He has left us no choice. He must be required to make one last sacrifice."

Kathryn put her hand to her chest. Her heart thundered with terror. *Surely, he cannot intend to follow through with his threat to do Arlon harm!*

"Karl, I am uncertain. I have doubts."

"A little late for that!" Karl stood aggressively, his fisted arms held firmly at his sides and his barrel chest thrust out. "We shall succeed, because we must. The alternative, as you rightly point out, is death. Just be prepared to do your duty when called upon."

Meekly, the voice replied, "You shall never find my support or my loyalty wanting, Karl." Despite the distortion, Kathryn thought the other man sounded trapped and a little desperate himself, probably exactly how Karl wanted him.

"And no more doubts. Now don't contact me in this fashion again. Of all things, *this* is being foolhardy!" The Duke of Jow turned on his heels and stormed down the covered passage, away from Kathryn. She watched him leave, burning holes of hatred in his back with her eyes.

I must get a warning to Arlon, she thought. *Something is afoot. Could an assassin be in the palace?*

Karl's conspirator stayed in the atrium for a moment, and Kathryn was forced to back away slowly, fearful that she might be discovered upon the balcony.

That was when she heard another pair of feet approaching along the passage below her, the soft-sandaled footfalls sounding hollow in the atrium passage. *A third conspirator?* She stopped short of the balcony over the walkway and looked down from the shadows. In the gloom below, it was almost impossible to identify the new arrival by his features, but Kathryn would recognise the familiar silhouette and shuffling gait of Professor Ergun anywhere.

What is he doing here?

The old professor stopped in the darkness of the far wall, seemingly to ambush the mysterious conspirator as he left the atrium. Before the stranger could step into Kathryn's view, Professor Ergun spoke, making him jump.

"What is going on, you fool!" Ergun said.

Whoever the conspirator was, they stopped their flight. Clearly Ergun knew them.

"Snooping around again, Ergun? How much did you overhear?"

Did she now recognise that voice?

"I heard enough, and I saw enough."

Kathryn was certain Ergun would have been too far away to overhear much. He was gambling on the other to incriminate themselves.

"Are you conspiring with Jow now? Has it come to this?"

"I don't conspire; I cooperate! It's the very essence of democracy!"

"Don't give me that nonsense. You're conducting secret meetings with your enemy."

"There are no enemies on the council."

"Rubbish! You are a member of the Council of Lords; you have a responsibility to Shenmadock to protect the nation from enemies, wherever they be found. That means from within, too! I warrant your duke has no knowledge of your dealings with Jow, these clandestine meetings?"

"Is the council aware of your regular meetings with Lord Ludovic," the stranger bit back, "or your secret sessions with the Knight Marshall himself? This is no different!" The man sounded cornered, panicky.

"I'm not on the council. I am a professor and an advisor. Right now, I advise you to confess your dealings here to the council, or I will be compelled to on your behalf."

"I know you, Ergun; you wouldn't betray me like that. Now get out of my way!"

The stranger finally lumbered into sight, clad in a dark cloak. Ergun stepped in his way, speaking quick, angry, earnest words that Kathryn couldn't hear.

Suddenly the pair were struggling—two old men by their movements. Then the stranger moved sharply in Ergun's direction and delivered a punch to the groin that doubled Ergun over and released the conspirator to make good his escape.

Kathryn rushed back along the balcony, all attempts at stealth gone in her need to reach Ergun.

As she came to the stairway, she could see the stranger's back as he fled through the winter sleet and snow. Suddenly she recognised his frame, and all the pieces fell into place.

He was slow, and Kathryn felt she could catch him, but instead she rushed down the corridor to the crumpled figure of Ergun, who still clutched his groin.

When Kathryn reached him, he rolled onto his side, pain written in lines on his old, grey face. "Professor, are you okay?"

Ergun's eyes took a second to recognise her, and then he spared a hand to grip her by the shoulder. "Kathryn, what are you doing here?"

"I had Lord Karl followed, like you asked me to. He came here on receipt of a note. I think he means to do

Arlon some harm, but I know not how. There must be more conspirators."

"No," Ergun told her weakly, nodding his sudden understanding. "That would reveal his broader intentions, and Karl can't do that. The attack will be in the form of a duel, a challenge between vexed lovers for the right to court Lady Marta. Karl already has the suitor lined up. I've been such a fool!"

"But that makes no sense," Kathryn told him, trying to lift him into a sitting position. "Arlon has no interest in Marta, so why fight for her honour?"

"Arlon has never expressed anything but contempt for Marta, but if it is an honourable duel, he won't be able to walk away. Karl has sought a connection to the position of Knight Marshall for some time now. Arlon has resisted and will be dealt with harshly. It will be an underhanded murder."

"We must stop them!" she said earnestly. "Get to your feet. I've obviously never been thumped in the goolies, but I imagine you're milking this a little."

He ignored her. "Kathryn, you need to do two things for me. First, get to Arlon and warn him immediately. His life is in grave danger."

It was then that Kathryn felt a tacky sensation on her upper arm, where his hand gripped her. She glanced down and saw dark red blood caking Ergun's hand. Her eyes widened and tears came unbidden. The flagstones behind the professor were flooding with dark blood. Darker than red; almost . . . black.

Before she could speak, Ergun said, "The same poison intended for Arlon now courses through my veins." Ergun released his hand from his groin, and Kathryn saw the handle of a punching dagger jutting from the top of his inner thigh. "Even without the poison, this was a mortal wound; he's severed my femoral artery. See how my blood darkens? The cold creeping through my legs must be Black

Spider Venom. I have scant moments, so listen hard! This poison must be administered to Arlon's blood flow. A deep wound like mine shall be almost certainly fatal; a scratch or flesh wound shall be long-suffering, but he might survive, strong as he is."

"I must fetch you help!"

"No," Ergun said through gritted teeth. "There is no time! Did you not listen? It is already too late for me."

Kathryn put a hand to his cheek to comfort his passing. She could see his eyes had already milked over.

"Enough, girl!" His words were harsh, but the tone weak and waning. "Get to Arlon; warn him of this conspiracy. Save his life. Shenmadock needs him." His hand dropped from her arm and fell weakly to the floor. Regret twisted his features. "Name my murderer, Kathryn. Reveal my brother, Fargil, for the traitor he is, and bring him and that snake Karl to justice before the council."

"I will. I promise," Kathryn said quietly. "You said you need two things from me," she reminded him gently, weeping now.

Ergun's eyes closed for a second. "Tell Arlon how you feel about him, Kathryn. Forget that you are a de Hayne and he a Knight Marshall. Be happy together. Or I swear, I'll haunt the pair of you."

Then he was gone.

The afternoon had limped into a long and miserable evening as the winter weather gripped the land with icy fingers. Sleet was on the early evening wind as Arlon stood in the courtyard of the palace grounds, near the very fountain that just the other day had played host to the conversation between Arlon, Lord Ludovic, and Professor Ergun. Although hardly a week had passed since the first mention of Handee's delay, the nation felt different, somehow fragmented. He only hoped the change was not irreparable.

The intrigue and manoeuvring in the council had now been replaced by a worrying silence. It was like watching still waters, knowing that sharks lurked just beneath the glassy surface.

The unrest on the border of Jow and Mashtock had apparently continued without any marked escalation or reduction, but word from the fact-finders had produced no more solid information. That these bandits were well armed and seemingly well organised was both apparent and concerning, but their origin, identity, and overall purpose remained a mystery.

Placing his sheathed sword next to him on the low fountain wall, Arlon sat for a quiet moment of introspection and a sip of water. The sleet and snow gathered in his messy hair, but he didn't let it bother him.

The thought struck him suddenly that he missed Kathryn. It had only been a matter of days since they had last spoken, but he missed her already, having been spoiled by her recent visit. It didn't help knowing that she had remained in the palace and was now engaged in espionage tasks at his and Ergun's bidding.

Interrupting his thoughts, Arlon heard footsteps approaching the courtyard, and he looked up to see a tall, broad man with a square jaw and mean eyes step into the darkening light of evening. This man was not just out for a stroll. Instead, he stopped and stared at Arlon for a long, uncomfortable moment. Arlon, tired and frustrated as he was, had no time for such interruptions.

"Knight Marshall Arlon?" the new arrival asked.

Arlon turned his head. "Do I know you, stranger?"

"You do not," he said. "I am Sir Failton Deed, baronet of Breen."

Great, Arlon thought. *Just what I need. A visit from Lady Marta's poor betrothed.*

"Hello, Failton," he said simply, unable to stop a small, pitiful smile playing across his lips. *At least he has the bulk to deal with her tantrums*, he thought somewhat petulantly.

"Don't mock me, Knight Marshall!" The anger in Failton's voice was more evident, and though Arlon had no idea where it came from, there was no mistaking the flushed face and white-knuckled fists.

He took a moment before replying. "I don't mock you, Failton. Why are you here? Surely you and I have no business. I am happy for you and Marta; my best wishes go with you."

"I'm here to demand the right of satisfaction."

Arlon paused. "Erm . . . I'm not sure it's me you need to be speaking to for that, lad." The fact that Arlon had replaced Sir Failton's honorific with the derogative "lad", despite them being of like age, clearly enraged the juggernaut further—which had been Arlon's intention.

A baronetcy was an hereditary title; ostensibly more senior to a normal knighthood, it nonetheless garnered little respect from Arlon. They might be traditionally granted the title *sir*, but they were not officially dubbed by the nation and therefore deserved no more of Arlon's respect or time than any other of Shenmadock's citizenry. Baronets were, by and large, spoiled children of lesser nobles who had achieved nothing of note but had still been afforded the honour—usually to satisfy pushy parents. The fact that Failton was obviously of the habit of lauding his title around like some badge of merit only served to reduce Arlon's opinion of the young man.

And now it seemed Failton was trying to challenge him. Arlon didn't fancy a fight but was more than ready to rise to it.

"I challenge you, sir! I shall not stand idly by as the good reputation of my betrothed is besmirched by your inappropriate attentions!"

His cup of water still in his hand and his scabbarded sword upon the fountain wall, Arlon stood in an attempt to placate the man. This only caused Failton to step forward aggressively, coming down the stairs with his hand upon the pommel of his sword.

"For goodness' sake!" Arlon tried, angered by Failton's threats. "Listen, I am fully aware Lord Karl has accepted your proposal, and I'm happy for you; I really am! You're barking up the wrong tree, for I have no interest in Lady Marta, other than the type of interest I have in a wasp that is intent on stinging me. And if you're worried about protecting her reputation, you might want to start with the lowliest squire in the palace and work your way up, just to be sure you avenge every indiscretion."

That Failton felt it was his place to bring his own insecurities to Arlon's door only annoyed him further, for the Knight Marshall had far larger fish to fry.

Failton's face crumbled with rage as he drew a long rapier—a deadly weapon in the hands of those well practiced in its use. The pair faced off across the courtyard, the falling sleet intensifying to an oppressive drizzle.

Failton had drawn steel. Arlon had to respond in kind; he had to touch blades, for this was an official challenge. Still, he had no desire to fight him, so he tried one last time. "Don't be foolish, boy. A fistfight is all well and good, but a real ruckus can only end in someone getting hurt."

"You cowardly rake!" Failton rushed across the flagstones and lunged at Arlon's chest with the tip of his rapier.

Arlon stepped to the side and threw his water into Failton's face, startling him into skidding on the sleet-covered flagstones. The bigger man lost his balance and stabbed too high with the point of his blade, cutting the air above Arlon's shoulder. With a shove, Arlon sent him staggering away.

Striving to remain relaxed and well balanced, he dropped his cup in the fountain and picked up his own sword, still leaving it in the scabbard. He remained keen to avoid a fight, because if he lost his temper . . . well, there was no telling what damage he might do.

"Don't do this, Failton. You've tried so hard to win Marta's hand; don't let your temper end your life before you can enjoy your good fortune."

Failton snarled and regained his composure. Arlon could see in his face that he would not make the same mistake twice.

Using his covered sword like a nightstick, Arlon deflected Failton's next two attacks and stepped to the side, shifting his perfectly balanced weight forward and skilfully blocking an attack behind his back intended to skewer his kidney.

Turning to face Failton again, Arlon twirled the scabbard twice in his hand as he backed away, deflecting three more strikes. Upon the third, Arlon drew his weapon and threw the scabbard aside.

The sleet was turning to heavy snow now as the seething clouds blocked out all remaining daylight.

"I warn you, Failton, I don't engage in swordplay lightly." Arlon deflected two more attacks and retreated up the stairs to the raised promenade around the edge of the courtyard. "I don't want to kill you."

Failton's breath came in puffs of white. He resembled nothing so much as a bull; he was huge but still in decent shape. Even crouching three steps above him, Arlon was almost eye to eye with the baronet.

Failton slashed out across Arlon's midriff—a blow he dodged back from—and then the rapier stabbed at Arlon's feet. He jumped that strike and punched Failton in the face with his sword hand. The hulk staggered back into the courtyard. Taking two steps, Arlon launched from the promenade and slammed his left knee into the side of Failton's face.

Failton tumbled onto his back, and Arlon caught his balance on the sleet-covered flagstones, his boots skidding on the increasingly treacherous surface. It took him a moment to register the stinging pain in his right thigh, a shallow groove where Failton's rapier had barely nicked him.

Blood rimmed Failton's teeth as he smiled—a cruel smile.

"So be it," said Arlon reluctantly.

Failton was visibly buoyed at having caught Arlon, even so slightly. He approached with even more confidence as they skirted the fountain, the courtyard filled with the clang and clatter of traded blows. Despite the cold, both swordsmen were working up a decent sweat.

As they fought on, a pair of palace lamp-lighters stepped out onto the balcony above on their nightly rounds. The sounds of combat immediately drew their attention. The older lamp-lighter ushered the younger man off to fetch help while he stayed to watch.

Failton slipped once more on the wet flags, and Arlon sought to press the advantage, punching Failton in the jaw and following up with a crash of his elbow across the ear. As Failton recoiled, Arlon slashed at his face, cleaving a nick into the point of his chin.

He was trying to avoid killing this fool, but his relentless determination was dangerous.

As he pressed the attack, he could feel fury threatening to boil up in him, like a surging tide barely contained by a sea wall. He caught Failton once more, high on the cheek, feeling the blade scrape along the jawbone as it tore his face open.

Failton lashed out wildly with his rapier as he fell back, a hand clasped to his ripped face. The rapier caught Arlon in the shoulder with a lucky glance, deeper this time.

Arlon cursed himself. *Patience*, he heard his old instructor's calm voice reminding him. *Passion is good, but never attack with anger, for that is devoid of balance and control.*

He shrugged off the wound and stood en guard, the point of his longsword aimed at Failton's chest. Arlon was the better fighter, and they both knew it; Arlon could see that in Failton's face.

Failton struggled to his feet, swaying a little before he jabbed forward with his rapier, attacking with the poise of a seasoned fencer. Arlon was hard-pressed to keep the point of the sword from nicking his flesh like an angry bee. Failton was trying to wear him down, tire him out like it was a fencing match, not a deadly swordfight.

Above, the second lamp-lighter returned to his friend's side as palace guards rushed toward the courtyard through the library. "Put down your weapons!" Arlon heard the guard leader shout, his voice deep with authority. Many more people had begun to gather at the balcony, drawn by rumours of a duel.

As the guards arrived, Arlon shouted out between parries and blocks, "Stand down, Captain! This is a challenge!"

The guards halted at the extreme of the courtyard. A few dogs on short leashes barked furiously. Although this was an official disturbance of the peace on their watch, and upon palace grounds too, they knew better than to intercede during a duel of honour. If Arlon had needed or wanted their help, he'd have asked for it.

Failton stepped away, snarled, and then launched back in to a flurry of strikes aimed at Arlon's torso, clearly frustrated. As Arlon worked to deflect each attack, the rapier occasionally nicked out and scored a graze in his forearm or bicep. The cuts were nothing serious, and yet he felt unusually weary, cold, and angry beneath the weight of the storm.

Failton wasn't going to give up. Soon, Arlon would have to end it. He was hoping to knock the man unconscious, but the blows he had already delivered weren't showing signs of slowing the man down. If the opportunity to incapacitate him didn't present itself, he would have to end it by other means. If that meant killing him, then at least he knew he'd tried.

Moving quickly, Arlon sprang away with his back to the fountain. As Failton followed and lunged at his stomach, Arlon sidestepped and kicked at Failton's foot. The big man slipped, and Arlon pushed his head under the water of the fountain pool.

The laughter of those on the balcony rang out as Arlon made to crash the pommel of his sword on Failton's head, but the rapier lashed out blindly, forcing him back.

He was inexplicably exhausted.

Perhaps his cousin's absence from the palace and his want of a sparring partner had left him out of shape. Arlon put it down to the fatigue from many days of poor sleep. His limbs felt heavy, and a bout of nausea struck him. He forced himself to focus, using his breath to concentrate.

Failton flipped his head up, water spraying from his sodden fringe. The humiliation on his red face was clear.

"Stop this, Failton. Walk away," Arlon said.

Failton lunged at Arlon again, ignoring his warning.

Somewhere beyond the palace guards and their barking dogs, Princess Kathryn de Hayne hurried through the growing crowd of onlookers, shouting Arlon's name. At first, Arlon couldn't make out what she was shouting above the rattle of clashing metal and baying dogs. Then he heard it.

He was suddenly filled with a deep dread.

"Poison!" she shouted again.

As the princess tried to explain things to the palace guard sergeant, imploring him to ignore the matter of honour, Arlon saw Failton's face shift from anger to desperation.

Poison? It didn't seem plausible.

But then again . . .

Failton jumped at Arlon, who was forced to take the blow on the flat of his sword, turning the huge man to the side. He lashed out with his own blade, running a red line along Failton's ribs.

The crowd had quieted as they realised something was amiss. The palace guard sergeant seemed unsure how to proceed.

Finally, the sergeant made his mind up, commanding the guards to close on the duelling pair. Failton bellowed with rage as the guards made their move and entered the courtyard, the dogs still barking loudly.

With impossible speed, Failton jabbed the rapier at Arlon's ribs. He jumped to the side, risking a wound to his flank. Closing the distance in one stride, Arlon slammed his forehead into Failton's nose, feeling it crumble under his skull.

As Failton staggered back again, Arlon swept out his sword and knocked the rapier from his opponent's hand. He slashed his longsword through the top of Failton's knee. The kneecap sprang away with a gristly pop.

Failton began to fall. Arlon punched his blade up under his chin and out through the crown of his skull, killing the baronet instantly.

Bloodied and breathless, the Knight Marshall released his weakening grip on his sword still impaled in his victim's head. He thumped backward to sit against the fountain wall as his snow-clouded vision swam.

As he glanced about, all he could see were swirling snowflakes. Then his darkening vision was filled with the most glorious sight—Princess Kathryn de Hayne, her hair dotted by snowflakes like stars in the night sky, her eyes full of love and concern.

His world shrank in upon him, and he tumbled backward into the fountain water, Kathryn's anguished screams chasing him to the torn depths.

Chapter Thirty

Remnant at the Gate

Dale, Guardigan, and the twins hurried on through the dark forest, finally cresting the last hill that led down to the Shen Utah plain. Dawn was more than an hour away, and rain had hammered down on them all night. Soaked through, miserable, exhausted, and crestfallen, they ploughed on through the mud.

Just as their resolve began to wane, the first sounds of pursuit had echoed through the night, chilling Dale to the bone. Flat and hollow on the night-time air that was thick with falling sleet, the rattle of armour and clatter of weapons had carried like a banshee wail. With the ghostly echo, it was impossible to tell if the pursuing elements numbered one or one hundred—but they were certainly close behind.

Any thoughts of giving up had fled their minds, as had any lingering hope that Aleks, Garrick, Corn, and Arrin had survived the ambush.

As Dale and Guardigan crashed between trees, stumbling down the slope, it was clear that the Wayfarers' brave sacrifice might not have been enough. It was impossible to tell if they had enough time to get the twins to the safety of Shen Utah before the pursuit overtook them.

Suddenly Dale burst through a stand of trees and emerged into an open field of grazing land. Cattle rested in a corner of the field, sheltering under a small stand of willow trees, and the ground still showed signs of the snowfall from hours before. The fields were mottled black and white all the way to the city. A gate stood in the far hedgerow.

A few miles away, upon the southern bank of the River Jow, Shen Utah huddled in the frozen rain. Only a smattering of burning torches illuminated the foulbergs outside the ancient city walls, but the streets and lanes inside burned brightly.

Guardigan and the twins stumbled out from between the trees behind him, and Dale hurried them toward the gate. The turf beneath their feet was hardening with frost but still gave dangerously, certainly enough to bog them or risk an ankle sprain. Although they were going to be able to move much quicker through the openness of farming land, the same would be true for their enemy.

The last chase was on.

The sleet had relented and the sky to the east was turning blood red with the approach of morning when Dale caught his first glimpse of their pursuers.

Jarn and Larissa were weakening to the point of collapse now, but they had reached the outer foulberg buildings moments before, and Dale turned to look up the hills behind them. Crashing down toward them, no more than three hundred yards at their backs, were six figures. The first of them was a dozen yards ahead of his colleagues and looked to be a monster of a man. Larissa let out an involuntary squeal.

"Dale!" Guardigan hissed. "Stop gawking!"

Guardigan ushered the twins through the wide paths of the settlements outside of the city proper. Although some candlelight could be seen in the windows, no one was abroad yet.

Following on, Dale huffed, "Guardigan, we'll never make it. It's more than five hundred yards to the South-eastern Gate, and we're exhausted."

Guardigan whirled round in anger. "Then what do you suggest? Should we leave them here? Should we fly over the walls with those wings we forgot we possess? Or do you want to stand and face six enemies on our own?"

"I think we must!"

Guardigan was aghast. "Have you gone mental?"

"Of course not," Dale said, recommencing their run toward the South-eastern Gate. "The twins are faster than us. They can get to the gate, alert the guard. All we have to do is hold them off long enough."

Guardigan linked once and then fervently agreed. "That's actually a good idea! You two, kick on for the gate! Run!"

Larissa looked worried, but Jarn pulled her forward. "Come on!" he shouted, and then pushed them into an exhausted sprint.

"Good luck!" Larissa shouted. "And thank you!"

And then it was just Dale and Guardigan. They tried to force themselves to pick up the pace, but they were exhausted. Suddenly, Guardigan stumbled to a stop, doubled over, and vomited up nought but water.

They were no more than two hundred yards from the gate when they came within sight of the distant torches atop the ancient walls of the capital, but it was still dark in the foulberg. Guardigan quickly recovered his poise, but it was clear he could go no further at their pace. Dale's own legs felt leaden and numb, as if he was running through chilled treacle.

Their race had been run. Now came their fight.

Just as he thought to start calling out to the unseen guard station at the gate—with breath he didn't possess—Dale was struck in the shoulder by some unseen object. He pitched onto his face, pain lancing through his arm. A cold sensation rushed through him and made him retch. Looking over his shoulder, he saw the hasp of a throwing dagger jutting up from his rent flesh. Blood leaked down his back as he cradled his arm. Even that small movement caused the sensation of metal scraping against the bone inside.

Behind them, striding between squat buildings, the huge tracker who had trailed them for perhaps a hundred miles approached. He carried a massive broadsword that bore a dull red hue in the pre-dawn darkness, as though fresh from the blacksmith's forge. He carried it to the side in a two-handed grip.

The hood of his robe was pulled back. Dale could see his features were unremarkable—his eyes cold and grey, his hair the colour of sand on a rainy day. He was chillingly expressionless.

Dale saw that Guardigan was clearly caught in a quandary—help his friend by facing this terrible foe or flee for the city gate and safety.

He glanced at Dale.

In that one look, the young soldier knew what his wizened comrade had decided, and felt like weeping when he saw Guardigan draw his sword and face their enemy. "Come on, whoreson!" Guardigan shouted bravely. "You don't frighten me, you big lummox!"

Dale got back to his feet, and then, gritting his teeth, he reached back and yanked the dagger from his back. A jet of blood squirted out behind him, and he swooned but managed to remain conscious. With a struggle, he tried to free his sword from its scabbard as Guardigan launched to the attack.

The old battler attacked low and quick, trying to avoid the longer reach of the broadsword. His attack missed, but so did the enemy's riposte. Backing quickly away, Guardigan glanced at Dale before working toward him.

The attacker stepped after Guardigan and swung a mighty attack at his head. The blade made a deep whooshing sound as it parted the morning air. The old City Guardsman hurled himself to the floor to avoid the blow.

The broadsword raised high above his head, the stranger made to cleave it down right through the prone Guardigan.

The thick blade of the broadsword clashed noisily onto Dale's sword. The sound rang out in the flatness of the morning air like a clarion bell, impossibly loud. Dale's arm flashed with pain at the terrible power of that blocked strike, and he broke out in a cold sweat, the wound seething in his back.

The stranger seemed confused by the inefficacy of his weapon. He snarled and aimed a kick at the meddlesome Dale, who sprang backward to avoid it. Again, the enemy swung his sword down at Guardigan, but found only soggy mud. The old guard had scrambled to his feet and turned on him again.

Their breath came in thick plumes as they pressed their heavily fatigued bodies into one last desperate bid. The enemy jumped forward, bringing his sword down in three hefty blows on Dale's sword. The weapon vibrated in his hand like a violin bow, and then cleanly snapped on the third block.

Dale fell back under the onslaught, ready to receive the final blow, but it never came. He glanced up and found that Guardigan had dealt a wound to the man's leg, trying to turn him away from Dale as he lay prone upon the ground.

Dale looked down at himself. His light armour had indeed been cut cleanly open by the third strike, and now Dale felt a strange wetness under his tunic. He reached a finger inside the rent armour and brought it out drenched in blood.

His chest was cut open. He had no idea how deep the wound could be, only that his breath now came in ragged gasps.

He knew he had to get up, but his legs would not obey. He collapsed back, morning rain pooling in his gasping mouth as he desperately tried to draw breath into damaged lungs.

Down the path, he could now see the huge man's remaining companions as they ran toward them.

Dale looked up helplessly as Guardigan tried in vain to fend off the giant man's attacks—a man who seemed utterly unaffected by the long journey they had all endured. Their enemy crashed on methodically, breaking against Guardigan's resolve like an ocean tide against ancient rocks.

As Dale tried again to get to his feet, he saw Guardigan lose his sword. The blade flipped from his grip, ringing as it flew out of sight. Without gloating or preamble, the enemy steadied himself to make the killing blow.

The man brought his sword up.

On the morning air, a whistle could be heard.

The insect-like buzz became the flutter of an arrow as it zipped through the air high above Dale's head and slammed into the man's temple. His head was punched sideways by the impact.

Another whistle.

A second arrow thumped home no more than an inch from the first. The man shuddered, his eyes wide with surprise as his fingers released his sword, the blade of which was now dull and unremarkable. His body crumpled in stages, first at the knees and then at the waist.

Suddenly, the air was alive with arrows that fell with deadly accuracy upon the rest of the pursuing squad, protecting the two battered Shen soldiers.

Dale sank back into the rain-sodden mud and felt the cold fire in his chest swell through him. As the rain grew in strength, Guardigan's face appeared above him. The old soldier smirked and said, "We did it, Dale. Just hold on, help is coming."

Chapter Thirty-One
Accusations

Ludovic awoke with a start.

Someone was knocking insistently on the door of his city home. Early as the hour was, he could hear the boom of each urgent knock. By the time his footman had come to his chamber door to rouse him, he was already dressed, buttoning his waistcoat as he opened the door to the landing.

"What is it?" Ludovic asked as he walked along the landing and down the main staircase. The dwelling wasn't as opulent or expansive as his others dotted around the countryside, but it was bigger than most in the area.

"My lord," said his footman, following after, "you have a visitor."

"Obviously, Arn; who are they, and what do they want at this ungodly hour?"

Arn held out his palms. "They wouldn't say, sir."

Stifling a growl of impatience, Ludovic stalked across the hallway and into the reception room to find a palace messenger waiting for him, a neatly folded note in his hand. The lad's forehead carried a film of sweat, proving he'd come at a run.

"What is it, then, boy?"

"Lord Ludovic, the Council of Lords convenes in less than an hour." He held out the parchment, and Ludovic took it, concern knitting his brow. He read the simple missive that declared an emergency session of the council. It elaborated no further.

"Very good, boy. Get gone now."

With a bow, the boy fled the mansion, leaving Ludovic alone with his thoughts. When Arn returned, his footman said, "Lord, I have already seen to preparations. Your wagon will be at the courtyard shortly."

"Good enough, Arn; thank you."

"Erm, one more thing, my lord. This arrived for you in the middle of the night." He handed Ludovic a second note, this one carefully folded and sealed with dirty wax. "It had been pushed under the buttery door, sir. I had the dogs give it a sniff, and it doesn't appear to be poisoned."

"Comforting," Ludovic mumbled as he took the note. As clumsily stamped as it was, he still recognised the seal. Without opening it, he placed the message in his pocket and went to find his boots. He would read it on the way to this emergency session.

He had a bad feeling.

As he entered the circular Council Chamber less than an hour later, Ludovic's bad feeling had grown stronger. Every officer and lord of Shenmadock's council appeared to be in attendance, even a few Ludovic was unfamiliar with. Minor nobles and even some of the more influential lords often chose to pass the winter season at their estates, so it was a surprise to see an emergency council meeting so well attended.

As he took his seat, Lord Ludovic surreptitiously unfolded once more the coded message he'd received under his door the previous night. More than anything, for his agent to have risked committing that minor act meant the contents of the message were vital. He had to trust the information, as troubling as it might prove to be.

Ludovic had lived his whole life in Shen Utah, and was an influential lord. He had spent many years cultivating a network of informants and lines of communication that most criminals would be proud of. As such, very little of note occurred in the city without Lord Ludovic learning of it.

On the face of it, the message in his hand told him very little, but when considered in light of all the facts at hand, the ramifications were wide-ranging. An apothecary in the city had been assassinated, but not before supplying someone with the dreaded Black Spider Venom. He had known of a plot to gain that most heinous of poisons, but had been reassured that the attempts to acquire it had been unsuccessful. Apparently, that was not the case; the poison was in the city and had—according to the last line of the secret note—been acquired by a lady of high birth.

Ludovic glanced around the room, allowing his gaze to linger on Lord Karl II, Duke of Jow. Some unknown representative of Jow had intended to allow a consignment of treasure and—more concerningly—naphtha to pass through their custom controls before the ship had been sunk in Shen Utah's harbour. The carrier Justin Dowling had also had the ship illegally passed through customs in the capital, at what must have been great expense. And then a customs inspector and his wife had turned up dead. All of this, to what end? What was that treasure intended to purchase?

And now this poison, this Black Spider Venom? There was a link to the ship; Ludovic was certain of that. As for this "lady of high birth" who had sought to acquire the Black Spider Venom . . . that Karl would have used his daughter Marta for such a purpose was not beyond the Jow duke. So, what was it for? If the trail did indeed run back to Karl—he had already shown a willingness to have men killed for their silence—why acquire such a poison? Unless to send a message . . .

His gaze landed on Councillor Horvarth of Unedar, whose expression belied concern in keeping with events. Unless Horvarth was a far better actor than Ludovic gave him credit for, Horvarth knew not the reason for this emergency session.

No, Ludovic was certain it was Karl who was behind much of what had occurred recently—especially the increasing unrest in the duchy of Mashtock. Ludovic had to figure out what the plan was before it was too late, and he had a strong suspicion that this emergency session was precisely Karl's design.

His bad feeling plunged to dread as the meeting was called to attention, for Ludovic could clearly see that neither Professor Ergun nor Knight Marshall Arlon were present. *Where were they?* It was surely no coincidence that Lord Karl was the member of the council who called proceedings to order.

"Order! Please, my fellow lords and councillors, come to order!" The chamber quickly fell silent, petering out to a rustle of clothing as those late to their seats hurried in.

Karl looked about the room for a moment, peering into individual faces before continuing. "We have grave and pressing business to preside over. Shenmadock faces peril of the most serious nature. For many days now, during a time of strife in Mashtock, the Senior Lord Handee has failed to return from his tour of the eastern duchies. We are yet to receive good news from Lord Handee's convoy, and must now assume the worst. For this very reason, this council has already petitioned the good Knight Marshall to declare *Senior Lord in Absentia*, to provide Knight Marshall

Arlon the emergency powers required to quell the unrest in Mashtock. A petition he has heretofore declined."

Still worried that Ergun and Arlon were both absent from the meeting, Ludovic interrupted Lord Karl. "Apologies, Lord Karl, but should we not wait for the Knight Marshall before we start accusing him of inaction?"

"We can ill afford to wait any longer," Karl said.

Ludovic held out his arms. "What's the rush? After all, we have still to receive information of a kind that would justify a call of *in absentia.* I appreciate that while the axiom 'no news is good news' might not be entirely accurate in these circumstances, the Knight Marshall was correct in not acting rashly to unseat Senior Lord Handee. The steps Arlon has taken to investigate the civil unrest in Mashtock were the correct ones, and required no intervention, and so no sovereignty shift. While we have no proof of an aggressor or even suggestion of conspiracy, we will not need to make any rash decisions."

There were several loud murmurs of agreement, and Lord Ludovic's heart was gladdened a little to know he wasn't alone in his concern. Still, that coded message was gripped in his fist. Karl would have an ace in his sleeve, for sure.

"Well, Lord Ludovic, I am afraid events have transpired that have forced our hand."

Lord Karl paused for effect. Ludovic looked on with a growing sense of apprehension.

"I have received word that Knight Marshall Arlon was challenged to a duel of honour this last evening by Baronet Failton Deed of Breen, whereupon the life of our nation's last great hero was taken, along with that of his challenger."

The entire room exploded with activity, lords and councillors chattering with the same fervour Ludovic had witnessed just days before. This time there was the distinct undercurrent of fear, and Ludovic shared that trepidation.

Arlon of Thes dead? The Heathenbane dead? What manner of warrior could vanquish such a man as Arlon? A man who the sagas describe as being a god amongst men?

It took several moments for Lord Karl to quieten the council in order to be heard, during which Ludovic stood like an island in a storm of alarm.

"Please, my esteemed councillors and lords—order!" The room again fell quiet, but there was a charge to the atmosphere since the announcement of Arlon's death.

What is happening? Ludovic thought. *What is his next move? I need time to think.*

Before Lord Karl could speak into the growing silence, Ludovic said aloud with genuine, sombre grief, "My friends, this nation has lost a hero. Please join me in a minute of silence in respect for the passing of Knight Marshall Arlon Hapthelt of King's End, Protector of Shen Utah, Heathenbane, Hero of Thes."

Lord Karl looked openly furious at the interruption, his words having died in his mouth, but there was nothing he could do. He had to endure the silence, a silence that gave Lord Ludovic time to contemplate just what it was Lord Karl was angling for. Had Karl used the Black Spider Venom to arrange Arlon's murder? It had to be the case! To what end?

There was only one possible motive, only one possible intention, and Ludovic didn't have to wait too long to have it confirmed, for the Duke of Jow interrupted the silence a little early for his liking. "A beautiful moment of respect, my lords, but we must press on. With the absence of Senior Lord Handee, the death of Knight Marshall Arlon, and the continued escalation of unrest across the border in Mashtock, we must act, and act decisively. I call now for an emergency ballot to elect a new Senior Lord, who can then assign the successor to Arlon of Thes in the position of Knight Marshall. The nation of Shenmadock must endure this tragedy!"

A long minute stretched out as lords and councillors raised their voices to be heard, all urgently discussing the call for a ballot. Ludovic sat down in his seat quietly, his heart heavy.

Arlon was dead, and now Karl had made his move to take power. Ludovic had no doubts that Karl would promote himself as Handee's successor, but he would need a nomination. Friends of Jow on the council were as rare as rocking horse dung, but a conversation with Arlon earlier in the week jumped into his mind. Horvarth. Arlon had feared a union between Unedar and Jow, but Ludovic had dismissed it at the time. What if Horvarth was lined up for this very moment?

If Karl received his nomination, and without proof against him of any underhand dealings, Ludovic's only hope to forestall his ascent would be to contest his bid for power. For that, he would need the cooperation of the other duchies. Mashtock, sensing that Jow were to blame for the unrest in their own duchy, should be no hard sell. But that would only split the vote two-a-piece. Choat would be left holding the casting vote. If they chose to support Karl's claim, Shenmadock would be in trouble.

On the floor of the chamber, another voice could be heard calling for attention. The voice sounded meek and feeble compared to the mighty orator that was Lord Karl. The lords around Ludovic sat and fell silent after a moment. Lord Ludovic could see Councillor Fargil of Mashtock standing in the centre of the chamber, looking like nothing more than a scared field mouse.

Hope sparked in Ludovic's chest. Fargil would be Mashtock's voice of reason and would give Ludovic and his allies the chance to oppose the ballot. Perhaps Choat would be won over by Fargil's pleas.

If only Handee were still here!

"I beseech the council, please hear me," Fargil began. Lord Ludovic watched as the little councillor steeled himself. "I, Councillor Fargil of Mashtock, speaking on behalf of my Lord Cordon Vale, Duke of Mashtock, officially support the proposition of a ballot to elect a new Senior Lord of Shenmadock."

Not ideal, thought Lord Ludovic, *but what other choice do we now have? All we must do is appoint the right successor to Handee. Duke Cordon Vale isn't a brilliant man, but he's an honest one.*

If Fargil nominates his own duke, would the rest of the duchies get behind his petition? They were about to find out.

"Furthermore," Fargil continued, "Mashtock supports the nomination of Lord Karl II, Duke of Jow, to the position of Senior Lord."

"What!" Lord Ludovic couldn't help but shout. All eyes turned on him as he stood, looking down upon the shrivelled form of Councillor Fargil. "I demand to see Lord Vale so he can explain this decision himself!"

"Enough, Lord Ludovic," interrupted Karl coolly. "Councillor Fargil speaks for Mashtock in this forum, and his support is so registered, humbly." Karl bowed deeply toward Fargil.

Deep dread and panic boiled in Ludovic's heart. He looked around the chamber in search of allies. His supporters and colleagues on the council looked back, their expressions of helplessness universally mirroring his own. Even the members of Choat's retinue looked confused. The primary reason to argue against Lord Karl's ascension—to support Mashtock—had just been compromised by Jow's very victim.

Then one of Ludovic's supporters shouted from the lower tiers, "I nominate Lord Ludovic of Shen Utah and sponsor his petition!" This angered Ludovic, for he had made no such petition.

"Silence, all of you! This is not legal!" Ludovic shouted. "We cannot elect a new Senior Lord, for Senior Lord

Handee has not officially been declared absent!" But none were listening, for most were too busy fighting like vultures for a bite of the carcass that was the Council of Lords. And his argument was a flaccid one, anyway. With Arlon dead, his point was moot. Ludovic tried in vain to seek some semblance of order, but it was to no avail.

What could he do now? Answer the nomination? Was it the move of a sane man to challenge Lord Karl's attempt at ascension by commencing his own? He could hardly argue the case to support Senior Lord Handee and at the same time put himself up as his successor! But what else could he do?

And yet it was futile. Karl would have the vote of Jow, Unedar, and now—incredibly—Mashtock. Ludovic had only Shen Utah and Choat. He would lose three to two.

Karl had won.

Suddenly, an enormous boom filled the political arena as the doors of the great chamber thundered open, the old hinges cracking. All voices fell silent, and all eyes turned to see who had the audacity to interrupt the council in session.

As one, the Council of Lords seemed to gasp, a sound like gas escaping from a fissure.

Arlon stood framed in the doorway, supported by the figure of Princess Kathryn de Hayne, the dawn light shining through the stained glass of the corridor behind them. Ludovic could have cried with relief, for his heart sang at the sight of the still-living Knight Marshall.

There's still a chance to avoid this insanity!

As he looked on, he could see that the Knight Marshall was indeed incredibly sick, his face drawn and pale, his skin moist with sweat. Despite being so much smaller than Arlon, Kathryn de Hayne supported him, one arm draped across her shoulders. Behind them, Ludovic could see a troop of palace guards standing to attention, awaiting orders.

"This meeting is a little premature," Arlon said simply. Even at this distance, Ludovic could see the fury in his bloodshot eyes.

From the far side of the chamber, another of Ludovic's supporters shouted, "Arlon of Thes lives! Thank the gods!"

Yet another demanded, "What is the meaning of all this?"

"In the matter of my death, it seems Lord Karl was misinformed," Arlon said, looking about the chamber. His eyes fell upon the form of Lord Karl, who now seemed so much smaller than just a moment before.

"With the Knight Marshall present, there can be no ballot!" declared Ludovic with glee. "Can I enquire of Lord Karl; precisely where did you get the information that the Knight Marshall had died?"

Karl's swine-like eyes turned up to Ludovic, narrowing with hate. "I was informed that a duel had taken place on the palace grounds, and that both individuals had sadly perished."

"Is this true?" Ludovic asked Arlon. "Was there a duel of honour?"

"There was a duel, but there was no honour in it."

"What was the purpose of this duel?"

"Failton Deed, baronet of Breen, challenged me to a duel to protect the honour of Lady Marta. I slew him, but not before he had dealt me several minor wounds . . . with a blade laced with Black Spider Venom."

The Council Chamber chattered with alarm.

"Such underhand behaviour from a baronet?" asked Karl with suspicion. "That is a weighty accusation, Knight Marshall. It is a tragedy that he did not survive for us to question him, so I assume you have proof?"

"Of course! And what's worse, I believe Failton was manipulated into challenging me, and that his poisoned sword was the work of another."

So it was true, then; Karl had been responsible for the Black Spider Venom. "An assassination attempt?" asked Ludovic.

"Surely not," another lord shouted.

"Whom do you suspect?" asked Ludovic, knowing what must surely be the truth.

Arlon nodded, steeling himself. It took a brave man to make an accusation in the Council Chamber. "I have reason to believe that Failton was pressed into this action by the father of his betrothed, Lord Karl II of Jow, to cement Karl's blessing for Failton's desired union."

The chamber erupted once more as supporters of both Shen Utah and Jow hurled accusations at one another.

"Enough!" bellowed Arlon, though it seemed to pain him to have to raise his voice.

"Arlon, such a serious accusation can only be made with evidence. Your mentor Professor Ergun would surely have taught you that much," Karl told him slyly.

"What is the proof you spoke of?" Ludovic asked hopefully.

"For once, Ergun *is* my evidence. My mentor, teacher, and friend, Professor Ergun, was slain last night. His murderer was witnessed conspiring with Lord Karl of Jow to arrange my assassination . . . *and* they were also heard discussing a conspiracy to have Senior Lord Handee detained by their accomplices in Unedar in order to usurp his position of leader of this nation. A conspiracy that has actually seen Handee murdered in Unedar!"

The noise in the chamber was rising with each allegation.

"That same witness then watched as the conspirator slew Professor Ergun in cold blood when the good professor chanced upon the meeting. Ergun's murderer then stood before this council and nominated Lord Karl for Senior Lord."

Lord Ludovic looked down on Councillor Fargil, who seemed to have shrunk even further. Instead of violent denials, Fargil simply began to weep.

Could it really be that Fargil murdered his own brother?

Lord Karl stepped past the grieving Fargil, placing a conciliatory hand on his shoulder as he went. "We share your loss," Karl told Fargil, as though it was only for Ergun that Fargil wept. Then Karl spoke to Arlon in deep, threatening tones. "Name your witness to these imaginings?"

Arlon went to speak, but instead, Kathryn stepped forward, releasing his arm. "I witnessed it all," she said defiantly. "Ergun interrupted his brother as he left his secret meeting with you in the royal atrium yesterday. The brothers argued, and Fargil stabbed the professor in the leg, severing the artery, before fleeing the scene. I was at Ergun's side as he died—a victim of the same poison intended for Arlon."

Karl looked at Kathryn de Hayne for a second, his eyes cold and contemplative. "I think I have the measure of it," he said, his voice full of confidence. Turning to the council, he continued, "It all makes sense. The Knight Marshall, once a suitor to my daughter, is now held in thrall by the Princess de Hayne!"

"I never paid suit to Marta," Arlon denied.

Karl ignored him. "He himself slew Failton out of jealousy! Arlon is clearly a monarchist, and he seeks a return to the old ways. *That* is why he has concocted this story in an attempt to destabilise this republic! *That* is why he has frequently refused to perform his duties as Knight Marshall of this land! *That* is why I suspect Arlon himself has had the Senior Lord assassinated!"

"That's preposterous!" shouted Arlon.

"Was it not your own cousin whom you sent to find evidence of Handee's return, without the consent of this council?"

Ludovic said, "The Knight Marshall doesn't need our permission to send his cousin into the field, Karl."

"Even so," Karl plunged on, "this could just as easily be seen as a mission to intercept and eliminate the returning Senior Lord, could it not? Carpion and his retinue are yet to return to the capital, just as Senior Lord Handee.

"Furthermore, if you examine Arlon's relationship with his cousin Carpion, and the myriad offices the captain holds, is Arlon not also in the perfect position to have certain witnesses silenced, and even to have orchestrated the unrest in Mashtock? If he sees fit to send Wayfarers east to seek out Handee, might he also send guerrilla troops north to cause havoc?"

Karl pointed out of the chamber, at the city walls beyond sight.

"And look to the walls! He deploys elves to this city's defences without our ratification! Disgraced Druidale Rangers, back on the walls of the capital!" He jabbed a fat finger in Arlon's direction. "You see fit to come here and accuse brave Fargil of murdering his own brother, when it seems clear to me that it was more than likely *you* who murdered your mentor! Perhaps not all of your wounds were caused in the one fight . . ."

"To what possible end?" implored Ludovic.

"Ergun loved the republic," Fargil said quietly from behind his clasped hands.

Karl proceeded unabashed, addressing Arlon and then the council in turn. "Ergun must have learned of your monarchist affiliations and your intentions to install yourself as king! He sought to dissuade you, to turn you back to this nation's cause! The record will show that I have only ever conducted myself within the laws of this land in an attempt to secure our nation's defence by placing sovereign power in Arlon's hands. It was *he* who refused that mantle. Why would I try to put you in power if I intended to kill you and seize power myself, as I am so accused?"

There were murmurings of doubt in the chamber. Eyes, darkened by growing suspicion, turned toward Arlon.

"But if we look at Arlon's conduct, we see a man who repeatedly rejected the laws of this land, time and again refused to declare *Senior Lord in Absentia.* He sent his own cousin to intercept the returning Senior Lord. He mans the walls of this city with elven archers, without engaging this political body in a discussion about such a decision. And as we all know, the last time elven archers stood atop the Shen Utah walls, the de Haynes sat upon the throne of Shenmadock! The archers of the Druidale Rangers were loyal to the monarchy only and were rightly supplanted during the revolution."

Ludovic looked at Arlon. His rage was palpable, but Kathryn de Hayne appeared openly worried at the developments.

"And this very morning, as we all stand here, it is Knight Marshall Arlon who has brought the first de Hayne into this chamber since the revolution. How much clearer could his affiliations possibly be!"

Karl turned on Arlon.

"I put it to you, Knight Marshall, that you are a royalist, a treasonous monarchist, who now seeks to usurp this council and return the line of de Hayne to power!"

"That's ludicrous!" Arlon raged, the colour returning to his face. "You're a silver-tongued traitor!"

"*You* are the traitor, Arlon! In the name of Shenmadock and the Council of Lords, I order your arrest pending charges of treason. Guards!" He gestured to those waiting outside the chamber. "Take the Knight Marshall to the dungeons!"

"No!" screamed Kathryn de Hayne. The guards hesitated, uncertain. Lord Ludovic looked about the room in search of an answer, but none was forthcoming.

Suddenly, a distant shout was heard from without the chamber, and all eyes turned toward the doorway. Some of the guards standing behind Arlon launched into action—but not to arrest the Knight Marshall. Instead, they rushed out of sight down the corridor.

As fast as he dared, Lord Ludovic moved from his seat and descended the stone stairs to the chamber floor. As he neared the foot of the stairs, the guards returned, accompanying a Druidale Ranger who in turn supported a sorry-looking figure covered in dirt and blood. Behind them limped another City Guard, a little older, in equally distressed condition.

Arlon moved toward the approaching guards. "Forgive me, sir," the elf carrying the injured man addressed the Knight Marshall. "These soldiers insisted upon seeing you, though this one is not in a good condition. We spied them running for the South-eastern Gate with two civilians. They were being harried by brigands, or so we thought."

"What of their attackers?" asked Arlon.

The elf smiled enigmatically. "Dealt with, sir."

"What occurs here?" demanded Karl, approaching across the chamber floor.

The wounded man looked up at Arlon, his unshaven face half covered in mud. A terrible gash had been cleaved into his chest, through his chest plate, and his breath rattled with fluid. "Arlon!" the younger soldier said with wonder, recognising the Knight Marshall.

The other guard took over. "Forgive my colleague, Knight Marshall. He's an idiot. This is Private Dale, and I am Sergeant Guardigan."

"I recognise you, I think," Arlon said.

"Perhaps," Sergeant Guardigan said guardedly. "We are Shen Utah City Guards reassigned to Carpion's Wayfarers for the mission to locate Senior Lord Handee. I bring dire news. An army is abroad in the Land of the

Lords. A great force marches through Unedar toward the duchy of Shen Utah, and I believe they march under the banner of Ipsica. They could be at the gates of the capital in less than a month, should they continue direct and unopposed."

There was a pregnant pause, the kind of silence that permeates the soul.

"How many?" asked Arlon quietly.

"Tens of thousands, sir. Conservative. Their lines extended to the horizon."

"My God," muttered Ludovic. Lord Karl looked suddenly ashen.

One of the Druidale Rangers handed Arlon a small rolled parchment and said, "A messenger bird from Miller's Brook, received this morning, confirms the same. The survivors of Adar whom these men rescued made it to Miller's Brook safely."

"We travelled as far as Adar and found the village being overrun by their advance elements," Guardigan continued. "The main force spanned the vista, sir. They rode down the rest of our troop and set Adar to flame. We rescued some of the villagers and fled, sending the women and children north to Miller's Brook. But your cousin fell, sir. He and the Wayfarers gave their lives to ensure our escape. I am sorry for your loss."

Ludovic was impressed that the staff sergeant had the presence of mind to say such a thing. A few in the chamber called out their incredulity. The gruff old soldier cut them off. "This army is laying waste to all in its path, sir. We found no sign of Lord Handee's caravan and can only assume his column has already fallen victim to this army, either dead or captured."

"We may never learn of Handee's true fate, I fear," Arlon muttered darkly.

"What have we done?" muttered a quiet voice from the seats behind them all.

Ludovic turned to see Fargil standing at the foot of the stairs, watching the injured warrior's report. His face, still stained by the tears he'd shed for his brother, was ashen and drawn.

"It's true!" Fargil's voice was a shrill wail. Suddenly, his face twisted with self-loathing. "It's all true! I murdered him! I killed my brother, and for what? Hollow promises of power. Veiled threats. Watching eyes in the darkness—always watching." His bloodshot eyes fixed Lord Karl with a maddened stare. "I loathe you! You poisoned my mind. You drove me to the unspeakable," he whispered.

"Shut up, worm!"

"No! I won't!" To Arlon, Fargil said, "It's all true. Everything the princess said is true. Through Horvarth, we bribed Reinhart to delay Handee in Hightower, even to kill him! Then Karl and I arranged the civil unrest on our borders to destabilise the council, buying weapons secretly from Choat so no one would suspect."

The treasure ship! Ludovic thought. *That fortune was to pay for secret weapons to fund a mock civil war!*

"With the Senior Lord absent, Karl wanted to marry you to Marta to strengthen his own claim, but you wouldn't have it. So instead, he tried to kill you. When you wouldn't lead them into the field where his assassin could kill you, instead he tried to have Failton do it."

Fargil laughed manically.

"You infuriated him!" Then he turned on Karl. "Didn't see that coming, did you!" Fargil derided him. "You always see in others the same dark ambition that's in your own heart! You never thought that Arlon could resist. You never imagined that he would be a *good* man!"

His eyes dropped to his feet in shame. "But you were right about me. I was weak and so easily manipulated, and no one is to blame for that but me."

"He's delirious!" barked Karl. "He knows not what he says! You've harangued him into a false confession."

Fargil ignored him. "And now an army marches across the Land of the Lords, and the things we did to gain power for ourselves have weakened the nation and made it vulnerable." He looked into Arlon's face. "Forgive me."

Ludovic watched as Fargil turned and ran up the stairs at the rear of the chamber.

Guards broke into a sprint to catch up with the surprisingly spry conspirator, as others moved to flank Karl and prevent his escape. The Lord of Jow's expression was one of pure fury, though Ludovic saw defeat in his pig-like eyes. But Fargil had too much of a head start on the guards, and no lords stepped to intercept him as he made for the upper tier of the chamber.

Suddenly, it dawned on Ludovic what Fargil intended to do. The large, stained-glass windows at the top of the room shone with dawn's light. Beyond the beautiful glass was the deadly drop to the palace courtyard, whereupon most of the last de Hayne Royal Family had been dropped decades before.

"The windows!" Ludovic called.

None on the floor of the chamber could help. It was clear the pursuing guards would not reach Fargil in time to stop him.

Suddenly, a narrow-shafted arrow thumped into the tendon of Fargil's right ankle. He fell heavily upon the top step, screaming in pain.

Ludovic turned to see the golden-haired Druidale Ranger, bow still in hand, his face stern. Ludovic hadn't even heard the twang of the bowstring. It was an impossible shot across a great distance at a moving target running uphill in a poorly lit chamber.

Ludovic looked upon the Druidale Ranger with new admiration, for he had never seen such a shot.

Arlon watched as Fargil dropped to the floor, his ankle tendon snapped cleanly by the Druidale arrow. Despite the shocked expressions around the room, Arlon was not surprised by the feat. There was a good reason that elven archers like the Druidale Rangers enjoyed the reputation they did, and it was only partly the exaggeration of folklore.

Feeling weak, Arlon looked around the chamber. The Council of Lords had turned on itself, and there was a real danger that their now fragile republic might crumble and fall to chaos.

He fought down his grief for his friend and mentor Ergun and for his dear cousin Carpion. There would be time in the future to feel regret for great men's passing. Judging by the City Guard's report of a foreign army abroad on their lands, there would be many more losses to mourn soon enough.

Arlon took stock as the crying, pathetic form of Fargil was dragged from the chamber to be locked in the palace gaol.

Lord Karl II, Duke of Jow, and Councillor Fargil of Mashtock had conspired to delay Handee's return and to place Arlon in power through means of a contrived conflict on the border between Jow and Mashtock. For that, they would both face charges; Arlon would see to it personally. Yet it was clear that neither Karl nor Fargil could possibly have foreseen this mysterious army seemingly invading from Ipsica.

The fates had conspired against the very men who themselves had conspired to commit treason. Shenmadock had been saved from an internal coup by a bloody invasion!

Between them, Ludovic, Ergun, and he had known something was afoot, but they'd underestimated the scale of their adversaries' ambitions. Did that simply show the degree of Arlon's innocence, or his naiveté? Karl had called him a royalist, and something in him resonated with the thought that one ruler and a feudal system at least avoided this type of rotten-to-the-core politicking and corruption.

Arlon shook his head and looked at Lord Ludovic, who stood nearby, an expression of open concern on his face. Arlon wanted to ask for his guidance; normally he would have turned to the sage advice of the late Professor Ergun.

An almost imperceptible nod and a knowing glance passed between Arlon and Ludovic, and then the latter called for order.

"My lords, attention, please! We have a true state of emergency!" The chamber fell silent. "An enemy marches across our lands, and the realm is under threat of invasion. Our Senior Lord is missing and must be assumed dead. Lord Karl," he addressed the disgraced Duke of Jow, "you and Councillor Fargil are both under arrest and will face charges of smuggling, murder, attempted murder, and high treason in due course."

Once more addressing the council, Lord Ludovic spoke with words galvanized by natural authority.

"As a result of this peril and the attempted coup in this very council, I propose we declare *Senior Lord in Absentia* and afford executive powers to the Knight Marshall, in order that he might lead the defence of these lands against the threat posed by Ipsica."

For the second time in minutes, Arlon felt the light of the council's attention fall solely on him. His heart thundered in his chest. He suddenly felt weak, even weaker than he did from the effects of the poison that had almost ended him.

But unlike days before, on the first call for *in absentia*, this time he could not refuse.

Kathryn moved toward him to support his arm once more, but reluctantly, he stepped away from her. He forced himself to stand tall, to ensure he was seen to be fit and well, despite his weakness.

He could see Kathryn's eyes registered the slight, but after the accusation that he was a royalist, Arlon knew their situation had just become even more complicated.

He told himself that she would understand. He had to have confidence in that. Now that the position of Knight Marshall held sovereign power, the threat of being accused a royalist might imperil them both. Although it broke his heart to do so, he had to distance himself from the woman he so deeply loved, for the good of Shenmadock.

The Council of Lords erupted into raucous applause, with shouts of support for the appointment.

"It gives me no joy to accept this call," he said carefully as the noise abated. "None at all. But I have never turned from my duty to this nation, my home. In time, we must dig out the rotten core of this council, once and for all. Seeing this man's neck stretched," he pointed at Lord Karl with his scarred and tattooed hand, "will be but a first step in that. But time enough for that. Lord Ludovic?"

"Yes, Lord Protector?"

"Best convene the military council; apparently, we are at war."

Kathryn watched as the chamber began to move in concentric circles of confusion—councillors, lords, guards, and messengers all rushing to and fro. Arlon was swept into the centre alongside Lord Ludovic and other members of the war council, leaving Kathryn to linger at the door.

At her side stood a member of the Druidale Rangers, ever loyal to her line.

Stepping back into the shadows of the doorway, Princess Kathryn de Hayne watched Arlon with tears in her eyes, her heart tearing in half.

She had never felt so alone.

Epilogue

Click sipped his green tea, trying to ignore the half-eaten meal in front of him. The Father wouldn't be happy at the wasted food, but he couldn't bring himself to finish.

Rumours being what they were, the Whisper had heard alarming news. Alarming for its potential to be *good* news, for once! A murmur from the palace indicated that there had been an attempted coup, and that the Knight Marshall had survived an assassination attempt—an assassination attempt using a poisoned blade. It had been Black Spider Venom.

Another whispering spoke of at least two members of the Council of Lords being implicated in the coup. For the first time in a long time, Click suspected he might be able to sleep soundly. It appeared he had helped unravel a complex plot to unseat the republic.

As was always the case with a small player in a bigger game, Click had no way to comprehend what this all might mean for him, or for his missing friend, Acaelian, but for now, it seemed the immediate danger had passed. As Martin Galvan strummed out a tune and Delgado set about finishing Click's uneaten dinner for him, he tried to put these things to the back of his mind.

There was one small concern, he had to admit—the assassin who had murdered Paldron Ward and Jorus, hoping to frame Click for the latter in the process. Who had that been? There were no rumours of a freebooter in the city, so the assassin would surely be a guild member, a Black Cat. Having failed to frame Click, would the assassin now try to deal with him more directly? He doubted it. Click had simply been a convenient patsy. And if the assassin had been in the employ of those who had failed in their attempted coup . . . well, they'd have bigger concerns than silencing a lowly spy who knew nothing, anyway.

A spy who knew nothing. Click laughed at that.

As Martin's music gathered tempo and Claudia stood up from the table, offering Click her hand for a dance, he forced himself to his feet.

No sense in wasting life just sitting.

Andi sat casually atop the railing of the quarterdeck of Bophamel's *Moistened Barnacle.* The ship was making good time along the Inlet of Theed upon the noon high tide.

Much to the group's surprise, Bophamel had been waiting for them outside the port of Mrnak when they finally vacated the dead city, the Tor Dewald in their possession. They had spied the big ship at anchor in the morning sun and had rushed to the abandoned harbour wall, where a small craft sped from the vessel in order to collect them. Once aboard, the rotund Bophamel had hugged each in turn and welcomed them warmly like long-lost friends.

"How did you know we would be there?" Andi asked. "You had repairs to run on your ship."

"We did, indeed," Bophamel admitted. "And we ran those repairs successfully in record time, though it wasn't cheap. The *Barnacle* is in serviceable enough condition. Once the work was completed, we sailed further down the Inlet of Theed than any other vessel has done for more than a century, just to come and give you a lift."

"Yes, I see that—but why?"

"The same reasons that you are here at all, I imagine. More than a year ago, I was in port at Hightower, enjoying a glass of wine or seven. When I staggered back toward my vessel, I came across an old man smoking a pipe at the end of our pontoon. I made to ignore him, but he beckoned me over. I'd never met him before, but he knew my name. Cutting a long story short—he told me that one day a woman would come to me in need of passage, someone requesting travel to the dead city of Mrnak. That woman would be fleeing grave danger and would need my help twice. Once to leave the Land of the Lords, and again to ensure she returns.

"When you came to me with the Hightower City Watch chasing you, something clicked in my mind. I had originally disregarded the old man as being a superstitious old salt, but something in your face, my lady—something in your very presence that morning had struck a chord with me, and I suddenly remembered the chance meeting with the strange old man. I took a gamble then to ship you to Jrnak. When you told me you would be heading for Mrnak thereafter, I knew my instincts had been correct and that you were the woman he had spoken of . . . and that you would need my help again, just as the old man said. And so, we have sat at anchor all night awaiting any sign of your passing."

Andi and the others hadn't needed to ask the name of the old man, but she had anyway.

"Oh, I'll never forget that," Bophamel said. "It is strangely seared in my brain. Barabel."

They had sailed clear of Mrnak, skirting the port of Jrnak, and headed out toward the open seas, awaiting the turn north that would take them home.

Sitting atop the railing above the rudder of the vessel, Andi laughed softly to herself. She felt manipulated by this mysterious Barabel, for it seemed he had an ability to see some portion of the future, and she was well aware that such a thing should have her worried. But if Barabel really could see the future, could he have possibly foreseen her death and her surreal encounter with the ethereal being of shadows at the gates of the afterlife? And, therefore, foreseen her miraculous return?

And then there was another unsettling coincidence—*the Baerv*. After hearing Manic's account of the battle with the golem, and how *the Baerv* had freed them from that trap, Andi agreed with the dwarf that Jakrat and the cowled figures must have been seeking to secure that mysterious gem so the forces working for good in this world would not be able to use it to retrieve the Tor Dewald. Andi and Manic had given the false gem to Jakrat and had stolen what they assumed to be merely the more valuable trinket for themselves. Little had they known precisely how valuable that pilfered gem would prove to be!

Yes, Andi felt swept along in a river of destiny, and yet that conversation with the being of shadow replayed in her mind. *Choices*. Existence was a series of interlinked choices. Just how much control did any of them really have over their own destiny?

Across the quarterdeck, Eidos stood alongside Captain Bophamel at the ship's wheel, watching the helmsman guide the vessel through the tricky reefs at the entrance to the Inlet of Theed. Manic and Fin walked to the back of the vessel and came to stand next to Andi, who afforded them both a sly smile.

"What do you scurrilous pair want?"

"Us? Scurrilous?" Fin protested in good humour.

Manic shrugged. "I don't even know what the word means, so I'm going to assume she just said I'm both handsome and witty."

"I was just marvelling at providence, Andi." Fin inclined his head. "On our voyage down here, we spoke at some length about your unique lineage, and I think it is fair to say we need no further proof that you are, indeed, of both elven and human descent."

Andi went to protest, but there was no conviction in it. It was just habit now—knee-jerk.

"I simply mean to point out that we are now on our return trip to a land we left on the verge of potential disaster, and you seem to be experiencing even more diverse changes."

"I've never seen someone move like that!" Manic said excitedly. "You were amazing. It was like you were emerging from the shadows themselves!"

Andi shrugged once. "Thanks, Manic. And yes, you're right, my green-skinned friend." Andi looked up as they made their turn north, the mainsail boom beginning to move across the quarterdeck. "But you've seen nothing yet."

As the pair watched quizzically, the ship's boom passed overhead and Andi disappeared *into* its shadow. Suddenly the pair stood alone, their mouths hanging open in surprise.

Smiling to herself with satisfaction, Andi wolf-whistled to them from her new position—hanging from the rigging in the shadow of the crow's nest sixty feet up the main mast. The pair turned and looked up at her, aghast.

Manic applauded like a child, and Fin was left to ask, openly perplexed, "How is that possible?"

Stefon sat astride his horse, the frost-covered ground crunching beneath its hooves. Alongside him rode his friends Rish and Jewl, whilst following were Brooss and Pryn aboard one of the engineer's war wagons.

The noon sun hid behind thick white clouds, and the Choat Ranges ahead were covered in snow. The ride would be arduous, but Stefon was now convinced it was necessary. He was riding out to find the mysterious woman of his nightmares, and all he had to guide him were the nightmares themselves.

"So, we lasted in *that* town long, didn't we?" Rish asked with a smile.

Pryn laughed. "At least a month this time."

"Do you think we'll ever find a place to actually settle?" Rish asked.

From behind, Jewl the dwarf shouted, "I think the trick is finding a town where people don't try to kill us after knowing us for twenty minutes!"

They all laughed, but Stefon felt no real humour in the banter.

"Stefon," Rish said, "are you going to miss her?"

For a moment, he didn't understand of whom he spoke. His confusion must have been clear on his face.

"I mean Coral."

"Ah," Stefon said. "No, Rish, I'm not going to miss her."

"But she was beautiful, and I'm sure she was sweet on you. She took me aside before we left and told me to look after you. Get that! It's my responsibility to look after *you*! A guy who can run up walls and carve whole garrisons to pieces!"

"I don't care about any of that," Stefon admitted honestly, flinching at the memory of the massacre in the market. "We've more pressing concerns."

"Like what we're going to do for a living, perhaps?"

Stefon shook his head. "Rish, if we're to believe these rumours about a civil war in the west, we might be involved in something a little more dangerous than simple mercenary work soon. I get the feeling we're riding into the heart of the storm. We'll do well to survive."

After a period of silence, Jewl began to sing quietly, an old song of the dwarven mines. As his dulcet tones carried on the chill air, Stefon fell into a deep introspection.

He rode on with darkness in his heart.

On the outskirts of Choat, Coral sat at a table upon the flat roof of an old monastery long since converted to a brewery. She sipped contentedly at a warm cup of apple cinnamon tea and hummed with satisfaction.

Looking out at the southwestern fells and the distant arm of the Choat Mountains beyond, Coral wondered about Stefon and his friends. By her side, her drinking companion asked again, "You told Rish to ensure he looks after the last Seer, yes?"

"For the hundredth time, yes! I made it clear to him that he must look after Stefon, no matter what the cost. I realise the risks if we lose the last Seer and the powers he commands. 'A Seer is vulnerable when the madness comes upon him, for his powers are not yet fully formed and the surge of prescience is almost too much for mortal beings to bear alone,'" she quoted. "See? You taught me well."

She took another thoughtful sip. "I still find it remarkable that this ancient race has been restored," she admitted. "What does it mean for the prophecy? Will the Seers now return in greater numbers, or is Stefon an anomaly? I don't believe it a coincidence that the Seers have returned now that the prophecy is coming to fruition. I don't know how he fits into things, but Stefon must be important."

"I think you're more right than you know, Daughter. Much of the future is still hidden to me, but from what little I have foreseen, if Rish fails in his duty, I predict the corruption of all that is pure in this world. If the last Seer falls, sooner or later, this world will pass into darkness—an eternal darkness, without respite or reprieve."

Coral shook her head. "You believe that the last Seer is one of the Five Principals in the prophecy." It wasn't a question.

"Indeed I do, and Rish is another."

"Which is which, though?" she asked rhetorically. Dutifully, she recited them, trying to gauge his thinking. "The First Principal, the Burning Rose, the Ultimate Weapon for Good. The Second Principal, the Darkening Blade, the Ultimate Weapon for Evil. The Third Principal, the Chrysalis, the Protector of Good. The Fourth Principal, the Black Vessel, Bearer of the Darkening Blade. The Fifth Principal, The Harbinger, Daemon of Pestilence . . . the Beginning of the End, the Bringer of Doom.

"We're all agreed that the Tor Dewald is the Burning Rose, the ultimate weapon for good. You believe that Stefon, the last Seer, is one of the other four?"

"Come now, my daughter. You saw with your own eyes his ability in the market. I believe that Stefon may be the Chrysalis, the Protector of the Burning Rose. If fortune smiles on us, Andi and her friends are bringing the Tor Dewald back from the deserts of Peena even now."

"I always thought you believed Andi to be the Chrysalis."

"As much as it pains me to say, I may have been mistaken. Andi is powerful, and I foresee that she will become more powerful than we can possibly imagine. But something has changed. I no longer believe she's one of the five. Something happened down in the desert, something of which I have only felt the slightest ripple. She's . . . something else."

Coral smiled at her father. "That is why you had me send Stefon to find Andi—because she shall be carrying the Ultimate Weapon for Good? Do you think the woman Stefon dreams of is this Andi?"

"Those are things I neither have knowledge of nor control over. It may just be the Seer madness coming upon him." Barabel closed his eyes and sipped his tea.

Coral nodded slowly. "Tell me the prophecy again."

"Must I?" he complained in mock reluctance. "All you do is argue the interpretation."

Coral's dark look convinced him, for she had always been cursed with her late mother's stubbornness. "Okay, once more," Barabel relented. "The Harbinger of Pestilence will come to your world, inhabiting the dark hearts of the deceased; suffering, rage, and unnatural death shall be his companions. Raising an army of the putrid, poisoned dead, the Harbinger shall march across the Lords' land. Come the reckoning, the souls of all existence shall be held in balance and will call the Five Principals to order.

"The Black Vessel, Bringer of Evil, shall deliver unto this world the Darkening Blade, Evil's Dread Weapon. Unto the good and holy shall be delivered the Might of the One True God, the Burning Rose, the Unseen and the Seen, the Sum of All Hope. Nurtured into this world into the hands of those who protect, this Tor Dewald shall defend existence, battle for souls, and overcome the Harbinger, vanquishing the Darkening Blade and delivering your world from evil."

Coral shook her head and took a sip of tea. Knowing that she risked winding her father up by entering into yet another debate, she said, "These things the prophecy speaks of—it's so indefinite. And the years of translation and retranslation must have confused elements. If it truly describes the battle for existence itself . . . well, it all seems so . . ."

"Farfetched?" her father finished for her. Barabel nodded his understanding. "The truth of our future is always clouded by the distance of time and the eternal possibility of choice. But right now, what we must concern ourselves with is my certainty that if Stefon dies, so shall we all."

Acknowledgements

This project was originally begun in 2005 and would never have been completed but for the encouragement and support of Bryony Harrison. Eternal gratitude to my editor, Michelle, for her unending encouragement, firm-handed guidance, and wisdom. It's fair to say this book would have been nonsense but for her.

And once again, the world of Peternu Lorzi itself, and many of the primary characters, too, are the beloved inspiration of a large group of people. To name the main protagonists: Steven Cubbon, Mark Jewell, Jip, James Farrell, Erik Lunt, Jessica Welch, Phaser, and Stephen Wood. Stephen is mentioned last for the sake of the alphabet, but his input and work in sowing the seeds of the world of this trilogy were nothing less than vital, and my thanks go to him.

Happy Days, Biscuit Boys!

www.ingramcontent.com/pod-product-compliance
Lightning Source LLC
LaVergne TN
LVHW041053080826
845145LV00007B/1562

* 9 7 8 1 8 4 9 8 2 2 8 7 9 *